THE STON
VEYLIN

BOOK 3:
THE BLOODSTONE OF TALAMU

SUE WOOLLEY

SCIMITAR EDGE

Published by Scimitar Edge

An imprint of Purple Unicorn Media

ISBN 978-1-915692-71-9

Cover design by Robin Stacey

www.scimitaredge.com

Dedication

For my grandsons,
Sam, Alexander, and Roman:
you have brought such joy into my life.

Author's Note

The following symbols have been used in chapter headings, to indicate the places they are set, or the peoples they concern. Their deeper meaning will become clear in the course of reading.

† Earth
Δ Talamdor
֍ The Commonweal of Veylindré

End Contents

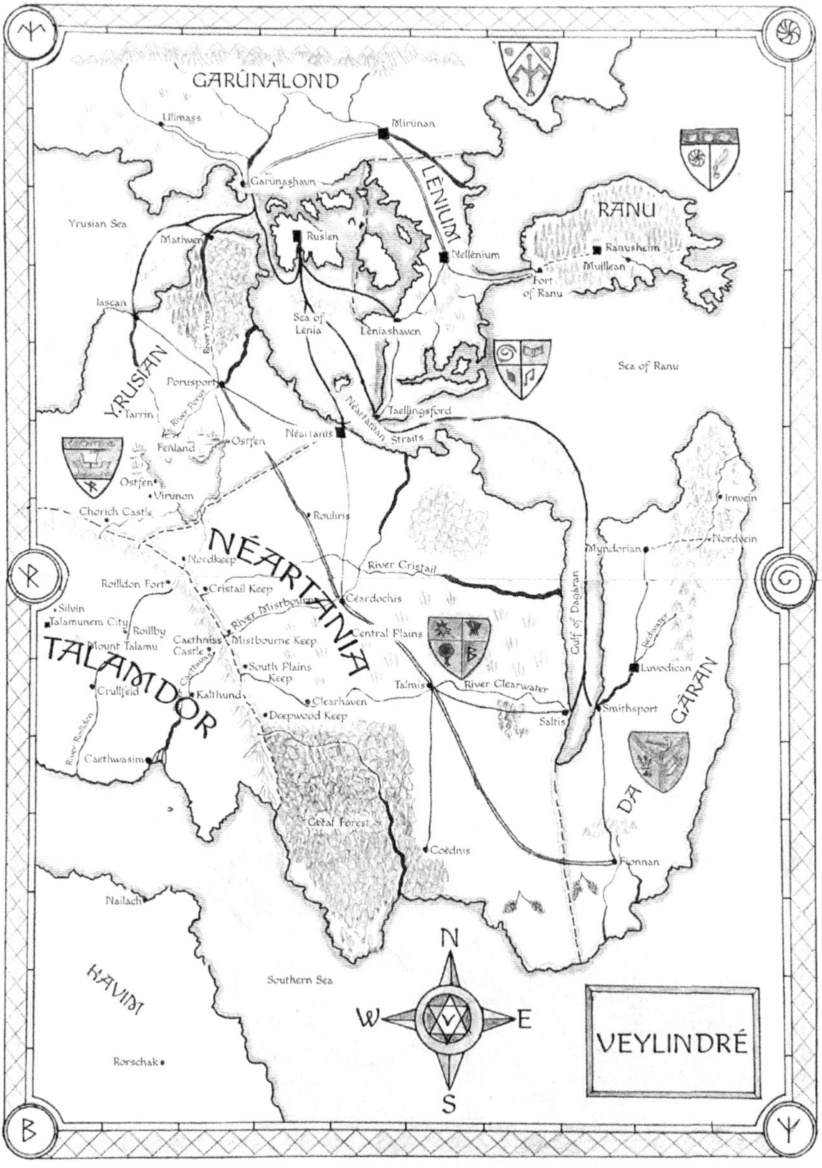
GARÛNALOND
Ullmass
Mirûnan
Garûnashavn
LÊNIUM
RANU
Ranusheim
Muillean
Fort of Ranu
Yrusian Sea
Mathven
Rusien
Nellenium
Iascan
Sea of Lênia
Lêniashaven
River Yrus
YRUSIAN
Porusport
River Porus
Tarrin
Fenland
Ostrfen
Néartanis
Taellingsford
Néartanian Straits
Sea of Ranu
Ostfen
Virunon
Chorich Castle
Rouliris
Irnvein
NÉARTANIA
Nordkeep
River Cristail
Myndorian
Nordvein
Roilldon Fort
Cristail Keep
Céardochis
Silvin
Talamunem City
Roillby
River Mistbourne
Central Plains
Mount Talamu
Caethniss Castle
Mistbourne Keep
Gulf of Dagaran
Redwater
TALAMDOR
South Plains Keep
Luvodican
Crullfeld
Kalthund
Talmis
River Clearwater
Clearhaven
Saltis
Smithsport
Deepwood Keep
DA GARAN
River Roilldon
Caethwasim
Great Forest
Coêdnis
Fionnan
Nailach
KAVIM
Southern Sea
N
W
E
S
VEYLINDRÉ
Rorschak

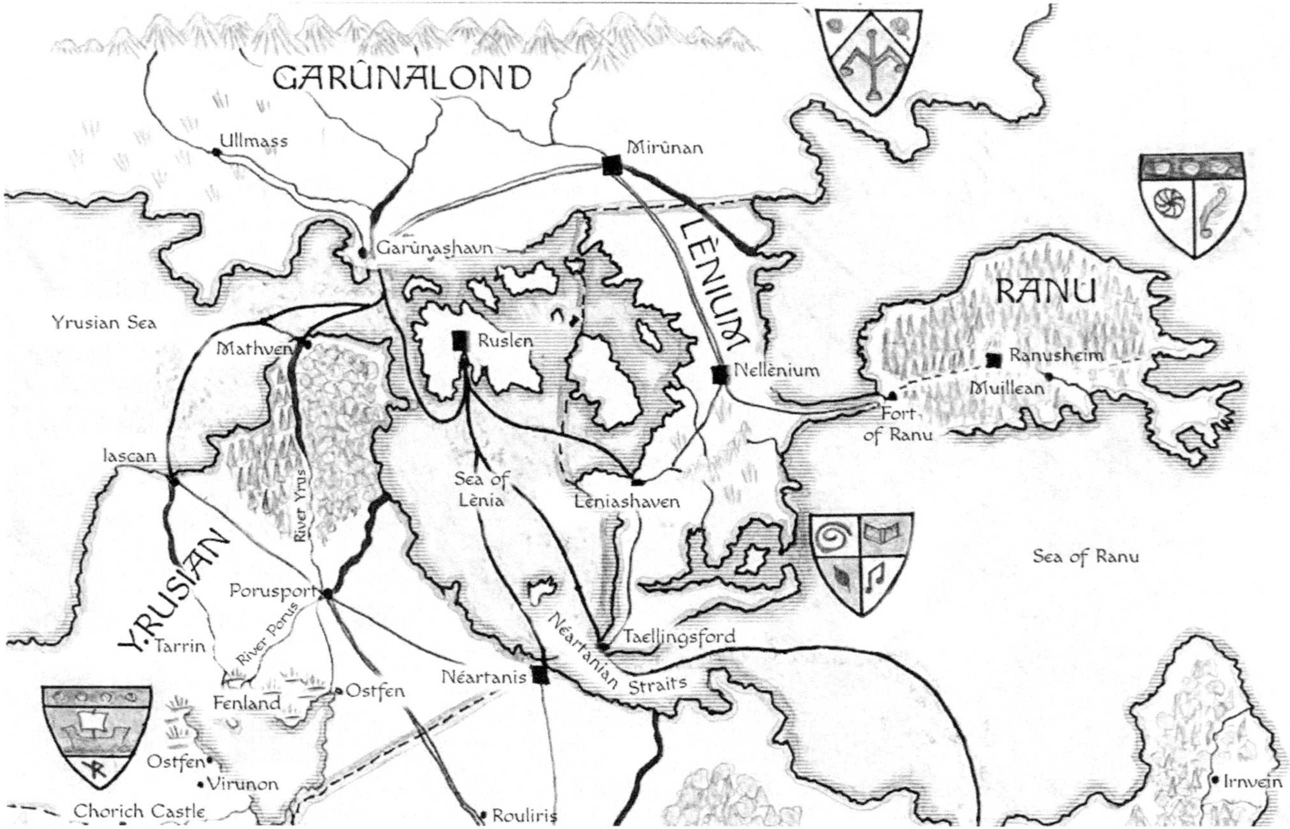
GARÛNALOND
Ullmass
Mirûnan
Garûnashavn
LÈNIUM
RANU
Yrusian Sea
Ruslen
Mathven
Nellènium
Ranusheim
Muillean
Fort of Ranu
Iascan
Sea of Lènia
Lèniashaven
River Yrus
Y.RUSIAN
Sea of Ranu
Porusport
River Porus
Tarrin
Néartanian Straits
Taellingsford
Néartanis
Fenland
Ostfen
Ostfen
Virunon
Chorich Castle
Rouliris
Irnvein

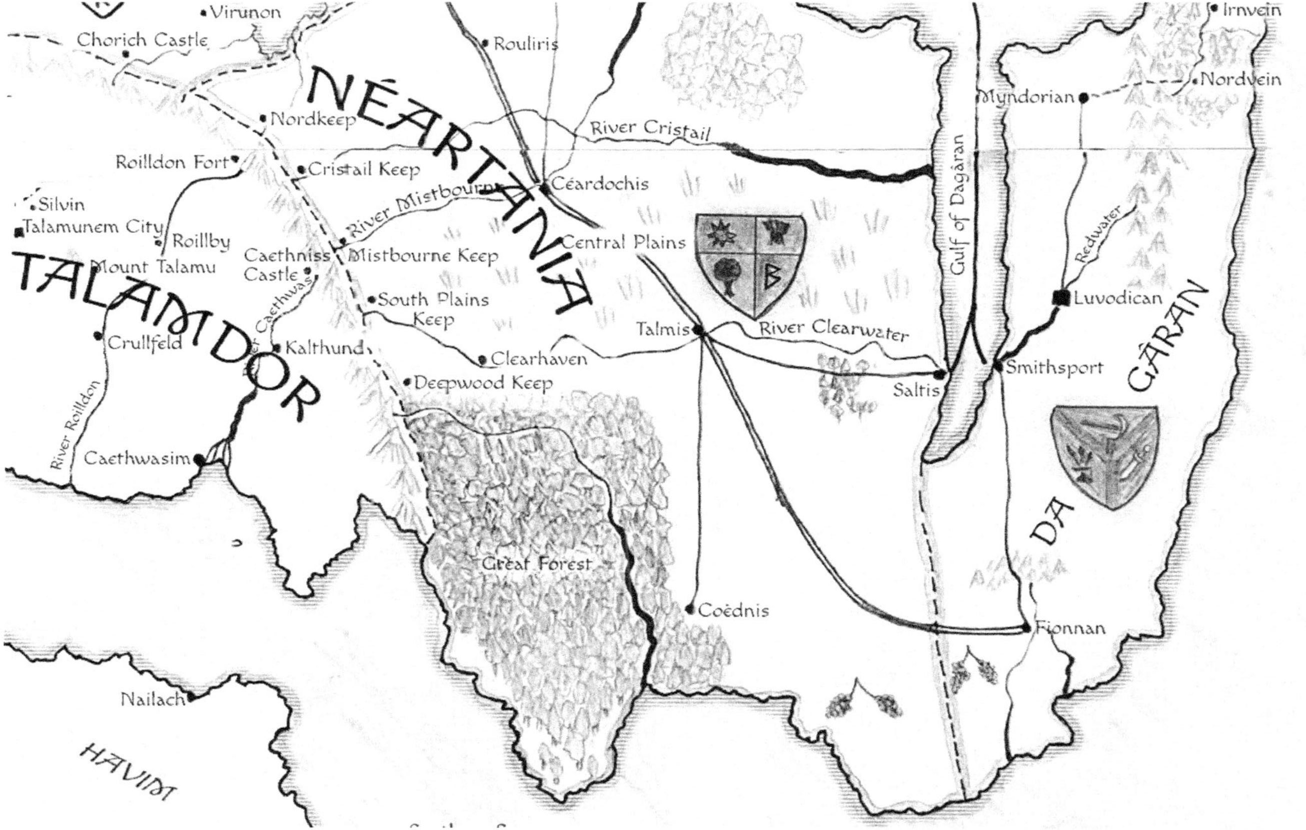

Virunon
Chorich Castle
NÉARTANIA
Rouliris
Irnvein
Nordvein
Myndorian
Nordkeep
River Cristail
Roilldon Fort
Cristail Keep
Céardochis
Gulf of Dagâran
Silvin
River Mistbourne
Talamunem City
Roillby
Central Plains
Redwater
Caethniss Castle
Mistbourne Keep
Mount Talamu
TALAMDOR
South Plains Keep
Luvodican
Talmis
River Clearwater
Crullfeld
Kalthund
Clearhaven
Smithsport
GÂRAN
Deepwood Keep
Saltis
River Roilldon
Caethwasim
DA
Great Forest
Coédnis
Fionnan
Nailach
HAVIM

The story so far...

The Goldstones and the Way

In April 1665, Abigail Winters and her family begin a journey to the New World, because her father, Presbyterian pastor Thomas Winters, is being persecuted by the government. On the way, there is a terrific storm, and at its height there is a green flash, and the ship is translated to a new world.

After they land on the east coast of Dagâran, Abigail and her boyfriend, Jacob Wallingford, are sent to seek a source of fresh water. When they return, the rest of the settlers have been massacred by pirates. There are also bodies of three strangers, whom Jacob searches. He finds a triangular red stone in a red buckskin pouch around the neck of one of them. They burn the bodies of their friends to give what respect they can, then set off through the neighbouring forest to find help.

Two young people from Nordvein, Aidren and Ellyn, come across them and realise Abigail and Jacob are not from Veylindré because they have no Waymark on their foreheads.

Back in Nordvein, they meet the Waymage, Shaunan, who becomes their mentor and guide. They show her the red stone and Shaunan recognises it as a Bloodstone. She warns them to keep it secret. Shaunan decides they need to be taken to Luvodican, the capital city of Dagâran, to be taught about the Way, and Aidren and Ellyn accompany them to gain some experience of the wider world. After some adventures, the five of them arrive in Luvodican and First Waymage Marinden allows them to lodge in the Visitors' Hall of the Temple. Abigail's and Jacob's learning begins – about the lands and peoples of the Commonweal of Veylindré and about the Way – the religious/magic system of this world, which is accessed by using Goldstones. Aidren and Ellyn continue their training as a warrior and a cordwainer respectively.

In the meantime, Portak, an agent of the Prophet of the One, ruler of Talamdor, has been despatched to find out if there were any survivors from the Havimi attack.

Abigail settles down well, apart from grieving for her family, but Jacob finds it harder to accept the Way, which has six goddesses, so different to Christianity. He is apprenticed to Master Kalen, a smith, which helps somewhat. Abigail is mentored by Shaunan, who realises she has special gifts. Shaunan resolves to take Abigail and Jacob to Ranusheim, the spiritual capital of all Veylindré.

At the Festival of Dagârastide, Abigail and Jacob undergo the Ceremony of Assignment and receive their Waymarks. Jacob's is Dagâran, as befits a smith. Abigail's is Ranusian, which means that one day, she could become a Waymage herself.

The five of them visit the rulers of Dagâran and learn that Havimi pirates have been sighted in the Gulf of Dagâran, so they decide to take the overland route to Ranusheim, through Néartania and Lènium. Ylonya, an Yrusian guide, joins the company.

After they have reached Talmis, a town in south-eastern Néartania, Shaunan takes them to the local temple to participate in worship. After the service, Jacob bolts. Aidren follows him and Jacob shares some of his struggles with the Six.

When Aidren leaves Jacob alone for a couple of minutes, he is abducted by Portak.

Abigail is distraught about Jacob's disappearance. When Ylonya fails to find him, Shaunan tells her that the only way to discover where he has gone is to ask the High Waymages at Ranusheim.

Jacob wakes up on a boat on the River Clearwater. His recent memories (since his arrival in Veylindré) have been wiped by Portak, whom he now sees as his only friend. He has also forgotten Abigail, except in dreams.

The company travels to Céardochis, a big trading centre in Néartania then on to Néartanis, the capital.

Jacob and Portak cross the Talamdorian Mountains using a secret pass. As they continue their journey towards Talamunem City, Jacob learns a little about Talamdor.

Just outside Néartanis, the company is attacked by three strangers and although Ylonya and Aidren win the fight, both are injured.

The Prophet and the Wayzenmoot

The company travel from Néartanis to Taellingsford, a coastal town in Lènium, using a secret tunnel under the Néartanian Straits. Ellyn has a panic attack, which leads to Aidren declaring his love for her.

Ylonya leads them to a house of a friend, Genira, who disguises Abigail by dyeing her hair and giving her

Garûnalonden clothes. They travel through Lènium to the Vale of Berlysian and visit the Healer's Hall.

Jacob and Portak arrive at Talamunem City and Portak takes Jacob to meet the Prophet of the One.

They arrive at Ranusheim, and Abigail tells her story to the Wayzenmoot (the ruling council of twelve High Waymages) and produces the Bloodstone that Jacob found. The Wayzenmoot realise that she may be able to attune herself to the Bloodstone because she is from outside Veylindré – it is inimical to any with Veylindréan blood in their veins.

Jacob meets the Prophet. Portak is jealous of the attention the Prophet pays Jacob but is ordered to teach him about Talamdor. An army is preparing to invade Veylindré.

Abigail, Shaunan, Ylonya, Aidren and Ellyn are given a quest by the Wayzenmoot: to wrest the Master Bloodstone from the Prophet of the One, and to bring it back to Ranusheim to be destroyed. Ednor of Néartania and Tremond of Garûnalond join the company.

Jacob's learning about Talamdor continues and he is given religious instruction by the Prophet, who reveals he was a witchfinder from England who came to this world more than thirty years ago and encountered Talamu, goddess of Talamdor, who called him to be her Prophet.

The company leaves Ranusheim after the Festival of Lèniastide and return to Taellingsford by a circuitous route.

The Festival of Ranusfest takes place in Talamunem City. The Prophet makes a speech, launching the offensive against Veylindré. Once the army has left, the

Prophet keeps Jacob close. Portak sends progress reports, using his Bloodstone.

The company crosses to Néartania once more, and stay with Kendris, a friend of Ylonya's, who gives them advice about the onward route. To Ednor's dismay, they are not going to travel south through Néartania, but instead go west into Yrusian, then through the Fenland. When they arrive at the Homing, the central settlement of the Fenland, they realise that the Fenland ruler, Lord Bredor, is under the power of Gilmak, an agent of the Prophet. They manage to escape but are pursued. Shaunan collapses with a heart attack. While Ednor, Tremond, Ylonya and Aidren are fighting the Fenlanders and Gilmak, Abigail tends Shaunan. Ellyn sees an arrow coming towards her friend's unprotected back and leaps to intercept it. She dies in Abigail's arms.

Back in Talamunem City, the Prophet hears that the army is about to cross into Néartania. He keeps Jacob closer than ever and tries to explain his plans for the future. Jacob is confused by this at first, then realises that the Prophet is grooming him to succeed him.

The company takes refuge in a village while Abigail does her best to comfort Aidren, who is mourning Ellyn, and to look after Shaunan, with the help of the local Waymage. Precious days are lost. But it may have put their pursuers off the trail. Once they reach Chorich Castle, the final journey into Talamdor is before them.

Now read on...

֍ Chapter 1 ֍

As they all dismounted and led their horses into the shadows between the twin towers of the gatehouse, Abigail looked around curiously. There had been no castle in Andover, where she came from and, apart from passing through the outer courtyard of the Fort of Ranu, she had never been inside one.

"...and I will inform the Castellan of your arrival," the guard said to Ylonya.

"Thank you. Please call your Healer also. If you would tell us where the stables are, we can care for our mounts while we wait."

The guard nodded. "Of course, Mistress Ylonya. This way."

He led them through an arch in the west wall of the outer courtyard into another large yard, this one surrounded with stables, most of them already occupied.

"Here is the barn," he said, showing them into a large stone building in one corner. "We don't have enough spare stables to accommodate you, but there are hitching posts within and all that you need for your horses' comfort. The hayloft is above."

Ylonya nodded at him. "My thanks, again."

The guard turned on his heel and strode back through to the main courtyard. The company tied their horses to the hitching posts and untacked them, before rubbing them down and feeding and watering them.

All except Shaunan.

"You sit there," Abigail said sternly, pointing to a corn bin. "We will tend to your horse."

To her surprise, the Waymage did as she was told. Abigail probed her with her healing sense but could only detect extreme weariness. Ylonya was right. They would have to leave Shaunan behind, much though she hated the idea.

They had just finished tending to the horses when the guard returned, followed by a tall, broad man with dark hair, brown eyes and tanned skin, clearly an Yrusian, although his Waymark was Dagâran. He was clad in chainmail with an Yrusian surcote over it and moved with the surety of one accustomed to command. This must be the Castellan. A small woman in the lilac robes of a Healer accompanied him

"Welcome to Chorich Castle," he said in a deep voice. "I am Trévon, Castellan of the Castle. What is your purpose here?"

"Trévon? Is it really you?" Ylonya's voice was full of joy.

The Castellan strode forward, smiling broadly, took both her hands in his. "It is good to see you again."

Ylonya turned to the others. "This is Trévon, a dear friend of mine from Porusport. I haven't seen him for years."

Trévon smiled at her. "If you would introduce me to the rest of your company..."

Ylonya opened her mouth to speak, but Abigail broke in.

"A moment, please, Castellan Trévon. If I might speak with your Healer? One of us is in sore need of her attention."

She sensed his displeasure at being interrupted, swiftly suppressed as he took in her Ranusian Waymark.

"Yes, Waymage. This is Healer Elyssa."

The woman came forward. "Which of you needs my care?"

"Our Waymage, Shaunan of Nordvein," Abigail said. "If we might come with you?"

"Of course. This way."

Elyssa led Abigail and Shaunan towards the main entrance to the castle proper, leaving the others with the Castellan.

Ednor waited impatiently while Ylonya introduced them all to the Castellan.

"Trévon, these are Tremond, a Watch officer from Mirunan and Aidren, a Warrior from Nordvein in north-east Dagâran. I think you may have heard of Ednor of Néartanis. He is the younger son of Lord Éadulf and Lady Aethed."

"I have indeed," Trévon said, with an inclination of his head. "It is good to finally meet you, Ednor. Welcome to Chorich Castle, all of you."

Ednor nodded in acknowledgement, then burst out, "How is the war going?"

Trévon's eyebrows shot up. "Where have you been, that you have not heard?"

"In the Fenland," Ylonya said. "It is a long story."

The Castellan took her arm. "Come within, and I will bring you up to date."

He led them all out of the stable yard and in through the main gate of the inner castle, past a small temple. Ednor had not had the occasion to visit Chorich Castle before – he had spent most of his recent tour of duty in the border keeps further south – and he was impressed with the air of calm battle readiness he sensed all around him. In the inner courtyard, a grizzled old sergeant was drilling some young soldiers in sword fighting techniques and the sight and sounds of swords clashing against each other reminded him of his years in Luvodican, where he had learned his craft and, in more recent times, of sparring with Aidren.

Trévon opened the door of the inner keep, which was flanked by two towers with arrow slits in their walls, a high rope footbridge between them, then led them up some spiral stairs, set into the wall of one of the towers. They came out into a large room, well-lit by oil lamps. Its most prominent feature was a fine table of Ranus wood, covered with maps and other papers. Ednor guessed it was the Castellan's headquarters. A number of chairs were scattered around.

"Sit," Trévon said. "May I offer you some refreshment?"

"That would be welcome indeed," Ylonya said. "Thank you."

Trévon pulled on a bell rope in one corner of the room and a young servant came in.

"I will be taking my evening meal here," Trévon told him. "Bring enough for five."

The young man bowed and left.

"Now," Trévon said to Ylonya. "What brings you here?"

"It's a long story," Ylonya began.

Ednor tried to contain his impatience. He could not wait to hear how the war was going but knew that he must. He listened as Ylonya gave a highly-edited version of their story – how they had travelled from Ranusheim through Lènium, then across the Fenland to here.

"We are on a quest, set for us by the High Waymages at Ranusheim," Ylonya wound up. "The six of us need to reach Talamunem City as soon as possible."

"Talamunem City?" Trévon exclaimed. "I would not advise it, Ylonya. We are at war with Talamdor."

"Nevertheless," she said, "that is where we are bound. And we were hoping that you would know of a way to cross the Talamdorian Mountains unseen."

She broke off as the young servant knocked on the door, then entered, carrying a laden tray. The smells of warm bread, spiced meats and cold ale reminded Ednor that he had not eaten since breakfast. He shrugged – news of the war could wait.

Abigail and Shaunan followed Elyssa as she led them out of the stable yard, through another gate, into the heart of the keep itself. The inner courtyard was full of life – some soldiers were practising their swordcraft and other people were crossing it, intent on their tasks.

Abigail hoped the Healer's quarters were not far. She could see the weary slump of Shaunan's shoulders, feel her mentor's exhaustion. Even this short walk from the stable yard had made Shaunan breathless, although Abigail could sense her efforts to hide it.

Elyssa opened a narrow door on the east side of the courtyard. "Here we are," she said. "Come in."

The Healer's room reminded Abigail of Tabor's, back in Virunon. Shelves holding books, dried herbs and bottles of various sizes lined the walls and there was a long workbench against one wall, a narrow bed against another. She stood back as Elyssa led Shaunan to a comfortable armchair.

"Sit here, Waymage Shaunan," Elyssa said, "and rest."

Shaunan did as she was told. Gradually, her breathing returned to normal, and her eyes closed. She was sleeping. Good.

"If you would tell me what symptoms she has, Waymage Abigail?" Elyssa asked.

Abigail flushed. "I'm not a Waymage," she said. "I only received my Waymark at Dagârastide and have had little formal training."

Elyssa's delicately shaped brows rose, but she made no comment. "Tell me anyway," she said in a low voice, which was yet light and musical.

"It started," Abigail counted back on her fingers, "nine days ago. We were attacked by a Talamdorian agent and some warriors from the Fenland and Shaunan had pain in her chest and collapsed. She found it hard to breathe. I think it is her heart. I had sensed she was hiding something a couple of days earlier, but she shrugged off my concern. The others managed to defeat our attackers, but Ellyn..."

Abigail could not continue. At the thought of Ellyn, tears had sprung to her eyes.

"Who was Ellyn?" Elyssa asked gently.

Abigail gulped, took a moment to fight back the tears, then continued, "Ellyn was Shaunan's niece and my best friend. She was protecting me while I tended her aunt, and she took – she took an arrow in the chest. I tried to save her, but she died under my hands. We – we buried her at Virunon last Ranusdag."

Elyssa reached out, took Abigail's hand. "I am so sorry for your loss."

"Thank you." Abigail managed a smile. "There is not much more to tell. Ylonya guided us to Virunon, where Waymage Tabor treated Shaunan and gave me a potion made from foxgloves to prevent a reoccurrence of her malady. But these last few days, since we left Virunon on Dagârsdag, she has been struggling. I fear – I fear her illness is more serious than we realised."

"I see," was all Elyssa said, but Abigail sensed that she understood. "We'll leave her to sleep for now," the Healer continued. "It is the best thing for her at present. If you would let me see the potion Waymage Tabor gave you?"

"Half a moment," Abigail said, "I have it in my pack."

She opened her Healer's bag and took out the small bottle. "Here," she said, handing it to Elyssa.

Elyssa eased the stopper free of the bottle and sniffed the potion. "Good," she said, "this is the right treatment for her."

"Healer Elyssa," Abigail said. "I need you to persuade the Waymage to stay here, to not come with us on the rest of our journey."

"Where are you bound?"

Abigail gave her a straight look. "To Talamunem City," she said, "and there may be fighting along the way. We cannot risk Shaunan any further."

"I – see," was all Elyssa said.

"I do not want to leave her behind," Abigail said, "but she is grieving so much for Ellyn – we all are – and I could not bear it if she died too."

"I think you are right to wish her to stay here. She will be safe here – or at least, as safe as anywhere in these troubled times."

"Thank you. Now, if you would tell me where the others are, I will leave her with you and return later."

The Healer nodded. "They will probably be in the Castellan's private quarters," she said. "Ask anyone in the courtyard and they will guide you. I will examine the Waymage more thoroughly when she wakes."

Abigail walked out of the Healer's quarters and looked around, unsure of where to find the others.

"Excuse me," she said to a passing soldier.

The young man – no, woman – turned, her face questioning. "Yes?"

"I'm a stranger here," Abigail said, smiling. "My name is Abigail. Could you direct me to the Castellan's quarters, please?"

"I am Jerica," the young woman said. "If I might test your Waymark, Waymage Abigail,"

"Of course."

This done, Jerica became less formal. "You must be one of the people who came with our Mistress Ylonya."

"You know Ylonya?" Abigail said, surprised. Yet why not – they were in Yrusian, after all.

"Everyone knows Mistress Ylonya," the young woman replied. "The Castellan's quarters are this way."

Jerica led Abigail across the courtyard to the gate she had come through with Elyssa, set between two high, granite towers. She opened the door of the right-hand tower and led her up some spiral stairs. Before long, Abigail could hear voices she recognised.

Jerica knocked on a sturdy wooden door.

"Come," a deep voice said.

"My Lord Castellan," Jerica said, "here is Waymage Abigail, another of Mistress Ylonya's company."

"Come within, Waymage Abigail," Trévon said.

"Thank you, sir." Abigail turned to Jerica, "and thank you, Jerica."

The young woman bowed, turned on her heel, and clattered back down the stairs.

"Close the door and sit down," Trévon said. "Ylonya has told me of your quest."

Abigail sat gratefully.

"How is Shaunan?" Tremond asked.

"She fell asleep as soon as she sat down in Healer Elyssa's quarters," Abigail said. "The Healer will examine her later, when she wakes."

"We were just having something to eat," Ylonya said. "There is plenty for you."

"Thank you." Abigail said, walking over to the table and helping herself. "What has been decided?"

"We have not got very far," Ylonya said. "I have explained to Trévon that we need to reach Talamunem City, then a servant arrived with our dinner."

"But now," the Castellan put in, "it is getting late, and you are all weary. I will ring for someone to show you to our guest quarters. We will speak again in the morning."

"But," Ednor began.

"He's right," Ylonya said, putting her hand on Ednor's arm. "I don't know about you, but I could do with a good night's sleep before we do our planning."

Ednor frowned, then nodded. "Very well."

Abigail finished eating and rose. "I must return to Shaunan."

Shaunan awoke with a start and had no idea where she was. Looking round, she saw she was in a Healer's room. Then memory came flooding back.

She started to rise, but a light voice from behind her said, "Stay where you are, Waymage Shaunan."

A dainty woman in the lilac robes of a Healer walked forward so that Shaunan could see her. "I am Healer Elyssa. You are at Chorich Castle. Abigail brought you here. She has gone to meet the others of your company."

"What has she told you?" Shaunan asked.

"That you collapsed nine days ago, with pain in your chest and found it hard to breathe. She gave me the potion that Waymage Tabor prepared for you. If I may examine you?"

Elyssa led her to a narrow bed in the corner of the room. "Lie here, please, Waymage Shaunan, propped up on these pillows."

Shaunan managed a smile through the tightness in her chest. "Shaunan will do, Elyssa."

But she did as she was told.

The Healer examined her thoroughly, then moved away. She returned with the potion bottle Tabor had given to Abigail and a glass of water. She added three drops of the potion to the water, then gave it to Shaunan, who obediently drank it down.

"Now, Shaunan," Elyssa said. "How long have you been having these pains?"

"For a few seisdags. But don't tell Abigail."

"I think she knows," Elyssa said with a wry smile. "You know it is your heart that is causing your symptoms."

Shaunan nodded. "Yes, but I hoped that Tabor's potion would heal me."

"Abigail has told me that your company has business in Talamdor," Elyssa said. "I think it would be best if you stayed here, waited for their return."

"But they need me with them," Shaunan protested. "Abigail has only had her Waymark since Dagârastide, and I have not had the chance to teach her much healing."

"You must tell me the tale, one day," Elyssa said. "But do you truly believe you are fit enough to accompany them?"

The Healer held Shaunan's gaze for a long moment.

Shaunan fought against accepting Elyssa's implicit diagnosis, but she knew it was true.

"I suppose not," she whispered. "If I fell ill at an inconvenient time, it could be fatal for the quest."

"I am sorry, Shaunan, but I fear you are right. Stay here, and I will tend you, so that you are fit enough to accompany them when they return."

"You have a Waymage here?" Shaunan asked. "I feel in need of spiritual direction."

"Yes, Waymage Rusilon," Elyssa replied. "I will bring her to you."

Aidren was not accustomed to the grandeur he saw all around him. He had been assigned a fair-sized chamber with Ednor and Tremond and the two men had fallen asleep quickly, filling the air with their snores. But Aidren could not sleep. The bed was too soft, and his heart was too heavy.

The next morning, after doing their Immersion practice, the three of them found their way to the Great Hall, where most of the castle's inhabitants were eating breakfast. He looked for Abigail and Ylonya and saw them sitting at a table on the dais at one end of the hall, Ylonya with the Castellan on her left. The blue banner of Yrusian swayed above them in the light breeze coming in through the open windows.

It was a grand room, nearly as long as the audience chamber of Lord Lesym and Lady Bélia, back in Luvodican. Bright shields hung on the walls. The rest of the tables were set at right angles to the dais and he and Ednor and Tremond found one with some space.

"May we join you?" Ednor asked.

The soldiers seated at the table shifted along on their benches to make room. Aidren recognised the elderly sergeant who had been drilling his troops the previous evening. He was easily old enough to be Aidren's grandfather and had a fine, waxed moustache.

Once the three of them had sat down, the men around the table passed them the basket of bread and platter of cold meats. Aidren didn't feel hungry but took some anyway. He knew he'd need his strength for the onward journey.

"What news of the war?" Ednor asked.

"Who's asking?" the sergeant said.

Ednor drew himself up. "I am Ednor of Néartania. My friends are Tremond of Garûnalonden and Aidren of Dagâran."

"*The* Ednor?" the man said, a flush mantling his cheeks. "Son of Lord Éadulf and Lady Aethed?"

Ednor nodded.

"My apologies, my Lord."

"Forget it," Ednor said. "You can repay me by telling me what is going on. We have been in the Fenland for the past couple of seisdags and I am out of touch."

The sergeant leaned forward, lowered his voice. "Rumour has it that things are not going well, my Lord. The Talamdorian army has crossed the mountains and attacked Cristail Keep in the north and Mistbourne Keep in the south, or so I've heard."

"What size is their army? What equipment do they have? How have we defended ourselves?" The questions came boiling out of Ednor.

The sergeant shrugged. "Some thousands of men, well-armed," he said. "That is all I know. If you need more, you had better ask the Castellan."

"Don't worry, I will."

Aidren sat back. More bad news.

At fourth hour, Ylonya went to see Trévon again, while the men packed and prepared the horses for departure. Abigail was once more with Shaunan.

"What advice can you give me for our onward journey?" Ylonya asked. "I have never been in Talamdor, so any information you have would be most helpful."

"I have been Castellan of Chorich Castle for the past five years," Trévon said, "but before then, as you know, I was one of Castellan Dravis's scouts. We often found our way over the mountains into Talamdor."

"You did?" Ylonya said, relieved. "What can you tell me?"

"Over the years, we have gained a reasonable knowledge of northern Talamdor," Trévon said. "Once, I saved the life of a young Talamdorian woman, Malke, who was being attacked by a wolf. She was quite badly injured, so I took her back to her village, Silvin, about ten miles north-east of Talamunem City. She was the daughter of the headman of the village. Since then, she has provided us with a safe hiding place for our scouts and sometimes sends us snippets of information through her brother, who trades with Yrusian. I will give you a token to give to her, so that she knows you have come from me."

"That could be very useful," Ylonya said. "But wouldn't the other villagers betray us?"

"No," Trévon said. "Malke is now headwoman, and they are completely loyal to her. To them, the affairs of Talamunem City and southern Talamdor are remote, especially since the Havimi conquered Talamdor. At that time, the villages of the north learned self-sufficiency. They live simply, supporting themselves on what they grow and hunt. You can trust her. I recommend you leave your horses with her and do the final miles on foot – you will be less conspicuous."

Ylonya nodded, "I suppose you're right. But it will be awkward if we have to get away in a hurry. Do you have a map which shows the location of this village?"

"Yes. I will give you a copy when you leave. I take it you still use your Finding skills?"

"Yes, why?"

"I will give you something from the village to guide you there."

"Thank you, my old friend."

"Furthermore," Trévon continued, "I do not recommend crossing the mountains from here. There is a secret crossing, only known to our scouts, about a dozen miles north of here. I will send one of them with you to show you the way."

"Thank you. We are in your debt." She paused, then continued, "I have another favour to ask you."

Trévon smiled at her, his eyes twinkling. "What is it?"

"That you will allow Shaunan to remain here in Elyssa's care. She is not fit enough to risk."

"Of course."

"I have spoken with Elyssa and with Waymage Rusilon," Shaunan said, "and have decided to stay here. I cannot risk becoming a burden to you all."

Abigail hugged her fiercely. "You are *never* a burden," she said. "I hate the idea of leaving you – how will we manage without you?"

"You have learned much in the past seisdags," Shaunan said "and know more than you think."

"You have been with me since the beginning of all this and without Ellyn too…" Abigail broke off, clapped her hand to her mouth. "I'm so sorry. It must be so much worse for you."

Shaunan sternly ordered her tears back to their source. Whatever happened, she must send Abigail off happy, not worried about her. "I will be fine," she said. "Do not concern yourself about me."

"What will I do if one of them is injured?" Abigail asked.

"Visualise me with you and ask yourself what I would do. The answer will come to you."

Shaunan sat up and reached for her healer's bag. "I am going to give you some of my more esoteric medicines," she said. "There is little time to explain their uses, but Waymage Rusilon is one who can speak over distance, so if there is need, you can contact her and, through her, me."

She saw Abigail's expression lighten. Then the girl asked, "Do you think we will succeed?"

Shaunan started to say that it would be the will of Ranu. Then a surety swept over her. "There will be great danger," she said, "and one of you will be injured. But you will find the strength to overcome all obstacles."

She sat back in her chair, shaken. The words had not been hers. But she recognised their truth.

"One of us will be injured," Abigail said. "Who?"

"I do not know, child," Shaunan said. "But I have seen no deaths. You will be able to deal with whatever comes. Now go and pack. I will see you off presently. May the Way be with you, my dear girl."

Abigail bent down and kissed her. "May the Way be with you also."

֍ Chapter 2 Δ

After a hasty lunch the company were in the stable yard, ready to mount up and leave. Abigail noticed that a canvas package, long and thin, had been tied to the back of each of their saddles with leather thongs. She was about to ask about it when the Castellan arrived, accompanied by a slim woman in her early twenties, clad all in brown, a bow in her hand, a long knife at her belt and a quiver full of arrows on her back.

"This is Crinan," he said, "one of our scouts. She will guide you to the secret pass through the Talamdorian Mountains, then return to us."

It was the first Abigail had heard of any secret pass. What had Ylonya told the Castellan?

"Thank you, Castellan Trévon," Ylonya said. "We are in your debt."

Abigail saw his eyes twinkle at her formality. She was so grateful to Ylonya for taking on the leadership of the company – no-one else was more fitted for it, with her friend's wide experience of journeying, her ability to rely on her wits and her many contacts to keep herself and the rest of them safe. And, perhaps more importantly, Ylonya had earned the respect of Ednor and Tremond.

Then Shaunan and Elyssa entered the stable yard and Abigail's heart contracted. Shaunan still looked so frail. How was she going to manage without her mentor's gentle wisdom? Stop it, Abigail. You're going to have to.

"I come to wish you success in your quest," Shaunan said. "May the Way guard and guide you." *Go well, Abigail – I have every faith in you.*

Abigail bowed her head in acknowledgement. *Thank you, Shaunan. I hope we will be back soon, with Jacob and the Master Bloodstone.*

May the Way guard and guide you, my dear.

While they had been speaking, Crinan had gone to the stables and returned leading a black horse, all tacked up and ready to go. She mounted it smoothly and took her place beside Ylonya.

"Go now and take care," Trévon said. "Remember that you can trust Malke, but no-one else. May the Way be with you all."

Abigail mounted her mare and exchanged a final glance with Shaunan. This was it – the final stage of the quest. There had been so many beginnings in the past seisdags – leaving England, leaving the settlement, meeting Aidren and Ellyn, and being given their quest at Ranusheim. As she watched the others swing onto their mounts, she felt a frisson of excitement – maybe this was the beginning of the end.

They clattered over the lowered drawbridge, Crinan in the lead. She swung her horse's head round to the left. "This way."

"How long have you been a scout?" Ylonya asked, as they rode parallel to the north-eastern granite wall of the castle.

"For more than five years, Mistress Ylonya."

"Ylonya will do. What drew you to the work?"

Unexpectedly, Crinan blushed. "I had heard many stories of your adventures," she said, "and wanted to be like you."

"You have the Finding gift?" Ylonya asked, hiding her amusement.

"I do. It has helped me find my way back to the Castle many times."

"Tell me what you have learned about Talamdor," Ylonya said.

Crinan's eyes were questioning.

"No," Ylonya said, "this isn't a test of your knowledge. I know little of Talamdor, so anything you can tell me will help me to guide our company truly."

The Yrusian girl relaxed. "We have not ventured far into Talamdor," she said. "I have come within five miles of Talamunem City, but no closer than that. So I can tell you about the north of the land, but nothing else."

"It is only about the north I need to know. We will be returning the same way we go in, if all goes well."

Ylonya could see the curiosity in the girl's eyes. "I'm sorry, Crinan, I cannot tell you of our quest. But if we return, you will hear then."

Crinan accepted this with a nod. "Perhaps it would be best if you asked me questions and I could share my knowledge that way."

"Thank you. First of all, what is the land like?"

"The secret pass is steep and narrow – it will take you a day to traverse it. Then you will see northern Talamdor before you. It is a bleak land, densely forested, with few people. Mining villages are scattered around, where the lodes are. The map the Castellan has given you shows their location, but you will need to rely on the food and drink you carry, plus anything you can forage, until you reach Silvin, the village of Malke."

"Yes," Ylonya said, "the Castellan told me about that. Have you met her?"

"A few times. She is not a typical Talamdorian – her skin is tanned like ours and her hair is dark brown, not black."

"Do you think she may have Yrusian blood in her veins?"

Crinan looked startled, but said only, "I suppose she might have."

"It would explain much," Ylonya said. "What is the route to Malke's village?"

"It is about ten or so miles north-east of Talamunem City, so about seventy miles south-west of the Talamdorian side of the secret pass. I could show you more easily on the map."

"Then I will look at it with you when we stop for dinner," Ylonya said. "I hope to reach the mouth of the pass on our side by then."

Crinan nodded. "Very well."

They continued to ride through the countryside of south-west Yrusian. This part of the land was sparsely populated – there were only a few villages dotted around the valleys on this side of the Talamdorian Mountains, with every possible inch under cultivation. But Ylonya knew it, nonetheless. Where they were going next, she would be travelling blind, relying on the knowledge of others. May Yrusia be with them.

They reached what Abigail assumed was the foot of the pass at twelfth hour, when the light was fading from the sky. She could see no entrance – just the jagged mountains towering above and around them. Crinan led them to a wooden hut, a few hundred yards beyond, concealed behind an outcropping of rock.

"It is too late to make a start now," she said. "We stay here sometimes, before making our forays into Talamdor."

Abigail looked around curiously. It reminded her a little of the charcoal burner's hut, back in Saltiswoods in south-east Néartania – it had the same slatted wood walls, the same air of disuse. But when she walked inside, there were three rooms instead of one – a central space, flanked by two sleeping areas.

"Women sleep there," Crinan said, pointing to the one on the left, "men, there."

Abigail poked her head into the women's bedroom, although to call it a bedroom was to give it almost too much status. There were four pallets arranged in a row on the floor, and a large wooden chest, which she assumed contained blankets. So she'd be sharing with Crinan and Ylonya.

It felt so strange, so heart-wrenchingly sad, not to be sharing with Ellyn – whispering secrets in their beds in the evenings, sharing the time of Immersion in the mornings. Would there ever be a day she did not miss her friend?

Crinan lit the fire in the hearth of the central space, and they all relaxed around it, feasting on some of the food the Castellan had given them – hunks of fresh bread, spread with butter and honey and last year's ripe apples, wrinkled but still sweet. They would save the rest for the journey ahead – well-wrapped loaves of *feolin,* strips of salted meat and dried fruit.

"Tell us some stories of your journeys into Talamdor," Abigail said.

"There's not much to tell," Crinan said. "We always go in groups of three, so that if one of us is injured, the second might stay with them, while the third returns to the Castle for aid."

"Is it such a dangerous land, then?" Ednor asked.

"Not in itself," Crinan said, "but we never forget that Talamdorians are enemies of Veylindré and the consequence of any meeting might be serious."

"Do Talamdorians from further south scout the north?" Ylonya asked.

"Sometimes, but I have not seen many – at least, not in recent seisdags. I think they believe the main threat to Talamdor will come from the north-east and east – from Néartania."

Ednor sat back. Abigail could sense his satisfaction with Crinan's words.

Ylonya fished the Castellan's map out of her pack. "Would you show us the best route to Malke's village?"

It was getting darker in the hut, so Abigail lit her Goldstone. And was a little surprised by how unremarkable it had become to rely on the power of the Way.

Ylonya nodded her thanks as she spread the map out in front of her.

Crinan moved closer to Ylonya, then sat down again. The rest of them crowded round so that they could see what she was showing them.

"We are here," she said, pointing to a small dot on the map, "and the secret pass starts here." She pointed again. "Once you are in Talamdor, you will need to avoid all of the marked villages except for Malke's, here."

"What is the terrain like?" Ylonya asked.

"Hilly and densely forested," Crinan said. "There are narrow valleys between the hills, in which the Talamdorians grow what they can. But the soil is poor – they trade the metals and minerals they mine for anything else they need."

"Whom do they trade with?" Ylonya said, her trading instincts obviously aroused.

"Mainly with the more fertile regions of Talamdor, I think," Crinan said. "And in recent years, we have heard that Talamdor has started to trade with Havim once more."

"Really?" Ylonya said. "It was only a few decades ago they were under the Havimi thumb."

Crinan shrugged. "Who knows what is in the mind of the Prophet?"

"Where will we find shelter?" Abigail said. "It is too cold to sleep outside in only our blankets."

"That will not be necessary," Crinan said, smiling at her. "We have given you some of our tents to help with that."

"Tents?"

Crinan went outside and came back in with one of the mysterious packages Abigail had noticed earlier. "This," she said, "is a tent. They were developed for us by Waymage Rusilon. Stand back, everyone, and I'll show you how they work."

The five of them scrambled to their feet and retreated to the walls of the room. Crinan laid the package on the floor and undid the leather thong that tied it together.

Then she clasped her Goldstone and said, "*Gal lo bynn fosgan.*"

Before their astonished gaze, the dun and green coloured canvas sprang to life, turning into a cylindrical shape with an opening at one end, ties hanging from it to fasten it closed.

"There is room within for one person and their pack," Crinan said, grinning at their surprise, "be they as tall as a Garûnalonden." She smiled at Tremond. "Waymage Rusilon has laid a charm upon them, so that once you have tied them shut, they will be warm enough within."

"Thank you, Crinan," Ylonya said, These are a generous gift."

"Then," Crinan said, "when you want to put them away, say, '*Streik an pakin.*'"

The tent leapt into the air and came down folded back into its original shape, ready for packing away.

"The colours were chosen to be inconspicuous against the landscape here," she said. "May they serve you well."

"We are grateful, Crinan," Abigail said. "Without the aid of others, we would not have come this far. We are in your debt. Please thank Waymage Rusilon for us."

"Go away," Aidren said, burrowing deeper under his blankets. It hardly seemed a moment since he had closed his eyes. He had been dreaming of Ellyn... Automatically, he cut off that train of thought. He could not afford to think about her, not now. Otherwise, his grief would be too much to bear.

Someone kept on shaking him. Reluctantly, he opened his eyes. "What? What is it?"

"It's time for breakfast," Tremond said. "We need to make an early start to get through the pass in one day."

Aidren sat up, suddenly wide awake. Of course, they were going to enter Talamdor today. Talamdor. Not in his wildest dreams had he ever thought he would be going there.

"I'll be with you in a minute," he said.

When he entered the central space, the others were eating breakfast.

"Come and eat, Aidren. We must be on our way soon," Ylonya said. "Crinan is going to come with us the first part of the way, then return to the Castle."

Within half an hour, they were mounted up, ready to leave. Crinan locked the door behind her, put the key in an inside pocket. They followed her back the way they had come the previous evening, then turned right into a narrow opening that looked as though it led nowhere. It was nearly as well hidden as the entrance to the Myner's Gap – that seemed so long ago.

The path upward was narrow, as Crinan had said, and they could only pass in single file – Crinan in the lead, followed by Ylonya, Tremond, Abigail, then Aidren himself, with Ednor bringing up the rear. The ground beneath their horses' hooves was covered with loose pebbles and small, jagged rocks – difficult to negotiate. Small bushes and plants lined the path, releasing their scent as the company pushed past them. The sun did not penetrate this pass, or at least not at this time of day, and a chill wind blew down from the top. Aidren found himself hunching his shoulders, in anticipation of an attack.

But nothing happened. They climbed and climbed. The sun rose higher in the sky and Aidren began to feel it warming his back. Then the path began to level off and he guessed they were almost at the head of the pass.

A few minutes later Crinan stopped at the summit, then turned to face them all. "This is where I leave you," she said. "Be careful of the path down – the scree makes the going slippery."

"Thank you for your aid," Ylonya said. "May your journey home be smooth and safe."

Crinan inclined her head. "There is a wider place a little further on, where you may stop and eat. May the Way guard and guide you all."

She started back down the pass to Yrusian. They were on their own.

It took them nearly as long to descend the other side of the pass as it had to climb up. They kept their pace to a walk – the ground was as treacherous as Crinan had warned. As they approached the mouth of the pass on the Talamdorian side, Abigail had a shock. Ahead of them was a smoky red light, blocking their path. Ylonya was about to walk her horse into it.

"Stop!" Abigail cried. "Can't you see it?"

Ylonya pulled on her reins, then turned her horse to face Abigail.

"See what?"

"The red light. It's all across the path."

"I see no light," Tremond said. "Does anyone else?"

They all shook their heads.

"You must believe me," Abigail said. "I sense it is evil. If you walk into it, you will die."

"Trévon said nothing about this," Ylonya said, "and neither did Crinan. But I trust your sight. How can we get past it?"

"Let me open my senses to it," Abigail said. "Then maybe I can work out how to pass it without danger."

As the others sat silent on their horses, Abigail let her reins drop and took out her Goldstone. She could feel the – whatever it was – prickling the skin of her face. Opening her mind, she pushed her thought out towards it. Then shied away, closing her mind as quickly as she could.

"It is a barrier," she said. "If we walk into it, something both powerful and evil will come to life to defend the pass against us."

Ylonya frowned. "But we must get through it," she said.

"I know," Abigail said. "Let me think…" And she closed her eyes once more.

Again the others gave her the gift of silence, so that she could concentrate.

She opened her eyes again. "The only way I can think of," she said slowly, "is to try to counter light with light. Ylonya and I can both conjure light with our Goldstones. What if we try to surround us all with the light, to protect us? Is that possible?"

"Why don't you use the Bloodstone?" Aidren asked.

Abigail bit her lip. "I don't know," she said. "I'm afraid it might give us away to any Talamdorians around."

"Then what's the point in having it," Ednor said, "if we can't use it as a weapon against them?"

"Is fighting the only thing you care about?" Abigail said, stung. "My main concern is to reach Talamunem

City unmolested, rescue Jacob and the Master Bloodstone, then get away again."

"Enough," Ylonya said, then to Ednor, "Abigail is the Ranusian here. The choice of whether and when to use the Bloodstone must be hers. I'd rather give her idea of using our Goldstones a try. Let's go back a way, so that we can make the attempt, out of sight of unfriendly eyes."

Without waiting to be asked, Tremond, who was at the rear, turned his horse and they followed him back up the path they had just traversed. Once they were round a corner, away from the mouth of the pass, he stopped.

Ylonya took out her Goldstone. "Tell me what to do," she said to Abigail.

"First, let's light our Goldstones."

And both said, "*Gal lo bynn leumin.*"

Both their Goldstones sprang into light, Ylonya's blue-white, Abigail's golden yellow.

"Now," Abigail said, "try to push the light out with your mind, so that it covers Aidren too. I'll do the same with Ednor and Tremond."

Gritting her teeth, Abigail concentrated on her Goldstone, repeating the spell in her mind. *Gal lo bynn leumin, gal lo bynn leumin.* And slowly, the light around her began to expand, reaching out to include the two men. Then faded, as Ylonya groaned.

"I'm sorry," she said. "I just can't do it."

"Then I'll have to try on my own."

Abigail closed her eyes again, bringing all her thoughts to the Goldstone in her hand. *Gal lo bynn leumin, gal lo bynn leumin.* Once again, the light spread out, surrounding first Aidren, then Ylonya, then Tremond.

She paused for a moment, exhausted by the effort. Then felt a hand on her shoulder, pouring strength into her.

Aidren. She felt all his determination to never let anyone down again, all his will to succeed.

Strengthened by his touch, Abigail pushed the light's protection out to include Ednor. She had done it. She opened her eyes, spoke to the others.

"Let's go. I'm not sure how long I can keep this up."

They wheeled their horses round and walked back down the path. Although it was cold, Abigail was sweating from the effort of maintaining the spell.

"Now!" she cried and kicked her horse into a trot. As she entered the aura of the red light, the prickling sensation increased ten-fold. *Gal lo bynn leumin, gal lo bynn leumin.*

She felt the resistance of the red light waver, then go out. They were through!

Once they were all past the barrier, Abigail let her Goldstone go out, sighing with relief. They had defeated the enemy. They were in Talamdor. Abigail saw a dark land – a stark contrast to the Yrusian they had left behind. That had been green and fertile; this was thickly forested, as far as she could see. How did they live, without fields to plant food in?

"We need to find somewhere sheltered to pitch our tents," Ylonya said. "Preferably near a source of fresh water." She looked at the men. "Could you go and find somewhere, please?"

Abigail gave her a puzzled glance as Ednor, Tremond and Aidren obediently scattered, leaving their horses behind.

"I needed to speak with you alone," Ylonya said.

"Why?"

"Have you been watching Ednor?"

"No more than any of the others. What about him?"

"I believe he is regretting not being part of the army defending Veylindré."

"And you think he may do something foolish, to prove himself as a warrior?"

"Exactly," Ylonya said. "You have senses that I do not. Keep an eye on him. We're going to need him."

Abigail could not believe her ears. "You're asking me to violate his privacy," she said.

Ylonya grimaced as though this straight talking was too much. "Yes," she said. "I would not ask if I did not believe it to be true."

Abigail knew she was right. She too had felt the young warrior repressing his impatience.

"Very well. I will do what I can."

"We could set up camp here," Tremond said, when they came to a clearing about half a mile from where they'd left the women.

"Good thinking," Ednor said.

Aidren shrugged. Once place was as good as another. He didn't really care. The only things he cared about were reaching Talamunem City, killing the Prophet and rescuing Jacob. And protecting Abigail.

"Let's fetch the others," Tremond said.

They rode back to where they had left Abigail and Ylonya. Abigail's cheeks were flushed and Ylonya's eyes were flashing – it looked as though they'd been having an argument.

"What's wrong?" Aidren asked Abigail quietly.

"I'm sorry, Aidren, I can't tell you."

Hurt, Aidren turned aside. She'd have told Ellyn.

Tremond led them to the clearing. "We thought here," he said.

Ylonya nodded her approval. "Good," she said. "Let's hobble the horses – there is enough grass around here to feed them. Did you find any water?"

"A small stream a few hundred yards further that way," Tremond said, pointing.

"Aidren and Ednor," Ylonya said, "fetch some water for the horses."

Aidren was missing Shaunan's gentler style of leadership. But there was no point in arguing with Ylonya.

When they returned, Ylonya nodded her thanks, then said, "Let's set up the tents."

They untied the tents from their saddle bows and laid them on the ground. Each in turn took their Goldstones in their hands and repeated the words Crinan had taught them, "*Gal lo bynn fosgan.*" The packages sprang into shape.

"I could get used to this," Ylonya said with a laugh. "It certainly saves time."

"Should we collect some firewood?" Ednor asked. "A hot meal would be welcome."

"No, I don't think we'll risk it," Ylonya said. "Fire may be seen over a great distance, particularly at night."

Ednor scowled, ready to make an issue of it.

Aidren touched his friend's arm. "Let it go," he said softly. "She is in no mood to be challenged."

After a cold and cheerless supper, and with no fire to sit round afterwards, the company prepared to sleep, leaving Ylonya and Ednor to take the first watch.

Abigail wrapped herself in her blanket, then eased her way into her tent. It was difficult to find a comfortable position, even with the blanket beneath her. She was worried – about both Aidren and Ednor. If only she could have told Aidren what was bothering her. She had sensed his hurt when he turned away – he had not deserved the rebuff. But it would have felt like disloyalty to Ylonya to tell him and she knew it was important for all of them to accept her friend's leadership. The five of them could not afford to be divided. Not if the quest was to have any chance of success.

She drifted into an uneasy sleep, full of dreams of those she had lost – first Jacob, then Ellyn and now Shaunan.

"Wake up, Abigail!"

Ylonya's voice was urgent.

"What's wrong?"

"Two riders from the south, heading this way."

Abigail sat up in a hurry. She crawled out of her tent, dragging her blanket and pack behind her. "*Streik an pakin,"* she said, and the tent was ready to go.

"What are we going to do?" she whispered.

"Hide," Ylonya said. "Although Ednor and Aidren both want to fight."

The five of them led the horses deeper into the trees, with cloaks wrapped around their muzzles so they couldn't call to the other horses and alert the Talamdorians to their presence.

Abigail held her breath and opened her mind cautiously. If she could overhear what the Talamdorians were saying, she might be able to gauge their purpose.

But she could only sense their intent.

"They are hunting for someone," she whispered.

"How do you know?" Tremond asked.

"I could sense it."

"Hush!" Ylonya said. "Here they come."

The sound of hoofbeats grew loud in her ears. She put her hand on the pommel of her knife. Whatever happened, she would not be captured easily.

Δ Chapter 3 ֍

Jacob didn't get much sleep in the hours that followed his encounter with Lord Domlok, tossing and turning in his narrow bed, sheets and blankets tangling up beneath and around him. Should he tell the Prophet what Domlok had said, or conceal it for now, but keep his eyes and ears open for other instances of discontent?

Because, little though he liked Domlok, he liked the idea of being the Prophet's spy even less. Such intrigue was foreign to him, dishonourable. Portak wouldn't have batted an eyelid – he'd have gone straight to the Prophet.

But he wasn't Portak. The conversation with the Talamdorian noble had shown him how precarious his position in Talamdorian society, in the Prophet's favour, really was, and he didn't want to anger him.

Yet, would his master – God, he was beginning to think like Portak – be more angry if he found out later that Jacob had known? What to do for the best? If only he had someone to talk it over with.

But Domlok's aggression had demonstrated vividly how unlikely this was.

"Our first skirmish has been triumphant," the Prophet said, as Jacob walked into the Chamber of Law, his eyes sandy from lack of sleep. "The Veylindréans tried to ambush our southern force in the pass over the mountains, but our troops vanquished them."

"That is good to hear, my Lord," Jacob said. But it was only one skirmish. One skirmish does not win a war.

"Why do you have no faith?" the Prophet snapped. "We have right on our side, the outcome cannot be in doubt."

"I'm sorry, my Lord. It – it reminded me of our Civil War, that's all."

"What do you mean?"

"Well, the Roundheads won at first and cut King Charles's head off. And they ruled for eleven years. I was born in that time, and it was all I knew. They must have thought the Commonwealth would last forever. But after Oliver Cromwell died, they only hung on a for a year or so, before the old king's son came back and became king again."

"And your point is?" The Prophet's eyes were stormy, and he looked angrier than Jacob had ever seen him. Jacob's heart began to race.

"I'm sorry, my Lord. But..."

"Yes?"

Jacob took a deep breath, summoned up his courage. "My Lord, my father told me that Oliver Cromwell was the only man strong enough to keep the Commonwealth together. After he died, it all fell apart."

"And?"

"My Lord, you are the ruler of Talamdor. Everyone looks to you and does what you tell them. I – I just wondered what would happen if you..." Jacob's voice trailed off. He dared not say it.

"If I died? Of course I'm going to die, one day. Which is why I need you to succeed me."

"But, my Lord," Jacob said, his heart thumping in his chest. How could he make the Prophet understand? "I don't think the Talamdorians will accept me. I wasn't born here, and I haven't been trained to rule anything. Surely a Talamdorian noble would better serve you."

The Prophet sat back. To Jacob's surprise the storm on his brow had subsided and he looked thoughtful rather than angry.

"You may have a point, Jacob. I will consider what you have said. Leave me."

"My Lord." Jacob bowed and beat a hasty retreat.

Portak estimated it must be more than ten miles to Mistbourne Keep from the mouth of the pass on the Néartanian side. But someone had made the journey in a hurry. He guessed one of their ambushers must have made off as soon as they engaged the Talamdorians and given the enemy warning of their arrival. By the time Portak and the vanguard of General Kreldik's army had made their way down the other side of the pass, a defending force was waiting for them.

Portak's heart sank. The men were already tired. They'd been marching all day, had been in a fight already. And now they would have to fight again, before they rested. He was taken unawares when General Kreldik shouted, "Charge!"

The Talamdorian cavalry did not hesitate. All weariness forgotten, it seemed, they hefted their weapons and charged towards the waiting Veylindréans. Portak was swept up among them and found himself in the midst of the battle before he had time to take a breath. The foot soldiers followed on behind.

He was fighting a tall Dagâran warrior, big and burly. But the man moved like lightning and Portak was hard put to it to defend himself. He had never been much of a warrior, preferring to work in other ways for the good of Talamdor. Sweat was standing on his brow as he traded sword strokes with the Dagâran.

Then, before he had time to block, the Dagâran got under his guard and thrust the point of his sword towards his heart. Portak managed to swerve, but the blade took him in the upper arm. The pain was severe and he nearly lost his seat. He tried to recover, to take the fight back to the Dagâran, but was relieved when one of the Talamdorian officers came to his aid.

All around were the cries of men – men in pain, men grunting and panting, men screaming defiance at the enemy. The Veylindréans seemed to be taken aback by the ferocity of the Talamdorian attack. A few minutes later, the enemy retreated. They had won. Portak sheathed his sword. Thank Talamu – it was over.

Once the Veylindréan army had withdrawn, Portak made his way wearily to General Kreldik. His arm was one great throb of pain – he wondered whether he would ever be able to use it again.

"Tell the men to spread out and set up camp over there," Kreldik was telling his officers, pointing to a flattish space about half a mile to the north. "And set up the healers' tents first – there is much work for them."

A healer. That was what he needed. Kreldik forgotten, Portak turned to follow the men and found a healer, clad in the pale red robes of his calling.

"Sit still," the man said.

He helped Portak remove his jerkin and shirt, which jarred the wounded arm. He had never experienced such pain – he had to bite his lips to stop himself crying out.

"Good luck," the healer told him. "It is a clean gash and should heal well."

He cleaned the encrusted dirt and blood away with an astringent lotion which stung like blazes – more lip biting – before applying a greenish salve, which soothed the worst of the pain. Then he bandaged it.

"Thank you, my friend," Portak said. "You have a gentle touch."

The man nodded his acknowledgement. "Put a clean shirt over it and come back in a couple of days for me to have another look at it."

"You have much work to do," Portak said, glancing across at the lines of camp beds, each with a wounded soldier on it. His ears were pierced by the cries and groans of the wounded – he had never seen so many at one time.

"War keeps us busy," the man said shortly. "We will heal those we can, with Holy Talamu's aid."

"What about the others?"

"If they are beyond saving, they will be given a drink of bitter herbs to send them gently into death."

Portak shuddered. "I will pray to Holy Talamu, that you may heal as many as possible."

Portak walked slowly back across the field to where General Kreldik's tent had been set up, the Talamdorian pennant snapping bravely in the breeze.

Kreldik and his staff officers were in the middle of what Portak guessed was a war council. Kreldik frowned when he saw Portak but gestured to him to join them.

"We are planning our next move," he told Portak.

"The Prophet ordered us to split into two forces and attack both Mistbourne Keep and South Plains Keep," Portak said.

"I'm well aware of that, thank you," Kreldik snapped. "But we're in a different game now. The element of surprise has been lost. The Veylindréan army knows that we are here, that we have invaded Néartania."

"So what is the plan?" Portak asked.

"We will lay siege to Mistbourne Keep," Kreldik said. "Using this place as a base, we will move our siege engines into place the day after tomorrow."

"Why not tomorrow?" Portak asked, before he could stop himself.

Kreldik scowled at him. "Because we need to entrench ourselves here first," he gestured to where men were digging trenches and building defences with the wood they had brought with them, "so that we will have a safe place to fall back to if we are defeated. And the men need to rest – they fought bravely today and are weary."

"You are not anticipating success, then?"

"The outcome of any campaign is not certain until it is over," Kreldik said.

"So what should I report to His Holiness?"

"That the situation is in hand."

Portak raised his eyebrows. "As you say."

The following morning, Jacob trailed back to the Chamber of Law, unsure of his reception. He hoped with all his heart that the Prophet had accepted his point about needing a Talamdorian to succeed him.

"Good morning, Jacob," the Prophet said.

His face was impossible to read.

"Good morning, my Lord," he said, before daring to ask, "Why is it good?"

"I have had another report from Portak. The Veylindréans were awaiting our brave troops when they arrived in Néartania. But General Kreldik was not daunted – he led a charge without hesitation. The Veylindréans were not expecting such ferocity and, after fighting for a short while, they turned and fled."

"Where did they fly to?" Jacob asked.

"Back to Mistbourne Keep. Our army now holds the area in front of the pass and will be able to re-group before taking the attack to our enemies."

This did not sound like a victory, but Jacob knew better than to say so.

"What are you going to tell the nobles?" He had blurted out the question before he had time to censor it.

The Prophet glared at him. "Only what they need to know."

Jacob bowed his head. "My Lord."

A few minutes later, what Jacob had begun to think of as the war council had assembled. It would be interesting to hear what gloss the Prophet would put on this latest news.

"What news, my Lord?" Domlok asked.

"Our army has reached Veylindré," the Prophet said. "We have engaged the Veylindréans and they have turned tail and run."

"Where have they run to?" Domlok asked.

"Back to Mistbourne Keep."

"Then the element of surprise has been lost?"

The Prophet nodded. "Yes, but Kreldik has formulated a plan. He is going to lay siege to Mistbourne Keep. We will starve the Veylindréans into submission."

The Talamdorian lord frowned. "Is our army equipped to mount a siege, my Lord?"

"Are you questioning the bravery of our troops, Lord Domlok?"

The biting sarcasm in the Prophet's voice made Jacob wince. He was glad it was not directed at him.

He watched the Prophet hold Domlok's gaze until the man bowed his head. "No, my Lord. Of course not."

"Then do not worry about it. Our army have siege engines with them and catapults and trebuchets. It will be only a matter of time until they have taken Mistbourne Keep."

The Prophet looked around at the assembled nobles. "Are there any other questions?"

No-one spoke. "Then this council is concluded. We will meet again in two days."

Δ Chapter 4 Δ

Abigail held her breath. Were they going to be found?

Aidren was standing next to her, all his attention fixed on their pursuers. She could feel him trembling. Surely he wasn't afraid?

She dipped into his mind as Ylonya had asked her to do to Ednor – hating herself for doing it – and realised it was not fear that was making her friend quiver like a plucked harp string. It was implacable hatred, pulsing out of him, dark and terrible. Shocked, she withdrew as unobtrusively as she could. She hadn't realised the force of Aidren's emotions. Was this what losing Ellyn had done to him?

Soon the Talamdorians were drawing close to the company, trotting towards their place of concealment. Abigail could hear their voices, harsh and guttural.

"What are we doing here anyway?"

"You heard what the captain said – the Guardians reported a group of strangers, mounted, astray in our land."

"Well, we've seen no sign of them. I'm tired – let's go back."

"With only half a job done – not likely. The captain would have my skin, and yours too."

Then, before Abigail could prevent, Ednor and Aidren were astride their mounts and bursting out of the covert to challenge the two Talamdorians.

"I told you to keep an eye on him," Ylonya hissed.

"I'm sorry. I was concentrating on Aidren."

As Abigail watched, her two friends drew their swords and began to fight. Although the Talamdorians were taken unawares, there was nothing wrong with their fighting instincts. They drew their own swords and fought back.

"I will wait with Abigail," Ylonya said to Tremond. "Go and help them."

Nothing loath, Tremond swung up onto his horse and joined the fray. It was soon over. Abigail saw Ednor parry a thrust from one of the enemy then, like lightning, give his own sword a tricky twist which sent the Talamdorian's sword spinning out of his grip. Then he went in for the kill. Tremond and Aidren dealt swiftly with the other.

At which point, Ylonya and Abigail rode out to join them.

"What in Ranu's name did you think you were doing?" Ylonya asked, clearly furious.

"Killing two Talamdorians," Ednor said.

"You need to stop keeping your brain in your scabbard," Ylonya retorted. "Hadn't you realised that when those two don't return, there will be others out hunting for them?"

Aidren looked abashed, Ednor did not.

"Then we had better make sure they are hard to find," he said, with a grim smile. "It is two less of the enemy to deal with."

"When you have hidden them, we had better get away from here. Fast," Ylonya said.

"How are we going to find our way to Malke's village?" Abigail asked.

"According to the map Crinan gave me," Ylonya said, "there should be a river a couple of miles south-east of here, which rises in the mountains and goes within a few miles of Silvin. If I can find it, all we have to do is follow it."

"Does this forest continue all the way?" Tremond asked.

"For most of it," Ylonya said. "So as long as we don't draw attention to ourselves," and here she scowled at Ednor and Aidren, "we should be all right."

And so it proved. To Abigail's relief, the rest of the journey to Silvin passed without further alarm. They moved cautiously through northern Talamdor, avoiding any settlements, finding sheltered places to camp near the river, and setting a watch. The land they were travelling through seemed to be sparsely inhabited, just rolling hills and narrow valleys, mostly blanketed with the ubiquitous trees. She didn't like the forest – it felt grim, foreboding even. No birds sang and they saw no sign of any other living creature. At night, however, they were kept awake by deep, resonant howls – wolves evidently lived here – natural guardians of this part of Talamdor.

Four days after breaking through the barrier of the pass, they arrived at the outskirts of Silvin in the middle of the afternoon. It looked scruffy and uncared for – there were piles of rubbish in the streets and most of the houses seemed to be in a state of disrepair.

"Are you sure this is the right place?" Ednor asked Ylonya.

"This is where Crinan's map says it is," Ylonya said, but even she seemed doubtful.

Abigail looked around her. There was something odd going on here. She took out her Goldstone, held it in her hand and looked again. The village transformed before her eyes into a tidy and prosperous settlement, with well cared-for dwellings and flowers in the gardens.

"It is not as it seems," she said. "When I look with the eyes of the Way, it looks completely different – tidy, well-maintained, neat. Take out your Goldstones and see."

"By the Six!" Ednor said. "How do they do that?"

"I expect we'll find out," Abigail said.

"You wait here," Ylonya said. "I will find Malke and give her Trévon's token. And," she added, frowning at Ednor and Aidren, "don't do anything stupid."

Abigail winced at her tone as she watched her friend walk her horse into the village, leaving the rest of them behind.

"Who does she think she is, telling me what to do?" Ednor said, his eyes flashing.

"Forgive her," Abigail said. "She bears the weight of leadership on her shoulders."

She nudged Ednor's mind gently and his scowl relaxed. "I suppose so."

Half an hour later, Ylonya returned, bringing two people with her: a tall woman and a man. The woman must be Malke. Looking at her, Abigail thought Ylonya's guess at her origins was correct – the woman did have Yrusian blood.

"I am Malke," the woman said. "Welcome to Silvin. Any friend of Trévon's is a friend of mine."

"Thank you," Abigail said. "We are grateful for your hospitality."

"Ylonya tells me you are a healer," Malke said. "My daughter is sick. Will you come and see her?"

"Of course. What is wrong with her?"

"She has a bad cough. It has troubled her for seisdags, keeping her awake at night."

"Take me to her."

"My thanks," Malke said. Then she turned to Ylonya and the others. "Go with Padrik. He will show you to the inn."

Abigail followed Malke as the woman led her to the centre of the village. She hoped she would be able to heal the girl.

Malke's house was the finest in the village, stoutly built of blocks of a black stone Abigail didn't recognise, with a thatched roof. Most of the other houses were of wattle and daub. The only other stone buildings were the temple and the inn.

"Come in," Malke said. "Jenne is upstairs."

As they climbed the stairs, Abigail could hear the child coughing – a deep, hacking sound. Then, as the coughing fit ended, a high-pitched whoop as the child tried to breathe. Straight away, she knew what the problem was – back in England, they would have called it the hundred-day cough. She had no idea what it was called here, nor how to treat it.

Malke opened the door of a small room at the head of the stairs. Abigail followed her in. Jenne, a small, pale child whose eyes had dark shadows beneath them, reached out her arms to her mother and Malke sat on the edge of the bed and cuddled her close.

"How long has she been coughing like this?" Abigail asked. "And are there any other symptoms?"

"It started about four seisdags ago," Malke said. "It seemed like an ordinary cold. Then after a couple of seisdags, the cough became worse. It makes her double up and she can't catch her breath and it seems to go on and on. She even vomits sometimes and says that her ribs hurt. And she has no appetite – she has lost weight."

"How long has she been whooping for?"

"Since the cough became worse."

Malke looked at Abigail with worried eyes. Abigail could sense her deep love for her daughter and her feelings of helplessness, that she could not make it all better for her.

"I think I know what the problem is," Abigail said. "But I will need to see her alone."

Malke nodded. "I will be downstairs. Call if you need me." She hugged her daughter once more, then quietly left the room.

Abigail fished her Goldstone out of its pouch around her neck and held it in her hand. Jenne looked frightened – she must reassure her first.

Abigail walked across to the bed and sat down on the edge, where Malke had been. "Don't worry, Jenne. I'm here to help you."

She examined the child with eyes, nose and healing sense. Then she clasped her Goldstone and sent her thought across the miles.

Waymage Rusilon? Can you hear me?

Who is this?

Abigail, Waymage Shaunan's initiate.

What is the problem? Has anyone been injured?

No. We have reached Malke's village, and her daughter is sick. She has asked me to cure her, but I don't know how.

What is wrong with her?

Abigail relayed the child's symptoms to Rusilon, finishing, *We call it the hundred-day cough at home, but I don't know what you call it here.*

She heard a laugh. *Hundred-day cough? That is a good name for it. We call it the Trader's Cough, as it is often spread by Yrusians travelling from place to place.*

How do you treat it?

There is no cure, but there are herbs which can make the cough less painful. If you mix hyssop with rue, rosemary and honey, that should help her. How long has she had it?

About four seisdags.

Poor child. She has a way to go. Did Waymage Shaunan give you any elecampane root powder?

Abigail rummaged in her bag. *Yes. How is it used?*

It can be made into a tea – one big spoonful in a large beaker of water, boiled and simmered for twenty minutes. Tell the mother to give it to the girl at night – it will make her drowsy and should make her sleep easier.

How long will it take before she is better?

You said it yourself – by the end of a hundred days. But you can shorten the time by using your Goldstone and casting a healing spell.

Thank you, Waymage. Give my love to Shaunan, please.

Abigail heard her laugh. *Of course I will.*

Abigail took her hand off her Goldstone, then spoke to Jenne. "I'm going to say some words, which should make you feel a little better."

Jenne took a deep breath, which made her cough again. Abigail waited until the spasm was over then, touching the child's thin chest gently with one hand, her Goldstone in the other, murmured, *Gal ens bynn wellent, gal ens bynn wellent.* She felt a flow of healing going into the child, who lay back and closed her eyes. Good, rest was what she needed most.

Abigail tiptoed to the door, opened it, walked through, and closed it behind her. Then she called softly, "Malke, would you come up, please?

She heard light footsteps running up the stairs. "Can you cure her?"

"No, but I can make her more comfortable. I will leave you some medicine to give her – one lot whenever the cough is bad, the other only at night. Do you have somewhere I can make it up?"

"Thank you, Waymage. I am in your debt. This way."

Abigail followed Malke down the stairs, where the rest of the company were waiting, having left their baggage at the inn.

"How is the child?" Ylonya asked.

"Resting. I need to make up some medicine to leave here."

"Good."

Abigail hoped this Talamdorian woman would be able help them. But surely the Castellan would not have sent them to her otherwise.

"How can I be of service?" Malke asked. "I am in your healer's debt."

"Let me introduce you to everyone first," Ylonya said. "You know Abigail. The others are Aidren, a Dagâran Warrior, Ednor of Néartania, also a Warrior and Tremond, a Watchman from Garûnalond."

Malke nodded at each of them. "I wonder what brings such a mixed company to Talamdor."

"It is probably better if you do not know, in case anyone asks," Ylonya said. "But Castellan Trévon said you would be willing to help us."

"I have said so," Malke said, sounding slightly irritated.

Abigail soothed her automatically.

"And we are grateful," Ylonya said. "We need two things: information about the layout of Talamunem City, and any advice you can give about getting in and out of there safely."

Malke's eyebrows shot up, but she said only, "Whatever I can do. I think it would be best if you go in disguise." Her eyes went from one to the others, then she said, "You don't look much like Talamdorians at present. But let us have dinner first."

Dinner proved to be a rich beef stew, with fluffy potatoes and herb dumplings. They sat round the oval table in Malke's kitchen and ate to their heart's content.

"That was delicious," Ednor said. "My thanks, Headwoman Malke."

"Malke will do."

"How are you going to disguise us?" Abigail asked.

"For a start, you will need something to put over your Waymarks," Malke said, "or you will be recognised as enemies straight away. Of course, if I had a Bloodstone, I could cast a glamour over them. But it might not last long enough. However, I don't, so disguising them will have to do. And you, Ylonya and Tremond will need to have your hair dyed black. After that, it will be a matter of providing you with suitable clothing and fake bangles of control."

Abigail could sense Malke was withholding something, but could not detect any malice. Should she tell her about the Bloodstone? No, better not – the Wayzenmoot had told her to keep it secret. Abigail brought her attention back to the others.

"Bangles of control?" Ednor was saying. "What are they?"

"They are silver-coloured bangles worn by lower-class Talamdorians," Malke said. "But they are not made of silver. They are made of talamunium. The Talamdorian elite use them to control the rest of us."

"Like the one Bredor wore in the Fenland," Aidren said.

Abigail noticed that Malke was wearing such a bangle and that everyone she had seen so far in the village was too and jumped to a conclusion. "Are all the bangles in this village fake ones?"

"Yes. We go our own way. You need to understand that anyone else wearing a bangle will be, at least to some extent, under the control of anyone with a Talamdorian Bloodmark."

"The red triangle?" Abigail asked.

"Yes. How did you know?"

"We encountered a Talamdorian noble in the Fenland in southern Yrusian," Ylonya said. "He used such a bangle to control the Lord of the Fenland."

"Then Jacob will probably be wearing one," Abigail said. "How are we going to convince him to come with us?"

"Who is Jacob?" Malke asked.

"Someone who was kidnapped by a Talamdorian agent, back in Néartania," Abigail said. "We are hoping to rescue him from the Prophet of the One."

"We'll cross that bridge when we come to it," Ylonya said. "At the moment, we are still a dozen miles away from Talamunem City. We need a plan to get in there, rescue Jacob, fulfil the rest of our quest and get out again."

"Which is why you need to know the layout of the City," Malke said.

"Yes," Ylonya said.

"I will draw you a map tomorrow."

"Here is the map," Malke said, spreading it out on the kitchen table. "Our village is here," she pointed to a small dot, "and as you can see, Talamunem City is south-east of us."

Ylonya peered at the map. "That is helpful – thank you. Do you also have a map of the layout of Talamunem City? And any idea where we might find the Prophet of the One?"

Malke turned the map over. "Here," she said. "I have only been to the City a handful of times, so I have had to draw this from memory. The North Gate is here," she pointed again, "then you will have to make your way through the streets to the Great Temple of Talamu. You will be able to see it from far away – it is the tallest building in the City and has twin spires which rise high into the air. The Prophet's apartments are somewhere inside."

"Do you know of anywhere just outside the walls where we could hide if necessary?"

Malke flipped the map over again. "There is a system of caves here," she said, pointing to a place about a mile outside the City's walls. "We use it sometimes to store trade goods."

"Thank you," Ylonya said. "That is exactly what we needed to know. My final request is whether you have anything from Talamunem City which I could use to supplement the map?"

Malke looked surprised. "You have the Finding sense?"

Ylonya nodded. "I do."

"Then I will find you something to use," Malke said. "But first, I will dye your and Abigail's and Tremond's hair."

"We are most grateful."

Abigail sat patiently on the wooden chair in Malke's bedroom, as the Talamdorian massaged some black dye into her hair. It reminded her of the time Genira had done a similar service, back in Taellingsford. But then, Ellyn had been with them. She felt the tears spring to her eyes. Think about something else.

"What is in this?" she asked.

"Powdered black walnuts, mixed with some other things to make it easy to apply," Malke replied. "It won't last forever but should work long enough for your purposes."

"I am most grateful to you – we all are," Abigail said. "Are there many villages like yours, which resist the rule of the Prophet of the One?"

Malke's fingers stopped their motion. "Why do you ask?"

"No reason. I was just curious."

"It is better that you do not know. I can only speak for the people here. We discovered that all Veylindréans were not evil when Trévon saved my life. Since then, we have met others – mainly from Chorich Castle. They seem to be ordinary people, like us. And I have long believed that the bangles of control are an evil in Talamdor."

"When did you find out how they worked?" Abigail asked.

"It was my father who discovered their secret," Malke said. "And gradually, he brought others in and began to substitute the bangles of control with identical silver ones, which look the same, but do not have the power to dominate hearts and minds. But if any Talamdorian noble comes this way, we have to act as though they do."

"Is that why the village looks other than it is to the casual glance?"

"Yes," Malke said. "It makes us uninteresting to any Talamdorian nobles who might pass this way.

"How did you do it?" Abigail said. "When we first arrived, it looked poor and neglected. It was only when I took my Goldstone in my hand and saw it with the eyes of the Way that I realised the truth."

Malke met her gaze in the mirror. "Trévon trusts you and you have helped ease Jenne's cough, so I will tell you. But please, I beg of you, keep this information to yourself. The whole village could be in danger if the Talamdorians discovered the truth."

"I promise," Abigail said.

Malke took a deep breath, then said, "I have a Bloodstone which enables me to cast a glamour over the whole village, which is automatically activated in the presence of strangers."

So that was what she had been withholding. "Ah, now I understand. That is so clever. And don't worry, your secret is safe with me – I understand why you didn't want the rest of my companions to know."

Malke smiled at her. "Thank you," she said. "It was first used by my great, great grandmother. Of course at that time, it was to avoid the attentions of the Havimi, but it works equally well to deter any agents of the Prophet from looking too closely. Both Bloodstone and the power to cast a glamour have been passed down the female line, as I will one day pass it down to Jenne."

It was on the tip of Abigail's tongue to share the purpose of the quest with Malke, but she had second thoughts. What the woman didn't know, she could not betray. It was probably an unfair judgement, but better safe than sorry.

"That's you done," Malke said. "You'll have to leave it on for an hour, then we'll wash it out. Could you send Ylonya up?"

"Surely," Abigail said. "Thank you again."

Tremond did not approve of this business of disguise – it seemed deceitful, somehow. When Ylonya came downstairs, looking almost unrecognisable, her brown hair a harsh black, he realised what he was in for.

"You're next," Ylonya told him.

Tremond heaved himself to his feet and walked up the stairs. The Talamdorian woman, Malke, was waiting for him, a bowl of a black, glutinous dye beside her on the table.

"Untie your hair, please," she said. "And I think we'll have to dye your beard, moustache and eyebrows too. Unless you'd rather shave them off?"

"Definitely not." Unthinkable.

Tremond fought not to scowl as she draped a linen cloth around his shoulders and set to work. It took a long time – not only was his hair long, it was also thick. Then she started on his facial hair. He stood for it as patiently as he could. If the disguise got them into Talamunem City safely, it would be worth it. He supposed.

By his estimation, two long and tedious hours had passed.

She passed him a reflector. "There. Even your best friend would not recognise you."

Tremond gazed into the reflector and was amazed at the difference having black hair made to his appearance. "My thanks, Mistress Malke."

"Another day gone," Ylonya said, "but it can't be helped. We needed to be disguised before we continued."

"You all look so different," Ednor said. "Especially you, Tremond."

The Garûnalonden grunted. "I'm glad it will wear off eventually."

Malke walked in with a large basket of clothes. "There should be enough for everyone here," she said. "Go and get changed."

Abigail was the first down. "May I go and see Jenne?" she said. "I'd like to check on her before we go."

"Of course," Malke said. "She had a better night – she only woke up coughing once. But I'd better go with you. She might not recognise you with black hair and different clothing."

Abigail followed her up the stairs and into Jenne's bedroom. "Here is the healer to see how you are," Malke said.

Jenne's eyes widened in surprise. "It is me," Abigail said. "Your mother has dyed my hair. How are you feeling?"

"Better, thank you," Jenne said.

"That is good to hear," Abigail said, examining her once more. "If you carry on taking your medicine like a good girl, you should feel much better before long."

Once everyone was back downstairs, looking self-conscious in the Talamdorian clothes, Malke said, "Now I need to disguise your Waymarks."

She applied a thick cream to each of their Waymarks, blending it in carefully so that it didn't show. Abigail noticed that she had even thought to provide a darker one for Aidren, which would blend with his dark brown skin. So thoughtful.

Then she gave the pots of paste to Abigail. "These will need reapplying regularly," she said, "at least once a day. And if it rains hard, they may wash off. Although you," she added, looking at Aidren, "had better keep the hood of your cloak up and your hands gloved when you reach the City – people with skin as dark as yours are rare in Talamdor."

"Thank you, Malke," Ylonya said, and her words were echoed by the rest of them.

"Now I just need to give you each a fake bangle of control," Malke said, "and you will be set to go. I would advise leaving the horses here – we don't have bloodstock like yours in the villages and they would be conspicuous. We will hide them and care for them until you return."

"It is getting too late for us to set out on foot for the caves today," Ylonya said, looking through the window at the dimming sun. "May we ask for your hospitality once more, Malke? We will leave at first light."

"Of course. I will call you at dawn."

Δ Chapter 5 Δ

Malke was as good as her word. She woke them at dawn, and after a hasty breakfast, they were finally on their way.

Abigail was beginning to feel excited. She had been missing Jacob for so long – his absence was a constant ache in her heart. And now they would be together again in a few days.

Or maybe not. She could not forget High Waymage Daefiel's words, that Jacob was with the Prophet of his own free will. What if he had changed? What if he didn't want to return to Veylindré with them? She wasn't sure she'd be able to bear it. She'd lost so much – her family, Ellyn. She couldn't abide the idea of losing Jacob too. If only Shaunan was with them…

Pull yourself together. If Jacob was under the Prophet's control, they'd just have to break him free. Somehow. She did not intend to leave Talamunem City without him.

But what if it came down to a choice between fulfilling the quest and leaving with the Master Bloodstone, and rescuing Jacob? Please God it would not.

It was odd to be on foot again. Already her shoulders and back were beginning to ache from the weight of her pack and her healer's bag. And the ground beneath her feet was uneven – she had to take care not to turn an ankle.

The countryside this close to Talamunem City was different to that further north. It was flatter, more open, with fields showing the new greening of the Season of

Growth, separated by hedgerows or dry-stone walls. In a funny way, it reminded her of home. But, like the fields of home, there were also fewer places to hide. She hoped they would reach the caves Malke had talked about without being spotted by the enemy.

"Are we going to reach the City today?" she asked.

"No," Ylonya said. "We'll hide up in the caves Malke told us about and work out a plan for getting to the Prophet."

"I agree," Tremond said. "Much better to sleep in the caves and move into the City fresh in the morning."

A shaft of resistance from Ednor, quickly suppressed. Was he in that much of a hurry to fight?

"How close are we now?" she asked Ylonya.

Ylonya closed her eyes briefly, her hand on her Goldstone. "About another three miles. We must move cautiously now – it would not do to be caught this close to the City."

"But surely we will be able to pass as Talamdorians."

Ylonya shrugged. "Perhaps. But it might take a lot of fast talking if anyone wants to know why we are here."

Abigail hadn't thought of that. "Have you thought of a story?"

"Yes. I spoke with Malke and we worked it out. We are a group of traders from northern Talamdor, from the mining village of Avarin, in the north-east, and are bringing a load of gemstones for sale."

"Gemstones?" Tremond said, overhearing her. "Where did you get gemstones from?"

"From Malke," Ylonya said. "I have assured her that we will return them or, if we fail and fall, she may apply to Guildmaster Brickon for their value in gold."

Abigail shivered. "Do you think we are going to fail?"

"Not if we are lucky," Tremond said. "But you never know. We are in enemy territory, after all."

By the time they reached the caves Malke had told them about, it was late afternoon. Aidren reckoned that if Malke had not given Ylonya a token to guide her to them, they would have missed them, hidden as they were in the middle of a small wood a mile or so north of the City.

"Here we are," she said. "As good a hiding place as any I have known."

They followed her into the main cave. Aidren looked around. The cave walls were irregular, its floor was of compacted earth. There was a neat stack of kindling against the back wall. Narrow passages led off it – to storage caverns, he assumed. Ellyn would have hated it. Don't think about that.

"Are we staying here tonight?" Abigail asked.

Aidren bit his lip. Why did they have to wait? Surely Abigail would want to find Jacob as soon as possible.

"Why don't we carry on and get the job done today?" Ednor asked.

"Yes. Why not?" Aidren was with him. He couldn't wait to get to the City and strike a blow for Ellyn.

"No," Ylonya said. "We are all tired. Get what rest you can, and we will start early tomorrow."

"I agree," Tremond said. "And we will be able to leave our packs here, too."

"But..." Aidren began.

"We wait until tomorrow," Ylonya said with finality in her voice.

As Aidren watched, Abigail shrugged off her pack and opened it, hauling out her blankets. So she was on Ylonya's side too.

There was nothing for it. He too took off his pack and chose a sheltered corner to sleep in.

"I think we could light a fire in here," Ylonya said, "so long as we use dry kindling, which won't give off too much smoke. I think we'd all welcome something hot to eat tonight."

After they had eaten a delicious hot soup made from some of the salted meat and vegetables donated by Malke, they sat around the fire together. Ednor took his whetstone out of his pack and began to sharpen his sword. Good idea. Aidren did the same.

"Now is the time to formulate our plan for getting into the Prophet's apartments and back out again," Ylonya said, bringing the map Malke had given her into the firelight.

"And for rescuing Jacob," Abigail said sharply.

"Of course," Ylonya said. "Let us hope we can do both."

What did she mean, 'let us hope we can do both'? If Ylonya thought that she, Abigail, was going to leave Talamunem City without Jacob, she had another think coming.

But what if it did come down to a choice? The fear of having to make that choice wouldn't leave her alone. It filled her mind, both waking and sleeping. Abigail was exhausted but found it hard to sleep. So many things could go wrong. What if, having come all this way, the quest failed? What if the Prophet was too strong to be beaten? What if Jacob didn't know them? She tossed and turned, turned and tossed, drifting into an uneasy sleep just before dawn. She awoke the next morning unrefreshed, almost entirely unready for the challenges ahead.

Aidren stoked up the fire and after they had eaten, Ylonya spoke.

"We need to think this through carefully," she said. "We have to formulate a plan for dealing with any dangers, both known and unknown, and also work out what to do if things go wrong."

"If the exit from the pass was guarded," Tremond said, "then all the gates of the City will almost certainly be. If it's just ordinary guards, Ednor, Aidren and I should be able to deal with them. But if Bloodmagic has been used, like we saw before, we'll have to be prepared to support and protect Abigail while she uses her powers to get past it."

"And we won't have time to decide who does what, in the heat of the moment," Ednor said. "So we'd better sort that out in advance."

"I will protect Abigail," Aidren said, "and lend her my strength."

Abigail smiled at him. "Thank you."

"Which leaves myself, Tremond and Ylonya to do the fighting," Ednor said. "Good."

"We must all stay together," Ylonya said.

"But what if we get separated?" Abigail asked. "What if some or all of us get captured?"

Ylonya frowned. "I hope that will not happen," she said. "But you're right, we need to think about that possibility."

"If we get separated, for whatever reason," Tremond said, "we should plan to meet up again here."

"And if we get captured?" Abigail said, in a small voice. Would their luck run out, this close to achieving their goals?

"Again," Ednor said, "it depends on how many Talamdorians are involved. If only a few, then we should be able to fight our way free. Or if only some of us get caught, the others may be able to free them."

"Always supposing," Aidren put in, "that whoever is left free knows where the others are being held."

There was a moment of quiet as they considered this possibility. The crackling of the fire was loud in the silence.

"I think we can guarantee," Abigail said, "that I at least will end up being taken to the Prophet."

"Why do you think that?" Ylonya asked.

"If they find a Bloodstone in my possession, that would be enough."

"I had almost forgotten about the Bloodstone," Ylonya said. "Do you think that this might be the time to use it?"

She remembered Ednor's bitter words, back at the mouth of the pass. Perhaps she should use it – what was the point of having it, otherwise? She rummaged in her pack, took out the red buckskin pouch.

"May I borrow your knife, Aidren?"

"Why do you need it?" Aidren asked, taking his knife out of its sheath at his waist and handing it over.

Abigail met his gaze. "I need to draw some blood from my finger – it's not called Bloodmagic for no reason. I will have to smear some blood on the stone to awaken its powers."

They all looked revolted at the thought. "In Ranu's name," Ylonya breathed. "Is that why? Where do they get that much blood?"

"From wearers of the silver bangles, I suspect."

"Then have mine," Aidren said. "We cannot risk you being weakened."

Abigail smiled, touched by his offer. "That is kind, but I think it will work better with my own."

Taking a deep breath, she pricked her finger, then allowed the blood to drip onto the Bloodstone. As before, in Valwyn's chambers, it felt cold in her hand and oddly slippery.

"The Bloodstone will fight against me," she said. "It will try to fill my mind with negative thoughts, so that I will fail. It would help if you could all think positive thoughts and augment my strength."

The four of them got out their Goldstones and each touched her. She could feel her mind becoming stronger, less vulnerable.

"Thank you," she said. "Please keep it up."

Then she closed her eyes, concentrated on the Bloodstone. Almost immediately, the negative thoughts began to fill her mind. *It's too dangerous. You can't do this. Who do you think you are?* But she could also sense the positive thoughts of her friends – Aidren's fierce care for her, Ylonya's desire to succeed, Tremond's love for Garûnalond and the rest of Veylindré, and Ednor's need to strike a blow against Talamdor. Their combined yearnings kept the negative thoughts at bay. Perhaps she could do this.

She sent her thought out across the land, towards Talamunem City. And sensed a fierce resistance.

Something or someone would not permit her to continue. She gritted her teeth, tried again.

Then felt a sharp shaft of attention. She gasped aloud and took her hand from the Bloodstone, threw her thought away from it, opened her eyes.

"What's wrong?" Aidren asked, his voice sharp.

"Someone became aware of me, of my presence. I think – I think it was the Prophet."

"How could you know that?" Ednor asked.

"I don't know. But who else could it be?"

"Anyone with a Bloodstone," Ylonya said.

Abigail shook her head. "I don't think so. From what High Waymage Valwyn told me, the use of Bloodstones is closely regulated by the Prophet and only the Master Bloodstone has the full power of Bloodmagic."

"Truly?" Aidren said. "How does he have such power over his people?"

"His rule in Talamdor is absolute," Ylonya said. "That much we have been able to discover."

"So what now?" Ednor said. "If we can't use the Bloodstone without alerting the Prophet, what use is it going to be?"

"Leave her alone," Aidren said. "Can't you see she's telling the truth?"

Ednor looked at him, eyebrows raised. "I meant no disrespect," he said. "But we are still no closer to formulating a plan of action and the night is growing old."

It took them another hour to work out a plan, or rather, plans. How to enter the City, how to find the Prophet's apartments, and fallback plans if things went awry.

"I think we should do our Immersion practice before we leave," Abigail said. "I for one will feel better for it."

She could sense Ednor's impatience but held his gaze until he acquiesced. The five of them knelt or sat cross-legged in a circle and took out their Goldstones. As she sank down into the soothing peace of Immersion, Abigail could feel mental strength and even some serenity filling her soul. Dear God, Beloved Ranu, give me the strength and will to do what has to be done. Keep us all safe. Amen.

After a few minutes, she opened her eyes, sighed. "That is better. Our quest is in the hands of the Six now." And God.

"Let's leave anything we won't need here," Ednor said as they ate a quick meal before leaving. "We'll be better off travelling light, so it is easy to fight."

"A good point," Tremond agreed. "We should only need the barest minimum of food and water, and our weapons."

"I'm not leaving my healer's bag behind," Abigail said. "What if one of us gets injured?"

"We will have to take the gemstones," Ylonya said. "They are our alibi for approaching the City."

They packed up all the things they were leaving in the caves – their sleeping rolls and most of the contents of their packs, the extra food and the tents. Then they hid them in one of the side caves, just in case.

Abigail shoved a *feolin* loaf and her water bottle into her healer's bag. Mustn't forget the Bloodstone. Although after this morning's experience, should she use it again? What if it brought them all to the Prophet's attention? But she said nothing to the others.

"Now for it," Ednor said, grinning fiercely. "Let's go."

The five of them swung their much lighter packs onto their backs and headed south, towards Talamunem City.

The northern walls of Talamunem City lay ahead of them, glistening darkly in the noonday sunlight. A huge mountain filled the rest of the horizon, behind and to the left of the City.

"What stone is that?" Abigail asked Ylonya, pointing to the walls. "I've never seen anything so black."

"Basalt," Ylonya said. "It is a volcanic stone, quarried from the slopes of Mount Talamu." She nodded in the direction of the mountain.

They were walking along a paved road made of the same black stone. In all her thoughts of how this moment would play out, Abigail had not imagined that they would be approaching the City openly and directly, as though they had the right to be there. She had thought they would be sneaking in under cover of darkness. But she trusted Ylonya.

She felt a twitch against her back. Something in her pack was vibrating. A voice in her mind: *I have been waiting for you, Abigail Winters.*

She fought not to cry out. How did the Prophet know her name? For she had no doubt that the voice in her head was his.

I knew you would come here in the end. That you would not be able to resist trying to rescue Jacob.

Her heart jumped. He knew about her and Jacob. How did he know? Had Jacob betrayed them? Surely not.

Do not try to resist me, Abigail. I am stronger than you will ever be. When you reach the City, you will come to me of your own free will. You will not be able to do anything else.

She tried to close her mind to him. He mustn't know how close they were, or they would be captured straight away.

"Talk to me," she said to Aidren, who was walking next to her. "Keep my mind occupied."

"Why?" he said, startled.

"Because the Prophet is trying to get into my head, trying to overpower my will."

Aidren's eyes widened. "He can do that?"

Abigail nodded. "Yes, but I think I can keep him out if I concentrate on what you tell me."

"What d'you want to talk about?"

"Tell me about how you came to know you were going to become a Warrior of Dagâra."

Aidren shot her a doubtful look, but obediently began to speak. "I was about ten, when a Warrior visited Nordvein, on his way back from Garûnalond. He was tall and strong and bore a mighty sword. As soon as I saw him, I knew that I wanted to be like him when I grew up."

"What was his name?"

"Belor. He had been serving Lord Phanuman and Lady Melandré, the rulers of Garûnalond."

"Why was he returning to Dagâran?"

"I'm not sure," Aidren said. "I think his term of service had ended and he was going back to Luvodican to be reassigned somewhere else."

"What was it about him that inspired you?" Abigail asked.

"His strength and his certainty. He knew that his strong arms and skill with the sword could help to protect people weaker than him. Meeting him filled me with the desire to do the same – to protect others by strength of arms."

"What happened next?"

"After he left – he only stayed for a day and a night – I summoned up my courage and spoke with my father."

"Your father was a miner, wasn't he?" Abigail remembered. "Was he disappointed that you didn't want to follow him?"

Your father must be sorely disappointed in you. His eldest daughter, following pagan goddesses…

Abigail's head whirled. How did the Prophet know exactly which sore spots in her heart to touch? *Go away.* She shut him out again, brought her attention back to Aidren.

"Maybe a little," Aidren was saying. "He told me to use the seasons until the Ceremony of Assignment to really think about my decision. Later, when it became clear that my mind was made up, that the Way was calling me to the path of a Warrior, he gave me his blessing."

"That must have been wonderful," Abigail said. "I didn't know that I was being called to Ranu until Shaunan proved it to me."

"How did she do that?"

"By putting a picture into my mind, then asking me to do the same to her. It seemed so natural to be able to do that. I was so surprised when she told me that it was a rare gift."

Not so rare, Abigail Winters. I too can put a picture into your mind. But you may not like what you see, unless you surrender your will to mine.

"No!" she said aloud.

"No what?" Aidren asked.

"It's the Prophet," Abigail said, "speaking in my mind. He wants me to surrender my will to him."

"You must fight him," Aidren said. "Don't let him in."

"I don't know how," Abigail said. "He's so strong."

"Fight him, Abigail," Aidren hissed, "otherwise Ellyn's sacrifice will have been for nothing."

Δ Chapter 6

When Portak wandered into General Kreldik's tent late the following morning, he discovered a planning meeting in progress. Although the foot soldiers had been given the rest day they needed, the General and his staff had not been idle.

"The scouts I sent to Mistbourne Keep last night have now returned," Kreldik was saying, "so we now have a good idea of the lie of the land and can plan our campaign. "Mindak," he continued, "tell us what you have learned."

The short, weather-beaten man bowed. He looked exhausted and his clothes were filthy. But he straightened up and saluted before he began to speak. "Sir. Mistbourne Keep is on the opposite side of the Mistbourne River from here. The river loops around it, forming a natural moat on three sides. It is flowing both fast and deep in this season. On the other side, the main gate of the Keep is located. There is a drawbridge, but it is up."

"Were you able to cross the river and discover the defences on the northern side?" Portak asked.

"No, my Lord," Mindak said. "Like I said, it runs both fast and deep and is, I guess, more than thirty feet across. I thought it best to return to share what we have learned. But I expect that, like the rest of the Keep, the northern side will be fortified."

"How high are the walls?" Kreldik asked.

"My guess would be about twenty to twenty five feet," Mindak said, "and there are taller towers at regular intervals, including one on each side of the main gate."

"Our thanks, Mindak," Kreldik said. "Go, rest."

The little man bowed and left the tent.

Kreldik turned to Portak and his senior officers. "It seems clear that our first objective must be to cross the river. Options?"

One of the captains, a grizzled veteran from the war against the Havimi, raised his hand. "Yes, Normek?"

"General Kreldik, sir. One way of getting across might be to build plank bridges and lay them across from bank to bank. We had some success with that, back in the day."

Kreldik stroked his chin with one hand, his face thoughtful. "Ye-es," he said. "The problem with that is how we would protect the bridge builders from the enemy trying to kill them from the Keep's battlements."

"And where would we get the wood from, to build such bridges?" Portak put in.

"We brought a certain amount with us, in the baggage train," Kreldik said, "but I would rather save that for constructing our siege towers and trebuchets. We must chop down some trees – there are plenty hereabouts – then cut planks from them to build the bridges."

"Is there no other alternative?" Portak asked.

"If this was a regular moat," Normek told him, "we could attempt to fill it with soil and rubble or try to drain it. But draining a river would be impossible."

"Even if we do manage to cross the river somehow, we will still need to break down the main gate," Kreldik said.

"That means we will need either a battering ram, siege towers or both," Normek said.

"We have brought the battering ram with us and have sufficient wood for the towers, so long as we can use local trees for the bridges," Kreldik said.

The discussion continued for half an hour longer, while the details were thrashed out. Then Kreldik dismissed them.

"Very well. That is our plan. This council is concluded."

It took another three days to prepare for the siege. Portak watched, fascinated, as two huge siege towers were built. Each was a tall, square, wooden construction, with stairs inside, built on a foundation of wheels, so the draft horses who had pulled the supply wagons could drag it to its destination. At the topmost level was a drawbridge, which could be lowered directly onto the battlements.

"How are we going to get them across the moat?" he asked one of the builders.

"Don't ask me, friend," the builder replied, shrugging. "My job is to build as ordered. Strategy is for higher ups."

The man obviously had no idea who he was, so Portak let it go. He turned on his heel and strode towards General Kreldik's tent.

"I've been watching the construction of the siege towers," he said. "How are we going to get them across the moat? And will there be enough space on the other side to set them up?"

Kreldik looked up from the papers on his desk and frowned. Why? It was an innocent question.

"Our battle plan is two-fold," he said. "One part of our force is going to march several miles downriver with the siege towers and cross the river unmolested, before heading back up the other bank to besiege the less-protected northern side of the keep. The rest of us will attack on foot from this side, using the plank bridges to cross it, ladders to scale the walls and a battering ram to reduce the gate to rubble. We also have three trebuchets to fling missiles at the walls."

"But all our weapons are made of wood," Portak said. "What if the enemy uses flaming arrows?"

"All the towers, trebuchets and bridges will be covered with wet hides, to repel any flame that attacks them."

"You seem to have thought of everything," Portak said. "His Holiness will be pleased."

"If you are going to speak to him, you may tell him that the siege will begin at sun-up the day after tomorrow."

"Not until then?"

"No," Kreldik snapped, "We need the rest of today and most of tomorrow to finish construction, then we will travel under the cloak of darkness to reach the Keep by first light."

Jacob simply could not face yet another meeting in the Chamber of Law. So he slipped out of his rooms and strolled down to the market square. He spent a pleasant hour, wandering round the stalls, the sunshine warm upon his face, immersing himself in the bustle of trading and trying to forget where he was.

A single word brought him back to himself. Havimi. He stopped walking, trying to make it look like a natural pause and strained his ears to find out who was speaking and what they were talking about. Two whip-thin traders, in a corner between a leather goods stall and a chandler's, speaking in low, urgent tones.

"And I heard they're planning to invade Talamdor, now our army's in Néartania. It'll be a pushover – no one here to defend us."

The second trader glanced around, and Jacob immediately glued his gaze to a fine belt on the leather goods stall.

Satisfied he was not being overheard, the man said, "That's not what I've heard. Didn't you hear about the Havimi trader," and here he turned his head aside and spat, "who was killed outside the South Gate the other day?"

The first man's eyes rounded in horror. "No. What happened?"

"A gigantic figure made of red metal came out of nowhere, grabbed hold of the Havimi and did him to death. Then disappeared, just like that. Poof!"

That sounded like one of the Guardians he and Portak had encountered at the Veylindréan side of the secret pass. Had the Prophet brought them here? Or were there more than the two he had seen? Then he remembered what the Prophet had said in the Chamber of Law: 'I have put other defences in place. I am pleased to hear they are working.'

Jacob shivered. If those Guardians were loose in the City, he'd better watch his step. He ought to return to the citadel and report what he had heard.

A quarter of an hour later, having run most of the way back, he was outside the Chamber of Law. "Let me in," he gasped, "I have an important message for the Prophet."

The two guards outside the Chamber glanced at each other, then lowered their spears.

Jacob burst into the Chamber. "My Lord," he said. "I have urgent news. I was down in the marketplace just now and overheard two traders talking. They said there was a rumour that the Havimi were planning to invade Talamdor, now that our armies are away in Veylindré."

"Sit down and be quiet," the Prophet said in a level tone, in which Jacob heard more menace than if the man had shouted at him. Oh, God! What had he done? How would the Prophet punish him? Thoughts of red, metal claws and flaming yellow eyes filled his mind and he had to suppress a shiver.

"We will speak of this later," the Prophet said, then turned his attention back to the Talamdorian nobles. "As I was saying, before we were interrupted by our impetuous young friend..."

Domlok raised his hand. "My Lord," he said with a courtier's smoothness, "I, and, I am sure, my colleagues also, would like to hear more about this rumour."

"Then want must be your master," the Prophet snapped. "You have my assurance that this rumour is false. And in any case, the City is well-defended."

"But my Lord..." Domlok began.

"Enough, Domlok," the Prophet said. "You," he continued, swinging round to face Jacob, "go back to my apartment and wait for me there. I will deal with you later."

Jacob felt himself go pale. He stumbled out of the room, closing the door behind him.

Portak was woken before dawn by having his shoulder shaken.

"What? What is it?"

"Time to get up, my Lord," his orderly said. "We march in half an hour."

Portak rolled out of bed, washed his hands and face in the ewer and got dressed. Then headed to the cooking fires to get some breakfast. It was going to be a long day and he needed some food in his belly.

He had watched the tall siege engines, drawn by the patient draft horses, leave with about a third of Kreldik's army late the previous evening. Which should mean they would be in place, ready to attack the less-defended northern side of the Keep, by the time the main part of the army arrived, later this morning.

He only had time for a hunk of bread and a mug of ale before the signal to march came. He guessed it would take them between two and three hours to reach the Keep. Hopefully they would be in time. How were they going to let the other half of the army know that they were in place?

He wished there was some way of staying in touch with them, apart from by runner. But he knew that, even if someone in the other part of Kreldik's army held a Bloodstone, they, like him, would only be able to speak directly with Tamin, the Prophet's Chief Messenger. The Bloodstones did not permit two-way communication. Or perhaps that was a limitation imposed by the Prophet, or by Holy Talamu herself. He dismissed the matter from his mind – it was not his job to question the will of either.

The sun was just beginning to lighten the eastern sky as the army began its slow march towards Mistbourne Keep. As Portak watched, she began to rise in a glorious display of red and orange, barred by deep grey clouds. He guessed that at their present pace, they should be in place by the end of second hour. Too late to catch the Veylindréans unawares, perhaps, but at least they might distract them from the peril coming from the north.

Jacob paced to and fro in a frenzy of agitation. What was the Prophet going to do to him? How long would he have to wait? Not for the first time, he wished he could simply run away, lose himself in the Talamdorian countryside and settle down to earn his living as an honest smith.

Outside the door, he heard the clash of spears as the two guards came to attention. The meeting must be over. He braced himself for the worst. Not that he could imagine what the worst might be…

The Prophet entered the room and strode towards his throne, black robes billowing out behind him. He seated himself, then glared at Jacob.

No words. Why wasn't he shouting? The tension in the room was unendurable. Jacob held himself stiffly to attention, chin up, eyes straight ahead. Waiting for… he knew not what.

"You." The single word dropped from the Prophet's lips like a piece of old ice. "Sit."

Jacob scurried to fetch his usual seat, then collapsed into it. He couldn't seem to get enough breath into his lungs.

"Never," the Prophet said in the same cold voice, that hurt Jacob far more than a raised one, "contradict me in public again. I have raised you high in my service. Do not forget that I can also bring you low."

"My Lord, I'm…" Jacob began.

"I did not give you permission to speak," the Prophet said. "You have disappointed me, Jacob. I had thought that I could begin to trust your judgement, that I could place some confidence in you." A pause. "Evidently I was mistaken."

Jacob sat in his chair, his eyes darkening and his face flushing as shame filled his mind and heart. However the Prophet chose to punish him, he surely deserved it. He kept his eyes lowered, not daring to meet his master's gaze.

"Look at me!" The voice cracked out like a whip.

Startled, Jacob raised his head, looked into the man's cold, dark eyes.

"Perhaps I have been too lenient with you, made too many allowances for your ignorance. Perhaps a little pain might teach you some wisdom. Yes, I think it might."

Before Jacob had time to draw breath to at least try to defend himself, the Prophet touched the Bloodstone at his throat.

Agony. Jacob doubled over like he'd been punched in the stomach. His belly felt like it had been filled with molten lead. And the surface of his skin was alive with a million pinpricks, shredding his nerves. He fought not to cry out, biting his lower lip bloody.

Then, as abruptly as it had begun, the pain left him. He sat back in his chair, sweating and exhausted.

"That is what happens to people who displease me," the Prophet said. "Do not forget this lesson."

Jacob bowed his head. "No, my Lord."

"Leave me."

Jacob got to his feet somehow and stumbled out of the room.

As Mistbourne Keep came into sight, Portak's heart sank. It was just as Mindak had described it – the tall, battlemented walls, the twin towers either side of the main gate and the river flowing fast and full in front of it. How in Talamu's name were they going to conquer it?

Kreldik made his depositions. The trebuchets were trundled into position, then the horses were taken back to a safe distance. Soldiers were standing by the improvised bridges, preparing to place them across the width of the river to gain access to the keep. The archers were behind a wall of shields, ready to shoot any defenders who showed themselves.

As Portak watched, the sling of the first trebuchet was loaded with heavy stones. "Fire!" came the order. The missiles flew through the air and hit the castle's walls. A heartbeat later, stones from the second trebuchet did the same from another direction.

It did not take long for the enemy to respond. Archers atop the battlements shot flaming arrows at the trebuchets, trying to set fire to them. The Talamdorian archers shot back – the air was full of arrows in flight, Portak's ears with the thrum of bowstrings.

Under cover of the aerial fire, the first land bridge was swung into place and soldiers began to swarm across it. To be met by another storm of arrows from the battlements. Only a small fraction of the soldiers reached the far side of the river. This wasn't going to work. The keep was too strongly defended.

Portak's doubts proved to be unfortunately well-founded. At the end of the first long unsuccessful day, he had an idea. He went to find General Kreldik.

"General," he said. "It appears our tactics are not meeting with success. I wonder whether there might be another way of gaining access to the Keep."

Kreldik surveyed him from under his beetling eyebrows. "What are you talking about, man?"

"Just this," Portak said. "His Holiness has used my un-Talamdorian appearance in the past to infiltrate Veylindré. I could disguise myself as a Garûnalonden and spy out the keep's defences from the inside. Perhaps even open the gates."

"You would risk yourself for us?"

For the first time, Portak saw a genuine look of respect on the General's face.

"Yes, General."

"Very well. We will try that tomorrow."

Jacob did not see anything of the Prophet for the next couple of days. He kept to his room, only leaving it to eat, and tried to work out how to mend his fences with his master. Would he be permitted to work his way back into the man's good graces?

A knock on the door. "Come in."

A man Jacob recognised as one of the Prophet's personal servants stuck his head round the door. "The Prophet requires your presence in his apartments."

Jacob stood up. "Thank you. I'm on my way."

Ten minutes later, he presented himself to the guards at the door of the Prophet's apartment. "His Holiness is expecting me."

"You may enter." The guards lowered their spears and Jacob set his hand to the doorknob. Then quailed, afraid to go any further.

"What are you waiting for?" one of the guards said. "Go on in."

There was nothing for it. Jacob squared his shoulders and walked into the familiar sooty gloom of the Prophet's apartment, his palms clammy and his heart going twenty to the dozen.

The Prophet was seated on his throne, waiting for him.

"You sent for me, my Lord?"

"Yes, Jacob. Come on in. Sit down."

The man's voice was calm and pleasant, as though the scene two days ago had never happened. Jacob shook his head – what was going on?

"Come, Jacob. I have news for you."

"My Lord?" Jacob reached his usual chair and sat down, facing the Prophet.

"Yes. It seems that the scouts in the north of our land have encountered some Veylindréan strangers, loose within our borders and heading south. Unfortunately they lost them again, by some devilish trick. It seems we have dangers on more than one front to deal with."

Jacob summoned up his courage, asked a question. "How many of them were there?"

"Five, they said."

"Then why didn't the scouts capture them, bring them back here?"

“A good question,” the Prophet congratulated him. “A very good question indeed. I will be asking that of the scouts on their return.”

“Are they a danger to us?” Jacob asked.

“That remains to be seen,” the Prophet said. “However, I know that I can count on you to defend me, should the need arise.”

Relief flooded through Jacob like a warm wave. The Prophet had forgiven him. He still had a chance to be of service. “Of course, my Lord. Whatever I can do, I will.”

The Prophet nodded. “That is what I had hoped.”

Δ Chapter 7 Δ

The voice continued, insidious, tempting.

Why do you resist me, Abigail? Don't you understand that I have divine right on my side? Surely you realise that the pagan Way of the Veylindréans is against the will of God? Does it not say in the Book of Exodus, 'Thou shalt have no other gods before me'? The Way of the Veylindréan witches is evil and false, and God will condemn them.

Oh God! Is he right? Remember how you felt when Jacob was lost – that he had been taken from you as a punishment? Yes, but Shaunan showed me that was false.

Abigail stopped walking. She pressed her forefingers to her temples, trying to concentrate on blocking the voice. Her heart was beating fast.

She heard Aidren's voice, "Fight him, Abigail, otherwise Ellyn's sacrifice will have been for nothing."

Tears sprang to her eyes as her mind filled with memories of Ellyn – her beaming smile, her love of life and adventure, her steadfast friendship. Ellyn, dying in her arms with an arrow in her chest, killed by an agent of this same Prophet, who was now trying to tempt her to give up. Never!

Get out of my head! I'm not going to listen to you.

"Thank you, Aidren. You're right. It is for me, for us, to make Ellyn's sacrifice mean something."

"Come on, you two – keep up!" Ylonya's voice, low and urgent. The Yrusian strode back along the path to where Abigail and Aidren were standing.

"What's wrong?"

"It's the Prophet," Abigail said. "He's getting into my head, trying to persuade me to give in, to come over to his side."

"Then you must shut him out."

"Don't you think I've been trying?"

Ylonya grasped her shoulders with both hands. Her grip was surprisingly firm. "I'm sure you have, but you cannot afford to have a divided mind, not now, not when we're so close to achieving the quest."

"Which one?" Abigail asked.

Ylonya looked puzzled. "What do you mean, 'which one'?"

"Recovering the Master Bloodstone or rescuing Jacob."

"Let us hope we can do both," Ylonya said, as she had before. "But Abigail, there may soon come a point when you need to choose to put the greater good of Veylindré first. We all hope we can rescue Jacob, but getting the Master Bloodstone away from the Prophet is the main reason we're here. It's what the whole quest has been about, ever since we left Ranusheim. In the end, rescuing Jacob must come second."

A band of iron circled Abigail's chest. She had to make the choice now, while they were not in imminent danger, so she didn't let the rest of them down, so she could live up to their expectations. So that Ellyn's sacrifice might mean something.

She squared her shoulders. "Thank you, Ylonya. I needed to hear it spelled out like that. I won't let you all down. I promise, by the Six and the Way."

Ylonya's face softened into a smile. "I know you won't."

Just the same, it was hard. So very hard to realise she had to put rescuing Jacob second. When her heart was telling her he was the main reason she was there. How would she survive without him – without his warm lips on hers, his strong arms around her? Yet she had, somehow, ever since Talmis.

If you surrender to me, Abigail, you and Jacob can live happily ever after in Talamdor.

Happily ever after? she shot back. *With no free will, no freedom? Forget it.*

You will change your mind when you see him, Abigail. Jacob is happy here.

Get out of my head.

Panting, Abigail once more closed the doors of her mind. Just in time. They were approaching the North Gate of Talamunem City. The high black walls towered above them, shutting out most of the sunlight. She shivered. What kind of place was this?

"I will do the talking," Ylonya said. "The rest of you stay quiet. And Aidren, keep that hood up."

Ylonya walked up across the iron road of the drawbridge to the Gate, ready to knock on the postern, while the rest of them crowded together at the far end. As she lifted her hand, two huge figures materialised out of nowhere. They towered over her, being at least eight feet tall, clad in shining red armour from head to foot, yellow eyes flaming through the eye slots of their visors.

Abigail took an involuntary step backwards. The figures seemed too big to be real. She could sense the evil pulsing out of them.

"Who comes to this place?" The voice was deep, cold, malevolent.

She could not tell which of the two had spoken and felt the hair on the back of her neck standing up. Why hadn't Malke told them of these supernatural guards? She and the three men hurried to join Ylonya, stopping a few feet behind her. She must not face these beings alone.

"We are traders from Avarin, a mining village in the north," Ylonya said, "bringing a load of gemstones for sale in the City."

"You lie." The voice was chilling in its judgement. "Not one of you has Talamdorian blood in their veins."

Ylonya walked back to where the rest of them were waiting. "What do we do now?" she asked out of the corner of her mouth. "Has Malke betrayed us?"

"I felt no sense of deceit in her mind," Abigail whispered. "Perhaps she didn't know about these – whatever they are – or perhaps they are new to the City."

Ylonya nodded in acceptance.

"There are five of us and two of them," Ednor said. "I vote we fight."

"You have to be joking – have you seen the size of them?" Abigail said.

"I think the attempt must be made," Ylonya said.

Abigail gaped at her. She had not expected this. How could they defeat these monsters?

"If we do not at least try to overcome them, we will not be able to enter the City," Ylonya said. "Then all the long miles of the quest, all the sorrow and grief we have undergone, will have been in vain. You stay back, Abigail. The rest of us will see what we can do."

As soon as Ednor drew his sword, the eyes of the creatures flared from yellow to red and, to Abigail's horror, razor-sharp claws at least six inches long sprang out from the ends of their mailed hands. How…?

"Ednor, look out!"

But Ednor had already danced back out of reach of the murderous swipe that would have dropped him where he stood. There was a feral grin on his face. "Two of us to each of them," he said. "Aidren, you're with me."

As Abigail watched in horror, the four of them moved forward to engage with the… whatever they were. Ylonya and Tremond tackled one, Ednor and Aidren the other. At first, they seemed to have some success – one of Tremond's arrows found the eye slot of the second creature's armour and one of its flaming red eyes went dark. It roared in pain and rage. Ylonya closed with it but was forced to retreat by another swipe of the creature's claws. Even so badly injured, it was a formidable opponent.

Ednor and Aidren were darting in with their swords, trying to find a vulnerable spot in the other creature's armour. It parried their thrusts easily, having longer arms than they did. Ednor was fighting brilliantly, his sword flickering in the afternoon sun.

"Ednor! Look out!" Abigail had seen the second creature abandon Ylonya and Tremond and head for the other fight. Before anyone could intervene, it had swung its claws at his back, cutting through his steel armour as though it was gauze. He cried out in agony and fell to the ground.

Ylonya and Tremond raced over and the Garûnalonden joined Aidren in the fight, while Ylonya picked Ednor up in her arms and brought him back to Abigail.

"Do something," she panted. "I must return to the others."

Abigail knelt beside Ednor's unconscious body. She was not going to lose another member of the company. Not after Ellyn. She put aside her fear and concentrated on Ednor. Taking out her Goldstone from its pouch around her neck, she examined him with eyes, hands and healing sense. The back plate of his armour had been scored right through and yellow fluid was oozing out of the deep scratches. She took her pack off her shoulders and began to hunt through its contents. Luckily, she had transferred most of her healing herbs. She closed her eyes to concentrate better.

Then opened them again as the sounds of the fight stopped abruptly. Half a dozen Talamdorian guards had issued from the postern gate to see what was going on. Already they had overpowered Aidren and Tremond. Ylonya was nowhere to be seen. Two of the guards ran over to where she was crouching beside Ednor and pulled her upright.

The red armoured creatures had disappeared, their job done. But six against three was too many. "Leave that carrion here," one of the guards said. "The ravens can have him."

"But he is injured. He needs help."

"Not for long," the guard smirked, a malicious twinkle in his eyes. "No-one survives a gash that deep from a Guardian's claw… unless you have the antidote."

"Leave me alone, you brutes," Abigail said, struggling to free herself. "I must save him."

"Less of your lip. Talk back again and he won't be the last of your friends to die today. Come, now. We ain't asking."

Their grip on her was strong, merciless. Tears sprang to her eyes. Without her aid, Ednor would surely die. The quest had failed. It was all no use.

Aidren and Tremond had already been hustled away the other four guards. Where was Ylonya?

As soon as the human guards appeared, Ylonya had melted into the shadows of one of the buttresses that held up the wall. She knew that someone would have to remain free to look after Ednor. Holding herself still and silent, she waited until they had taken Abigail, Aidren and Tremond through the gate into the city. Then forced herself to count back from a thousand to be sure they weren't coming back.

She raced across to Ednor and put her fingers on his neck to check for a pulse. He was still alive. Her eyes fell on Abigail's pack, left behind when they had taken her prisoner. Somehow, she would have to get Ednor back to the caves and try to save his life.

Ednor's eyes opened. "What – what happened?"

He tried to rise, then sank back to the ground with a moan of pain.

"Lie still," Ylonya said. "The other creature hit your back, scored right through the armour."

"The others?"

"Captured. I hid so I could look after you."

"We – we must save them."

"You are in no condition to save anything or anyone. I'm going to try to get you back to the caves. Can you stand?"

With Ylonya's help, Ednor staggered to his feet. He was as pale as a Garûnalonden, his teeth clenched against another moan of pain.

Ylonya shouldered Abigail's pack over her own and put an arm around Ednor's waist. "I probably shouldn't be moving you at all," she said, "but we cannot stay here."

The distance back to the caves, which they had covered so blithely and swiftly earlier that day, took more than an hour to walk. Ylonya had to fight against looking back over her shoulder every other minute – if they were pursued, they were lost. Ednor was almost too heavy for her in his armour and was evidently in a lot of pain. Was she doing the right thing, forcing him to walk this distance? But what else could she do? If they had stayed where they were, they would have been captured for sure.

By this time, Ednor's lower lip was bloody from suppressing his cries of pain. She could tell he was nearly at the end of his strength.

"Not far now," Ylonya said, trying to sound encouraging.

Ednor merely nodded. He was past speech.

At last, they reached the wood in which the caves were hidden. When they reached them, Ylonya half-helped, half-lifted Ednor inside. He sank to the earthen floor, completely exhausted. His pale face was now grey with pain, apart from red spots high on his cheeks.

The guard had said the wounds were poisoned. Was she too late to save him? She offered him a drink from her flask, which he accepted with a nod.

"I'm going to have to take your armour off, to see the wounds," she said. "I'll be as gentle as I can. Can you sit up?"

Another nod. Ednor fixed his gaze on the far wall of the cave, an expression of fierce concentration on his face. Ylonya unstrapped the back plate of his armour, removed the stiff leather gambeson beneath it, then eased his undershirt up as gently as she could.

The creature's claws had scored four parallel lines across his back, deep and long. Each was oozing a foul-smelling yellow fluid and the surrounding skin was red and swollen as Ednor's body strove to fight the infection.

Ylonya rummaged in Abigail's bag. She didn't know much about healing – that was the domain of Healers and Waymages – but as a traveller, she had built up a basic knowledge of first aid. She took out a soft cloth and a bottle labelled 'comfrey'. Then began to clean Ednor's wounds.

She was as careful as she could be, but each time she touched his back, a hiss of pain escaped his clenched teeth. "I'm sorry," she said, "but I must get these clean if you are to have any chance of healing."

"Do what you have to."

Doggedly, Ylonya continued with her ministrations. At last, the wounds were as clean as she could make them.

"Stay still," she told Ednor. "I'm going to look in Abigail's bag again."

"What are you looking for?" he said, each word a gasp.

"Lènia's Nimbane," she said. "The herb that saved Modsdara's life. I think Shaunan gave it to Abigail when we left Chorich Castle. It is potent against poisons."

She had nearly given up hope when she found the small bottle half-full of dark purple liquid at the bottom of Abigail's bag, and a spoon. She gave Ednor one small spoonful, not daring to give more. The correct use of this rare herb was outside her rudimentary knowledge of healing.

"Now," she said. "I'm going to lay out a sleeping pad. I want you to lie on your stomach and try to sleep."

To her surprise, he fell asleep straight away. Perhaps the herb brought sleep to speed healing. She hoped she had not given him too much. She collected some firewood from the far corner of the cave and built a small fire. Then she rummaged again in Abigail's bag, trying to find the leaves of Lènia's Nimbane, remembering that Shaunan had made them into a poultice for the Fenlander girl.

"Oh, Shaunan. I wish you were here," she said under her breath. "I am no healer."

She heated some water over the fire and dropped in half a dozen of the leaves. Once they had softened, she poured the water away and waited for the leaves to cool. Then she applied them to Ednor's back, wrapped a bandage round him, then covered him with a light blanket. It was too cold at night to sleep uncovered.

He did not stir, seemed to be hardly breathing – had she given him too much of the potion? Oh, Yrusia! Had she killed him? She shook her head – it was too late to worry about that. She took out her Goldstone and touched him, praying, *Gal em bynn wellent, gal em bynn wellent.* But she was no Healer, didn't know whether her rough first aid would work.

She had done as much as she could. The rest was up to Ranu. Wearily, she took a *feolin* loaf out of her pack and began to munch it. She had no real appetite, but knew she had to keep up her strength. She would watch over Ednor until he woke, then return to the City to rescue the others. How, she did not know.

Ylonya woke with a start feeling cold and stiff, from a sleep she had never intended to take. Where was she? Then she remembered and jumped to her feet to check on Ednor. The fire had died down to embers and it was dark both inside and outside the cave. She fished out her Goldstone and murmured, *leumin.* Its clear, blue-white light welled through her fingers, and she hurried over to where Ednor was lying.

So far as she could tell, he had not moved since she had left him. She stooped to check he was still breathing. He was. She gently drew back the blanket to inspect the bandage. It was clean, unstained by blood or pus. Good. At least she hadn't killed him. She covered him up again, then tiptoed across to the fire and built it up into a good blaze. She took a blanket from her own pack and wrapped it around her shoulders.

When would Ednor wake up? And would it be to clarity or delirium? How she wished Shaunan – or even Abigail – were here. She had done her best for Ednor, but she was no Healer. Only time would tell whether he would recover from the wound those evil claws had dealt him.

And until he regained consciousness, she was trapped here. She couldn't leave him alone until she knew he would survive being left. In the meantime, who knew what was happening to Abigail and the others? If only there was someone else here to look after Ednor, so that she could try to rescue them. Gritting her teeth in frustration, she held her hands out to the blaze. In this enclosed space, the small fire had warmed the surrounding air quickly.

She shrugged her shoulders. There was nothing else to do but wait for morning, until Ednor woke up. Huddled under her blanket, she gazed into the flickering flames and hoped for the best.

Δ Chapter 8 Δ

Abigail's shoulders ached. The Talamdorian guards had pulled her hands behind her back and tied them tightly together with thin rope, which was cutting into her wrists. She, Aidren and Tremond were being hustled through the streets of Talamunem City, heading she knew not where.

And she could not find it in her heart to care. She trudged along, helpless and hopeless. The quest had failed. They had been captured before they even got into the city. Ylonya had disappeared and Ednor had been killed. His death, like that of Ellyn, was crushing her with guilt. Why had the High Waymages put this responsibility on her? Perhaps they thought she and the others were expendable and the real fight was taking place in Néartania.

Or was this the Prophet again, trying once again to undermine her sense of purpose? Aidren's words came back to her, "Fight him, Abigail, otherwise Ellyn's sacrifice will have been for nothing." She would not give up. Would not. She drew in a deep breath, raised her head and began to look around.

It was an imposing city. Fine buildings of three storeys and higher, organised in a neat grid pattern – so unlike other cities she had seen with their narrow chaos of streets leading every which way – built of the same black stone as the road they had walked along that morning. Basalt, Ylonya had called it. How had she managed to disappear? At least one of them was still free.

Their little procession was attracting some attention – the Talamdorians were not exactly lining the streets to watch, but she could sense a fierce curiosity in everyone they passed. Most were wearing the silver bangles that announced their subservient status.

"Make way there!" the guard shouted. "We are on the Prophet's business."

The Talamdorians melted away out of sight. What it must be like, to live in such fear. Her heart ached for them.

Then she heard Aidren gasp, "By the Six!"

What had he seen? She glanced up, then she too gasped. A huge cathedral-like building, black and intimidating, dominating the buildings around it. Its twin spires rose to a great height and its front was decorated with columns, spare and elegant. So different to the cathedrals back home, which would have been richly decorated. Such idolatry. Her Presbyterian soul preferred the plainness of this building. In the centre were wide, bronze doors, intricately carved with the triangular motifs of Talamdor.

A fierce tug on her arm brought her back to reality. The guards were not taking them to the cathedral. Instead, they swung left and marched the three of them down a side street towards another tall building. The captain of the guard took a ring of keys off his belt and opened the door.

Inside, it was dark, with a hot, metallic stench that made her uneasy. Blood. She could almost taste it. In an instant she was back in the cove in eastern Dagâran, looking at the piled up corpses of her family and the rest of the settlers. She pressed her lips together to stop herself vomiting. Were they going to be killed out of hand like they had been?

The guards marched them down some steep, narrow stairs, which ended in a long corridor, lined with iron-barred cells. The captain opened one of them.

"Get in."

"Will you not untie us first?" Tremond said. "We cannot escape."

The captain snorted. "Count yourself lucky not to be in fetters."

He slammed the door and locked it, then he and his fellows marched away.

"When will Portak report back again?" Jacob asked the Prophet. They were, as usual, sitting in the Prophet's dark apartment. Jacob still found the darkness oppressive, but knew better than to say so, or even to think so.

"All in good time. The campaign is going well."

The Prophet fingered the red jewel around his neck. He seemed to be in a good mood today.

A knock on the door. "Come," the Prophet said.

A guard in the uniform of a captain strode into the room and saluted.

"My Lord," the man said. "We have taken some prisoners, at the North Gate. They were fighting with the Guardians. We left one for dead outside the gate."

"Are they Talamdorian?"

"I – I am unsure, my Lord. I think not – one of them has skin as dark as night, like no Talamdorian I have ever seen."

"Did they have marks on their foreheads?"

"No, my Lord. They are all wearing the silver bangle."

The Prophet sighed, a sharp, percussive sound. "Return to the prison and wipe their faces with a damp cloth," he said. "Then come back and report to me."

The man saluted again. "Yes, my Lord. Right away."

Jacob was confused. "Why did you ask him to wipe the prisoners' faces?"

"Because I suspect they are Veylindréan spies, with their Waymarks disguised."

"Oh, I see."

A few minutes later, the captain returned. "They struggled mightily, my Lord, but I called on my guards to reinforce me. Each has a Waymark on their foreheads."

"Describe them."

"One, on the skin of the black one, was Dagâran, one was Garûnan and the third was Ranusian."

Jacob watched the Prophet's face. He had been with him so much, these past weeks – no, seisdags – he could sense his moods, up to a point. And there was little doubt that this news pleased him immensely, for some reason.

"A Dagâran, a Garûnan and a Ranusian. Very good, very good."

The Prophet closed his eyes as if in thought. Jacob wished he could be of more help.

Then the Prophet's eyes snapped open. There was a fierce, exultant smile on his narrow lips. "Bring the Ranusian girl to me early tomorrow."

How had he known the Ranusian spy was a girl?

"How are we going to get out of here?" Aidren asked.

He, Abigail and Tremond were sitting on the hard stone bench beds of the dark, dank cell. It only had one barred window, high up and out of reach of them all, even the tall Garûnalonden. So far as he could judge by the scant light that reached them, it was late afternoon.

"I don't know," Abigail said. "I'm so worried about Ednor – that guard said his wounds were poisoned. I'm the only healer among us and I can't do anything to help him."

"Ylonya is still free," Tremond said in his deep voice. "I'm sure she will have hidden when the guards came, so she could look after Ednor. Do not despair, Abigail. Most Yrusians have a rudimentary knowledge of healing."

Abigail's head came up. "How do you know that?"

"Because they spend so much of their time travelling," Aidren said, trying to sound reassuring, "they have to know how to look after themselves if one of them is injured or sick. And your healer's bag was left behind, wasn't it?"

Abigail's face brightened. "That is true. Maybe Ylonya will be able to save him." Then she gasped again.

"What's wrong?" Aidren asked.

"The Bloodstone. It was in my pack. How are we going to find the Prophet without it?"

"At present," Tremond said drily, "we cannot go anywhere or find anyone. The Talamdorians are calling the tune now, and we must wait and see what happens next."

How could he be so patient, so resigned? Aidren was grinding his teeth in frustration and the usual words of self-blame were whirling round his head. *You should have seen them coming. You should have managed to escape. You should have…*

"Abigail," he said. "Does the Prophet speak to you in your mind?"

"Yes, why?"

"Because my mind is filled with negative thoughts, and I don't know where they came from."

"Try to ignore them," she said. "Think of Ellyn. We cannot give up now."

His darling girl. Buried in alien soil. All that brightness, all that love, gone. Aidren sank into a reverie, barely listening to Abigail and Tremond as they spoke quietly to each other.

"I'm quite glad I don't have the Bloodstone," Abigail said. "It will be one less thing for them to hold against us, when we are brought to the Prophet."

"What makes you think he will deal with us himself?"

"I just know," Abigail said. "He knows I am here."

"Abigail," Tremond said, "come over here so that you are back to back with me. Then see if you can undo the cords around my wrist by feel. Your fingers are smaller and defter than mine."

"I'll try," she said, "but it may take some time."

"Time," Tremond said with one of his rare smiles, "is something we are not short of."

It seemed like forever to Aidren before Abigail managed to undo the knots tying Tremond's wrists.

"Give me a minute," Tremond said.

Aidren possessed his soul in patience as the Garûnalonden bit his lip against the pain of returning circulation. Then he untied first Abigail, then Aidren himself.

"Let us make some loops," Tremond said, "so that it looks like we are still in fetters."

Even this limited freedom felt good. They settled themselves for sleep, wrapped in every garment they possessed.

When Aidren awoke, Abigail and Tremond were already up, talking quietly together. Then Tremond broke off what he was saying. "Hush, someone is coming. Put your arms behind you, quickly."

Aidren listened to the footsteps coming down the stairs to their cell. It was the same captain of the guard as had captured them, with two of his fellows, all three with swords. Too many to rush them. Aidren wished he knew where his sword had been taken. He felt naked without it.

The man took his keys off his belt, opened the door and grabbed Abigail roughly by the arm. "You, come with me."

Before Aidren or Tremond could do anything to prevent, Abigail was gone. He had sworn to protect her, and he had failed.

"Now what do we do?" he asked Tremond.

To his surprise, Tremond smiled. "We wait for Ylonya," he said. "She will be along presently to rescue us. I have a great respect for her cunning."

Ylonya was woken by the early morning sunlight filtering in through the mouth of the cave. For a moment, she could not remember where she was. Then recollection came flooding back, and she jumped to her feet to check on Ednor.

He was still sleeping, but the hectic flush had left his cheeks and his breathing was slow and even. It looked as though the Lènia's Nimbane had done its work. Relief swept through her – he was going to live. She rose to her feet and began preparations for breakfast. She put more wood on the fire and tended it until it was hot and alive once more.

By the time she had eaten, Ednor was stirring. Ylonya hastened to his side. "Wake up, Ednor. It's tomorrow."

His eyes fluttered open, and he pushed against the floor of the cave, trying to raise himself to a sitting position. Then gasped with pain and slumped back down.

"What – what happened?"

Ylonya helped him to sit up before she answered. "You were attacked from behind by one of those monsters, at the north gate of the city. I brought you back here."

"Where are the others?" he asked, urgency in his voice.

"In the City, somewhere," she said. "When you were attacked, half a dozen human guards came out of the gate and seized Abigail and the others. I don't know where they've taken them."

"Why didn't they fight?"

"Because six against three is not good odds," Ylonya said with some exasperation. "And you were lying there, left for dead. I hid, so I could take care of you."

"The wound on my back – you have tended it," he said. "But you are not a Healer."

"No, I am Yrusian. And we know how to take care of ourselves."

"We must go and rescue them."

"You," she said, "are not going anywhere. Don't you realise that wound was poisoned? If it hadn't been for the fact that Shaunan had given Abigail her supply of Lènia's Nimbane, I would have lost you."

She bit her lip.

"Why, Ylonya, I didn't know you cared."

Ednor's voice was light, teasing. But his eyes on her were piercing. She could feel herself flushing.

"Of course I do," she said. "And I will not lose you again."

"What are we going to do next?"

"Once we have eaten, and I have renewed the poultice on your back, we will plan what to do next. But first, breakfast."

She bustled around, producing *feolin* loaves from her pack and a flask of light ale.

She was glad to see that Ednor's appetite had returned. He ate ravenously. She put some water on to heat on the fire.

"Now," she said, "sit still. I will have to take the dressing off, then sponge away the old poultice. I'm sorry, this may hurt."

"Do what you must," he said. "I am grateful."

As gently as she could, Ylonya removed the old bandage and the now-discoloured leaves. Then she added a few more of the Nimbane leaves to the water and sat back on her heels, waiting for them to steep. When she thought they had softened enough, she scooped them out and laid them on her pack to cool, before applying them to Ednor's back.

He sat rock-still, submitting to all. When she had finished the re-bandaging, he caught her hand and kissed it. "My thanks, Ylonya. You have a gentle touch."

She nodded, unable to speak. The touch of his lips had been so gentle, but also like fire. She cleared her throat, fought for balance. "Now, my friend, we must decide what to do next."

"We must return to the city and rescue our friends."

"Not we, me."

Ednor opened his mouth to protest, but she cut him off. "I can move more secretly alone," she said. "And you are not yet healed. You will stay here and await our return."

He scowled at her, but she held his gaze until his eyes dropped.

"Very well," he said. "I suppose I must submit. But how do you plan to circumvent those monsters?"

"I have thought of that," Ylonya said, rummaging in Abigail's pack. "I am going to use this." And she produced the Bloodstone in its red velvet pouch. "I will hang it around my neck, like a Goldstone. And I think its presence will fool those monsters. But I will need your help before I leave."

"Anything," he said.

She took the concealing cream out of her pack. "Apply this to my forehead. And when it is dry, I will see what I can find to paint a Talamdorian Bloodmark on top of it."

"How will you find Abigail and the others?"

"I am Yrusian," she said again.

"Of course. You have the Finding gift. But what if you are discovered?"

"I won't be. Trust me, Ednor. I can do this."

Abigail stumbled and was dragged back to her feet by the rope looped around her wrists. Thank goodness they hadn't realised it was just for show.

"You don't have to be so rough," she said.

"Keep quiet."

"Where are you taking me?"

"I said, keep quiet."

There was hardly anyone about – it must be early still. Dark clouds covered the sky, so she could not tell from the sun. They were heading back up the side street to the cathedral-like building she and Aidren had noticed yesterday. It must be the Talamdorian equivalent of the High Temple in Ranusheim. Almost against her will, she was impressed by its stern grandeur.

The guard knocked on one of the wide bronze doors. A tall man in red robes and a prideful face opened it and looked down his nose at them.

"Who comes to the Great Temple?"

"Captain Dornik of the City Guard. I am here to bring a prisoner to His Holiness."

"Does he know you are coming?"

"Yes. Now let us in."

The priest – if that was what he was – sneered at the guard but stepped aside to allow them entrance.

The magnificence within the temple took Abigail's breath away. Two tall rows of columns made of black basalt split the massive space into three – a nave and two side aisles. It reminded her even more of a cathedral back home. The walls were covered with huge tapestries, their colours unclear in the dimness. Then she stopped dead as her eye was caught by a massive painting of a stately woman with pale skin and dark, piercing eyes above the high altar. This must be Talamu.

"Hurry up!" Another tug on the rope interrupted her reverie. She continued to stare at Talamu, caught in her gaze like a rabbit before a fox, as the guard led her up the aisle, then turned left before hustling her through a side door which led to a straight corridor ending in another door. Two guards in red and black livery stood in front of it, their spears crossed.

"Who seeks audience with the Holy Prophet?" one of them asked.

"Captain Dornik of the City Guard, with a prisoner. His Holiness asked me to bring her to him."

"Leave your weapons here. None may come into the Prophet's presence bearing arms."

Dornik took off his sword belt and gave it to the guard.

"You may enter." And the spears were uncrossed.

Abigail found she was trembling. After all this time, she was going to come face to face with the Prophet of the One.

Δ Chapter 9 Δ

"When the girl arrives," the Prophet told Jacob, "I want you to keep her secured. Do not listen to anything she says – she is a Veylindréan witch and may be dangerous."

Jacob felt his spine stiffen. He would keep his master safe, whatever happened.

Presently, they heard the challenge of the guards outside.

"She is here."

Jacob braced himself for action. The same soldier as yesterday, middle-aged and weather-beaten, dressed in the livery of the City Guard, entered the room, propelling before him a slender girl, pale of face, in dirty clothes. She didn't look very threatening. But the Prophet knew what he was talking about.

"Bring her to me, Jacob."

Jacob strode down the room to where the girl was being held in the firm grasp of the guard. He would not fail his master.

Abigail stood where the guard had left her, in a vast dark space lit only by a sooty red light at the far end. Then forgot everything as she heard Jacob's well-loved voice, saw him striding down the room towards her. She opened her mouth to greet him, but something in his eyes stopped her.

"I will take her from here," he said to the guard, and seized her arm.

The Prophet forgotten, Abigail had no eyes for anything or anyone except Jacob. He looked well-fed and healthy with a certain glossy assurance he had not had formerly. Why was he being so rough with her? Surely he recognised her.

It was all too much. Tears began to pour down her face and she twisted round in his grasp to face him. "Jacob, don't you know me? I'm Abigail."

He frowned as though trying to remember. "There was a girl once. Small and slight, with a great sheaf of blonde hair. Not like yours. But she died in the shipwreck. Portak told me. Why do you torment me with this memory?"

Come over to our side and I will give him back that part of his memory.

The Prophet's voice was in her head, insidious, tempting.

A good Presbyterian girl like you should have nothing to do with evil witches. Throw your lot in with us and together we can eradicate this evil from the lands and bring all Veylindré together under our control.

"Bring her here, Jacob. We have much to discuss."

"Yes, my Lord."

What was going on? How had this man managed to influence Jacob so much? Then she saw the bangle on his wrist. Her heart ached as the implications sank into her mind. She would get no help from Jacob.

"I still don't like it," Ednor said as Ylonya prepared to leave. "How are you going to get into the city unobserved?"

Ylonya grinned at him. "I'm going to make my way round to the East Gate," she said and try to slip in with a group of other people."

"But what if they stop you, challenge you?"

"They won't," Ylonya said.

Ednor was taken aback by her confidence. "You can't know that."

"I'm going to use a technique we've developed at the Guild," she said. "Watch."

And before his very eyes, she seemed to change. Although his common sense told him she was still right in front of him, his eyes seemed to glide over her, as though his brain was telling him *boring, of no interest, ignore.*

"By the Six!" he said as she faded back into view. "How do you do that?"

"Trade secret, my friend. But it takes a lot of concentration, so I only use it when I have to. I won't be able to keep it up for long. I should be able to blend in once I'm in the city and will only need to use the trick to get past any guards."

Ednor was convinced. "Stay safe, my friend."

"Don't worry, I will."

Abigail stood where she had yearned to be for so long, in Jacob's arms. But those arms were not holding her lovingly. They were restraining her. He was under the Prophet's influence and didn't know her.

Of all the blows she had foreseen or guessed at, this was the hardest to take. In her daydreams, she had imagined Jacob being held against his will, that she and the others would rescue him from the Prophet's clutches, and all would be as before. Something inside her broke as that dream died.

All will never be as before, Abigail Winters. Jacob is mine.

So he could read her mind. As hope died in her heart, she felt a new strength coming from somewhere. She was Abigail Winters, a Ranusian initiate, and she had not come this far to give in before she had fairly begun. Abigail stood up straight and met the Prophet's gaze.

"Jacob is not yours, save by coercion," she said quietly. "And I will never be yours."

A pale smile touched the Prophet's thin lips. "You have courage," he said. "I admire that. But you are wrong. Jacob is wholly mine, by his own free will." He touched a red jewel at his throat. "Hurt her, Jacob."

Jacob pulled her arms up behind her and pain shot through her shoulders. His hands, which she remembered being so gentle on her body, were now fierce and merciless. She clenched her teeth together, determined not to give the Prophet the satisfaction of hearing her cry out. Then Jacob, in response to a nod from the man, forced her hands up higher and her shoulders screamed. A gasp of pain escaped her as involuntary tears sprang to her eyes.

"Enough," the Prophet said. "Stop hurting her but keep fast hold of her."

Jacob eased his hold on her arms. She choked back her tears. She must be strong. This is not Jacob. This is what the Prophet has turned him into.

"You see? Jacob will do anything I ask him to. He is my faithful servant."

"So I see," Abigail said. "But it does not follow that I will be also."

Her defiance seemed to amuse him. His laughter was cruel and triumphal, piercing her mind like knives. She twisted in Jacob's grasp, trying to find a way to break free. But his hold on her was too strong.

"You fool! Did you really think that dyed hair and stolen clothing would disguise you from me? I have known you were in Talamdor for days, ever since you broke through the barrier."

His tone changed. "Out of interest, how did you do that?"

She looked up at him. His expression was open, curious. Yet behind it she could sense his implacable will. He *would* have an answer.

"I used my Goldstone," she said.

"You lie. A Goldstone does not have that kind of power."

Anger flooded through her, replacing fear. "I am not lying. I used my Goldstone. Read my mind and see the truth."

"You interest me, child. How do you, a girl of no account, come to wield a Goldstone with such surety and power?"

"I-I don't know," she replied truthfully. "Perhaps it is because I am not from this world."

"But here I have you. You might as well give up, Abigail. My rule here is absolute. I have guards within call who can take you to the deepest dungeon in the citadel and chain you up there and leave you to rot."

"Why would you want to do that?" she asked.

"Because there is only room for one rule in Talamdor, and that is the rule of Holy Talamu, which I enforce."

Abigail remembered something that had puzzled her. "How did you know I was Presbyterian? And how do you know what 'Presbyterian' even means?"

His gaze on her was amused, even mocking. "Jacob told me. And because I, like you and Jacob, am from England."

"From England?" This was astounding. "But..."

"Yes, from England. I came here more than thirty years ago."

"Then why do you worship Talamu? Were you not a Christian?"

"Of course I was. Then I had an encounter with Holy Talamu in a cave and have been Her Prophet since that day."

"Her prophet?" Abigail could hear the truth in his words. Her mind was reeling. "What task did she lay on you?"

"She told me to set Her people free and to overcome the evil rule of the witches of Veylindré."

How did she know him? Even as he held her imprisoned between his hands, Jacob was so confused. He listened as she and the Prophet talked. She said she was from England, that she had known him there. Why couldn't he remember?

He racked his brains. Could this girl, who was calmly defying his master, be the girl of his dreams? It didn't seem possible. That girl had been blonde, slighter, quieter, far less forceful. This girl could not be the one... She was beautiful, though, even if he did prefer blondes.

And in any case, she was one of them – a Veylindréan witch, one of those his master had warned him about. His girl had been English, like him. He was positive of that. And she had drowned in the shipwreck. Portak had told him.

Unless Portak had been lying to him all this time. Had he been in this world for ages before Portak found him, instead of just a few days? No, why would Portak have deceived him?

But what if she is the one? A small voice at the back of his mind raised the question. And if she was, how had they got separated? How come Portak had found only him?

She couldn't be the same girl. And if she was, she would have arrived in this world at the same time as he did, which was, by his best guess, only about three months ago. She wouldn't have had time to be trained as a witch, let alone to have the skill his master seemed to think she had. And the Abigail he had known would never have embraced witchcraft, never have turned her back on Lord Jesus.

But his master now followed Holy Talamu, not Jesus. He still didn't understand how that had happened. How could anyone from England stop being a Christian? He was so confused. He wished he was back working in his father's forge, far away from this world of intrigue and lies and witchcraft and strange gods.

Abigail had been gone for a good hour, by Tremond's estimation. Anything could be happening to her. He ground his teeth – where was Ylonya? He guessed she would have taken Ednor back to the caves. If he yet lived. Surely she would not give them up for lost. Aidren was visibly chafing at not knowing what was going on. Tremond guessed he was blaming himself – it was what he would have done at Aidren's age.

"Don't give up hope," he told the younger man. "Abigail is Ranusian and is stronger than you think. She will resist the power of the Prophet. And Ylonya will be here soon, I'm sure of it."

Then his quick ear caught the sound of tramping footsteps, the jingle of keys. "Hush, someone's coming."

When the guard came into view, Tremond saw that he was carrying a wooden tray. On cue, his stomach rumbled. He was immediately ravenous.

"Stand away from the door! I'm coming in."

Could they rush him? He was only one, and they were two.

Then the moment was past. The guard lowered his tray onto Abigail's bench bed. "Food," he said, then turned and left the cell, locking the door behind him.

"Wait," Tremond said. "How are we supposed to eat with our hands tied?"

"As best you can." Then the guard left.

"What have they given us?" Tremond asked.

Aidren stood up, walked over to the bench bed. A cast iron pot was on the tray, with two wooden bowls, two wooden spoons and a hunk of bread. Carefully, he slipped his hands out of the loop of rope, took the lid off the pot, then drew back. "It smells horrible."

Tremond joined him, sniffed in his turn. "I don't think it's poisoned," he said, looking at the scum-covered, watery contents. We'd better eat – who knows when they'll feed us again."

Reluctantly, they transferred the contents of the pot into the two bowls. Tremond tore the bread into two and gave the larger portion to Aidren. It smelled stale and they could both see spots of mould on the crust.

"Sop it in the soup," Tremond said. "That will soften it."

Tremond forced himself to swallow the thin, unappetising broth, choke down the stale bread, and was relieved when Aidren did the same. They would need all their strength if they were to escape. Or be rescued.

"You mean, like Moses in the land of Egypt?" Abigail said.

A smile touched the Prophet's thin lips. "Exactly like Moses. When Holy Talamu took me for her Prophet and gave me my task, this land was under the cruel domination of the Havimi, who had turned all highborn Talamdorians into slaves and bled the country dry. Setting them free was the simple part. It has taken me more than thirty long years to bring Talamdor back to prosperity."

"Thirty years? That's not possible. You can only be in your forties now."

Another thin smile. "You see clearly, Abigail Winters, but not clearly enough. The hand of Holy Talamu is upon me. I do not age. I would have died long ago back in England. I have more than seventy winters, but the service of Holy Talamu keeps me young."

"Yet," Abigail said, "does it not say in the 90th Psalm that 'the years of our life are seventy'?"

"What a well-read child you are, especially for a girl," the Prophet congratulated her, "but it also says in the sixth chapter of Genesis that, 'My Spirit shall not abide in man forever, for he is flesh; his days shall be 120 years.' So I have many years yet to live."

"The gift of life comes from God," Abigail said, "but you have turned your back on Him to follow Talamu."

A flash of something in the Prophet's eyes – anger? doubt? She could not tell.

"You are insolent," he said and she shivered at the ice in his voice. "You are not here to debate the span of human life, but to be instructed." He sat upright on his throne, fingering the red jewel around his neck. That must be the Master Bloodstone. "I was given a sacred commission by Holy Talamu, which had two parts. The first, to set Her people free, I have achieved. The second, to overcome the heretical witches of Veylindré, I am in the process of achieving."

"The people of Veylindré are not heretics," Abigail said. "They are good and kind and compassionate."

"So young, yet so deluded," the Prophet said. "I see I will have work to do, to persuade you of the rightness of our crusade. But there is time. Surely you do not believe that witchcraft is 'good and kind and compassionate'? Surely I am justified in destroying those who practice it, for the greater good of all?"

She could hear the mockery in his voice and hated him for it. Then some useful anger came to her aid and her spine stiffened.

"Greater good?" she spat. "For whom? It was not a 'greater good' to murder my family and friends, violating the women, even killing the little children..." her voice broke as she remembered little Daniel and Faith, "...as your agent and his brutal pirates did." She could see their broken bodies in her mind's eye, could taste again the grief their loss had brought her. "And for what? What possible justification can you give me for that?"

He gazed down at her. "That was a regrettable error," he said. "My agent was sent to investigate these people, to see who they were, as we had heard they bore no Waymark on their foreheads. Perhaps he used more force than was strictly necessary, but the men of your settlement must have been foolish enough to resist."

Then his voice changed. "Come, Abigail. That was long in the past. What matters now is that you give up your mistaken allegiance to Ranu and join myself and Jacob in the worship of Holy Talamu. Together, we could rule the whole Commonweal of Veylindré. You will be as Eve to Jacob's Adam, able to preserve my great legacy for posterity."

Once more, Abigail felt the hypnotic influence this man was able to exert over the minds of others. Did Jacob really worship Talamu? Or was that only because he was wearing the silver bangle?

You are wrong, Abigail. Jacob is mine, heart and soul. He has changed much since he came here.

Another blow to her heart. But even if that was so, it didn't mean this Prophet had the right to rule all Veylindré.

"I have not found the Veylindréans to be evil," she said, aiming for a voice of sweet reason. "Does it not say in the Gospel of Matthew, 'by their fruits shall ye know them'? Every Veylindréan I have met has been good and kind and hospitable. They took Jacob and me in, when we were lost in the forest and helped us to find our places in this world. How can I believe they are evil witches?"

"You disappoint me, Abigail. Do they not carry out magic with their Goldstones? Did not Moses name people who used charms, or divination or other magic 'abominations of the Lord'? And Saint Paul, in his Letter to the Galatians, named witchcraft as a work of the flesh and stated that 'they which do such things shall not inherit the kingdom of God'? They are an evil in this land, and I intend to root them out and burn them, as witches should be burned."

Abigail gaped at him. "You are planning to murder every man, woman and child in Veylindré?"

"They will be given a choice – those who choose to convert to the worship of Holy Talamu shall live, under Talamdorian rule; those who hold to their evil ways and refuse to recant will die."

"And yet our blessed Lord told his disciples that 'In my father's house are many mansions'", Abigail said. She was beginning to feel desperate. Somehow she had to make him understand how wrong, how cruel, his beliefs were. "Surely there is room for people to follow their hearts, to believe as they wish. Why must you have dominion over them?"

"Because that is the will of Holy Talamu." The Prophet's voice rang out, full of conviction. "There is no more to be said. I am Her Prophet and will seek to fulfil her commission for the rest of my life."

"Then I will resist you, with every ounce of strength in my heart and mind," she said.

"Then you will burn, like the rest of your heretical friends."

Abigail bowed her head. She had done her best. But she had failed.

She had failed.

Jacob had to admire the girl's eloquence and courage. Unlike the Talamdorian nobles, Portak, and Jacob himself – much though he hated to admit it – this slip of a girl did not seem to fear his master. As she argued with the Prophet, her voice soared, passionate in its conviction. He could feel her quivering in his grasp.

He couldn't believe his ears when she started using Bible quotations in her arguments. She must truly be from England, from his world. Could the rest of what she was saying be true also? Had she known him before – before the shipwreck? Had there even been a shipwreck? Had his whole life here been founded on a lie?

No, that was ridiculous. Why would Portak lie to him? Why would the Prophet lie to him? His master had told him that he, Jacob, was his heir, the one who would carry on the crusade to obliterate witchcraft from the face of this world. And he knew his father had feared and hated witches more than almost anything else.

But how could this girl be a witch? Witches were bent up old crones, who went around muttering to themselves, not beautiful young girls. The Prophet's voice interrupted his thoughts.

"No, Jacob, you are wrong. That may be true in our world, but remember what St Paul wrote in his Second Epistle to the Corinthians: 'Satan himself is transformed into an angel of light.' This girl may appear virtuous and beautiful in her outward semblance, but in her heart she worships the false goddesses of Veylindré and is no better than Satan. In fact, she is worse, because she was once a Christian and chose to embrace these false goddesses and learn witchcraft from their minions."

"No!" The girl's voice was fervent. "Jacob, you cannot believe that is true. Look at me." She was twisting in his arms, trying to make eye contact. "I am Abigail – Abigail. I don't know what this man has done to you, but everything he says is false, evil. You must believe me."

It was all too much. Both of them couldn't be lying, but which was telling the truth?

Δ Chapter 10 Δ

Before Ylonya left the cave, she double-checked that she had everything she needed: the Bloodstone in its red buckskin pouch and her Goldstone, both hidden away in different inside pockets of her jerkin, the packet of gemstones, small items from Abigail's, Aidren's and Tremond's packs, to help with the Finding, a couple of *feolin* loaves and a water flask. Hopefully the presence of the Bloodstone would get her past the red armoured monsters, but she didn't dare wear it openly – no ordinary Talamdorian trader would carry one.

"Take this," Ednor said, as he unstrapped his poniard from his belt. "It has been an heirloom of my house for generations. Our legends say it was wrought from tempered steel by a Dagâran Mastersmith who was taught his craft by Dagâra herself, before the Six left Veylindré. It is runed with charms to help whoever wields it prevail against the agents of Talamu."

Ylonya drew it out of its fine leather sheath. It was a superb piece of craftsmanship, honed to sharpness and gleaming in the light of the early morning sun.

"Why haven't you used it before?" she asked.

"I had planned to use it to kill the Prophet, to the honour of my house. But now I must stay here. So you must go in my stead."

Ylonya took his hand, guessing how much this gesture had cost him. "Thank you, Ednor. I will not dishonour it."

"May Dagâra be with you."

Once out of the cave, she put up the hood of her cloak. She skirted round the edge of the wood and set off south-west, aiming to join the road that led to the West Gate. Before she had gone far, the sky clouded over, and it began to rain. It didn't take long for her to be soaked to the skin. Never mind, a bit of dampness wouldn't hurt her. Her plan was to wait until a party of traders from western Talamdor came along and then to blend in with them at the Gate. Risky, but it was all she and Ednor could come up with. If she failed, if her presence was discovered, Abigail, Aidren and Tremond could die. She could not, would not allow that to happen.

She took cover behind a convenient rock a few yards back from the road. *Belannath Yrusia, gal ma bynn teidenvoll.* May I have the skill to succeed.

She waited for more than two hours, judging by the movement of the sun, which had shown her face again once the rain had blown over. Her sharp ears caught the jingle of harness and the hum of voices. At last. She remained hidden until the riders were in plain sight. Yes, a group of traders. Half a dozen heavily laden mules, several people on foot and a couple of outriders on horses. Perfect.

Once they had passed by, she tailed them, flitting from rock to rock. It was a precarious process – the outriders glanced behind occasionally and she had to take cover. When the traders reached the West Gate, she closed up to a few yards behind them. And watched as the fearsome red figures materialised from… nowhere. What were these creatures? How did the Prophet control them? She shuddered; she had no illusions as to her fate if she was caught by them.

She couldn't catch what the traders said, but their answers seemed to satisfy the monsters and they stepped back into the stone of the walls. Thank Yrusia. Ordinary guards she could deal with. But she hoped she wouldn't have to.

The gate opened and the group started to pass in. She concentrated fiercely and managed to fade into the background. Would this work? She held her breath as she approached the gate.

A few more steps and she was in. Now all she had to do was find the others.

She ducked down an alley before preparing to search for them, making sure she was unobserved. She took out the belongings she had taken from their packs – Aidren's whetstone, the twine that Tremond used to fletch his arrows and Abigail's comb. She held them in her left hand, her Goldstone in her right and murmured, *gal euren bynnen cenfent, gal euren bynnen cenfent.* May they be found. And felt a tug from her Goldstone.

She crept out of the alley, then put the hand with the Goldstone in her pocket, walking up the street in the direction of the tug. It was leading straight to the heart of the city. After a few minutes, she came out into a huge square, which was dominated by a great black building, which must be the Great Temple of Talamu.

She repeated the spell, *gal euren bynnen cenfent.* But either her Finding skills were leaving her, or something else was amiss. Maybe they had been split up. She retreated to the edge of the square, huddled in a corner. By juggling the objects, she discovered that Abigail must be in the Temple, but Aidren and Tremond were not with her. What to do? After a moment's thought, the answer came to her: rescue Aidren and Tremond, then together, they could go after Abigail.

Aidren was pacing back and forth, unable to sit still. Where was Ylonya? And where was Abigail? Visions of both of them captured, tortured, or worse, filled his mind.

"Sit down," Tremond said. "We need to husband our strength in case we need to fight our way out of here."

Aidren snorted. "That's a joke," he said. "Even if Ylonya makes it into the city, she'll go to find Abi, not us."

"I don't think so. She will need both of us if she is to rescue Abigail, and Jacob too."

"But Abi's been gone for hours. Anything could be happening to her. And I'm stuck in here, unable to protect her."

"Peace, my friend. I'm sure…" Tremond stopped, held up his hand for silence.

Aidren held his breath and heard the sounds of a scuffle, away up the corridor. Then a thud as though something heavy had hit the floor. He crowded up to the barred window, trying to see what was going in.

Light footsteps, running towards them. Ylonya! And in her hands were some heavy keys.

"Ylonya, thank Ranu you're –" Aidren began.

"Time for talking later," Ylonya said as she unlocked the door to their cell. "We need to get out of here. When is your next meal due?"

"We don't know what hour it is, but they only feed us morning and evening," Tremond said.

"Then we should have time to escape. I've dealt with the guards. Where are your weapons?"

"They took them and our Goldstones away when they put us in here," Aidren said. "Ylonya, they've got Abigail. They took her to the Prophet."

"I'll fetch them," Ylonya said, ignoring him. Wait here."

The minutes crawled by, each as long as an hour to Aidren. But in reality, it could not have been more than ten minutes before Ylonya returned, bearing their swords, Tremond's bow and arrows and his knife, the three Goldstones and some dark cloaks.

"Come, my friends," she said as they reached out for them. "Draw the cloaks close around you and put your hoods up. We must try to evade notice."

"I've got a better idea," Tremond said. "Why don't we take the guards' uniforms and wear them instead?"

"But there are only two of them," Aidren said.

"Good idea," Ylonya said, over-riding his objections. "You and I can wear the uniforms, Tremond, and we'll act as though we are taking Aidren as our prisoner to the Prophet."

The three of them carried the guards back to the cell and stripped them down to their underthings. Ylonya's uniform fitted well, but tall Tremond had to make some exotic adjustments to make his look anything like regulation. One of the guards was showing signs of coming round, so Ylonya hit him quite carefully on the side of the head, and he slumped back to the floor. They tied them both up for good measure and gagged them, using strips of material torn from the lining of one of the cloaks.

"Let's go."

The three of them emerged warily from the prison. Aidren held his hands behind his back, as though they were tied up, a loose loop of cord around his wrists to convince the casual passer-by. Ylonya and Tremond were holding one of his arms each and they marched him briskly up the square towards the huge black building. Were they actually going to get away with this?

"Come on, you," Tremond said in a harsh Talamdorian accent, hauling on his arm.

They had reached the entrance. Abigail must be in here somewhere.

"Tremond," Ylonya said quietly, "Once, we're inside, I'll need you to hold Aidren for a minute. I have to locate Abigail."

She pushed open the door and the three of them slipped inside.

"What are you doing here?"

The voice made Aidren almost jump out of his skin. A tall, skinny man clad in red robes was striding down the aisle towards them.

"Orders of the Prophet," Tremond said, drawing himself up to attention. "We've had word that the prisoner is needed in his private apartments."

Aidren admired his friend's quick wits. Was it going to be that easy? Would the priest believe him?

As the priest – if that was what he was – glared suspiciously at them, his attention on Tremond, Ylonya swiftly moved behind him. A moment later, the man collapsed backwards into her arms.

"What did you do to him?" Aidren asked.

"Something Kendris taught me, back in the day," Ylonya said. "Let's get him out of sight."

Aidren and Tremond helped her to drag the inert body into the shelter of a pew and left him there. Then Ylonya took out her Goldstone and Abigail's comb. She performed her Finding spell as he had seen her do before, back in Talmis.

"This way," she said, leading them up the aisle, then left to a small door. "She's through here."

They found themselves in a long corridor, leading to another door. But this one was guarded.

"Quickly, Aidren. You need to be a prisoner again."

Back in formation, the three of them marched towards the guards, who stood with their spears crossed, denying them entrance.

"Who seeks audience with the Holy Prophet?" one of them asked.

"We bring the Veylindréan prisoner," Ylonya said, "by order of His Holiness."

"Wait," one of them said. "who are y–?"

Too late. The three of them leapt forward and dispatched both the guards. Then dumped their recumbent bodies in a shadowy corner. Ylonya put her ear to the door.

"Let's go."

"But have you seen the Way in action?" Abigail was pleading now. "Spoken to real Veylindréans? I have, and I cannot believe that the Way is a power for evil."

"You stupid girl," the Prophet said. "They have gulled you properly, I see. Else you would not believe that this Way" and he spat the word, "is a force for good. They are witches, complex and deceptive."

There was a knock at the door.

"Come."

His anger at being interrupted was plain to Abigail. She tried to see who was coming in, but Jacob was holding her too tightly. But it sounded like more than one person. Could it possibly be…?

"I did not call for you." Then she saw him look again. "Who are you?" he demanded. "Guards!"

"They won't be coming."

Abigail was thrilled to recognise Ylonya's voice, even with the fake Talamdorian accent. Her friend continued, "Free Abigail."

Someone else – Abigail could not see who – strode forward and held his dagger to Jacob's neck.

"Release her, or I will cut your throat." Tremond.

Jacob let go of her so abruptly she almost stumbled, and Tremond swiftly slashed through the ropes looped around her hands.

"Thank you."

She turned and saw Aidren too, who was staring at Jacob in utter disbelief. "Jacob, what are you doing here?"

Ylonya walked up to her. "Here's your Goldstone."

Abigail turned back to face the Prophet. She held her Goldstone tightly, the power of the Way thrumming through her, giving her the courage to defy him once more. "You may imprison us," she said evenly, "but you'll never conquer Veylindré, never break our spirits. The people of Veylindré are free to choose whom they worship."

As she defied him, a bright yellow light flared out from the Goldstone in her hand.

"You young fool," the Prophet said. "You cannot defeat me. You cannot defeat Holy Talamu. We *will* prevail."

The power of his voice made her quail inwardly, but she was not going to show him she was afraid. He lashed her with his gaze, ignoring all else.

"Hold him still and silent, and bind his arms behind him," she heard Ylonya tell Tremond. She must be talking about Jacob.

"Down on the floor, on your stomach." Tremond said.

"Aidren, quick!" Ylonya said.

What was going on?

Then, more swiftly than she would have thought possible for a man of his age, the Prophet leapt off his throne and seized her, twisting her hair in his strong fingers, forcing unwelcome tears to her eyes. She struggled to get away, then froze.

His other hand was holding a dagger, whose keen edge stroked her throat.

"Back off," the Prophet said, "or I will kill her where she stands." And then to Tremond, "Release him."

It was too late. It was all too late. Or was it? She had one last chance to accomplish the quest. She went limp in the Prophet's grasp, as though she had given up resisting, and he loosened his hold on her hair, moving to clutch her arm.

Belannath Ranu, gal ma bynn dreit. A flood of new energy filled her.

Heedless of the knife at her throat, she twisted in his arms like an eel and seized the Master Bloodstone with her free hand, tugging with all her goddess-augmented strength. The chain broke. She had it.

The Prophet slashed at her with the knife, slicing through the flesh of her upper arm. She screamed in pain.

Then Aidren was there, pulling her from the Prophet's grasp. His face was contorted with a mixture of white-hot anger and savage determination. "You'll not have Abigail too," he panted. "This is for Ellyn."

His sword, the one Master Kalen had given Jacob, was in his hand. Through her pain and exhaustion, Abigail remembered the Mastersmith's words: 'It is made of finest Luvodican steel and carved with runes for strength and protection'. Aidren put her behind him and closed with the Prophet. From the corner of her eye, Abigail could see Ylonya darting forward, a poniard in her hand. They both attacked him.

But at almost the same time as their strokes landed, the Prophet began to scream, a high, thin, wailing sound. She could hear words in that scream, "Holy Talamu, no! You promised me…"

As they watched in horror, his face started to age, skin stretching tight over sharp cheekbones, then exploding into dust. Bleeding from his wounds, he crumpled to the floor, an old, dying man with no powers left.

Abigail realised that his life must have been linked to the power of the Master Bloodstone, which was why he had looked so young, a man in his prime. Shocked by his disintegration, the pain of her wound forgotten, she knelt at his side and closed his eyes.

They had killed his master. Jacob lay on the dusty floor, pinned by the foot of the Garûnalonden, his arms tied behind his back. They had killed his master. Why hadn't they killed him too?

He heard the light steps of the girl. "We must cut off the silver bangle," she said. "It is what has kept him bound to the Prophet."

"First we must bind your arm," the woman said. "Jacob can wait."

Yes, he could wait. What was the point of anything, now that the Prophet was dead? He closed his eyes, tears leaking from between their lids, oblivious to whatever was happening around him. There was no room for anything except for grief that his master was dead.

He heard a gasp of pain. Then the girl's voice, ragged with emotion. "*Gal ma bynn wellent, gal ma bynn wellent.*"

She was casting a spell. Jacob shivered in revulsion.

Then the other woman, "Is it working?"

"Partly. But healing myself is far more difficult than healing another."

"That's because you're trying to focus on two things at once – ignoring your pain and healing yourself. Try acknowledging the pain, then focus on healing it."

Another deeply indrawn breath. "All right. I'll try."

Once again he heard her spell words. This couldn't be his Abigail. No-one could change that much in such a short time. Then a sigh of relief.

"That's better. Bind it tightly, Ylonya. We'll deal with it when we're back at the cave."

Footsteps. Then, "Jacob, wake up."

The girl's voice. Again, it reminded him of something he had forgotten. He knit his brows in perplexity. If only he could think.

"Aidren," the girl said, "do you have something I can thread between the bangle and Jacob's wrist? I don't want him injured."

"Stay away from me, you Veylindréan witch."

The girl's eyes filled with tears, but she stepped back, gestured to the young warrior to take her place.

He knelt by Jacob's side, forcing a wad of cloth between his bangle and his arm. He tried to resist, but the tall one, the Garûnalonden, growled, "Hold still, you."

Turning his head to one side, he watched the woman approach, a sharp poniard in her hand. He forced himself to meet her gaze – he would not die cowering. But with unexpected gentleness, she eased her dagger between his bangle and his wrist. As the blade came into contact with his bangle, he saw the runes which had been engraved along it flash into life. The blade sheared through the talamunium and the bangle fell apart.

His ears popped. He was dizzy, disorientated. What was going on?

"Let him sit up now," the woman said. Her voice now seemed distantly familiar. Where had he heard it before?

Someone helped him to sit up. The young warrior. "Aidren? Is that you?"

Aidren grinned. "Yes, it's me. And Abigail and Ylonya are here too. The Garûnalonden is Tremond."

"But where is Ellyn? And the Waymage?"

A fleeting expression of anguish crossed Aidren's features. What had happened while he had been here? It seemed there were more tales to tell than his.

"This is not the place for long stories," the woman – Ylonya – said. She looked so different with black hair and Talamdorian clothing. "Do you know a different way out of here, Jacob?"

"A different way? What's wrong with the door?" He wished he could think clearly. What were they all doing in Talamdor? Why had they killed the Prophet? They were obviously Veylindréans – that was clear from their Waymarks. He drew breath to call the guards, but the Garûnalonden – Tremond, Aidren had called him – clapped a hand over his mouth.

Then the girl was in front of him, her eyes fixed on his face. "Jacob, it's me, Abigail. We're on your side. We came to rescue you. You have to trust us."

He shook his head. Abigail? No, it can't be. She died in the shipwreck. Portak told me.

"You have to trust us," Aidren said. "We are here to take you back home to Dagâran."

What? He had never been to Dagâran. Portak had found him in Néartania. But some part of him recognised Aidren as a friend. God, he was so confused.

"If we let you speak, will you promise not to call out?" Ylonya said. "Otherwise we will have to gag you. And we need your help."

Jacob shrugged, then nodded. The hand over his mouth was taken away and he ducked to wipe his lips on his shoulder.

"What do you want from me?" he asked.

"Is there another way out of here?" Ylonya said again. "We need to escape from this city as soon as possible."

"Why?" He didn't understand.

"Because we have killed the Prophet," Aidren said.

"Why did you do that?"

"We can discuss that another time," Ylonya said. "For now, we need to get out of here before someone comes."

"I suppose we could go back to the Visitor's Hall through the other passage," Jacob said.

"Good," Ylonya said. "Show us."

"And no calling out, no acting up," the Garûnalonden said. "I will be right behind you."

Jacob shrugged again. "Untie my arms," he said.

He saw Ylonya nod, felt the Garûnalonden's knife cutting through his bonds. He brought his hands round to the front, rubbed his wrists.

"Let's go."

֍ Chapter 11 Δ

The siege of Mistbourne Keep was not going well. No matter how many rocks the Talamdorian trebuchets threw at the castle walls, the stone held. And whenever they tried to raise a siege ladder, somehow the defenders were in just the right place to throw it down. Were they using magic? Portak would not have been surprised –Talamdorians would have done the same, if they had been invaded.

He began to make his way back to base camp, to prepare his disguise. Risky, but it had to be done. Then in his ears, the words, "Holy Talamu, no! You promised me..." screamed at the extreme of someone's anguish. His stomach clenched as he recognised his master's voice. He seized his Bloodstone, closed his eyes, and tried to link to the Prophet.

Nothing. There was nothing to link to. A vast empty space where the Prophet's mind used to be. What? Portak turned his horse around, clapped his heels into its sides and rode back to the siege at the best pace the tired animal could manage.

Once there, he looked around urgently, trying to locate General Kreldik. And recognised one of the General's staff officers – Normek, the man's name was – an expression of shock on his weathered face. He strode up to Portak, laid a hand on his horse's reins.

"Come with me. General's orders."

Portak tethered his horse to a nearby tree and followed him. He could sense the turmoil in the man's mind and tried automatically to soothe him. With no success. What was wrong with his Bloodstone? No matter how hard he tried, he could no longer access most of its power. If the same had happened to General Kreldik, he could understand why the General wanted to see him. To explain what was wrong.

But how could he, when he had no idea himself? Arriving at General Kreldik's pavilion, the staff headquarters for the siege, Portak ducked his head and walked in. Straightaway, his arm – fortunately the uninjured one – was seized in a strong grip. Someone was clutching it like a drowning man. To his astonishment, it was Kreldik.

"Come with me," the general said in a low voice. "I must speak with you without other ears."

Then, raising his voice, "I will speak with the Prophet's agent alone. Hold yourselves ready for further instructions."

The staff officers rose to their feet and saluted, as Kreldik hauled him out of the tent.

Once they were alone, Kreldik barked, "What in Talamu's name is going on? I was directing the troops through my Bloodstone, when I heard the Prophet's voice crying out in pain. He seemed to be speaking to Holy Talamu. Didn't know the man was capable of such emotion."

"General," Portak began, but Kreldik talked right over him, raising his hand for silence.

"And then, my Bloodstone seemed to jump under my fingers. Since then, I have not been able to do anything through it. What's going on?"

The general glared at him, obviously expecting an answer.

"Sir," Portak said, "I am as much at a loss as you. I heard the self-same words in my ears."

"And then?"

Portak bowed his head. "I have attempted to link my mind to His Holiness but," and here Portak's hands started to shake and the ache in the pit of his stomach grew abruptly worse. He fought to ignore the symptoms, didn't understand – would not understand – what they might mean.

"But what?" Kreldik said. "Speak up, man!"

"But nothing," Portak said, in a voice so quiet it was almost a whisper. "I tried to link with the Master Bloodstone and felt… and felt…"

"Felt what? Dammit, man, you must tell me."

Portak met the General's eyes, saw the desperation in them. In normal times, he would have put him off, kept the truth a secret. But these were not normal times – his master was gone and his own future was uncertain. He decided to tell him the truth.

"I fear that His Holiness is dead. I cannot reach his mind. There is a vast empty space when I try."

He watched the General's expression change from impatience and anger to the blankness of someone who has received a bad shock. He knew the feeling.

"I will attempt to contact Tamin, Chief Messenger of the Prophet, in Talamunem City. He, if anyone, will know what has happened."

"Do so. But speak to no-one except myself, when you have the answer."

Portak nodded and left him.

Finding a quiet corner in which to concentrate was a problem Portak had not foreseen. The cries of men, the creak of the trebuchets, the neighing of horses and all the other sounds of a determined assault filled his ears and mind.

He would have to leave the area, find somewhere peaceful. But where?

Back to the base camp at the foot of the pass. There would be somewhere on the way that he could stop. Surely.

He hurried back to his horse, which was cropping the grass, tightened the girth and gathered up the reins. Then swung himself up into the saddle and put his heels to the horse's sides.

Within minutes, the sounds of the assault had subsided into low background noise. He glanced around. The landscape he was riding through was green and fair, untamed by the hand of man. He came to a stream with willow trees just coming into leaf lining its banks. This would do. He dismounted, tethered his horse to a stout branch and sat with his back against one of the trees.

Then he took his Bloodstone out of its pouch and held it in his hand. It felt so different – not thrumming with energy, as it usually did. It felt... lifeless. Nevertheless, he must try, although he felt a curious reluctance. As long as he did not know for sure, there was still room for hope. He shook his head – this was ridiculous.

He pricked his finger with the point of his dagger and allowed the blood to drip onto the Bloodstone. Then pressed his thumb over the cut to stop the bleeding. He breathed deeply as he had been taught and, closing his eyes, began to reach out to Chief Messenger Tamin.

Tamin. Tamin. Answer me. Answer me. Tamin. Tamin.

Again, the sense of emptiness, powerlessness. Something had changed – something important. At last, the stone in his hand twitched. Portak concentrated with all his strength and a message began to flow into his mind.

The Prophet is dead. The Master Bloodstone has been stolen by Veylindréan agents. Domlok has taken control. Call off the siege and return to Talamunem City.

No! It could not be true. Tears sprang to his eyes, and there was a roaring in his ears. He felt as though he was about to pass out. Stubbornly, he fought to maintain his focus, so that he could respond to Tamin.

I hear you. I will tell General Kreldik.

Come swiftly.

Then the connection died. His legs would no longer hold him. He sank to his knees, a scream of anguish and loss tearing his throat. Hot tears poured down his face. He found he was rocking to and fro, his hands clamped over his face. Grief took him.

Portak did not know how much time had passed when he came back to himself. His legs felt numb, as though he had been kneeling in one position for a long time and he had a thumping headache. He looked around – the light was beginning to fail, and his horse was standing as still as a statue, as though it was sleeping. He changed his position to sitting with his legs stretched out in front of him, then bit his lips as the pins and needles of returning circulation shot through them. He waited until the pain had died down before attempting to rise to his feet.

He wanted Balmak so much. The feel of his friend's gentle arms around him, the press of his lips on his own. If he ever got back to Talamunem City, he would never leave again.

His master was dead. Why had he left his side? If he had been there, he could have prevented it. Would have given his own life to do so. Why hadn't he stayed in the City? But it was futile to dwell on what ifs. And the Master Bloodstone had been stolen – no wonder he had struggled to contact Tamin. Disaster on disaster. He had better get back to Kreldik.

He shuffled over to the horse and mounted, turning its head back towards Mistbourne Keep. He had better make haste – Kreldik would be wondering what had happened to him.

By the time he reached the outskirts of the Keep, it was full dusk. Wearily he slid off his horse's back, tethered it in the horse lines and started the long walk to Kreldik's tent. He was not looking forward to this at all.

When he entered, Kreldik was alone, quill in hand, working on some documents.

"General Kreldik?"

"You took your time, man. I was about to send out a search party for you."

Then Kreldik stopped, looked at him more closely. "What has happened? What is the news? I can see it is not good."

"May I sit, General?"

Kreldik gestured to a chair. Gratefully, Portak sank into it.

"Your report, Portak."

"You are correct, General," Portak said, fighting to keep his voice even, free from emotion. "I had to leave the camp in order to find a quiet place, so that I could concentrate on reaching out to Chief Messenger Tamin. It – it took longer than usual to make that connection, and now I know why."

"Tell me," Kreldik demanded.

Best to get the worst news out first. "My master, the Prophet, is no more."

As he watched, Kreldik's face went very still, paling under his tan. "How? He should have been safe in the fastness of the Great Temple."

"Tamin did not explain what had happened – I think he found making the connection as difficult as I did." Time to share the rest. "And I know the reason for that too – whoever killed my master stole the Master Bloodstone from around his neck. Much of the power of my Bloodstone has been lost."

Kreldik gaped at him. "The Prophet and the Master Bloodstone lost? Holy Talamu, how could this have happened?"

"I do not know. But I must give you the rest of Tamin's message. Lord Domlok has taken control of the Council and is ordering us to give up the siege and return to Talamunem City as soon as we can."

Kreldik's eyes went flat. "Abandon the siege and return home? This makes a mockery of all we have achieved – so many lives lost, and for nothing. If we give up now, the Veylindréans will be in Talamdor within seisdags."

Portak could understand his dismay. "Nevertheless, that is the order of the Council. But," he added, "I'm not sure you're right. I have travelled around Veylindré on – on my master's business," he had to pause, beat down the grief that was tightening his throat before continuing, "and I do not believe they are interested in invading us."

"Let us hope you are right," Kreldik said. "Leave me now. I must confer with my staff."

The siege had been called off and the army had withdrawn to the base camp at the foot of the pass. As Portak walked through the camp, he could hear the low hum of many conversations, as the men speculated why this had happened. They would find out soon enough.

There was a stir outside the General's pavilion. Portak watched as the General emerged, his face old and drawn. How would he address the troops, without the power of his Bloodstone? The loss of the Master Bloodstone had so many implications, none of them good.

But it seemed he was not going to try. Portak realised that representatives of each company had been gathered in front of the tent. The General would speak to them, and they would let the men know. Swiftly, Portak moved to a position from which he would be able to gauge their reactions.

"Our orders have changed," the General began. "Word has come from Talamunem City that," and he paused, visibly gathering his courage, "that our leader, His Holiness the Prophet, has been slain by Veylindréan agents. Our orders…"

Pandemonium. "It cannot be true." "How did it happen?" "Our leader – lost." "We must make them pay." Anger. Grief. Confusion. Disbelief.

The General stopped speaking, allowed them a moment to absorb the news. Then he held up his hand, ordering silence.

"Our orders," he repeated, "come from Lord Domlok, who has taken control of the Council. We are commanded to abandon the invasion and return to Talamunem City with all haste. I know this will not be welcome news for many of you, but as loyal soldiers, we serve the rulers of Talamdor and must follow their directives. Ready your men and pack the equipment onto the wagons. We leave at first light tomorrow."

More protests. "Abandon the invasion? That's ridiculous." "But we're so close to gaining power in the Commonweal." "Then all those lives will have been lost for nothing." More anger. More confusion. More disbelief.

Portak watched as the General stood erect, waiting for the emotions of his men to run their course. Knowing that the man was in full agreement with them.

"What about the wounded?" asked a man garbed in the red robes of a healer, as the cries of protest died down. "Some of them should not be moved."

"Space must be found for them on board the wagons."

"But..."

"This is not a matter for debate." The General drew himself up to his full commanding height. "You have your orders. Dismissed."

Δ Chapter 12 Δ

Abigail pulled Ylonya to one side, leaving Aidren talking quietly to Jacob under Tremond's watchful gaze.

"How did you manage to rescue Aidren and Tremond without being caught?"

"Through an old trick I was taught by Kendris, when he was my mentor in the Guild of Intelligencers," Ylonya replied. "It makes me appear boring, not worthy of notice. People ignore me, their eyes slide off me and they forget they have ever seen me."

"That's it," Abigail said, snapping her fingers. "That's how we'll escape."

"But I can only do it for me – how will that help the rest of you?"

"Do you remember how I used my Goldstone to get past the monstrous creatures of the pass?"

"Yes, of course," Ylonya said, her face lighting up. "You surrounded us all with light from your Goldstone."

"That's right. I think you could use a similar trick to extend your – what would you call it? a mask of concealment? – to cover all of us in the same way."

Ylonya looked doubtful. "If you remember, I was unable to do it at the pass."

Abigail smiled. "Ah, but you did not have my power augmenting your own then. I'm sure we can do this together."

"If you speak a single word out of turn, Tremond will kill you where you stand," Ylonya told Jacob.

"You don't have to be so hard on him," Abigail said. "It's Jacob."

"But not the Jacob we lost in Talmis," Ylonya said. Then to Jacob, "Lead on."

The five of them – Jacob, with Tremond immediately behind him, knife in hand, then Aidren, with Abigail and Ylonya herself at the rear – crept down the corridor to the Visitors' Hall, out through the far door and into the streets of the city. Dusk was falling and Ylonya trusted that the fading light and the hoods of their cloaks would help camouflage their un-Talamdorian features. But she need not have worried. Word that something serious had occurred had obviously got out in the short time that had elapsed – already, hundreds of people were milling around the square outside the Great Temple, waiting for news. And more were heading that way. With luck, they would be able to lose themselves in the crowd.

It was difficult to make headway against the human tide, more difficult to get through unnoticed, but Ylonya's trick, augmented by Abigail's power, got them through. Although it took longer than Ylonya would have liked – it was a real strain to maintain the mask. But she could sense the energy thrumming through her from Abigail's hand on her shoulder, which gave her the power she needed.

She led them to the West Gate, which had only one guard – no doubt the others had decided to head for the main square with the rest of Talamunem City's citizens. Aidren crept up behind him and knocked him out with one blow from the pommel of his dagger. But they would still have the terrible red constructs to contend with.

"How are we going to get past them?" Aidren asked.

"With this," Ylonya said, producing the Bloodstone Abigail had carried for so long. "It worked when I came in this way."

Holding her breath, she clutched the Bloodstone in her right hand, praying that its presence would fool them into believing that the five of them were Talamdorian. She tiptoed out through the Gate. Nothing. The mail-clad giants must have been controlled by the Master Bloodstone. She gestured to the others to come through quickly – who knew how long the power of the Bloodstone would work, now that the Master Bloodstone was not controlled by the Prophet.

"Now what?" Abigail asked.

"Now we walk slowly and casually away, until we are out of sight of the Gate. Then we get off the road."

"It's getting dark – how are you going to find your way back to the cave?" Aidren asked.

Ylonya waved her poniard at him. "This is Ednor's," she said. "I'll use my Finding powers to guide us back."

"You seem to have thought of everything," Aidren said, and she could hear the admiration in his voice.

"I do my best."

It had been a long and tedious day. Ednor had tried to rest but gnawing worry about the others kept him up and pacing for most of it. A couple of times he ventured out of the cave, to see whether there was any sign of them returning. But the pain from his wound and his promise to Ylonya stopped him from going far. He cursed the accident that meant he, a trained Warrior, was forced to watch and wait, instead of taking the fight to the Talamdorians.

He rummaged through his pack, brought out a *feolin* loaf and a flask of thin, red wine. He forced himself to bite, to swallow, but the tension in his gut made it hard work. Surely they should be back by now?

When the light began to fade, the waiting became near unbearable. He would have gone after her, but he didn't know what route she had taken. They must return soon. He'd better keep the fire going – it was getting cold.

It was fully dark before he heard the sound of footsteps and quiet voices. But even in his eagerness, he did not forget caution. Picking up his sword, he got to his feet and crept towards the cave's entrance. If necessary, he would die to defend it.

Ylonya stepped into the firelight. She looked tired, but he could see no wounds. He felt a certain tension in his gut relax. Thank Ranu. He moved back to let them all enter.

"Have you done it?"

Ylonya clapped him on the shoulder. Then her face was transformed by a gorgeously wide grin, which made his heart beat faster. "Yes, my friend, our quest – or at least, the first part of it – is achieved. Let us sit down – there is much to tell you."

Then he noticed the tall stranger – a youth with dark, curly hair, dressed in Talamdorian fashion. And that Tremond was standing close to him, his knife in his hand.

"Who is this?"

"This is Jacob," Abigail said. "We have rescued him from the City."

Ednor could tell there was something amiss – he would have expected her to be full of joy. But her face was pale and drawn and he thought he could see the glimmer of unshed tears in her eyes.

"Peace, my friend," Tremond said. "There will be time for tales once we have eaten."

Ednor bowed his head. "Of course. I have kept the fire going."

Before long, the six of them had eaten their fill and quenched their thirst.

"Now," said Ednor, "what of your tale?"

"Ylonya told me you were wounded at the North Gate," Abigail said. "I will tend it while we share our story."

As he watched, she fetched her healer's bag from a corner of the cave. "Let me see your wounds."

Obediently, he turned his back to her, felt her gentle hands raising his shirt to get to the bandage underneath. Then hissed in pain as she eased it free and began to sponge away the poultice covering the wounds.

"These look nice and clean," she said. "What did you use on them, Ylonya?"

"Comfrey first, to clean them," Ylonya said. "Then I gave him a mouthful of the Lènia's Nimbane potion and made a poultice out of the leaves. But I am no Healer – I'm glad you are here to tend to him."

"You have done well, my friend," and Ednor could hear the warm approval in Abigail's voice. "This is exactly what I would have done. I'll make a fresh poultice, then bandage it anew."

The relief in Ylonya's face was almost comical. But Ednor knew she had saved his life. He touched her hand, trying to convey his gratitude. She flushed and looked away. Time to change the subject.

"While Abigail does her work," he said, "would someone please tell me what happened before I burst with suspense?"

Aidren grinned at him. "The guards took us to a prison and locked the three of us up," he began.

As the tale unfolded, Ednor listened with a mixture of envy and astonishment. So much had happened and he had been stuck here, useless.

He heard Abigail's voice behind him, murmuring, "*Belannath Ranu, gal em bynn wellent.*" Her hands gentle on his back. Then, the miraculous surcease from pain.

As she rebandaged his wounds, he thanked her.

She smiled. "It is part of my calling. Keep them covered for the next couple of days, then we'll let the air heal them the rest of the way."

"Here is your poniard, my friend," Ylonya said. "It struck one of the blows that wounded the Prophet."

Ednor nodded, feeling a warm glow of satisfaction. "Good."

"But it was Abigail's wresting of the Master Bloodstone from around his neck that killed him," Aidren said. "I have never seen anything like it. He seemed to age tens of years in seconds."

"Yes," Abigail said, sounding almost sad. "His life force was linked to his possession of the Master Bloodstone. Once I took it from his neck, that link was broken. It was a horrible way to die."

"You could have done nothing else," Aidren said.

She bowed her head. "I know," she said, "but all the same..."

"Now we must rest," Ylonya said. "Ednor, will you take first watch?" Then she came close and said softly, "Have an eye to Jacob. He must not be allowed to escape."

Aidren was about to settle down to sleep, when he felt a hand on his shoulder. Ylonya.

"What do you want?"

"I want you to keep a close eye on Jacob and listen to him, if he wants to talk. For some reason he trusts you, which is more than he does any of the rest of us. Probably because you are the only person who is recognisably someone he knew before Talmis. Once we get back to Chorich Castle, Abigail and I will be able to drop our Talamdorian disguises, which might help. And of course he will see Shaunan again. But until that time, please be his friend."

"I am his friend," Aidren said. "But why doesn't he recognise Abi? He has known her much longer than he's known me."

Ylonya's face grew thoughtful. "Who knows how much his memories and mind have been damaged by wearing that bangle all this time. Also," she continued, "he watched and heard Abigail defy the Prophet, whom he seems to have had great respect for. And from what he's said, he seems to fear her."

"Poor Abigail. How will she bear it?"

"She will cope. She is stronger than you think. But I fear it will be a long while before she gets her Jacob back, if it happens at all."

"How do you know all this?" Aidren asked.

Ylonya laughed. "An Yrusian needs to know how to understand what motivates people, if she is to trade with them."

Of course. "I'd forgotten about that – your gift of Empathy." Then he met Ylonya's gaze. "I'll do my best."

She clapped him on the shoulder. "Thank you, my friend."

Abigail hadn't been asleep for long when she awoke suddenly, all five senses alert. Darkness was all around her, apart from the dim glow from the embers of the banked fire.

What had woken her? She held her breath and listened. Two low voices speaking just above a whisper, both intimately familiar. Jacob and Aidren.

She knew Aidren had been due to take the second watch, but what was Jacob doing awake? Some instinct warned her to keep quiet and still and listen.

"...and I don't know who I am any more. The time I spent with you and the others is starting to come back to me, but it's still like seeing through a dense fog. Like it happened to someone else, in a fairy tale long ago."

"That must be hard, my friend." Abigail could hear the sympathy in Aidren's voice. "We have been searching for you all this time, never dreaming that the Prophet had taken away the memories of your life in Veylindré. I got quite a shock when I saw you bore no Waymark."

"There you go," Jacob said with a deep sigh, "talking about Waymarks again. When the only mark I'd heard of, up until yesterday, was the Talamdorian Bloodmark. And I knew I'd never have one of those –

I'm not a trueblood." His voice was muffled, as though he had covered his face.

"How can I help you?"

Something in the tone of Aidren's voice reminded Abigail of another night-time conversation, way back in Dagâran. When she had been wakeful during their journey through the Myner's Gap and Aidren had patiently answered her questions about how he had become a Warrior. How long ago it seemed. It was hard to believe that all Jacob's memories of that time had been erased.

Together with his memories of her. Her heart ached – how long would it take him to recollect the love they had shared? Or had she lost that Jacob forever? No, she would not believe that. Shaunan would be able to heal him, restore his memories, once they got back to Chorich Castle. Shaunan could do anything.

But what if she couldn't? What if Jacob continued to fear her? Some part of her was reluctantly beginning to realise that the Jacob she had missed for so long, the boy she had loved so dearly, had cried herself to sleep about, no longer existed. Except in her memory. This new Jacob was someone she would have to get to know. She – they – would have to start again. She would have to earn his trust.

At least he recognised Aidren as a friend. Abigail held on to this as a promise of things to come and carried on listening.

"He told me she was dead," Jacob was saying, and she could hear real anguish in his voice, "that she and all the rest had perished in the shipwreck."

"Who told you that?" Aidren asked.

"Portak, the man who rescued me, who brought me to Talamdor."

"Is that why you went with him?"

"What else could I have done? I was alone in a strange land, with no idea how I had got there. Portak was my only friend."

"What else did he tell you?"

"That Veylindré was ruled by evil witches, who controlled their people using magic."

Abigail's fists clenched. The man had been diabolically clever. He must have overheard Jacob's conversation with Aidren in the inn at Talmis and used what he had learned to turn Jacob against Veylindré. Against the Way. She remembered how difficult he had found it to accept the Way in the first place, back in Luvodican all those seisdags ago.

And now he saw her as a Veylindréan witch. Someone to be feared.

"But the Way is used only for good," Aidren said.

"That is not what I was taught," Jacob said. "Portak rescued me from falling into their hands and the Prophet explained how the Veylindréan witches had persecuted Holy Talamu, long ages ago."

Abigail's heart sank. It seemed clear that Jacob had been thoroughly indoctrinated to fear and mistrust both Veylindréans and the Way.

"What about Abigail?" Aidren asked. "Surely you remember her?"

"I don't know," Jacob said, his voice full of pain. "The girl I remember had a sheaf of golden hair and was docile and loving. I don't know this one who calls herself Abigail. She may look something like my Abi, apart from the hair. But she doesn't act like my Abi – I saw and heard her defy my master. And it was her theft of the Master Bloodstone that killed him."

Abigail could hear the anger in his voice. She fought to stay silent, to not betray that she was eavesdropping. Was *that* what he thought of her? She turned her face into her cloak, which served her as a pillow, and stifled the sobs that were shaking her whole body. It sounded like the only things this Jacob needed from her were patience and forbearance. The disappointment was crushing.

She flipped her blanket over her head. She didn't want to hear any more.

"Wake up, sleepyhead." Abigail heard Ylonya's voice summoning her from the depths of sleep.

She awoke with a beast of a headache and sore, scratchy eyes. For a moment, she couldn't think why. Then the memory of the previous night's conversation came flooding back. What she had learned about Jacob. Don't think about that now.

"What time is it?"

"Nearly sixth hour," Ylonya said with a chuckle, "I thought I'd better let you rest, after your exertions yesterday."

Abigail shot up into a sitting position, wincing as pain lanced through her head. "Nearly sixth hour? Then I've wasted the whole morning for us."

"Don't worry about it," Ylonya said. "We're not moving out until it is fully dark."

"Why not?"

"I slipped out earlier for a look around and there are Talamdorian scouts out searching."

"Searching?" Abigail said, fear leaping into her throat. "For us?"

"I expect so. But the entrance to this cave is well-disguised and we've been keeping quiet."

"How are we going to get out of here, if there are Talamdorian patrols?"

"The moon is a couple of nights from full and the skies will be clear tonight."

"How do you –" Abigail began, then remembered. "You used your weather sense?"

Ylonya chuckled again. "Yes. I estimate it will take us the best part of five hours to reach Malke's village."

"How will you find the way in the dark?"

"I have the map Malke drew for us. I can use it to hold us on course."

"But how will you be able to read it in the dark? We won't be able to use our Goldstones for light."

"Worry not. I'll use my Finding sense."

Abigail's heart filled with gratitude. Without Ylonya's many skills, the company would have foundered long ago.

They were ready to leave long before dusk. But Ylonya insisted that they wait until it was fully dark. She knew it would take all of her skill to keep them safe and unseen.

"Do you think we will be pursued for long?" Aidren asked.

To Ylonya's surprise, Jacob spoke up, somewhat scornfully. "Of course you will. It will be Domlok who has taken control of the Council and I know Domlok. He will not give up easily. Not only will he be seeking to avenge the death of my –" and he bit off what he was going to say, "– I mean, of the Prophet. You've also stolen the Master Bloodstone. Domlok will pursue you to the ends of the earth to retrieve it. He will never feel secure as head of the Council until he possesses it. It is the most holy artefact of Talamdor and the pure blood Talamdorian who controls it is seen as the rightful ruler."

A silence fell over the company as they took this in.

"Thank you, my friend," Ylonya said, "for your insight. Abigail, come with me please."

"Why? What do you want?"

"You will see. And Ednor, may I borrow your poniard?"

"Of course." He handed it over, sheath first.

Ylonya strode to the back of the cave, where a natural outcropping would give them some concealment. "I do not want Jacob to see this," she said in a low voice. "Or Tremond," she added under her breath.

Abigail's eyebrows contracted at this. "But he's just helped us."

Ylonya nodded. "Jacob? That is true. But I still do not entirely trust him. He has been conditioned to believe in the Prophet's cause. It is better he should not know where the Bloodstones are concealed. Fetch your pack."

Abigail did so, then asked, "Why don't you want Tremond to know?"

"He is a good friend, but he is also a Watchman. My fellow Yrusians would never forgive me."

She picked up her pack and began to empty it, laying her belongings on top of her blanket. Then she drew Ednor's poniard from its sheath and began to patiently unpick the stitching at the bottom of the inside of her pack. Underneath was a shallow compartment completely filled with a box made of thin Ranuswood. She opened it and took out the pouches and strips of cloth that filled it.

"I paid a small fortune to a Néartanian woodcarver to have this made, but it has paid for itself many times over."

In spite of her sorrow about Jacob, Abigail began to laugh. "Now I understand why you didn't want Tremond to see it."

"Pass me the Bloodstones."

As Abigail watched, she wrapped both stones securely but separately until their shapes were entirely obscured. She placed them at opposite sides of the Ranuswood box before filling up the gaps with the rest of the cloths. Then she began to restitch the false bottom into place.

"There. Now no-one should be able to detect them."

Δ Chapter 13 Δ

To Jacob's surprise, Ylonya walked over to where he was sitting when she and Abigail returned from their mysterious errand at the back of the cave. She squatted down beside him.

"Jacob, you told us Domlok will have taken charge in Talamunem City."

"Yes. What of it?"

"I was wondering how well you know him. For example, can you guess which direction he'll expect us to go to escape from Talamdor?"

Jacob furrowed his brow. "I think," he said, "he'd expect us to flee eastward, towards the Néartanian border, to meet up with the Veylindréan army."

Why was he helping them? He should be trying to escape, to return to the City.

"Then, if we go north, we have a better chance of avoiding notice?"

"I honestly don't know. I didn't know Domlok that well. In fact, he hated me."

"Why?" Abigail asked.

"Because he was jealous of my relationship with the Prophet. That I had the Prophet's ear."

Jacob noticed a fleeting expression of shock on Abigail's face. Why was she reacting like that? He was proud of how close he had been to the Prophet. Or was that a lie too? He wanted to trust Aidren, but everything his friend had told him contradicted his whole life in Talamdor. God! He was so confused.

As the light began to fade from the sky, Ylonya stood up and faced the others.

"I think we can count on being hunted, once we leave the safety of these caves. We have achieved the first part of our quest, but there are many long and dangerous miles between here and Ranusheim. It is more vital than ever that we work as one, so we are not recaptured."

"Why are you going to Ranusheim?" Jacob asked.

"We have to –" Abigail began, but Ylonya interrupted her.

"Never mind that now. The important thing is that you all follow my instructions, between here and Silvin. Whether that is to move, stay still, or run. Our lives and the success of the quest may depend on your instant obedience. If we fall into Talamdorian hands now, everything we've achieved so far will have been for naught. We need to get out of Talamdor as soon as possible."

Ylonya looked at each of them in turn. Aidren looked determined, Ednor and Tremond acquiescent – they understood the danger, although she sensed that Ednor would rather fight than hide. Abigail looked confused, as though she didn't understand why she had stopped her from blurting out the truth about the Master Bloodstone. And Jacob – Jacob was sitting a little apart from the others, as though he wanted to disassociate himself from them. She did not trust him.

"Abigail, if I might have a word?"

"If you like." The girl scrambled to her feet and Ylonya led her back to the secluded part of the cave.

"What's wrong?"

"I still don't trust Jacob. You must keep the final aim of the quest to yourself. I think it could be dangerous for him to know about it."

The girl's face twisted in unwilling acceptance. "I suppose you're right. But it is so hard to think of him as anyone else except... Jacob."

"You have to forget the Jacob you knew," Ylonya said. "I can sense he is on the edge of something. Perhaps he is hoping to escape and return to Talamunem City, to the only life he knows here."

"I suppose you're right. Of all the outcomes of our quest, I hadn't counted on this."

Abigail's voice was full of sorrow. Ylonya wished she could be more empathic, but the success of the quest was more important than anything else.

"Abigail," she said, "I want you to probe Jacob's mind. It is vital that he does not betray us. If you find any hint of a desire to escape," and she took a deep breath, steeling herself to continue, "we'll have to keep him under control somehow."

The girl looked horrified. "What do you mean?"

Ylonya gave her a straight look. "Do you have something in your healer's bag that we can dose him with, to keep him compliant?"

"We've just rescued him from the domination of the Prophet and now you want to control him again?" Abigail's voice was incredulous.

"Yes. I'm sorry, but this is too important for us to be ethical. If we fail," and Ylonya used the surest argument she knew, hating herself for being so manipulative, "Ellyn's death will have been for nothing."

The colour drained from Abigail's face and she bowed her head. "I hate this so much. Is there no other way?"

"Not if the quest is to succeed."

"Very well. I'll speak to Shaunan through Waymage Rusilon."

"Do it now."

Abigail took her Goldstone out of its pouch, held it in her right hand and closed her eyes. Ylonya held her breath. There had to be something.

After a couple of minutes, Abigail opened her eyes again, looked at her friend. "Shaunan says there is a syrup made from honey and the juice of poppies which brings calm and placidity. She has told me which bottle to find it in and how much to give him. Ylonya, must I do this?"

"I'm sorry, Abigail, you must."

"But he's not going to drink something just because I ask him to. Especially not if *I* ask him to. I'm the one who killed his precious master. Can't we find some other way to do this?"

Ylonya thought for a moment. "All right. Then you must keep your mind open to him. I'll ask Tremond to stay close to him, so that he can act instantly if the need arises."

Abigail's shoulders relaxed. Odd that the girl preferred to invade Jacob's mind over drugging him into submission, which would be much surer. She would never understand Ranusians.

It was a clear, starlit night and in other circumstances Abigail would have gloried in it. But not this night. Ylonya had convinced her of the danger they were in and her nerves were stretched as tight as lute strings. They were all trying to be as quiet as possible, but only Ylonya and Tremond had the skill. The rest of them stumbled occasionally and each sound made her startle like a wild hare. But there was nowhere to run to, nowhere to hide.

Ylonya led them in a series of short flits from cover to cover, moving as silently as a bitch fox. Jacob and Aidren came next, followed closely by herself and Tremond, with Ednor bringing up the rear, his hand on the pommel of his sword.

Before they left the security of the cave, Tremond had confronted Jacob. “You must do exactly what Ylonya says. If you make a sound or a move out of place, I will kill you. Is that clear?”

She had never seen Tremond so fierce before. And was not surprised when Jacob nodded his head. She would have obeyed Tremond too, if he’d spoken to her in that tone.

And Ylonya had told Ednor and Aidren in no uncertain terms, “This is not the time for fighting. This is the time for staying concealed and escaping. Can I trust you both?”

Abigail had noticed the mutinous expressions on both their faces and gently nudged them into reluctant assent. Two more to keep an eye on.

They were more than an hour on the way and the moon had risen when Ylonya stopped dead, holding up her hand for silence. Abigail froze in her tracks and felt, rather than saw, Tremond easing his long knife out of its sheath and taking hold of Jacob’s arm.

The sound they had dreaded – hoofbeats, coming from behind them. From Talamunem City. Ylonya led them behind a patch of scrubby bushes.

Abigail opened her mind to their surroundings. And was assailed by the emotions of the others – Ylonya's determination not to get caught, Ednor's and Aidren's desire to fight, Tremond's stolid concentration on Jacob, and Jacob's... she felt a sudden, wild shaft of excitement from him. Ylonya had been right – Jacob was hoping to escape and she only had moments to stop him. She darted towards Tremond and whispered, "Hold your knife to his throat."

Hating herself, but betraying him anyway.

Then she tiptoed over to Ylonya and murmured, "Can you do your concealment trick again, if I augment your strength?"

Ylonya nodded. Abigail put her left hand flat on her friend's shoulder, took her Goldstone in her right hand and concentrated, pouring all her strength and determination to escape from Talamdor into Ylonya. In the nick of time – the Talamdorians came into view moments later.

There were three of them, all on horseback. The company froze behind their concealing bushes. Would they suffice to keep them hidden? Abigail renewed her focus on her Goldstone, on transferring strength to Ylonya.

"How can we be expected to track anyone in this darkness," one soldier said in a whining voice. "I don't think they've come this way at all. Why in Talamu's name would they go north, when they could link up with the enemy army if they go east? That's what I'd do, anyway."

"Oh, so you're a strategist now, are you?" a second voice sneered. "Myself, I think they're hiding up somewhere close, until all the clamour has died down."

"And how do they expect us to find anything or anyone in this confounded darkness?" the first soldier complained. "Why couldn't we have waited until morning?"

"You have a point there, mate," the second voice replied.

"Quiet there." A third voice, gruffer and deeper than the others, and slightly sibilant. "Our instructions come from Lord Domlok himself. We are to search north, so search north we will. Unless you'd rather spend the next few years of your lives in prison."

"Sorry, Captain Grenlik, I didn't mean no harm."

"I should think not. Now keep your whining to yourselves and keep your ears open. We are to continue the search, then meet up with the other half of the patrol in Silvin at fourth hour."

As the hoofbeats receded into the distance, Abigail let out the breath she hadn't realised she had been holding and took her hand off Ylonya's shoulder. That had been far too close for comfort.

"Come on," Ylonya said in a low voice. "We must reach Silvin before dawn."

"Yes, they must be warned," Tremond said.

"How are we going to retrieve the horses, if that patrol is in Silvin?" Abigail asked.

"We'll have to get there before them, that's all. You heard the man – he's not planning to reach the village before fourth hour."

"By which time we must be long gone," Abigail said. "We'll ask Malke for supplies, then leave straight after breaking our fast."

"I had hoped we would be able to spend some time there," Ylonya said. "So we could try to make Jacob understand that we have his best interests at heart."

"No," Abigail said. "It would be a poor repayment for Malke's hospitality if we brought her and the rest of the villagers into danger through our presence."

Ylonya shrugged. "Very well. In which case, we'd better put our best feet forward."

They reached Silvin just as dawn was beginning to lighten the eastern sky, without encountering any other patrols. Abigail was relieved, but also determined not to bring Malke and her community into peril. She and Ylonya left the others and went to find the headwoman.

But there was no need – Malke was hurrying down the village's one street to meet them. "I am glad to see you all. Have you been travelling all night to reach here so early?"

"Just about," Abigail said. "Malke, we narrowly avoided being caught by a patrol, which was out searching for us. And I overheard they were planning to come here at fourth hour. So we need to be out of here before then."

"Why are the Talamdorians after you?"

"It is best that you do not know," Abigail replied. "The last thing I want is to put you and yours in danger."

The headwoman nodded. "Very well. What do you need from me?"

"If we could break our fast here, that would be wonderful. And I'd like to have another look at Jenne before I leave. How has she been?"

"She's still coughing, but the medicine you left has helped greatly. I am in your debt."

"No," Abigail said, "we are in yours."

Ylonya put a word in. "We need to ask a further favour. We have another person in our company, whom we rescued from Talamunem City. Do you have a horse we could borrow? I promise we'll send it back from Chorich Castle."

"Yes, that I can do. And I'll give you food enough for the three day journey."

"Bless you, Malke," Abigail said. "You have been a true friend to us."

Aidren yawned. "I'm so tired," he said to Jacob, as they waited for Ylonya and Abigail to finish talking to Malke. "I hope we'll be able to rest here awhile before carrying on with our journey."

"I don't even know where we're going," Jacob grumbled. "You lot are as bad as Portak was on the way to Talamunem City – he wouldn't tell me anything either."

"I'm sorry, my friend," Aidren said. "But until we are safely back on Veylindréan soil, it is best that you are content to simply follow us."

Jacob startled, the whites of his eyes showing like a horse's. "We are going to Veylindré? But it isn't safe. We'll be captured by the witches."

Aidren put his hand on the other young man's arm. "It's not like that in Veylindré. I promise you. Nobody will hurt you, nor put a spell on you against your will. All that is a lie the Talamdorian nobility spin to keep their people quiet and obedient."

Jacob folded his arms, but he said nothing. It was plain to Aidren that he didn't believe him. He caught Tremond's eye and beckoned him over. "Keep an eye on Jacob," he murmured. "I need to have a word with Ylonya and Abigail."

He strode up to the two women, who were on their way back to the rest of them. "Jacob is frightened of going to Veylindré," he said. "He thinks he'll be captured and ill-treated."

"Thank you for letting us know," Ylonya said. Then to Abigail, "It's time. We cannot risk him attempting to escape."

Time for what? Aidren watched Abigail's face – it was plain that she didn't like Ylonya's plan, whatever that was. Why did Abigail shut him out? It wasn't fair – he'd known her longer than Ylonya had. Didn't she understand that he had sworn to protect her, no matter what? How could he do that if she excluded him from her plans?

Abigail rummaged in her healer's bag, found the vial of poppy juice. There wasn't much in it – would it be enough to last the three days they needed to escape from Talamdor? It would have to be. She closed her hand around it and went to find Malke.

"What are you giving us to drink?" she asked.

"Mead. Why are you asking?"

"Because," Abigail said, hating herself, "I need to dose our new companion's drink, to make him quiescent."

Malke shot her a startled glance. "Why do you need to do that?"

"He was under the control of the Prophet and has been told lies about Veylindré and Veylindréans. He believes we are all evil witches who will try to harm him."

"But isn't that what you are doing – drugging him into submission?"

This question hit Abigail like a blow to the heart. She felt her eyes prickle with tears and bit her lip before answering. "I know. And I absolutely hate doing it to him. But Malke, it's vital that we escape from Talamdor. And I know he is planning to get away from us if he can. But I love him. Or, at least, I loved the person he was before he was captured, so many seisdags ago."

Malke's expression softened in comprehension. "Very well," she said. "I have trusted you this far, so I will trust you again. Come with me. I was going to bring the mead in a jug, but we'll pour it into mugs first and you can dose the young man's before he gets it."

Abigail put her hand on Malke's arm. "Thank you, my friend."

Aidren watched Abigail as she walked down the main street of Silvin, accompanied by Malke. Between them, they were carrying two heavy trays, one with food on it, the other with half a dozen mugs of drink. He hurried to meet them and took the tray of drinks from Abigail. Why did one of them have a piece of twine tied to the handle?

"What's going on?" he asked Abigail.

She met his eyes. "We have to make sure that Jacob doesn't try to escape," she said in a low voice. "So I've dosed one of the mugs with poppy juice to make him quiet and compliant. It's the one with the twine round the handle. Can you take it off and give it to him?"

Thank Ranu. Abigail was trusting him again. He nodded at her before untying the twine and taking that mug over to Jacob.

"Here's some mead for our breakfast," he said.

Jacob took it and sipped it warily. "This is good," he said, "but sweeter than I'm used to."

Aidren took a swig of his. "You're right," he said. "It is. But a good brew, nonetheless."

The six of them sat outside Silvin's pub at a couple of wooden trestle tables in the early morning sunshine, eating and drinking their fill. Malke had provided fresh bread rolls with butter and honey to go with them. They tasted so good.

As Aidren watched Jacob, the pupils of his friend's eyes got bigger and the wariness faded from his face. Good, the poppy juice was doing its work. How had Abigail known what to give him?

When they had finished breaking their fast, Ylonya stood up. "We need to get our horses and leave."

"What about Jacob?" Aidren asked.

"Malke is lending us a horse for him. We'll return it once we reach Chorich Castle."

In a matter of minutes, they were mounted up and ready to go.

"Thank you for your hospitality and your many kindnesses," Abigail said to Malke, giving her a hug.

"You are welcome," the headwoman replied. "Go well. Your secret is safe with us."

Δ Chapter 14 ֍

Almost as soon as they were clear of Silvin, the forest that covered most of northern Talamdor began. Not being able to see for any distance made Ylonya jumpy – there were so many places of concealment in which the enemy could hide. Once they were among the dense ranks of trees, it did not take her long to find the river they had used to guide them from northern Talamdor to Malke's village, only a couple of seisdags ago. It seemed like a lifetime.

"Here it is," she told the others. "Now all we have to do is follow this path, staying close to the river, and it will take us almost to the pass."

It felt good to be back on horseback, but she knew never to relax into it. The trees all around them made it difficult to see far – the enemy could be hiding anywhere, ready to spring out on them. Ylonya was on high alert every moment for signs of pursuit. Or ambush. The Master Bloodstone and Abigail must be kept safe whatever happened. Ednor, Tremond and Aidren rode with only their left hands on the reins, keeping their right hands free to unsheathe their swords at an instant's notice. Excellent. They were ready for action.

The forest felt stuffy. It was hard to breathe. And it would take them two whole days to reach the foot of the pass on the Talamdorian side. She dropped back to speak to Abigail.

"Do you think the entrance to the pass will be guarded, like it was when we crossed before?"

"I don't know for sure, but I think not. I suspect the force we felt then had been put there by the Prophet. With any luck, it will have been powered by his possession of the Master Bloodstone and will be gone."

"I hope you're right."

"Let's wait and see. We have to get there first."

They were riding past one of the frequent outcroppings of rock on the right side of the path, and their forward vision was temporarily blocked. Ylonya was about to answer when half a dozen Talamdorian soldiers burst out from behind the rocks. Ednor, Tremond and Aidren immediately drew their swords and began to fight. They had been together for so long now that each instinctively supported the other two, and all three strove to keep the attackers away from Abigail.

Ylonya was torn – should she join the fray or defend Abigail? The Talamdorians were on foot, but it was still three against six – not good odds. Four against six would be better. Make that four against five. Ednor had thrust the point of his sword into the gap between one Talamdorian's breastplate and helmet. One down, five to go.

She'd better stay with Abigail. Then she remembered the Bloodstones in the bottom of her pack – she must keep them safe and uncaptured, whatever else happened. She had to trust that her three companions would beat off their attackers. They had the advantage of being mounted and both Ednor and Aidren were trained warriors. Belannath Ranu, lend strength to their arms.

What was Jacob doing? He had moved his horse next to Abigail's, and his knife was drawn. Was he defending her? His eyes were wide, his expression confused. Of course, Abigail had given him the poppy syrup in the mead. He'd be no use at all. Ylonya set her heels into her horse's sides and joined them.

"What are you doing here?" Abigail shouted above the noise of the fight. "You need to help them. Jacob will take care of me."

Ylonya swung her pack off her shoulders. "Look after this then."

Abigail took the pack, tied it to the pommel of her saddle. "Go!"

Nothing loath, Ylonya drew her own sword and cantered into the fray. It did not take long. Ednor and Aidren between them dispatched three more of the remaining five and she and Tremond saw to the other two. A nasty little fight, but soon over.

"Are any of you injured?" Abigail asked urgently.

"Not a scratch," Ednor told her, a fierce grin on his face.

The other three shook their heads. The Talamdorians had not expected such a fierce defence, had not been a match for them.

Abigail sighed with relief. "Let's hope they will be the last to pursue us. We still have nearly two days in Talamdor before we reach the pass."

They settled back into the journey. That evening, they found a cave deep in the forest to sleep in.

"Do you think we can risk a fire?" Abigail asked Ylonya.

"So long as we light it towards the back of the cave – there's a hole in the roof which should act like a chimney."

"But won't anyone outside be able to see the smoke?"

"We'll wait until nightfall. I think we deserve a hot meal after our little tussle."

"Little tussle?" Abigail's voice rose a full octave. "Is that what you call it?"

Ednor, who had been listening to them, laughed. "Hardly worth getting our swords out for."

"Don't get over-confident," Abigail said. "I for one will be glad once we are back on Veylindréan soil."

Ednor's expression sobered. "You're right. But don't worry, Abigail. We'll make sure we get there safely."

The next day passed without incident, for which Abigail was profoundly grateful. The mountains were drawing nearer, the trees beginning to thin out, and she guessed they'd reach the foot of the pass before night.

Which was a good job – only one dose of the poppy juice remained. She'd give it to Jacob this evening. How she hated doing this to him. But it had worked – it had made him docile and compliant. And he had stayed by her side during the fight.

She longed to reach inside his mind again, to discover what he was thinking. But shrank from it – it felt like a violation of his privacy. She would only do it at the extreme of need. She had already done it more often than she was comfortable with. She couldn't wait to get back to Chorich Castle and Shaunan. She was sure her mentor would be able to cure Jacob. That she would get her dearest love back.

But a little voice inside her head kept asking, *What if you don't? What if he never gets his memories back?*

"No," she said aloud. "I won't believe it."

"Won't believe what?" Aidren asked.

"That Jacob is incurable," she said in a low voice.

He hugged her. "The Waymage will be able to cure him."

She hugged him back. "Thank you."

They spent their last night in Talamdor in sight of the pass. Aidren would be glad to be back on Veylindréan soil. He'd seen enough of Talamdor to last him a lifetime.

"Tell me more about where we're going," Jacob asked him, as they set up camp in a grove of trees. In fact, it was the same place they had stayed during their first night in Talamdor. Hopefully they wouldn't be disturbed this time.

"It will take us the whole of tomorrow to cross the pass," Aidren said. "Then I expect we'll stay the night in the scouts' hut on the Yrusian side before heading for Chorich Castle. If we can get in – they keep it locked. That's a thought – I need to have a word with Abigail."

He left Jacob and walked over to where Abigail was talking to Ylonya.

"...and I hope that we will not have to pass through the barrier again," Abigail was saying.

"Surely not," Aidren said. "Didn't you say that the power of the Master Bloodstone was broken?"

Abigail turned to face him. "I hope so, but we won't find out for sure until we get there tomorrow morning."

"I've just thought of something," Aidren said. "Are we planning to stay the night in the scouts' hut the other side of the pass?"

"Yes," Ylonya said. "Why do you ask?"

"It'll be locked unless they know we're coming," Aidren said. "Don't you remember? Crinan locked it up when we left."

"Good point," Ylonya said. "Abigail, can you ask Waymage Rusilon to send someone there to welcome us?"

Abigail took out her Goldstone, closed her eyes. Aidren watched in fascination as her Goldstone began to glow with a golden light and her expression became remote, distant. A few moments later, she opened them again. "She knows. She will send Crinan."

"Excellent. Then all we have to do is get over the pass tomorrow."

"How is Jacob?" Abigail asked Aidren.

"I think he's frightened about leaving Talamdor. The influence of the Prophet still lies heavily on him."

A shadow passed across Abigail's face. "Do what you can to reassure him," she said. "He still doesn't trust me."

"Nevertheless," Ylonya said. "You will have to control him. We cannot risk him trying to escape.

Abigail bit her lip. "I know," she said softly. "But how I hate having to do this to him."

Aidren could not bear her to be so sad. "Don't worry," he said, giving her a clumsy hug. "Shaunan will sort him out, once we're at Chorich Castle."

Early the next morning, they broke camp and headed for the foot of the pass. Aidren was excited by the prospect of finally being on the way home. Or at least, if not on the way home, back in Veylindré again. It would be many seisdags before he saw Nordvein again – if he ever did. Don't think about that – concentrate on Jacob. He didn't need the power of empathy to sense his friend's unease. He was biting his nails and kept glancing behind.

"Do not fret, my friend," he told him. "Once we're back at Chorich Castle, Shaunan will be able to heal you."

"There's nothing wrong with me," Jacob snapped, "except that I'm being taken away from the only place I know in this world, into the lands of the witches."

Aidren had to suppress a sigh. How many times did Jacob need to be told? The Way only worked for good, and Waymages were not these 'evil witches' his friend kept bleating about. "Please, Jacob, try to trust us. We would not bring you into danger. You knew Shaunan well, back in Dagâran. She would never harm you."

"That's easy for you to say," Jacob said. "You know these people. I don't."

"I know that's what you believe," Aidren said, hanging on to his patience. "But you really did know her, before."

The sooner they were over the pass, the better. Luckily, Ylonya's fears about the barrier they had had to break through when they had entered Talamdor proved ill-founded. By noon they had reached the place near the top of the pass, where they had stopped to eat just after Crinan had left them. Was it only two seisdags ago? It seemed like a lot longer, so much had happened.

"We'll stop here," Ylonya said. "We know we can reach Yrusian by nightfall."

Aidren swung off his horse, loosened its girth and tied the reins to the stump of a bush.

"Come on," he said to Jacob. "I'm hungry."

But his friend only picked at his food. Aidren saw Abigail and Ylonya exchange a worried glance. Then

Abigail took out her Goldstone, murmured something and Jacob sighed, then began to eat.

Half an hour later, they were back on the horses, picking their way down the narrow track that led to Yrusian. Ylonya and Ednor were in the lead, followed by Abigail, then himself behind Jacob, with Tremond bringing up the rear. The going was easier on this side of the pass, with less scree, so they made good time.

Dusk was falling by the time they reached the scouts' hut. There was light streaming from the windows. Good, Crinan must be there already.

Aidren turned to Jacob. "Come, my friend. Let us care for the horses before we eat."

Jacob shrugged, but at the same time seemed to relax slightly. Maybe the act of doing something familiar was a comfort to him. Aidren hoped so.

They reached the grey bulk of Chorich Castle by seventh hour the next day. Abigail was hungry – she had had little appetite for breakfast. Not when Jacob had been so defensive, fending off any attempt to reassure him. She couldn't wait to see Shaunan again.

When they clattered into the stable yard, their horses' hooves loud on the cobbles, Shaunan was there, waiting for them. Abigail slipped off her horse, ran into her mentor's waiting arms.

"Oh, Shaunan! I'm so very glad to see you. I've got so much to tell you."

She was delighted to see that Shaunan had her old colour back and had even put on a little weight. "You're looking much better – are you?"

"Yes," Shaunan replied. "A couple of seisdags' rest and the care of Healer Elyssa and Waymage Rusilon was all I needed." She glanced across to the others, who were being greeted by the Castellan. "I see you have managed to persuade Jacob to come with you."

Abigail sighed. "I suppose so. But he doesn't trust me, or Ylonya. Only Aidren, and him only a little bit. Oh, Shaunan! Do you think you'll be able to heal his mind? He has no memory of anything before his time in Talamdor and fears Veylindréan witches so much. I thought – I thought that once we'd rescued him, everything would be all right. But nothing's all right. I never dreamed it would end like this."

"This is not the end," Shaunan said gently. "I am sure that with time, Jacob will get his memories back. And," she added, glancing at Abigail's darkened hair, "I think that the sooner we strip that dye from your hair and make you a blonde once more, the sooner Jacob will be able to recognise you as the Abigail he knew."

Abigail felt her heart lift. "Thank you," she said. "You have no idea how much I've missed you."

"I am proud of all you have achieved, my dear. To put an end to the Prophet's rule and to recover the Master Bloodstone was no mean feat."

"We couldn't have done it without Ylonya. She's been so resourceful – we wouldn't have made it without her."

Ylonya, too, was relieved to have reached Chorich Castle. Crinan sped off to fetch Castellan Trévon, who strode into the stable yard a few minutes later. He gripped her shoulder, his touch warm and welcoming.

"Ylonya! It is good to see you back, safe and sound."

"Thank you. It's been an exciting couple of seisdags."

"You must tell me all about it, once you've settled your mounts and had some lunch." Then he raised his voice, addressed all of them. "Come to my chambers at ninth hour. I'm sure you have much to tell me. And I have much to tell you."

What did that mean? It would be interesting to hear news of the war. Ylonya disliked being out of touch with what was happening in Veylindré – the last two seisdags had been very odd in that respect. She was just about to lead her horse to the hitching posts and untack her, when she felt a touch on her arm. She swung round. Shaunan. The Waymage looked very much like her old self, except for the sadness in her eyes.

"Well done, my friend," Shaunan said. "Rusilon and I will look after Jacob, while the rest of you speak with the Castellan."

"Thank you," Ylonya said. "You'll find him much changed."

"Abigail has already told me that the Prophet erased all his memories of his time with us. You have done well to get him this far."

Ylonya felt herself relax. "It's hard to believe we've done it," she said. "There were times when I feared the quest was going to fail."

"I had every faith in you."

After an excellent lunch in the great hall, Ednor and the others made their way to Castellan Trévon's quarters. Ednor could not wait to hear what was happening in the war. But he guessed the Castellan would insist on hearing their own tale first.

"Sit down, all of you," Trévon said, "and tell me about your journey."

Ednor listened with fascination as Ylonya related a carefully curated version of their story – enlarging on how helpful Malke had been, but making no mention of the Master Bloodstone. She was good at this.

"...and once we had managed to rescue Jacob from the Prophet's clutches and slay the Prophet himself, we escaped from the City and made our way back here."

Ednor watched Trévon taking in every word. It was hard to tell what the man was thinking, but he seemed impressed. As he should be.

"You seem to have had an action-packed couple of seisdags," Trévon said. "All of Veylindré will be in your debt for ending the Prophet's reign. Who rules at Talamunem City now?"

"Jacob told us it will be Lord Domlok," Ylonya said.

"Yes, Jacob," Trévon said. "Who is this young man and where is he now?"

"He was my dearest love," Abigail said, "and the main reason for our journey to Talamunem City. So that we could rescue him."

"But he is not here now," Trévon said.

"No," Abigail said. "He is with the Waymages. The Prophet damaged his mind, erasing all his memories of his time in Veylindré."

"I see," Trévon said. "He was close to the Prophet?"

"Yes," Ylonya replied.

"Then I must speak with him and find out what he knows of Talamdor, how they are likely to react, now that the Prophet is gone."

Abigail looked aghast. "But he's not ready for any such conversation," she said. "He mistrusts us all."

"I am prepared to wait awhile," Trévon said, "until the Waymages have healed him. But speak with him I must. An insider perspective on Talamdorian affairs could be invaluable."

Ednor could not wait any longer. "How is the war going?"

Trévon turned to him, a smile on his face. "It is over," he said. "Or at least, mostly over. A seisdag ago, the two Talamdorian armies disengaged from their sieges of Mistbourne Keep and Cristail Keep and began the long march back to Talamdor."

"They've given up?" Ednor could not believe his ears. The first war in decades and he had missed it all.

"From what you have told me," Trévon said, "their withdrawal seems to have coincided with the fall of the Prophet."

Ylonya nodded. "That makes sense," she said. "Jacob told us Lord Domlok sees the Havimi as Talamdor's true enemies. No doubt he has called the armies back to Talamdor for that purpose."

"Please sit down, my friend," Shaunan told Jacob.

The young man slumped down in his chair, seeming uninterested in his surroundings. Yet she could sense an undercurrent of fear in his mind. What had the Prophet done to him?

"What do you want from me?" Jacob asked.

Shaunan smiled at him. "I do not want anything from you, Jacob. I want to help you to regain your memories of the time you spent in Veylindré before you were abducted and taken to Talamdor."

Jacob sat up straight, scowling. "What is it with you people? All of you – Aidren, Ylonya, Abigail. I don't remember. Portak rescued me when I was wandering, lost and alone, after the shipwreck. I woke up on a boat on the way up the River Clearhaven. And… that's all."

Shaunan touched his arm, soothed him. And felt him shrink away from her touch. "Peace, my friend. I am not trying to hurt you, nor to put a spell on you. Abigail has told me you believe all Veylindréans are witches, that the Way is evil."

"Well," he said belligerently, "isn't it? The first I knew of you all was when Abigail and the others were in my master's apartment. She defied him and she and the others killed him. And now I've been taken away from everyone I knew and brought here. How in God's name am I supposed to trust you?"

Shaunan had not quite realised the extent of Jacob's distrust. Nor his closeness to the Prophet. This would need careful handling. She tried again.

"But you recognised Aidren as a friend, did you not?"

"Yes, I suppose so. But I have no idea where I know him from."

"I understand that this is difficult for you, Jacob. Let us leave it there for now. Have you been assigned a room here?"

"I'm sharing with Aidren."

"Then I suggest you return there and get some rest. We can talk again tomorrow."

The young man shrugged, stood up and left without another word.

Rusilon came into the room. “It’s a problem, isn’t it?”

“I do not know how to get through to him,” Shaunan said. “This is beyond my healing skills, Rusilon. Can you think of any way we could restore his memories? Because if we cannot, it will be difficult to persuade him to come with us. And I do not want to keep him doped with poppy juice for the whole journey.”

Rusilon thought for a moment, then said, “I think we need to contact the High Waymages at Ranusheim. They might know how to remove the block from his mind.”

“You think that is what has been done to him?” Shaunan shuddered. “How horrible.”

“I fear so,” Rusilon said. “In his place, wouldn’t you distrust us?”

“I suppose so. But it is breaking Abigail’s heart, that he does not want to know her.”

“I wonder whether stripping the dye from her hair would help. Perhaps if he could see her blonde, as he remembers her, that might help.”

“Yes, I had thought of that. I will do it tomorrow. There must be some way of getting through to him.”

“I hope so,” Rusilon said, shuddering. “I had no idea the Master Bloodstone had such power.”

Δ Chapter 15 Δ

Portak was summoned to General Kreldik's tent, once the man had finished addressing the troops.

"After conferring with my staff," Kreldik said, "I have decided to leave early tomorrow morning, to give the healers time to make arrangements for the conveyance of the wounded. Contact the Council and give them that message."

"Is that needful?" Portak asked. "Surely they know that we will be back as soon as possible."

Kreldik scowled. "It is. I would not be asking you otherwise. It is vital that the Council knows we are returning in good order."

Portak bowed his head and left. Returning in good order – that was a joke. When the army started the long trek back to Talamunem City, they would be leaving behind hundreds if not thousands of dead, and would be delayed along the way by having to care for the many injured. How many more would die on the journey?

Had it only been four seisdags since they had set out from Talamunem City with such high hopes? How had it all gone so wrong? If only he had been at the Prophet's side. He would have defended his master with his life. Where had Jacob been? If Jacob had been involved in the death of the Prophet, he, Portak, would not rest until he had hunted him down and killed him, as slowly and painfully as possible.

He hunkered down in a quiet spot some distance away from the base camp and cradled his maimed Bloodstone in his right hand. Then closed his eyes and concentrated on reaching out to the mind of the Chief Messenger. *Tamin. Tamin.*

Before they began the long journey back, Portak joined Kreldik and his staff to hear the report from the healers. The numbers of dead and dying were rising and morale among the healers was at rock bottom.

"General Kreldik, sir," a healer said, visibly trembling at his own temerity, "we must allow the wounded to rest. Otherwise more and more are going to die."

"That may be so," Kreldik said, "but we are under orders from the Council to return to Talamunem City as swiftly as we can."

"Then may we at least leave the most badly injured at Caethniss Castle?"

Kreldik stroked his chin. "Hmm." He turned to Captain Normek. "What do you think, Normek? How many wounded do you think Caethniss Castle could accommodate?"

"Up to three score, I would say," Normek replied, "five score if they use every space available."

"What do you say?" Kreldik asked the healer.

"Up to five score? That would help a good deal. But some of us will have to stay with them, to treat their wounds. They do not have many experienced healers at the Castle."

Kreldik nodded, and Portak knew he had come to a decision. "Very well. The five score most sorely wounded may remain at Caethniss Castle. How many healers will have to stay with them?"

"Nine, maybe ten," the healer said, "if we are to have any chance of saving them."

"Which will leave how many of you to carry on with the journey?"

"About the same, General, sir."

"Very well, do that." Kreldik said, rising from his seat. "This Council is concluded."

It had taken the Talamdorian army just over two seisdags to reach Veylindré. The journey back to Talamunem City would take them nearly four. The only spot of light relief during that grim period had been the look of almost comic dismay on the face of the portly Major Turnik, when he had been told he must find space and provisions for five-score wounded and their healers. But even when they had left the worst of the wounded at Caethniss Castle, the remainder of the army would still have to travel more slowly. Portak was desperate to return to Talamunem City, even without the Prophet. He was aching to see Balmak.

The evening before they were due to leave Caethniss Castle, he was summoned by Kreldik. What did the man want now? The General was sitting alone in the quarters Turnik had hastily vacated, brooding.

"Portak," he said, "I want you to find a way to raise the morale of the troops. I hear they are in low spirits."

Portak raised his eyes to meet Kreldik's. The man looked as weary and defeated as his army. "How?" he said, too bitter to feign feeling otherwise. "What is there for them to be cheerful about? We've abandoned the invasion, lost hundreds of men for nothing, and now have the ordeal of the long march back home, a defeated army. And my master is dead."

"That is enough!" Kreldik surged to his feet, his face scarlet. "I will not have you making matters worse with such defeatist talk."

Portak shrugged. "I speak as I find."

"Then you have some work to do."

The words seared into Portak's consciousness. The man was right. He could not lose himself in his grief, not while Talamdor needed him.

Kreldik brushed his hand across his eyes and his anger subsided. He leaned forward, holding Portak's gaze. "Don't you understand?" he asked, his voice quiet but intense. "They have lost so much. We need to give them some hope – something to hold onto. Because once we get back to Talamunem City, more will be required of them."

Portak bowed his head. "I know. I'm sorry. Life goes on and so must Talamdor. I will do what I can. But in return…"

Did he dare ask? Why not?

"In return, what?"

"Sir, once I have spoken with the troops, I would like to go on ahead to the City. I need to know what's happening there. Whether there is anything I can do to help."

Kreldik eyes bored into his own – Portak found himself struggling to maintain eye contact. But what he saw there seemed to satisfy him.

"Very well. You may leave on the morrow, once you have addressed the army."

Portak stood up and, for the first time, saluted the general with respect in his heart. "Thank you, sir."

At last, after four days and more than a hundred and thirty miles of hard riding, switching horses at staging posts, the black basalt walls of Talamunem City came into view. Portak could not wait to get back to civilian life, to leave the army behind. It had been an interesting experience, but by no means a good one.

When he rode in through the East Gate, the streets of the city were comparatively empty. Such a contrast to when the army had marched out, when there had been cheering crowds and his master high up on the battlements. Don't think about that. That part of his life was over. He needed to see Balmak. If he could just rest for a while in his dear friend's love, perhaps he would be able to regain some kind of balance.

Portak threaded his way through the well-known streets and knocked on the door. Balmak opened it. He looked pale and sad, new lines of grief had etched themselves into his cheeks. But when he saw Portak, a broad beam transformed his face.

"You're back! I wasn't expecting you for at least another seisdag. Come in." He took Portak's hand, drew him inside.

Portak barely had enough self-control to wait until the door to the outside world was shut. As soon as it was, he took Balmak in his arms, buried his face in his shoulder. "I've missed you so much."

"And I you, my dear. Come and sit down."

Balmak gently disengaged himself from Portak's embrace and led him into the living room. "Do you want something to drink? To eat?"

"A glass of wine would be nice." He was so tired.

Balmak fetched a flask of wine and two glasses. "Now, he said, "Tell me all about it."

Where to begin? At least with Balmak, there would be no need to edit, no need to censor his words. "It all started so well," he began.

Balmak listened in silence, his hand in Portak's. The touch of his hand was calming – it gave Portak the strength to tell his story. When he was done, he leaned back in his chair, drained but strangely peaceful.

"I needed you so much," he said, "when I heard the news of the Prophet's death."

"I'm sorry I wasn't there for you," Balmak said. "But now you need to hear what has been going on in the City, since the Prophet's passing."

Portak sat up again. "Yes," he said, "I do. For a start, was Jacob involved? Because if he was, I will not rest until I've hunted him down and killed him."

"I am unsure," Balmak said. "He certainly left with the Veylindréan terrorists – or so the rumour has it – but whether that was willingly, or under duress, I do not know."

"Someone must know. And I will find out."

"What difference will it make? It will not bring the Prophet back."

Portak's shoulders slumped as he took in the truth of that. "I know," he said, "but someone has to pay."

"I wish you could let it go," Balmak said. "You've been gone for so long and so often lately. I don't want to lose you again."

Portak sighed. "And I've missed you so much too. I have no idea what the new Council will want of me... If they want me at all. I have served the Prophet for more than thirty years. I don't know who I am now."

"Don't worry about it now," Balmak said. "You are home. That's what matters."

The next morning, Portak returned to his own apartment early. The city felt different – there were few people on the streets and those who were kept their heads down, making no eye contact. He could sense the uncertainty and fear everywhere. It felt almost as though the city itself was under siege.

He knew that news of his return would have reached Domlok and wanted to be where any message from the Council would reach him. He and Balmak had kept their relationship secret for so long, he didn't want to risk it being exposed. At half-past second hour, there was a knock on the door. He strode down the hall and opened it.

"Yes?"

A guard in City livery saluted, handed him a scroll. "You are to report to the Council at fourth hour."

"I will be there."

The guard clicked his heels and left. Portak walked into his living room, sat down and unrolled the scroll. Who wanted him? The note was terse: 'Portak. Report to the Chamber of Law at fourth hour. By order of Lord Domlok, Head of the Council.'

Portak scrubbed his face with his hands. He'd better have a wash and get changed. He had certain standards, even if the Prophet was no longer there to keep him to them.

He knocked on the door of the Chamber of Law at five minutes before fourth hour.

"Come."

He walked in, looked around. Fifteen men, dressed in fine red and black robes, serious expressions on their faces. He recognised most of them as members of the first families, seated around the familiar triangular table, with Domlok in the seat of power. It hadn't taken him long, then. It felt all wrong to see Domlok sitting there, in the Prophet's place. Portak had to bite back an instinctive protest.

"Portak," Domlok said, "sit down. We are anxious to hear your report."

"When the army left," he began, "its morale was high and its objectives clear..."

The grilling lasted for over an hour – the Council wanted his opinion about every stage of the campaign. He watched for their reactions, but had never seen such a collection of closed faces – he couldn't tell whether he was saying what they wanted to hear, or far otherwise.

"... and then the order came for our return. The journey back was long and arduous – we had many wounded. Even though we left five score of the worst at Caethniss Castle, many more will have died along the way. And morale was low – there was a sense that all the loss of life had been a waste, since we had not succeeded in taking Mistbourne Keep. And all were devastated by the news from here."

Domlok nodded. "Thank you, Portak. Now, I want to speak to you about another matter – the young man, Jacob. Tell us what you know of him."

Portak's head came up. "What about him? Was he involved in the death of my master?"

"I am asking the questions. It was you who brought him here, you who have known him longest."

Portak gaped at him. Surely he was not being blamed for the Prophet's death. "I brought him here at the behest of the Prophet. I was told to find any survivors from a Havimi raid on the east coast of Dagâran, and to bring them back here. Which I did."

"We are aware of that, Portak. What we want to know is, was he the kind of man who would conspire with the enemy to kill the Prophet?"

Portak shook his head. "It goes counter to all I know of him. He hated and feared the Veylindréans, seeing them as evil witches."

Domlok pursed his lips. "Hmm," he said. "And do you know why the Prophet wanted to keep him close?"

"My master did not confide that to me."

Domlok fixed him with a freezing stare. "I am your master now. The Prophet (Talamu rest him) is no more and policies have changed."

"In what way?" Portak asked, careful to keep his voice neutral. His master was barely four seisdags dead and already his achievements were being undermined.

"We need to recover the Master Bloodstone – that is our top priority. You will hunt down Jacob and his companions. With your distinctive colouring…" Portak could hear the disdain in the man's voice and hated him for it. It took him back to the time when they had all been boys together and Domlok and his cronies had ganged up on himself and Balmak, mocking them for their differences. "…you will be ideally placed to track them into Veylindré. You must retrieve the Master Bloodstone and bring Jacob back to us for judgement and retribution."

"Do we know in which direction they have gone?" Portak asked.

"If we knew the direction, do you think we would be having this conversation?" Domlok snapped. "In the confusion that followed the Prophet's demise, they managed to escape from the city unseen. We sent out patrols in all directions, but to no avail."

Portak stared at him in disbelief, too taken aback to be circumspect. "Then how am I to begin to search for them, if their destination is unknown?"

"That is your problem," Domlok said dismissively. "We expect you to use the wits Talamu gave you, plus your knowledge of the young man."

"But –"

"This is not a discussion, Portak. This is an order. Do not return without both stone and boy."

Portak pulled himself together, bowed to the assembled nobles. "Yes, my Lord. When should I leave?"

"The sooner the better. You may take a horse and whatever provisions you need. I expect you will be gone for some time."

When Portak left the Chamber of Law, he headed straight to Balmak's apartment, to share the latest news.

"When do you have to leave?"

Portak hated the stricken expression on Balmak's face. He took him in his arms. "Tomorrow. I'm so sorry, my dear. I like this no more than you do. It seems that all Domlok cares about is power. He needs the Master

Bloodstone so that he can control others, but I believe he only wants Jacob back so that he can be seen to be doing something about the Prophet's death."

"You may well be right," Balmak replied. "Not all in the city are loyal to him. There are some who believe he should not have recalled the armies from Veylindré, that they are the true enemy, not the Havimi. But Domlok will not hear any views that go counter to his."

"And he has given me no idea of what direction to search," Portak said. "They could be anywhere. You should have heard him, Balmak." And here Portak's light voice took on the deeper, more aggressive tones of Domlok's, "'We expect you to use the wits Talamu gave you, plus your knowledge of the young man. Do not return without both stone and boy.'"

"Then where will you go?"

"To the scout barracks. I know Domlok sent scouts out when he learned that the Master Bloodstone had been stolen. So I'm going to ask around, see if someone found any trace of them."

"Good idea," Balmak said. "But, oh! How I hate you going away again so soon."

"I know. I hate it too. So the sooner I manage to find them, and bring them back, the better."

"But what if you don't? What if they have got away entirely?"

"I'll cross that bridge when I come to it," Portak said. "It may be that we will have to leave the city, start a new life somewhere else."

Balmak gave him a wistful smile. "That would be so good," he said. "Go well, my dear friend. Come back to me soon."

It took Portak the rest of the day to find, and then question, all the scouts who had been sent after the Veylindréans. He had almost given up hope when he encountered Grenlik.

"We found some clear tracks heading north out of the City, my Lord," he said.

"Heading in what direction?" Portak asked, trying to keep his voice casual.

"Towards Silvin. But when we got there, we saw no sign of them and the headwoman swore they had not come that way."

"My thanks, Grenlik. I will start there."

By the following morning, Portak was ready to leave. He had a horse, adequate provisions and a fire in his belly. If Jacob had been involved in the death of the Prophet, he, Portak, would see that he paid. He rode out of the North Gate towards Silvin.

Chapter 16

Shaunan spent the evening sitting around the fire with Ylonya and Abigail, in the comfortable room that Castellan Trévon had assigned her once Elyssa had judged her well enough to be alone. It had come to feel like home to her in the last couple of seisdags. The two of them brought her up to date with all that had happened since they had left Chorich Castle. Shaunan marvelled at what they had managed to achieve.

The next morning, Waymage Rusilon swung into her quarters, with news in her face.

"What did the High Waymages say?" Shaunan asked.

"They were shocked by the extent of his memory loss, and horrified that the talamunium bangles enforce such control. There are some herbs, such as sage, turmeric, and lemon balm, which may help, if he can be persuaded to drink a tisane containing them regularly. But there would only be a slow improvement. They said that our best chance of restoring his mind would be to dose him with Lènia's Bruagan, then use our Goldstones to invade his mind, find the block and break it down."

A shiver went down Shaunan's spine. "Is that not dangerous?"

"Yes, very," Rusilon replied, with a wry smile. "And not only to the young man. High Waymage Shonala warned me that the memory loss might transfer to one of us, if we do not carefully shield our minds while we work with him."

Shaunan sank back in her chair, trying to absorb this news. "Lènia's Bruagan," she said. "I have heard of it, but have never used it, nor seen it used. What properties does it have?"

"I have used it, with care, to treat anxiety and low moods," Rusilon answered. "But according to Shonala, it can also open the outer shields of his mind, so that we can do what we have to. But if we get it wrong, we could damage his mind permanently."

Shaunan's intake of breath was loud even in her own ears. She could feel the blood pounding in her veins, and fought to breathe slowly and deeply, to calm herself.

"Are you all right?" Rusilon asked, striding over to where she was sitting.

Shaunan waved her away. "Yes. It was just the shock of realising we could damage him beyond hope of repair. It is such a risk, Rusilon. Do you think we have the right to take it?"

"I think it is the only way to restore his memories."

"Then we must at least attempt it. I had better warn Abigail."

"Do you think that is wise?"

Shaunan sat up straight. "Yes. She must be told. She would never forgive me for keeping this from her."

"Very well. I will prepare the Lènia's Bruagan later today, and we will make the attempt tomorrow."

Shaunan caught Rusilon's hand as the younger woman prepared to leave. "Are you willing to do this, despite the risk?"

Rusilon smiled down at her. "I am," she said. "It is a Waymage's duty to heal the sick. You should rest, now, so that you are fresh on the morrow."

"When I have spoken with Abigail."

Abigail brought Jacob to Waymage Rusilon's quarters the next morning, her heart in her boots. She had reluctantly accepted that this Lènia's Bruagan was the only hope of bringing back her own Jacob, but was horrified by the level of risk, not only to Jacob himself, but also to Shaunan and the Yrusian Waymage.

Rusilon drew her to one side and said quietly, "You may stay and watch, Abigail, but do not attempt to interfere. Shaunan and I have talked this through and know what we have to do. But it will be a fine balance between protecting ourselves and healing the young man. It is essential that you watch only."

Abigail bowed her head. "I promise."

"Drink this," Shaunan told Jacob. "It will help you to get your memories back."

Jacob backed away. Fear and mistrust were emanating from him.

"How do I know that?" he asked, his voice belligerent. "What are you going to do to me?"

Abigail knew she had to persuade him somehow. She took his hand, met his angry gaze. "We wouldn't harm you. Please, Jacob, do it for me."

His brown eyes searched her face, then he nodded. "All right."

"Sit here," Shaunan said, soothing him, "so that you are comfortable."

Jacob sat in the armchair, then took the glass of potion from Shaunan and drank it off. His eyes closed.

At once, Rusilon and Shaunan chanted together, *"Belannath Ranu, gal lo bynn wellwich, gal em bynn wellent."* Both closed their eyes, grasping their Goldstones in their right hands, an expression of intense concentration on their faces, repeating the words over and over.

Abigail held her breath. Was this going to work? What would she do if anything happened to Shaunan? She murmured a prayer of her own, but managed to resist the temptation to help. Not that she knew how to.

Then, to her horror, Jacob sprang out of the chair and fell to his knees, screaming and clutching his head, before collapsing in a heap on the floor.

Promise forgotten, Abigail jumped to her feet, rushed over and took her beloved in her arms. “Stop it, stop it! Can’t you see you’re hurting him?”

“Get away from him, Abigail,” Rusilon said, real anger in her voice. “Stay away completely. We’re nearly there.”

What had she done? Shocked, she put Jacob gently down, retreated to the door. She looked at Shaunan, who was slumped in her own chair. But keeping the chant going, rippling from her lips.

Please, God, please, Ranu, help this to work. Help this to work. Keep them all safe. Please, God, please, Ranu.

When Jacob came round, he was lying on the floor of a strange room. What had happened to him?

He heard a vaguely familiar voice. “Go, Abigail. You may touch him now.”

A rush of footsteps, then he felt arms around him. “Jacob, Jacob! Wake up, my love.”

This couldn’t be real. She was dead. Where was he?

“Jacob!” It *was* Abigail. Her voice was full of joy as she bent over him. Why was he lying down? What was going on?

He gently loosened her hold on him and sat up. "Abigail? Is that you? And Shaunan? Where are we? What is going on?"

"You know us! Oh, thank God! Thank Ranu." Abigail's voice was thick with tears.

"Don't cry, my little love," he said, then asked again, "Where are we?"

"In Chorich Castle, in Yrusian," an unfamiliar voice said. "I am Waymage Rusilon, and we have restored your memory."

Jacob shook his head trying to clear his mind. He had been in Talamdor, he was sure of it. With his master.

"I don't understand," he said. "How have I got here? I was in Talamunem City, with the Prophet…"

Then his more recent memories came flooding back and he pushed Abigail away. "You killed him," he said. "Between you all, you killed him."

He saw Abigail's face crumple, tears pour down her face.

A calm voice from behind them said, "No, Jacob. Losing the Master Bloodstone was what killed him. His power was linked to it, and when it was taken from around his neck, all the years he had cheated came to him at once."

It was too much to take in. There was a roaring in his ears and everything went dark.

"It hasn't worked," Abigail sobbed. "I'll never get him back. Oh, Shaunan, what am I going to do?"

Shaunan took her in her arms. "It has worked, but it will take time and patience to reconcile his memories from Talamdor with all that has happened to us since he left us in Talmis. He was happy in Talamdor, I could sense that clearly. Do not expect him to be the Jacob you remember. That is not going to happen. But you will be able to build new memories with him."

"How long will it take?"

"As long as it needs to."

Not a comforting answer. "But how will we be able to do it?"

"It will be a matter of telling him our story, slowly, over days, even seisdags, so that he has time to absorb it. Do not expect too much of him yet. We have managed to remove the block from his mind, so he will be willing to accept us as friends, willing to listen, but his memories of his time in Talamdor are as true and real as any others. And he is grieving for the Prophet. I could tell that they were close, perhaps even as close as father and son."

Abigail could sense how weary Shaunan was feeling. Gently, she disengaged herself from her mentor's arms. "I'm sorry," she said, "I'm being selfish. I haven't even thanked you for what you've done. And you too, Waymage Rusilon."

"He will sleep for some time," Rusilon said. "Leave him with us." Then to Shaunan, "And you, my friend, also need to rest. Otherwise you will undo much of the healing I have been able to achieve."

What had she done? "Shaunan! Are you all right? Oh, I'm so sorry."

Shaunan smiled at her, a tired smile, but a smile, nonetheless. "I am fine, Abigail. I will sleep now, and awaken refreshed."

Abigail could hear no lie in her voice. She planted a kiss on Shaunan's brow. "Rest for as long as you need to."

Then she exchanged a glance with Waymage Rusilon, silently demanding that she look after Shaunan. The woman nodded, a crooked smile on her face. *Don't worry, Abigail. I will care for them both.*

I know you will. Thank you, Waymage.

"How is he?" Ylonya asked Abigail later that day. She had looked for the girl everywhere, and finally run her to ground in the room they were sharing. She was staring out of the window, one elbow leaning on the stone window ledge.

"I'm not sure," Abigail said, turning to face her. "Shaunan and Rusilon managed to remove the block on his memory, so he knows me again. But his memories of his time in Talamdor are still there too, and he was happy there."

Ylonya winced at the desolation in her friend's voice. "Give him time," she said gently. "He must be feeling very disorientated at present. You will need to be patient with him."

"That's what Shaunan said. But it's so hard. I thought that once we had rescued him, everything would go back to how it was."

"That was never going to happen. Surely you realised that? Both of you have spent long seisdags apart, and have had very different experiences in that time. It is a long way from Talmis."

Abigail smiled ruefully. "I know. And yes, I will be patient. I know it's my only hope of building a new relationship with him."

Time to change the subject. "When do you think he will be ready to speak with Trévon?"

"Why does the Castellan want to speak to him?"

"For an insider perspective on the situation in Talamunem City, of course. It's the chance of a lifetime to get information from someone who was close to the centre of power in Talamdor."

"I suppose so. I'll have to ask Shaunan and Rusilon. We don't want to put too much stress on Jacob, not now."

Ylonya grimaced. "I suppose not. But I know that Trévon will not let us leave here before he has questioned Jacob. And we still have to get the Master Bloodstone back to Ranusheim. The quest is not over yet."

"I'll go and ask Shaunan."

Jacob was gradually beginning to get his bearings. Talking with and listening to Abigail and Shaunan, Aidren and Ylonya had helped to bring back his memories of their time in Dagâran. He was beginning to comprehend what Portak had done to him, even to understand that his silver bangle had been a means of controlling him.

Yet he still grieved for the Prophet. Whatever else was true – and he was still struggling to come to terms with all the contradictions – the Prophet had, in some sense, treated him like a son. He had been a strict father figure, even a frightening one, sometimes, but a father figure, nonetheless.

He was sharing a room with Aidren and was starting to unconsciously fall back into the patterns of their old friendship. Yet Aidren had also changed, matured. His grief for Ellyn was ever present. Jacob too had been saddened by the news of her death – she had been such a bright, lively girl. He knew that if it had been Abigail, he would have been devastated.

He and Aidren were sitting in the great hall eating breakfast, when Waymage Rusilon came up to them. He was wary of her – she was a Waymage after all, and he still distrusted their power.

"Castellan Trévon would like to speak with you," she said.

"With me? What about?"

"About your time in Talamdor. Any knowledge you can share will help us to defend Yrusian, defend Veylindré, against the Talamdorians."

Jacob frowned. He retained some lingering loyalty to Talamdor and did not like the sound of this. Then he remembered – again – all that he had been told in the past three days. That the people of Talamdor, not Veylindré, were the enemy. About the Talamdorian agent, Gilmak, who had killed Ellyn. That he belonged here, not in Talamunem City.

He stood up. "Very well. I will come."

"Thank you."

Rusilon led him out of the great hall, across the courtyard and into one of the two towers which flanked the entrance. Then up several flights of stairs. She knocked at the door.

"Come."

The two of them walked in, and Rusilon said, “Here is Jacob.” Then she bowed and left him standing there.

“Come in, Jacob,” the Castellan said, his voice deep yet warm, “and sit down.”

Jacob looked up and saw a tall, well-built man with dark hair, eyes as brown as his own, and tanned skin. He was wearing chainmail with a dark blue surcote over it. The symbol on it was the same as Ylonya’s Waymark – a pointy P with a diagonal slash through it. But the symbol on his forehead was the same as Aidren’s – so this man was a warrior, first and foremost.

Then he noticed, standing in the shadows of the wood-panelled room, someone he had learned to distrust. Tremond. The one who had threatened to kill him unless he did what he was told.

“Why is he here?” Jacob said, nodding towards Tremond.

“Tremond is an officer of the Watch and also a member of your company. I have asked him to be present in both capacities.”

Jacob tensed up, on the defensive at once. What did that mean? Would he be hauled off to a dungeon if he didn’t give the right answers? He leaned back in his chair, his armed folded across his chest.

“I understand from Waymage Rusilon that you have spent some seisdags in Talamdor,” the Castellan began. “And although the invasion is over and the armies have returned to Talamdor, it would be invaluable to learn more about them from someone who has lived with them. “

“Why do you want to know?”

“So that we may be ready to defend ourselves if something similar ever happened again.”

“But I hardly know anything about Talamdor,” Jacob objected. “I spent most of my time with the Prophet.”

“Waymage Rusilon tells me you sat in on the meetings of his Council,” Trévon said. “Anything you can tell me about what their policies might be, now that the Prophet is gone, would be most helpful.”

Jacob shrugged. That seemed harmless enough. And he certainly didn’t owe Domlok any loyalty.

“Domlok will be the leader of the Council now,” he began. “He didn’t like me.”

“Why was that, Jacob?” Tremond asked.

Jacob glared at him before answering. “Because he was jealous of my closeness to the Prophet. He wanted me to use my influence with the Prophet to persuade him to fight against the Havimi instead.”

“Can you remember exactly what he said?” Trévon asked.

Jacob closed his eyes, trying to remember that angry conversation in the Hall of Visitors. “He said something about the enemy of Talamdor being Havim, not Veylindré.”

“Did he say why?” Trévon asked.

Something in his voice made Jacob open his eyes, look carefully at the Castellan’s face. It gave little away, but he could sense that the answer he gave would be important.

“Let me think.” He closed his eyes again, and the words came floating into his mind. He was surprised they had made that much impression on him, but he could clearly remember the fear he had felt, the anger in the

Talamdorian lord's face, the wildness in his eyes. "He said, 'They are the ones who took over our land. They are the ones who forced true blooded Talamdorians into slavery. They are the ones who should be put down.'"

"You are certain of this?" Tremond asked. "He has no interest in Veylindré?"

Jacob scowled at him. "I've told you the truth. Why do you doubt me?"

"Softly, Jacob," Trévon said. "We believe you. Did Domlok say anything else?"

Jacob turned to face Trévon, ignoring Tremond. "He asked me to persuade the Prophet to abandon the campaign and recall the armies."

"What did you say to that?" Trévon asked.

"I reminded him that the invasion of Veylindré was at the command of Holy Talamu. He didn't like that. I knew I had made an enemy. But it didn't matter, so long as the Prophet was alive. He protected me."

He saw the two men exchange a glance at this, but didn't know what it meant. When would this be over?

The Castellan sat back in his chair. "That is very helpful – thank you. Now, could you tell us about the feelings of ordinary Talamdorians?"

Again, Jacob shrugged. "I didn't have much to do with them," he said. "I spent most of my time with either Portak or the Prophet. And in any case, it didn't matter what they thought. All those with the silver bangle did what they were told by the trueblood nobles. I didn't understand what my bangle meant until I met Melnok."

"Melnok?" Tremond echoed. "Who was he?"

"He was a smith, who I worked with for a while until the armies left the City." He paused, then said, "All I wanted to do was to apprentice myself to a smith and do some honest work. But the Prophet wanted me to learn all kinds of things about Talamdor, and I didn't understand why. Not at first, anyway."

"So why did he want that?" Trévon asked.

Jacob bit his lip. Should he tell them? But the Prophet was dead, so what did it matter? "He wanted me to be his heir," he said, "because I came from England like he did, and feared and hated witches, like he did."

The look of astonishment on both men's faces was almost comical. Trévon recovered himself first. "The Prophet came from your world?"

"Yes. Didn't you know?"

"No, we did not. We knew there was something… odd about him, because he didn't seem to age like normal men. But we put that down to the intervention of Talamu."

"It was the Master Bloodstone that gave him the gift of not ageing," Jacob said, shuddering at the memory of his master's death. "When Abigail wrenched it from his neck, all the extra years he had been given crashed down on him. It was a terrible way to die."

Despite all he had learned since that day, Jacob could not keep the accusation out of his voice. Desolation at the loss of the Prophet and anger at his own inability to do anything to protect him filled his mind.

"He," and he nodded towards Tremond, "stopped me from saving him. I will never forgive him."

Tremond frowned. "I am sorry," he said stiffly. "It was necessary."

There was a pause, before the Castellan continued, "Can you tell us more about Melnok?"

"What about him?"

"What was his view about the war against Veylindré?"

"He thought," Jacob said, trying to remember, "that the job of ordinary folk like him was to do as they were told."

"Ordinary folk like him?" There was a question in Trévon's voice.

"He said, 'Those of us who wear the silver bangle. Those of us Holy Talamu found wanting.' Everyone in Talamdor has to do a Test of Faith at the age of twelve, and if they fail it, they have to wear the silver bangle and do what any trueblooded Talamdorian tells them to. I don't think they would ever question something a trueblood told them. It's not in their nature."

"I see," Trévon said. "Thank you, Jacob. That is most helpful. So you think that with Domlok in control, the prospect of another invasion of Veylindré is unlikely?"

"I suppose so," Jacob said. "But don't take my word for it. I've told you all I know."

"And we appreciate that."

"Can I go now?"

Trévon stood up, then, to Jacob's surprise, bowed to him. "We are in your debt. Our thanks."

Jacob stood in his turn and bowed back. Then turned and left the room, trying hard not to run. His legs were full of lead and his head was pounding. He never wanted to go through that again.

Tremond left the Castellan's quarters and began to walk back to the room he was sharing with Ednor. The young man had given him a lot to think about. If it was true that the new Talamdorian council saw the Havimi the enemy, not the Veylindréans, there might be an opportunity to establish some common ground between them, later on.

Of course they'd have to get the Master Bloodstone back to Ranusheim first. But after that... Tremond hated the Havimi as much as any Talamdorian – it had been they who had introduced the plague that had taken his wife and daughter from him. If he, Tremond, could help them to defeat the Havimi, he'd do it with a heart and a half.

But it would take some careful negotiation. He would have to convince the Lords and Ladies of Justice.

Yes, that had been a most fruitful interview.

Ylonya knew herself well enough to recognise the signs. They had been in Chorich Castle for two seisdags and she was beginning to feel the familiar itch – the need to keep moving. It had been worse in Ranusheim – by the time they had left the Isle she had been ready to bolt.

But this time she had valid reasons for her impatience. They were still long miles and seisdags away from fulfilling the quest and the presence of the Master Bloodstone in her pack was a constant source of unease. It felt as though it might burn through the Ranuswood box and betray its presence somehow.

Go and see Shaunan. She found the Waymage in her quarters, with Abigail and Rusilon, the Castle's Waymage. Shaunan gave her a welcoming smile, but she was too distracted to return it.

"We need to leave," she said, "soon."

Shaunan met her gaze, one eyebrow raised. "I suppose you are right," she said. "Garûnastide is over and now would be a good time for travelling. But I am still working with Rusilon on Jacob's recovery. Is there that much need to hurry?"

"Yes!" Ylonya heard herself almost shouting. "Yes," she repeated more quietly. Somehow she must make Shaunan understand. "We cannot stay here any longer. We are still far too close to Talamunem City for my liking, and there are many long miles between here and Ranusheim."

Abigail, whose expression had lightened when Shaunan had questioned Ylonya's urgency, sank back in her chair, visibly disappointed.

"Shaunan," Ylonya continued, "are you well enough to travel? Because if you are, the sooner we are on the move again, the harder we will be to find."

To her relief, the Waymage nodded. "You are right," she said, standing up. "Let us go and find the others."

They found Aidren sparring with Jacob in the courtyard, with Ednor looking on, offering both of them advice. Tremond was nowhere to be seen.

"Do you know where Tremond is?" Ylonya asked them.

"No. Why?" Ednor said.

"We need to have a meeting of the whole company, to decide our onward route."

"I'll go and find him," Aidren said, sheathing his practice sword. "I think he may be with the Castellan."

"Thank you. Bring him to Shaunan's quarters as soon as you can."

Aidren hurried off. In a matter of a few minutes, all seven of them were squashed into Shaunan's room – Shaunan in her chair, Abigail, Jacob and Aidren on the Waymage's bed, and the rest of them perched on any available flat surface. Ylonya stood, backing up to the door so she could see them all.

"I think," she began, "and Shaunan agrees, that we need to leave here as soon as possible. So we need to decide what route we're going to take to Ranusheim."

"I agree," Tremond said. "Now that Garûnastide is over, and my Goldstone is recharged, there is no reason to wait."

"Good," Ylonya said, "because I sense that the longer we are in one place, the greater the danger of us being followed and found."

Tremond nodded in agreement. "What do you advise?"

"Shaunan," Ylonya said, "do you still have the map Jacob was looking at in the inn at Smithsport?"

"Yes. It is in my pack. Half a moment." Shaunan brought out the map and unfolded it.

"We cannot go back through the Fenland," Ylonya said, "so I recommend travelling north to Iascan, then taking a ship from there."

"What's wrong with going back the way we came?" Abigail asked. "We could skirt around the north of the Fenland, pick up our horses from Hamnis, then carry on to Néartanis."

"Good idea," Ednor said.

"That is the way the Talamdorians will expect us to take," Ylonya said. "And whatever happens, we need to keep the Master Bloodstone safe and untaken. I think it would be safer to travel by sea from Iascan to Garûnashavn, then either continue through the Sea of Lènia to Lèniashaven, or take the overland route through

Garûnalond to Mirunan, then down through Lènium to the Land Bridge."

"Surely that will take much longer," Ednor objected.

"Actually," Ylonya said, "the distance is about the same. But travelling by sea will make us harder to get at and will also be easier for Shaunan. Whichever way we choose, we must leave on the morrow."

After much poring over of the map, the majority of the company agreed with her, as she had hoped. Abigail had been convinced as soon as she had mentioned that the sea voyage would be easier for Shaunan, and both Aidren and Jacob had followed her lead. Once Ednor had realised the rest of the company were set on the sea route, he had fallen in with the majority. They would leave the next day, at first light.

Chapter 17

The company left Chorich Castle early the next day, loaded down with provisions for the journey, thanks to the Castellan. This part of western Yrusian was lush and green, with crops as well as woodlands, as the Season of Awakening made way for the Season of Growth. It had always been Shaunan's favourite time of year, when the trees – oak, ash, beech, birch and, of course, the Ranus tree, put out their leaves – so many shades of new green lining the tracks on which they rode. The cherry trees in the orchards they passed were heavy with blossom. In the verges, the early daffodils were dying back, being replaced by pale yellow primroses, fragrant cowslips, purple and yellow crocuses, and sweet violets. She felt new hope in her heart.

She was glad they had waited to leave until after Garûnastide – it would have seemed so odd to have missed the festival. She was going to miss Rusilon very much. They had grown close over the past few seisdags.

She understood Ylonya's sense of urgency – indeed, she shared it. Yet she was not looking forward to the long journey to Ranusheim. Although she felt much better for the seisdags of enforced rest, some of her old resilience had gone for good and she tired easily. Her grief about Ellyn seemed to have sapped her energy beyond what she had expected from her illness.

"How long will it take us to reach Iascan?"

Abigail's voice roused Shaunan from her thoughts. "About a seisdag, I think. Ylonya would know better than I."

"How are you?" Abigail asked. Shaunan could hear the concern in her voice. "Are you strong enough for all this travelling?"

"Do not worry about me." Shaunan forced a smile, hoping her initiate would not probe. "My time at Chorich Castle has made a new woman of me and I have a plentiful supply of the potions I need to strengthen my heart. Rusilon saw to that."

Remembering the insistence of the younger Waymage turned the fake smile into a real one. "And we will be travelling by sea from Iascan to Garûnashavn and maybe beyond. Which will be more restful."

"What about the Havimi?" Abigail asked. "What if they are still lurking? They might attack us."

"I have never heard of Havimi ships in the Sea of Lènia," Shaunan said. "Let us hope they have not grown bolder during the seisdags we've been away."

"Well, I for one will be glad to be out at sea," Abigail said, accepting her reassurance. "Even though Ylonya thinks the Talamdorians will be looking for us in Néartania, I cannot shake the fear of being followed, now that we have left the safety of the castle."

"Have you sensed something?"

"No. It is just a feeling. But maybe we'd better take it in turns to sweep the road behind us with our minds."

And all around us, Shaunan thought, but did not say. She too believed the Talamdorians would not have given up the chase that easily.

It was as well they had decided to take this precaution. On the third day out from Chorich Castle, an early Season of Growth rain was soaking them all, and the wind was rising. Abigail suddenly stiffened in her saddle. She closed her eyes, the better to ignore the impending storm, and sent her senses out into the surrounding landscape.

They were being followed. Abigail concentrated, seeking to sense how many of the enemy there were. It had taken practice to hone her skill, to be able to differentiate a human mind from those of innocent animals. But she had it now. The feel of a human mind was denser somehow, more complex, and she was beginning to be able to sense emotions too. Whoever this was, was angry, so angry that she winced away from the contact, feeling his anger in her own gut. His? Yes, it was a man.

Only one? That seemed unlikely. She concentrated again, but try as she might, she could not discern anyone else. Better let the others know.

She urged her horse into a trot and came up alongside Ylonya. "Someone is following us." She had to shout over the noise of the beating rain and strong wind.

"How many can you sense?" Ylonya asked, on the alert immediately.

"Only one man."

"But why in Ranu's name would they send a lone man out after us?" Ednor asked. "They must know that there are at least six of us."

"I don't know," Abigail said, "but I can only sense one."

"Could you sense anything about him?" Ylonya asked.

"I felt a mixture of anger, determination and betrayal." Abigail paused, confused by what she had sensed. "Why betrayal?"

"I've no idea," Ylonya said. "But we need to find somewhere to hide."

"And of course, you know of somewhere," Ednor said, his tone light and teasing.

Abigail had noticed a big change in the Néartanian's relationship with Ylonya, since they had left the City. The old antagonism between them had vanished, to be replaced by what she could only describe as a friendly fondness. Interesting.

Ylonya gave Ednor a quirky smile. "Of course," she said. "This way." And she led them away from the track and around the base of a nearby hillock. She dismounted, giving her reins to Abigail and walked confidently towards what looked like an impenetrable thicket of bushes.

But too late. A voice behind them, "Stop, in the name of Talamu."

It had taken Portak days to pick up their trail. When he had reached the village of Silvin, the headwoman, Malke, had almost convinced him that no Veylindréans had been seen in the vicinity. His first instinct was to interrogate her more fiercely, force her to reveal what she knew, but time was against him. He had a mission to fulfil – somehow he must catch them up. Undeterred, he had continued north, sparing neither himself nor his horse. They already had several days' lead on him, but he must catch them somehow. He slept only a few hours each night, and that only to give his horse time to recover from the punishing pace he was setting. He knew there was a pass through the mountains which led to Yrusian. He hadn't used it himself, but knew others who had.

What was driving him? He had no loyalty towards Domlok and didn't care about retrieving Jacob. Unless Jacob had killed his master, which would be another matter entirely. If he had, death would be too good for him, and he, Portak, intended to be the chosen instrument.

Yet he couldn't see it somehow. He had travelled far with the boy and had also spent considerable time with him in the city, teaching him about Talamdor. How far off those days seemed now. He remembered how the boy had shuddered at the thought of the Veylindréans. Surely he would not have gone with them willingly.

Maybe that was it. Maybe they had forced him to go along with them, and he, Portak, would be rescuing him. The irony of that almost made him laugh out loud, considering he had kidnapped him in the first place. A grim smile curved his lips.

But the Master Bloodstone was a different matter. Without it, the power of Talamdor was crippled. And, whatever else he felt, Portak loved his country. He might detest Domlok, but his loyalty to Talamdor was never in question. The Master Bloodstone had enabled them to throw off the yoke of the Havimi, to grow back into power, to take their rightful place once more as an independent, proud country. Somehow, he must get it back. Because if he didn't, the individual Bloodstones were of little use and without them, he did not see how they could defeat the Havimi.

At a village some miles beyond the foot of the pass, he heard that a party of strangers had been seen. He was on the right track.

Jacob knew that sibilant voice. Portak. What on earth was he doing here? He started to ride back towards him, but was prevented by Tremond's hand on his reins.

"Where do you think you're going?"

"It's only Portak. He won't harm me."

But the Garûnalonden did not release him. Instead, he raised his voice, "What do you want?"

Portak brought his horse to a halt several paces away. "You have stolen two things from Talamdor. I have come to take them back."

Jacob's heart sank. He guessed that one of the 'things' was himself. Did he want to go back? He felt confused. He had believed that Portak was his only friend for many seisdags. Yet if Abigail and Aidren were to be trusted, he had not been a true friend, but had controlled him with the silver bangle. And it had been a Talamdorian agent who had killed Ellyn. He sensed the other members of the company closing up around him.

"Jacob," Abigail said, "this man is not your friend. He is your enemy."

Jacob stiffened. Had she been reading his mind? Unacceptable. "Stay out of my mind," he snarled.

Then watched as Abigail rode forward a couple of paces to confront Portak. "He is not coming with you," she said. "You abducted him in Talmis and you're not going to do the same thing again."

Portak sneered at her. “So you say. Why should he want to be with you, when he had a better life in Talamdor?”

Abigail lifted her chin – a distinctive gesture Jacob remembered from when time was. “His life in Talamdor was a lie,” she said. “He belongs with me.”

“Lost your tongue, Jacob?” Portak asked. “Have you forgotten so quickly that I saved you from the shipwreck? Brought you to Talamdor, where you were fed, clothed and educated? You owe Talamdor, owe me, a debt of gratitude.”

Yes. He remembered all that. But he also remembered what Shaunan and the others had told him. Yet they had killed his master, the Prophet. What should he do?

“Don’t do this, Jacob,” Aidren said. “It was a Talamdorian who killed Ellyn.”

A picture of Ellyn came into Jacob’s mind. A beautiful laughing girl with dancing eyes. And now she was dead, because of him. Because of Talamdor.

“No,” he said. “I owe you nothing. You took me against my will. You took *away* my will. And one of your people killed Ellyn.”

“You stupid boy.” Portak’s face was contorted with rage. Then, with a huge effort, it seemed, he brought himself back under control. “Very well. You will not come with me. You have chosen to spend your life with the witches of Veylindré. You disappoint me, Jacob.”

Jacob shrugged. “Go back to Talamunem City, Portak,” he said. “I belong here.” At last, his heart was made up.

"I do not take or eschew action at your command," Portak spat. "And there is the little matter of the Master Bloodstone. I will not leave here without it."

"Not a chance," Ednor said. "Give it up and go home. If you do not, we will kill you, like we killed your precious master."

Jacob watched Portak's face blanch to a pure white, and knew it was rage, not fear. He was about to caution Ednor not to anger him, when Tremond spoke.

"Let him alone," he said. "We are seven against one. He cannot prevail against us."

Ednor bit his lip, then shrugged. "Go, Talamdorian. But follow us no more. You will not find us so merciful if you do."

Portak glared at Jacob. "Traitor," he spat. Then he wheeled his horse round and cantered away.

Surely he would not give up so easily. Jacob opened his mouth to warn them, when he was stopped by a cry from Abigail.

"Shaunan! What is wrong?"

Abigail slid off her horse and ran towards Shaunan, who was swaying in her saddle. She caught her as she fell.

"Help me," she said, and Ylonya rushed to her side and helped her to lay Shaunan gently on the ground, a hastily snatched blanket beneath her.

The Waymage's face was a muddy grey, her lips blue.

"She needs to be more upright," Abigail said. "Go and fetch a couple of packs for her to lean against."

That done, Abigail rummaged through her healer's bag, found the foxglove potion and measured out a dose. Holding it to Shaunan's lips, she said, "Drink this."

Shaunan obediently swallowed her medicine. Abigail took her Goldstone in her right hand, laid her left hand on Shaunan's chest and began to examine her. Why hadn't she realised that her mentor was still so weak? Shaunan must have kept her out on purpose. Why didn't she trust her?

Shaunan opened her eyes, met Abigail's gaze. "It is not a matter of trust, but of expediency," she said. "We must get the Master Bloodstone back to Ranusheim. I thought that I was over the worst. And I did not want to be left behind."

"Your health and wellbeing matter far more to me than the Master Bloodstone," Abigail said.

"No, Abigail," Shaunan whispered. "Destroying the Master Bloodstone is more important than anything. Do not worry about me. I will be fine once I have rested."

Abigail swung around to face Ylonya, who was watching them anxiously. "We'll need to spend the night here," she said. "Shaunan should not be moved."

"I had hoped to reach the next village," Ylonya said. "We would be safer there than camping in the open."

"I know," Abigail sighed. "But I don't think it would be wise to move her until she has recovered from this latest attack."

"Very well. I will tell the others."

As she watched Shaunan drift into a peaceful sleep, her face returning to its normal dark brown, her lips losing their blue tinge, Abigail became aware that an argument was going on between Tremond and Ednor.

"Why didn't you kill him when we had the chance?" Ednor demanded.

Tremond straightened up, met the Néartanian's eyes. "When I was a young Watch officer, still learning my trade, Guildmaster Géorn once told me that it was the first duty of the Watch to serve the cause of justice with absolute impartiality."

"What's that got to do with anything?" Abigail could hear the frustration in Ednor's voice.

"Serving the cause of justice," Tremond replied, "sometimes means being compassionate, merciful, even if it seems unwise. So I chose to give him the benefit of the doubt."

His expression darkened and Abigail could sense some deep regret inside him.

"We cannot afford to be that idealistic," Ednor said. "What if he goes and fetches other Talamdorians?"

Tremond nodded. "You have a point, my friend," he said. "I too once believed that the Guildmaster's advice was ridiculously high-minded, but I learned… I learned otherwise."

"How?"

Tremond bowed his head in thought and Abigail could sense he was deciding whether to share some part of his story. Then he met Ednor's eyes.

"Very well, you have earned the right. I had just completed my training, when a… situation arose, and I had to decide whether to give someone who had betrayed me the benefit of the doubt. At that time, I chose justice over mercy and turned him in to the Watch. He was severely punished, having his rank stripped from him and being set to do menial work. I have always regretted it."

Ednor snorted. "Well, I hope you don't regret this."

Once he was out of sight of the company, Portak turned around and began to track them once more. If they thought he would give up that easily, they were greater fools than he had believed them to be. And there had been something in Jacob's eyes. Portak was now sure he had been involved in the Prophet's death. Which had to be avenged.

He left his horse tethered and hobbled, and began to track the company on silent feet. They were easy enough to follow – this was not a well-used route and the hooves of six horses left plenty of evidence. When he found them, he could not believe his luck. The fools had decided to camp out in the open. Good. That would make his task easier. One way or another, he would retrieve the Master Bloodstone and get his revenge on Jacob. After all he had done for him… if Jacob thought he could get away with this betrayal, he had another think coming.

He watched and waited, keeping a tight rein on his impatience, as the company prepared for sleep, paying particular attention to where each person was sleeping. And noted that they had given the first watch to the big Garûnalonden. He should be easy enough to trick. When the man's back was turned, Portak picked up a small rock and lobbed it to the far side of the camp. It made a satisfying clatter as it landed. As he had hoped, the Garûnalonden headed off to investigate. This was his chance.

Wasting no more time, Portak tiptoed towards where he knew Jacob was lying. Drawing his needle-thin talamunium dagger, he plunged it savagely into Jacob's breast. That for the Prophet. The boy would not have the chance to betray anyone else. Now for the Master Bloodstone.

Then the breath whooshed out of his lungs as he felt a knife enter his own body from behind. How…

Abigail was awoken by a shout from Tremond. "Abigail, Shaunan, quickly!"

She untangled herself from her blankets and wriggled out of her tent. "What? What has happened?"

Then she saw the two bodies. Jacob and the Talamdorian. No, this could not be happening. Could not. She shook her head, willing her eyes to tell her a different tale. She ran over to Tremond. "What's going on?"

"Never mind that," Tremond said. "The Talamdorian has stabbed Jacob in his sleep. Only you can save him."

Abigail rushed back to her tent, picked up her healer's bag and dashed back to where her beloved was lying, the bright blood pooling beneath him from the narrow wound in his chest. Clutching her Goldstone, she plunged her healing senses into him, but could only sense a flickering life force within.

"Get Shaunan," she snapped at Tremond. "This will take more skill than I have."

Then she took hold of Jacob's hand, stroking his dearly loved face, running her fingers through his dark curls, willing him to hang on. "Don't leave me now," she whispered. "I couldn't bear it."

Fiercely, she fought to nurture that life force, but she could sense it wavering, flickering, no matter what she tried.

It seemed an age before she felt Shaunan's gentle hand on her shoulder. *What has happened?*

The Talamdorian – Portak – has stabbed Jacob. Shaunan, we have to save him.

"If Ranu permits," Shaunan said aloud.

The Waymage sank to her knees beside Jacob, and Abigail could sense her adding her strength and healing powers to her own. For a moment, the life force within Jacob seemed to rally, to strengthen a little. Please God, please Ranu, save him. I cannot lose him. I love him.

She threw her senses into him, willing him to respond. But it was as though there was some barrier, preventing the flow of healing. She fought to break through it, to heal her beloved. But it was too late. Too late. He sighed once without opening his eyes, then was still, dead beneath their hands. She felt the same horrified disbelief as she had when Ellyn had died. She could not go through this again. Could not. After all they had done to rescue him. When he had finally decided to trust her again. Her throat tore as she screamed, unable to keep the pain inside a moment longer.

Tremond. It was all his fault. Springing to her feet, she flew at him, hands extended like claws. "You were supposed to be watching," she hissed. "How could you let this happen?"

Tremond's face was a mask of pain and regret. "I'm so sorry, Abigail. He –"

"I don't care about your sorrow," she snapped. "Jacob is dead, and it's all your fault."

Jacob was dead. She could not bear it. She clamped both hands over her face, collapsed in a storm of tears, felt Shaunan's arm around her shoulders.

"Come, my dear. Come over to the fire. You're shivering."

Numbly, Abigail did as she was told. Nothing mattered any more. Jacob was dead. The tears continued to pour down her face, and she made no attempt to wipe them away. Her life was over. She became tangentially aware that Shaunan was saying something.

"What?"

"Drink this."

"Why?"

"Because it will help you to sleep."

"What's the point? I'll only have to wake up again later."

"Drink this, Abigail."

Dimly, Abigail sensed Shaunan's nudge for her to comply. She shrugged. It would make no difference whether she was asleep or awake. She drank the potion, gagging a little at the bitterness. As she lost consciousness, she heard Shaunan say, "It is the best thing for her now."

Nothing was the 'best thing' now.

Chapter 18

Ylonya leaned against Ednor, aghast at this turn of events. Her brain scrambled to make some kind of sense of it, to work out what to do next. It was still the middle of the night and the darkness around them seemed vast and full of unknown dangers.

"We need to leave, now," she said.

"We cannot leave until morning," Ednor said. "Shaunan has just managed to get Abigail to sleep."

"I have failed. I should have insisted that we carried on to Tarrin. We would have been safe there."

"It is not your fault," Ednor said gently, reaching out to touch her shoulder. "It was Abigail who insisted that we camp here, because of Shaunan's illness."

Ylonya scrubbed her face with both hands. "Nonetheless," she said, "we have now lost Jacob. I do not think Abigail will ever forgive us."

"Surely she won't be so irrational."

"You don't know Abigail. When we lost Jacob the first time, when Portak abducted him in Talmis, her grief was deep and prolonged. And you must remember her attitude in Ranusheim, when she prioritised rescuing Jacob over stealing the Master Bloodstone."

"True. I'd forgotten that. But she has shown herself to be a person of integrity since then. When you reminded her that she would have to choose between rescuing Jacob, she promised not to let you down. And she didn't."

"That is true," Ylonya said, a little hope returning to her heart. "When we reached the Prophet's throne room, she was shocked by the change in Jacob. I think it may even have given her the courage to defy the Prophet."

"There you are then," Ednor said.

"Yet now she has lost not only her best friend – and I know how much she has grieved – is still grieving – for Ellyn, but also the man she was in love with, the only other person from her world, who alone knew her before she came here. I believe his loss will hit her even harder than Ellyn's did."

"Perhaps Aidren will be able to help her," Ednor said. "After all, he is near to her in age and has also lost the person he loved."

Ednor's words sank like a balm into Ylonya's mind. "Thank you. That's a brilliant idea. I'll talk to Aidren later."

"Come and rest now, for what remains of the night. You don't need to carry the whole burden of the company alone."

Ylonya reached up to kiss him lightly on the lips. "Thank you."

Abigail awoke the next morning with sore eyes and a blinding headache. For a moment, she couldn't think why, then her heart contracted as the events of the previous night flooding back into her memory.

Jacob. She had lost Jacob. They had travelled all that way to rescue him, and now he was gone, snuffed out in an instant of malice. Once more her eyes filled with tears and she clamped her hands over her mouth to stop herself screaming her loss to the skies. Losing him in Talmis had been bad enough – now she had no hope left.

She felt a gentle hand on her shoulder. Shaunan. With a despairing wail, she gave up any attempt of self-control, sat up and leaned into her mentor's waiting arms, keening her grief for all to hear.

Eventually, the storm subsided, although her body still shook with the violence of it.

"How do you feel?" Shaunan asked.

Abigail had no words for it. No words of hers could describe the depths of her misery. Unbidden, verses from the twenty-second psalm came into her mind. It had been one of her father's favourites. In a wobbly monotone, she quoted them, "My God, my God, why hast thou forsaken me? Why art thou so far from helping me, and from the words of my roaring? O my God, I cry in the day time, but thou hearest not; and in the night season, and am not silent… I am poured out like water, and all my bones are out of joint: my heart is like wax; it is melted in the midst of my bowels…. Thou hast brought me into the dust of death."

"Those are powerful words," Shaunan said, "but I think they are not your own."

Abigail met her gaze, saw the sympathy there, and fresh tears scalded her eyes, hot and insistent. She bit her lip, forced them back down and answered, "No, they are from our Bible, our holy text. But they describe how I feel perfectly."

"I am so very sorry, my dear."

"Why didn't Tremond stop him?" Abigail burst out. "He was supposed to be on watch."

"The Talamdorian was cunning," Shaunan said. "He threw a rock across the camp, so that Tremond would go and investigate the noise. Then he slipped in and… did what he did."

But Abigail was scarcely listening. "First my family," she whispered, "then Ellyn, now Jacob. I'm not sure how much more I can bear."

Shaunan hugged her close. There was nothing she could say to that.

The remaining six members of the company reached Tarrin at sixth hour that day. Jacob's body was carried there in a sling fashioned of two tents tied together, between the horses of Tremond and Ednor. As they entered the village, a young boy spotted them and rushed off, presumably to announce their arrival.

"Let us wait here," Shaunan said, nodding at Ylonya. "It appears that news of our coming is already being told."

Sure enough, the boy came back into view a few minutes later, followed by a young Waymage who looked vaguely familiar. Where had she seen him before?

"Welcome to Tarrin," the young man said. "I am Waymage Ferdin. Be welcome in Tarrin. How can I help you?"

Ferdin. Of course. He was one of the latest class of Waymages to complete their studies at the Colaste a'r Teisen. They had seen him during the Ceremony of Assignment at Ranusheim, during Lèniastide.

"Waymage Ferdin," she said. "It is good to see you again."

The young man nodded his acknowledgement of her courtesy. "I am sorry, Waymage. I do not remember meeting you before."

Shaunan smiled at him. "I am Waymage Shaunan, of Nordvein in Dagâran. We were at Ranusheim last Lèniastide, when you were assigned to the post of Waymage here."

Ferdin's eyes widened. "Then you must be the company who set off on a quest to Talamdor."

"That is correct," Shaunan said, and decided to come straight to the point. "And now one of us has perished. We come to you to ask for your hospitality and for permission to bury him here."

The young Waymage bowed his head. "I am sorry to hear that," he said. "It will be an honour for the village to have you staying here among us." He turned to the young boy. "Run and fetch Grimon."

"Grimon is the headman here," he said. "He will want to welcome you all to Tarrin."

Shaunan hid a smile. She found Ferdin's thinly disguised awe at finding himself in their company amusing. He had a lot to learn. But there were more important matters to deal with.

"I ask your permission to lay our friend to rest in the Temple," she said.

Ferdin flushed. "Of course. I should have thought of that. Please, come this way."

He turned to lead the way to Tarrin's temple, a small building about the same size of Shaunan's own temple at Nordvein. It seemed an age since she had been there.

While Ylonya held their horses, Ednor and Tremond dismounted and began to untie the ropes connecting the sling that held Jacob's body to their saddles. Then they and Shaunan followed Ferdin into the Temple, leaving Ylonya and Aidren with Abigail.

“Where should we lay him?” Ednor asked Shaunan in an undertone. “He does not have a Waymark.”

“In front of the altar of Dagâra,” Shaunan said. “His former Waymark was Dagâran.”

Ferdin overheard Ednor’s question. “He does not have a Waymark?” The young man’s eyes were wary as he stepped away from them. “I cannot in all conscience bury him without a Waymark.”

Shaunan sighed. She had hoped to avoid this conversation. “His Waymark was Dagâran,” she said. “But he was a prisoner for some seisdags in Talamdor and it was removed at that time.”

“Who has the power to remove someone’s Waymark?” Ferdin asked, his face paling, his voice high and unsteady.

“The Prophet of the One,” Shaunan replied evenly. “I assure you that his former Waymark was Dagâran. You must let us bury him here.”

“I need to consult Waymage Aedyn in Iascan,” Ferdin said.

“Come, Ferdin,” Shaunan said, losing patience with him. “You know that no Waymage can lie. And you have vowed to remember that all are children of the Six. One of our company was very close to this young man. Do not cause her more grief by making difficulties for us.”

“I’m sorry,” Ferdin said, his pale face flushing scarlet at her implied rebuke. “Of course, you are right.” He turned to Ednor and Tremond. “Please lay him in front of the altar of Dagâra.”

Shaunan nodded. “Good. Now I must return to Abigail.”

Aidren was out in the stables of Tarrin's single inn the next morning, grooming the horses, breathing in the comforting scents of horse and hay. But his mind was far way, his hands doing their work automatically.

Of all the twists and turns of their quest, this one had taken him completely by surprise. He should have known that the Talamdorian would not give up that easily, should have been on his guard. And now they had lost Jacob. He should have taken better care of him. He ground his teeth.

The horse's tail swished and it raised one hind foot in protest. "Sorry, my friend," Aidren said, realising his thoughts had made him use the brush rather harder than he had meant to. He stroked the animal's silky smooth neck, and it calmed down.

"Here you are," Ylonya said. "I was wondering where you had got to."

Aidren focused his attention on the horse, not wanting to face her. "The horses still need caring for, no matter what."

"You're right. But Aidren, would you stop for a moment? I need to talk to you."

What was this about? He turned to face her.

"It's Abigail," Ylonya said.

Aidren snorted. No surprise there. "What about her?"

Ylonya looked down for a moment, as though considering what she was going to say. Then she met his gaze. "Jacob's death has devastated her," she said, "and I don't know how to reach her."

"What do you mean?"

"We have to persuade her to continue the journey, to take the Master Bloodstone to the Wayzenmoot."

"She wants to stay here?" Aidren knew that feeling, knew it well. When Ellyn had died, he had not wanted to leave her either. But they had made him.

"Why are you telling me?" he asked. He was not going to make it easy for her.

"Because you, of all of us, know what it means to lose the person you love. I think you could reach Abigail, if you tried."

Aidren hated the gentleness in her voice. He stalled for time. "What does the Waymage say?"

"She agrees with me. We cannot stay here. It is too close to Talamdor. If it is known that we escaped in this direction – which it must be, as the Talamdorian followed us here – then it is even more urgent that we leave Yrusian as soon as possible."

He knew she was right. But the enormity of the task she was laying on him was daunting. His heart had still not healed from the loss of Ellyn – it had only been a few short seisdags after all – and he knew Abigail had been grieving for her too. How could one broken person help another?

Perhaps it was the last thing he could do for his friend. When he thought of it like that, he knew he at least had to try. "All right. I'll speak to her."

"Thank you, my friend," Ylonya said. "She has known you longer than any of us and knows that you were Jacob's friend. I believe you could bring her comfort."

Inside the inn, in a dark corner where he hoped to remain unnoticed, Tremond was drinking steadily. He had started with pints of ale, but that was too slow to take effect. So he had switched to a strong spirit. All he wanted was to be drunk enough to pass out, to escape his guilt and regret, at least for a little while.

"Don't you think you've had enough?" a light voice said behind him. Ednor.

"Not nearly enough. Need to be drunk enough not to remember."

"Why would you want to do that?"

Tremond couldn't believe his ears. "Are you stupid?" he said, trying to meet Ednor's gaze. But his eyes kept blurring. "This is all my fault. All my fault. If I hadn't failed in my duty, Jacob would still – would still be alive."

Ednor sat down opposite him. "It is not your fault," he said. "You mustn't think that."

"'Course it is. I've let you all down. 'Specially Abigail. What must she think of me? I should've listened to you. You didn't want to let him go. You wanted to kill him. An' you were right. I told you to let him go. An' he came back, murdered Jacob. 'Course it's my fault."

How could he have been so stupid, so naïve? Talking so fine and large about compassion and mercy. Look where that had got them.

He realised he was trying to drink from an empty glass and attempted to stand up, order another drink, only to be pushed back down again by Ednor.

"Lemme go. I want another drink."

"Oh no, my friend. I think you've had quite enough." Ednor's voice was firm. Then his tone changed, became gentler. "Don't you understand? Getting drunk won't help. It will only add a blinding headache to all the rest. And we must leave as soon as the Waymage here has buried Jacob."

"They're burying him here?"

“Yes. What else did you expect?”

Tremond shrugged. “I dunno. And Abigail has accepted that?”

It was Ednor’s turn to look away. “I don’t know,” he said. “But it is the only way. We must return to Ranusheim.”

“’M not going to Ranusheim. I’m going to leave you all at Garûnashavn, make my way to Mirunan to report to the Lords an’ Ladies of Justice.”

“Just as you like. But you need to sleep now. I expect the funeral will be tomorrow.”

Tremond didn’t want to sleep. He wanted to drink. But he’d been travelling with Ednor for long enough to recognise the younger man’s mind was made up, that he wouldn’t be allowed to stay here. Blearily, he wondered why he couldn’t resist, but it was too hard to think about.

“Come, my friend,” Ednor said. “It’s time to lie down, have a little sleep.”

Tremond heaved himself to his feet and stood there, swaying. “A little sleep. Yeah, alright.”

“I’ve just poured Tremond into bed,” Ednor told Ylonya and Shaunan as they ate a lonely lunch in the inn’s common room. Neither seemed to have much appetite, and he didn’t blame them. He felt the same. “He blames himself for Jacob’s death.”

“How did he get that drunk, this early?” Ylonya asked.

“I don’t know. But there was a row of pint glasses on the table in front of him, and by the time I found him, over there,” and Ednor nodded towards the dark corner of the common room, “he was drinking a strong spirit. His breath was rank enough to fell an ox.”

"I will try to reason with him later," Shaunan said. "Jacob's death was no-one's fault except Portak's. He might as well blame me, for falling ill on the road."

"No," Ylonya said. "How could we blame you?"

Shaunan smiled at her – a sad smile. "I did not say I blamed myself. But if we had reached here by the day's end, we would not have been camping out and would have been safe."

"I'm not sure that's true," Ylonya said. "I believe that Portak's mind was set on vengeance, and he would have followed us until he got it."

That was what he liked about Ylonya – her shrewd intelligence always saw to the heart of the matter. That among other things.

"Where are Abigail and Aidren?" he asked.

"Abigail is asleep in her room," Shaunan said. "I gave her a strong sleeping draught this morning, after she confessed she had not slept all night."

Ednor nodded. That was about what he had expected. "And Aidren?"

"I saw him earlier, in the stables," Ylonya said. "and suggested he might be able to help Abigail to come to terms with her grief."

"Why Aidren?" Ednor asked.

"Because he has known her and Jacob longer than the rest of us, longer even than Shaunan. And he was Jacob's friend. But also because he lost Ellyn, so he knows how she is feeling."

"Where is he now?" Ednor asked.

"If he has finished in the stables, I imagine he has gone for a walk," Ylonya said, "to think through what he will say to her."

"I have noticed that too," Shaunan said. "Aidren thinks best when he is outside."

"When will the funeral be?" Ylonya asked.

Shaunan sighed. "That will depend, at least to some extent, on Abigail. She would never forgive me if we did not allow her to be present, and I am unsure how long it will take her to be ready to let him go."

"And *I'm* not sure we can wait that long," Ylonya said in a low voice. "We need to leave here as soon as we can. The object I'm carrying will not improve with keeping. And we are still too close to Talamdor for my comfort."

Shaunan nodded. "You are right," she said, standing up. "I will go and sit with her, and speak to her when she wakes up."

Once the Waymage had left, Ylonya said, "She must persuade her. I have a bad feeling about staying too long in any one place."

"What do you mean?" Was she speaking from knowledge, or just intuition?

"It's like I felt on the journey to Talamdor," she said. "That we have to keep moving, that we need to be hard to find. I will be happier once we are at sea."

Ednor put his arm around her. "I'm sure Shaunan will be able to persuade Abigail. She is her mentor, after all."

Ylonya relaxed in his embrace. "I hope you're right. She doesn't seem amenable to persuasion at present."

"We cannot leave him here." Abigail was adamant about this. She sat up in bed, crossing her arms firmly to emphasise her resolve. If they buried him in this little out-of-the-way village, she would be leaving him behind forever. Which didn't bear thinking about.

"We must," Shaunan said, "just as Aidren had to leave Ellyn in Virunon."

"And look how he has grieved for that," Abigail countered.

Shaunan nodded. "That is true," she said. "Nevertheless, he was able to see that we needed him in order to fulfil the quest."

"Well, it's done now, isn't it? We've got the Master Bloodstone. How much more do you expect of me? I want to stay here with him."

Shaunan met her eyes. "Much more, Abigail. You forget, the quest will not be ended until we have taken it to Ranusheim and it has been destroyed."

"I don't care about that. It's all too much. I've lost nearly everyone I love. I – I can't bear it anymore."

"You must find a way. We need to leave here tomorrow, and you must be with us."

Abigail could not believe her ears. "How can you be so cruel? Why don't you understand?"

"I do understand," Shaunan said in a gentler tone. "But life must go on. You are stronger than you think you are. But if you would prefer it, I will ask Ferdin if he minds my conducting the funeral instead of him."

Abigail felt numb. The decision had been taken out of her hands. "Yes, please. At least you knew him. And – could you include a psalm from the Christian Bible? I think Jacob would like that."

"Of course I will, if you will write down the words for me." Shaunan paused, then said, "Would you like me to send Aidren to you?"

"Not now. I need to be alone."

"Very well. I will go and make the arrangements."

Jacob's funeral reminded Aidren almost unbearably of Ellyn's. A similar green and silent graveyard, in another small Yrusian village, quiet and nowhere special. Except that this time, Shaunan was presiding, rather than the local Waymage. He guessed that she had offered, to make it a little more acceptable to Abigail.

He looked over to where the girl was standing. Her face was marble pale, her eyes vacant, and each hand was clutching the opposite elbow, as though she was trying to hold herself together.

He knew how she felt. He knew it only too well. It was less than seven seisdags since he had been in her position. And of course, she too had grieved for Ellyn, as he did for Jacob.

As the service continued, Aidren watched her. To his surprise, there were no tears. Had she cried herself out?

"Jacob was a fine young man," Shaunan was saying. "By the time we got to know him and Abigail in Nordvein, he had already proved himself to be an unselfish lover, one who cared more about Abigail than about anything else." She paused. "This made his life difficult on occasion, as it was hard for him to understand why she was so strongly attracted to our Way. But he overcame his mistrust when he was apprenticed to Mastersmith Kalen in Luvodican, who believed he had much promise. Like Abigail, he was welcomed in to our society last Dagârastide, and was assigned a Dagâran Waymark.

"He was abducted by an agent of the Prophet of the One many seisdags ago, and part of our quest was to rescue him from the Prophet's clutches. Which we did. Only to find that the long days he had spent in Talamunem City had changed him, had made him distrust all Veylindréans. He was in the process of regaining that trust, when he was foully slain by the Talamdorian. All of us, particularly Abigail, will miss him greatly."

Then she began to speak the words of committal, words which Aidren recalled only too clearly from Ellyn's funeral. He remembered how unbearable he had found them, and moved closer to Abigail.

At last, tears began to track down her cheeks. Aidren put his hand on her shoulder and she glanced at him. "Help me," she whispered.

"I am here for you."

Chapter 19

The journey to Iascan took more than three days, which Ylonya had found hard. She had been on high alert the whole time, convinced that the Talamdorians would not give up that easily. But her fears had been groundless, or so it seemed.

As they drew closer to Iascan, the sparsely inhabited countryside of western Yrusian became more populous, with a village every few miles. The Season of Growth was advancing and the fields surrounding the villages were full of new crops in varying shades of green. She knew this part of the world well and had no trouble finding somewhere for the company to stay each night.

But she could not wait to be on board a ship, safely out at sea. There at least they would be reasonably safe from pursuit. Or so she hoped. The sooner they left Yrusian soil, the happier she would be. As soon as she had settled the others in a backstreet inn, owned by a Guild member, she headed for the harbour.

Her heart lifted as the noise level rose. Like most ports, the harbour of Iascan was bustling with activity, as fishing boats and trading ships arrived and left. Mixed in with the clean, salt scent of the sea were other, more strident smells – a recently unloaded catch of mackerel, a whiff of spices, and the stench of unwashed bodies as sailors poured off a trading ship, eager for shore leave.

She stood still for a moment, absorbed by all the comings and goings. Then shook herself. This would never do. She needed to find a captain willing to take them and their horses to Garûnashavn, preferably tomorrow morning. She took a long look round, then her eyes lit up. She strode purposefully towards a small trading ship. It was somewhat ostentatiously named *The Pride of Iascan,* and her captain was an old friend. She walked up the gangplank and was met by an elderly sailor, who had evidently been left on board as watchman.

"What is your business here?"

"Is Captain Jorkin on board?"

"He is, but I have orders not to disturb him."

Ylonya drew herself up. "Please tell him that Ylonya would like to speak with him. He will remember me."

The old man's eyes widened. "That same Ylonya who is daughter of Mistress Margera?"

Of course. She was in Yrusian. No wonder he had heard of her. "Yes."

"I'll fetch him at once."

He louted and left her, returning a few minutes later with Jorkin. Ylonya smiled to see his weather-beaten face in which a pair of bright blue eyes sparkled; the years had not been unkind to him. "Jorkin, it is good to see you again."

Jorkin rolled up the deck towards her in his typical seaman's gait and enveloped her in a rough hug. "Ylonya! You are a welcome sight. What brings you to Iascan?"

"Business, my friend," Ylonya said, one eye on the listening seaman.

"Come down to my cabin," Jorkin said, taking her by the elbow, "then we can talk in peace."

Once there, Jorkin settled her into a chair and said, "Can I offer you a glass of wine? It's a young red from Fionnan."

"That would be welcome, thank you." She knew Jorkin was a great stickler for courtesies, so she played along, answering his polite enquiries about her family, and learning what he had been up to in recent seisdags.

Once the necessary civilities had been exchanged, Jorkin sat up straighter, his eyes fixed on hers. "Now, what do you need from me?"

"Passage for six, and six horses, to Garûnashavn, please."

"We have only just arrived, back from a trading journey to Dagâran."

"Dagâran? That explains the wine." She grinned at him impishly.

"How well you know me." He smiled back at her, then grew serious once more. "How soon do you need to leave? Soon, if I know you…"

"Without delay. Our company needs to leave Yrusian as soon as possible."

Jorkin lifted one eyebrow, then said, "It will take me a while to round up the crew. I've just given them forty-eight hours' shore leave."

Ylonya's heart sank. Every extra hour they spent on Yrusian soil gave the Talamdorians another chance to catch up with them. All her instincts were telling her they needed to get away, and quickly. Somehow she must persuade Jorkin.

"We cannot wait that long. Our mission is urgent."

"May I ask why?"

"Guild business. Sorry, Jorkin, but you know how it is."

He accepted her words with a nod. "Fair enough. I know you well enough to understand that you would not ask unless it was important." He rubbed his chin thoughtfully, his fingers rasping against the stubble. "If I send someone to find the crew now, we could be ready to leave at first light tomorrow."

Ylonya nodded, accepting the inevitability of the delay. "Thank you, Jorkin. You have my gratitude, and that of the Guild."

He bowed to her. "One day, I'd like to hear the full story."

"When all this is over, I'll tell you."

The Pride of Iascan was not a passenger ship. Abigail was ineluctably reminded of *The Sweet Sarah,* the ship she and Jacob had set out from England on, all that time ago. There too, the passengers had been the least important part of the cargo. They were squashed in, three to a cabin – she with Ylonya and Shaunan, and the men together in another. Oh, Jacob! She missed him so much.

She had come up on deck to be alone, unable to bear even Shaunan's gentle sympathy. And she had a bad headache – perhaps the clean, fresh air would help. Try as she might, she could not think about anything except Jacob. The quest, her friends, everything, receded into the background of her mind. She remembered Jacob's deep voice, his gentle hands, his dark curls, his beautiful brown eyes, the feel of his lips on hers. How could Tremond have been so stupid as to fall for such a simple ruse? If he had had his wits about him, Jacob would still be alive.

She wasn't sure she would ever be able to forgive him. She wished she had never left England, never lost her family, never heard of the Way. She wanted to crawl down a deep hole and close it up behind her. There was no point in carrying on. Jacob was gone.

Later on, Shaunan and Abigail were sitting in the cabin they shared with Ylonya. Shaunan was getting worried about the girl – she seemed to be locked in a deep melancholy. Somehow, she would have to find a way to lift her out of it – the quest was not yet fulfilled.

A knock on the door. "Come in."

It was Tremond, looking unwontedly apprehensive, as though he was about to face judgement.

"What can we do for you, my friend?" Shaunan asked.

"What will you be doing when we reach Garûnashavn?"

Such a curious question – what will *you* be doing? As though he was planning to leave them. Shaunan opened her lips to reply, but before she could, Ylonya burst in.

"I have bad news," she began. Then she noticed Tremond. "What are you doing here?"

"Never mind," he said. "What is this news you have heard?"

"There've been rumours about sightings of Havimi ships in the Sea of Lènia. Jorkin's just told me. One of his sailors heard about it in one of the dockside taverns and was told to let Jorkin know. But," and Shaunan could sense her frustration, "the man was so well soused when they brought him back on board that it slipped his mind.

Only now, two days later, is he sober enough to remember."

The hiss of Tremond's indrawn breath was loud in the little cabin. "Havimi in the Sea of Lènia? That has never happened before. How do they dare?"

Ylonya nodded her agreement. "I know. It seems that their alliance with the Talamdorians has made them bold."

Abigail too gasped. "Havimi? The ones who slaughtered my family? We cannot risk encountering them. Not with the Master Bloodstone in our possession."

Shaunan frowned, mulling over the news in her mind. "I had hoped we would be able to sail all the way to Lèniashaven, which would have shortened the time of our journey considerably. But now… what do you advise, Ylonya?"

"I think we will have to change our plans and travel along the Great North Caravan Route, through Garûnalond to Mirunan, then south to Nellènium, and approach the Isle of Ranu from the north instead of the west. I am sorry, Shaunan," she added. "I wish I could have spared you the land journey, but I honestly do not believe it would be safe to continue by sea."

"I will see that she doesn't overtire herself," Abigail said, fixing Shaunan with a fierce glare.

Shaunan laughed, in spite of her apprehension. "You see, Ylonya? I will be well taken care of. But will it be safe to use the Caravan Route? I am sure you know some backroads we could use instead."

Ylonya nodded. "You are right. We had better not draw attention to ourselves."

"Then I will stay with you as far as Mirunan," Tremond put in.

"You were not thinking of leaving us?" Shaunan asked.

He looked down at his feet, not meeting her eyes. Then drew himself up to stand at attention. "I am no longer worthy to be a member of the company," he said in a flat monotone. "I am an officer of the Watch, who failed in his duty. Through my negligence, one of us was killed. I was going to leave you at Garûnashavn, and make my way to Mirunan to report to the Lords and Ladies of Justice. But now I will continue to serve you as far as there, if you will have me."

"Look at me, Tremond." Shaunan made her voice as persuasive as she could.

He met her gaze and Shaunan could see the dark shadow of shame in his eyes.

"You have been a worthy member of our company," she said. "Do not judge yourself so harshly. Portak would have continued to track us until he had wreaked his revenge on Jacob, regardless of how carefully we kept watch. I dipped into his mind and saw the implacable will for vengeance there."

Then Abigail took a deep breath and said, "I do not blame you either, Tremond. It is as Shaunan said."

Shaunan was so proud of her, that she had been able to overcome her grief sufficiently to let go of blame – or at least, enough to forgive Tremond.

"Truly?" Tremond asked. "You do not blame me?"

"No, I do not."

He bowed his head to hide the tears Shaunan knew were glimmering in his eyes. “Thank you,” he said. “I will try to be worthy of your trust.”

“How long will it take us to reach Mirunan?” Abigail asked Ylonya as they disembarked.

“Not so loudly,” Ylonya said in an undertone. “If we dared to use the Great North Caravan Route, it would take us less than a seisdag. It’s about a hundred and twenty miles. But as Shaunan suggested, I will take us on backroads on a winding route to avoid attention. So perhaps eight days.”

Abigail nodded. “Then I will have seen all six countries of Veylindré. I never dreamed I would travel so far in my whole life.”

Ylonya grinned at her. “It is the best life in the world,” she said. “Each day a new horizon.”

“Don’t you ever get tired of travelling?”

“Never. I remember Ellyn…” and she paused, a fleeting expression of sorrow crossing her mobile face, “…asking me a similar question, way back in Néartania. I think it was when we were in Talmis. She was so excited by the prospect of journeying outside Dagâran. It was when I promised to buy her a ring, the one that Aidren wears now.”

Abigail sighed. “I remember that day so well,” she said. “You took us to Gadaria’s shop in Céardochis and bought me this.” She touched the yellow ring of Ranu on her right hand.

She changed the subject. “What river is this?”

“It is the River Elvan, which flows from the mountains in the north of this land to the sea, here. It goes through

Ullmass, which marks the beginning of the Great North Caravan Route."

The harbour was humming with activity. As well as the tanned Yrusian sailors in their clothing of many shades of blue, there were many tall Garûnalonden, their fair hair flowing loose down their shoulders, or neatly braided. They seemed to favour blue or green clothing – Genira had told her that. Together with the various brown woods of the ships and the grey stone of thc quays, it was a colourful sight.

And loud. Not only with the calls and shouts of the people, but also with the creaking of windlasses, either loading or unloading cargo from the ships and the rumbling of barrows and carts, taking the unloaded cargo away to warehouses farther down the wharf. And above it all, the raucous calls of the sea birds.

Once the horses were unloaded and Aidren and Tremond had checked them over to see that they were sound after the voyage, the company mounted up and headed out of the town. Soon the rowdy harbour and Garûnashavn were left behind and they were travelling on a quiet, country road, flanked by fields of new grass, on which sheep cropped contentedly, with green hills fading to purple in the distance. Abigail recalled that western Garûnalond was famous for its wool. Hadn't Waymage Findoran come from here? She could see the stately, red-haired Waymage in her mind's eye, with her pale skin and natural dignity. How long ago that seemed. And Jacob had been with them, then. Jacob…

The grief rose up in her, as ferocious as a bear. No, that's enough. She knew she had to try to move on. Getting buried in her grief would not help. The spring –

no, Season of Growth – sunshine was warm on her face as they continued on their journey. She knew that Ylonya would be able to find them somewhere to stay each night, so she tried to relax into it.

Living in the present was less painful than remembering the past.

They kept to the backroads, with Ylonya ensuring that they stayed with trusted acquaintances each night. They were making progress, so far as Abigail could tell. She and Shaunan took it in turns to sweep the landscape behind them with their minds, but it seemed as though they had managed to shake off any pursuit.

Abigail was getting tired of forever being on the move. Apart from the seisdags they had spent in Luvodican, and their brief rest at Ranusheim, it seemed like they had been journeying forever.

"I will be so glad to reach Ranusheim," she said to Shaunan. "I'm sick of all this travelling."

"I too will be glad of a rest," Shaunan said.

At once, alarm bells began to ring in Abigail's mind. She sent a quick, probing thought to her mentor. *Are you feeling all right?*

Yes. Do not worry. I will let you know if I am not.

No chest pains? No shortness of breath?

"No," Shaunan said aloud. "So long as we keep to this pace, I am well able to manage."

Abigail shot her a doubtful glance, but Shaunan's face was serene.

"And in any case, we will be in Mirunan in a couple of days' time. I expect we will stay there for more than a night. So I will be able to rest then."

"What are the Lords and Ladies of Justice like?" Abigail asked.

"Why do you ask? We will not be seeing them."

"I'm just curious."

"They are the secular rulers of Veylindré, as the Wayzenmoot are the spiritual rulers. They sit in the Hall of Justice, which is where the laws for the whole Commonweal of Veylindré are debated and decided. Each land has six representatives, three men and three women, who are elected every six years."

"Like the High Waymages in Ranusheim?"

"Yes, very like them. Except that the Lords and Ladies of Justice are responsible for the secular laws of Veylindré, whereas the High Waymages oversee the lore of the Way."

"Do you know any of them?"

"No, but I expect Ylonya does, and Ednor and Tremond too." Shaunan smiled at Abigail, such a sweet, sad smile. "Before you came along and turned my life upside down, my only venture out of Dagâran was when I did my Waymage training."

Abigail's heart hurt as she thought of Ellyn. She and Aidren weren't the only ones to lose someone they loved. "It hasn't worked out very well, has it?"

"You must not blame yourself, Abigail." Shaunan's voice was gentle, but Abigail could hear the steel beneath it. "I told Tremond and now I am telling you. It was not your fault that Ellyn and Jacob died as they did. All of us have been caught up in something bigger than ourselves and we must continue to serve it until our journey is over."

Abigail bowed her head in acknowledgement. She knew in her head that Shaunan was right, but her heart wasn't working in tandem.

"Nonetheless," she said, "I will be glad when we are safely back in Nordvein."

Once they had settled in to an inn in Mirunan, Tremond left quietly. He was glad his days with the company were coming to an end. When they had set out, he had been sure he would be able to make a positive contribution. But all he had done was in vain – his foolish naïveté had resulted in the death of one of them. Abigail might be able to forgive him – and he wasn't convinced that she had – but he could not forgive himself.

He left the inn and began to walk along Mirunan's well-known streets, with their tall buildings of dark grey stone. Automatically, his pace became regular and slow, as though he was on patrol. He was heading for the Academy of the Watch to submit himself to the judgement of Guildmaster Géorn.

On the way to the Academy, he passed the Hall of Justice – an imposing building, built of blocks of the same dark grey stone, square and stern, with little in the way of decoration. The flag of Garûnalond, with the symbol of Garûna in dark green against a paler green ground, flapped in the stiff breeze. He would need to make his report there later.

But now for Géorn. Tremond swung in through the gates of the Academy, greeting the man on guard. "Ho, Armond," he said. They had joined the Watch at the same time and shared many adventures.

“Tremond, is that you?” Armond, said, clasping his arm.

He smiled with an effort. “Yes, I’m back.”

“Where have you been? The last I heard, you were heading for Ranusheim to report some information to the High Waymages. But that was seasons ago.”

“I have been travelling with a company set to accomplish a quest by the Wayzenmoot.” Better not say any more than that. “I need to report to Guildmaster Géorn.”

“Then I won’t delay you any longer,” Armond said, clapping him on the shoulder. “But I can’t wait to hear what you’ve been up to.”

“I’ll come and find you.”

Slightly cheered by the encounter, Tremond carried on, through the courtyard, into the heart of the Academy.

It did not take long for him to be admitted to the Guildmaster’s presence. Being his nephew helped. But Tremond knew that Géorn’s judgement would not be any more lenient on that account.

Chapter 20

Tremond tapped on the door of the office Géorn used to conduct his business.

"Come."

It was a large, wood-panelled room with a map chest to one side and a large desk in front of the only window, through which the afternoon sunlight was streaming. Géorn was sitting behind it, busy with some paperwork. He was a tall man in his late sixties, with a lined face that spoke of years of diligent care for others. He had been Guildmaster of the Academy for the past twenty years, and all respected him.

"So, you have returned," he said, gesturing to Tremond to sit. "Make your report."

Tremond sat to attention and began, glad that the sun in his eyes prevented him from seeing Géorn's face clearly. "When I reached Ranusheim, the Wayzenmoot were also receiving other visitors. As a result of the news they brought, a quest was laid upon them. I judged it right to offer my services and have travelled many miles with them, even so far as Talamunem City."

Géorn listened with close attention while Tremond told his story. Now for the difficult bit. Tremond took a deep breath and continued, "Eleven days ago, an agent of the Talamdorian government caught up with us and demanded the return of both Jacob and the Master Bloodstone. It need not be said that we refused. Ednor wanted to kill him, but I persuaded him to stay his hand."

"Why was that?" Géorn asked.

"Because I remembered what you once told me, when I was a young man."

"I told you many things. Clarify."

"You said – you said –" Tremond bit his lip, why was this so hard? "– it was the first duty of the Watch to serve the cause of justice with absolute impartiality, that doing so sometimes meant combining justice with compassion and mercy. So I chose to give him the benefit of the doubt, to believe that he would give up the fruitless chase."

"And then what happened?"

"I was wrong!" Try as he might, Tremond could not keep the anguish out of his voice. "He returned in the middle of the night and tricked me into investigating a noise on the far side of the camp."

"Surely it would have been safer to stay in a village. There are many in that part of Yrusian."

"The Waymage, Shaunan, has a heart condition and she became ill from the stress. Her initiate ruled that she could not be moved that night."

"I see. Continue."

"While I was searching for the source of the noise, he slipped into the camp and murdered Jacob with a knife of talamunium, which poisoned the blood in his veins. I had failed in my duty as a Watch officer. I have told them that I can no longer continue as a member of the company. I am not worthy."

Tremond sank back in his chair, feeling drained. What would his punishment be?

Géorn held his silence for so long that Tremond feared the worst. Would he be stripped of his rank? Imprisoned?

"Your duty to the company has not finished," Géorn said at last. "You must continue to guard them as best you can until they reach Ranusheim."

"But I've told them I am leaving," Tremond said.

"Then you must take that back. Come, Tremond. It is unlike you to eschew a duty."

"I am so ashamed," Tremond whispered. "Because of my negligence, Jacob is dead."

"That is as may be," Géorn said. "Nevertheless, I am ordering you to finish the job." Then his tone softened a little, as uncle replaced Guildmaster. "Don't you see? If you run away from this, you will never trust yourself again."

Tremond nodded. "Very well. I will return to them. Please say nothing to the Lords and Ladies of Justice of our journey. The Wayzenmoot will let them know in good time."

"Go well, nephew. May the Way guard and guide you."

Abigail was examining Shaunan with her health sense, to take her mind off Jacob and to check that the eight days of their journey from Garûnashavn had not exhausted her mentor, when there was a knock on the door. Who could it be?

"Come in," Shaunan said.

Tremond. What did he want?

"Waymage Shaunan," Tremond began. "I have been at the Academy of the Watch, reporting to Guildmaster Géorn. Don't worry," he continued, raising one hand as Shaunan half-rose from her seat, "I have been discreet. But I am here to tell you that the Guildmaster has ordered me to remain with the company until we reach Ranusheim. So I have come to ask whether my continued presence will be welcomed."

He was so stiff with apprehension that Abigail began to feel the first stirrings of pity for him, in spite of her pain.

"Sit down, Tremond. You are not on trial here." *Will he be welcome, Abigail?*

I suppose so. But I'm going to find it hard to trust him again.

"Of course your presence will be welcomed," Shaunan said aloud. "I told you before, you were not to blame for what happened to Jacob."

But Tremond was not looking at Shaunan, he was looking at her. What did he want from her? Some kind of absolution? She wasn't sure she could give it – if he hadn't fallen for Portak's ruse, Jacob would still be alive.

With an effort, she met his eyes and lied. "Yes. For my part, you are welcome to continue with us."

She sensed the relief filling the Garûnalonden's mind. In her head, she knew Shaunan was right, that Jacob's death had not been Tremond's fault, but part of her still wanted to lash out at him, to blame someone for the end to all her hopes of happiness. She lowered her lashes, not wanting him to read her feelings in her eyes.

Tremond stood, saluted them both, and said, "My thanks. I will not let you down again." Then he left.

"Why is it so hard to let go of blame?" Abigail asked.

"It is a natural part of the grieving process," Shaunan said, "hunting around to find someone to blame, to ease our own sorrow and feelings of guilt. But it does us no good. In order to grow into our best selves, so that we can serve the Way purely, we have to learn to let it go, to move on."

"Didn't you blame someone when Donan was killed?"

"At first, perhaps. But then I had Ellyn to look after and I knew I must not sour her young life by hanging on to my bitterness."

Abigail thought about that for a while. It seemed to make sense. "All right," she said, "I will try."

That evening, Ylonya gathered them all together in the bedroom she and Abigail were sharing. There wasn't much space, so Abigail and Aidren sat on one bed, with Shaunan – at Abigail's insistence – propped up comfortably with every pillow from both beds on the other. Ylonya sat in the room's one chair and Ednor and Tremond leaned against the walls.

"I have news," she said, her eyes on Shaunan. The Waymage seemed well enough, but Ylonya knew she was still far from robust.

"What news?" Ednor asked. "I thought you'd been gone for a long while."

Ylonya grinned at him. "It is my duty to gather information wherever I go."

"So," Ednor repeated, "what news?"

"Quite a bundle, actually." Then she stopped teasing him and began to share what she had learned from the Guild representative in Mirunan. "First, most of the people in our armies – or at least all those who are not Warriors," and she nodded at Ednor and Aidren, "have returned to their homes, because the armies' leaders have judged that the likelihood of Talamdorian invasion has waned enough to make that practical. As you all know, the Talamdorian armies have retreated back to Talamdor."

"But that doesn't mean the threat of invasion no longer holds," Ednor protested. "What about the border forts?"

"My informant reports that all the garrisons of the border forts have been strengthened and that there are new plans to patrol the whole length of the Talamdorian border with Néartania and Yrusian. And I've also heard a whisper that the Lords and Ladies of Justice are planning to revive the old town and city militias to protect the coastal areas from the depredations of the Havimi."

Ednor's eyebrows shot up. "That is going to take a lot of manpower."

"True," Ylonya said. "I expect that neither of you," and she grinned at him and Aidren, "are in immediate danger of being out of a job."

She noticed the instant sparkle in the eyes of both men at the prospect, which saddened her. She had hoped that Ednor… well, never mind.

"Is that all your news?" Shaunan asked.

"No, indeed," Ylonya said. "I also have an update about the Havimi presence in the Sea of Lènia."

"What about them?" Abigail asked, her voice thin and high.

Ylonya remembered that the girl's family and community had been slaughtered by the Havimi when they had only just arrived in Veylindré. No wonder she was worried about them. Aidren touched her shoulder, which seemed to calm her. Interesting.

She made her voice as reassuring as she could. "The Lords and Ladies of Justice have ordered that our few warships should patrol the Sea of Lènia and prevent the Havimi from landing anywhere."

"Are there enough warships for that?" Tremond asked.

"No, there are not. But they are doing the best they can. The task of building more is a not inconsiderable one, which will take much time."

"What are the implications for our onward journey?" Shaunan asked.

"I think we will be safe enough if we continue as we have begun," Ylonya said. "I will lead you on little-used backroads through south-eastern Garûnalond and down through Lènium to the Land Bridge. Once we are on there, we should be safe enough. But we should not stay long in any one place. I suggest we leave in the morning."

"I feel so torn," Ednor said to Aidren, as the two of them ambled back down the stairs to the inn's common room. "Part of me wants to take a fast horse and head for the nearest port, where my skills as a Warrior of Dagâra would be useful. Or go home to Néartania and help my brother Réothed at the border forts."

"But you're not going to, are you?" Aidren said in a shocked voice. "We will need you to help us reach Ranusheim safely."

Ednor clapped the younger man on the shoulder. "No, I will stay with the company until we reach the Isle. As you say, it is my – or I should say, our – duty to defend the company against all comers."

He noticed a fleeting expression of apprehension on Aidren's face, and continued, "Not that I think there will be any further trouble. It took us eight days to get as far as here, and there's not been a sniff of danger." He lowered his voice. "Maybe Portak was acting on his own initiative and the Talamdorians have abandoned any hope of recovering the Master Bloodstone."

Aidren did not look convinced. "I don't think so," he said. "If it's as important as the Waymage seems to think, as – as Jacob told us, it's unlikely they'd give up the chase so easily. I for one will be on high alert until we are safely at Ranusheim."

"Perhaps you're right," Ednor said. "In which case, we'd better put in some sparring practice. Are you game?"

The younger man nodded and they went back upstairs to fetch their practice swords. No need to mention the other reason he had never seriously considered deserting the company.

The onward journey from Mirunan, through the south-eastern portion of Garûnalond, to Nellènium, in the heart of Lònium, took nearly another seisdag, being something over a hundred miles. They had to travel slowly, for Shaunan's sake.

Aidren and Tremond were ranging around the company, now behind them, now out to the sides, while Ylonya and Ednor rode at the front. Although part of Aidren's mind was on possible pursuers, he could not help being bowled over by the natural beauty surrounding him.

"I'd no idea this part of Garûnalond was so stunning," he said.

"It is my favourite part of our land," Tremond said, "I grew up not far from here."

They were riding south-east, shading their eyes in the morning sunlight. Behind them, in the far distance, the colossal mountains of the Northern Range dominated the skyline, their peaks still capped with snow. They were beautiful, but looked high and cruel to Aidren. His own Dagâran Range was a lot less – grand, but also less daunting. He shivered.

"Do any people live north of those mountains?"

"Not many. We call the area that lies beyond the Northern Range, the Northern Wastes. It is bitterly cold there all the year round, so few people live there. Most Garûnalonden live in the southern third of the land."

"But some live there?"

"A few hardy souls who herd the reindeer, whose pelts are valued because they offer such good protection from cold and wind. They are a proud people – fierce in their stalwart independence. There are many rivers flowing north from the far side of the Range, and they hunt and fish for most of their needs, supplementing their diet with berries and roots. They only come down from the Wastes on rare occasions, to trade the pelts for the things they need to make their lives a little less hard."

Aidren was fascinated. "What kind of things?"

"Mainly craft items from Néartania, and root vegetables."

"It must be a fine thing to be so independent."

Tremond cocked an eyebrow at him. "Do you think so? I would rather be a part of the Commonweal, where we can move freely throughout the lands and benefit from the bounty of all of them."

Aidren shrugged. “I suppose so.”

“I know so.”

A sense of impending peril she could not shake off made Ylonya jumpy. She was having to fight against baulking at any sound. Her heartbeat was loud in her ears and her stomach felt tight. She knew that Aidren and Tremond were scouting around them, that Abigail and Shaunan were scanning the landscape with their minds, to sense any malevolent presence before it could draw near to them.

She still felt uneasy.

As before she was using side trails, rather than the Great North Caravan Route. When they crossed into Lènium on the second day out from Mirunan, she began to notice a difference in the landscape. It seemed that the Season of Growth was further advanced here than in the still chilly southern portion of Garûnalond. She threw her hood back, welcoming the sunlight on her face, the fresh breeze coming in from the Eastern Sea. Yet the sense of imminent danger would not allow her to relax.

She estimated it would take another four or five days to skirt around Nellènium to the west and reach the Land Bridge. How fast they travelled would depend on Shaunan.

“Ednor,” she said, “when we stop this evening, would you distract the Waymage while I speak to Abigail?”

“Surely,” Ednor said easily.

Once more, the day passed without incident. Was she being unduly cautious? No, she was convinced that the Talamdorians would not give up the Master Bloodstone so easily.

That evening, once they were settled in the farmhouse she had chosen for them, she managed to have a quiet word in Abigail's ear.

"Can I speak with you?

The girl looked up, a question in her eyes.

"Without other ears," Ylonya said softly.

"Of course."

Abigail rose from her seat and followed her out to the stables. As they left, Ylonya saw Ednor take the vacant chair and begin to talk to Shaunan. Good.

"What is wrong?" Abigail asked.

"I have a strong presentiment of danger," Ylonya said, "which I cannot shake off, no matter how I try."

"You don't believe the Talamdorians have given up following us."

It was a statement rather than a question.

"No, I do not. If the Master Bloodstone is even a fraction as powerful as the Golden Stone of Ranu, it will be vital for them to get it back, at whatever cost."

"I think you're right. But what do you want from me?"

Ylonya looked at her young friend. She looked pale still, with dark shadows under her eyes. She had endured so much in such a short time. But she could not afford to spare her.

"How is Shaunan?"

"All right, I think, although she still tires easily. Why do you ask?"

"Because I'm convinced we will not be able to cross the Land Bridge unassailed."

She saw the whites of the girl's eyes. "You think they are lying in wait for us?"

"I do." No point in skirting around the truth.

"And you're worried that Shaunan will have another heart attack if we are?"

"Yes."

Ylonya watched Abigail closely, saw her accept her words. "I will speak with High Waymage Valwyn," she said, "and ask her advice about increasing the dose of Shaunan's medication. And I will watch her carefully." She paused, closing her eyes. "I cannot lose her too."

"It will not come to that."

"I hope you are right. Are you going to warn the others?"

"Yes."

The attack came as they were about to turn east, to cross the Land Bridge. Half a dozen warriors, clad in the customary Talamdorian red and black, boiled up out of the undergrowth at both sides of the track and surrounded them.

Abigail was horrified – why hadn't she sensed their presence? Too late for that now.

The leader, a tall, pale-faced man with black hair which he wore tied back from his face, strode towards them, stopping just out of bowshot.

"What do you want?" Ednor asked, riding forward a couple of paces. The Talamdorian retreated, maintaining the distance between them.

"You know very well what we want," he said, his voice thin and sibilant. "Return the Master Bloodstone to us, and we will allow you to go on your way unmolested. It is sacred to Holy Talamu. You have no need of it."

Abigail was distracted from the confrontation by Ylonya, who was untying the thong that held her pack to her saddlebow, quietly dropping the pack in the grass. Of course! It contained the Master Bloodstone. Casually, Abigail made her horse sidle closer, slipped off its back when the Talamdorians' attention was on Ednor and picked the pack up before remounting and tying it to her own saddle. Whatever happened, they weren't going to get this.

"What makes you think we have what you seek?" Ylonya asked. Good, she was playing for time.

The man snorted. "Don't play games with me. Your company has been described to us in some detail – we know you are the ones who stole the Master Bloodstone from our holy Prophet, then murdered him."

Without thinking, Abigail retorted, "It was not murder. He was threatening my death. My companions had no choice but to attack him."

"You lie," the man said. Then he bowed ironically. "But thank you for the confirmation that you are the ones we seek." Oh, God. What had she done?

The man's voice changed, becoming harsher, more menacing. "Now give us back the Master Bloodstone."

"Never," Abigail said.

That had done it. Abigail sensed rather than saw Tremond, Aidren and Ylonya riding up behind her, forming a protective circle around herself and Shaunan, with Ednor at the front. Why hadn't she kept her mouth shut? Ylonya might have been able to talk their way out of it. But now the fight was inevitable. And it was six against four. But the enemy were on foot, whereas the company were mounted – surely that should make a difference.

All this went through Abigail's mind in an instant. Then the fight began and there was no time for thought, only for desperate prayer.

Shaunan touched her hand. Her face was grey, but she was still on her horse. *Are you all right? What is it?*

I'm fine. Abigail, you are able to speak at a distance. Call for help.

Of course. Abigail shut her eyes and concentrated as hard as she could. *Help us! We are being attacked by Talamdorians. Come quickly.*

Then she listened, both ears and mind straining to hear a response. Nothing. And the fight was going badly. The Talamdorians were fighting with a deep ferocity and as she watched, one of them swiped at Tremond with his sword. If the Garûnalonden's reactions hadn't been so quick, it would have been a killing blow. As it was, he received a deep slash to his shoulder, and fell back with a cry of pain.

This couldn't be happening. The quest could not fail, not this close to Ranusheim. This could not be the one fight they lost.

In desperation, she called again, *Help us! We're being attacked. Come quickly.*

Then, to her astonishment, a response. *We're coming. Where are you?*

Chapter 21

Who are you? Abigail sent the thought out to her unknown rescuer.

Rynam. Where are you?

On the approach to the Land Bridge, on the road from the north. Please, come quickly. There are six of us, but only four of us can fight and one is already badly injured. How close are you?

Not far, I hope. Wait a minute. I'm telling the others.

An abrupt absence, as the link between them closed. She had heard the strain in the young man's response. Perhaps he wasn't used to speaking over distance, mind to mind.

Heart pounding, she waited for his voice to return. And was almost dizzy with relief when it did. *I'm with a party of Yrusian traders. We're nearly at the entrance to the Land Bridge now, on the Ranusian side. We should be with you in a few minutes.*

Hurry, please! I'm not sure how much longer we can hold on.

On our way.

"Abigail, Abigail!" Shaunan's voice. She opened her eyes, looked at Shaunan, who was biting her lip, her face full of strain.

"It's all right," she said. "I've made contact with a young Waymage, who is with a party of Yrusian traders. He said they should be here soon."

"Let us hope so. We cannot fail, not now. Not so close."

"I know." Abigail reached out her hand, touched her mentor's shoulder, trying to quieten the older woman's heartbeat.

Shaunan shook her off. "Go and see to Tremond. I will follow."

"No. You stay here and watch my horse." *The Master Bloodstone is in Ylonya's pack, here on my saddlebow.*

Shaunan's eyes widened as she understood.

Slinging her healer's pack over one shoulder, Abigail ran towards where Tremond was lying, his face grey, his eyes closed. No. She could not lose him. Could not lose anyone else. Would not. She threw her healing sense into him, pressing her hands over the gaping wound in his shoulder, ignoring the bright red blood. *Belannath Ranu, gal em bynn wellent, gal em bynn wellent.*

Gradually, the flow of blood slowed, and the wound began to knit. Even after all this time, it still amazed her, this healing power. It was such a precious gift. In her world, Tremond would probably have died, or at least lost the use of his arm. She rummaged in her pack for comfrey and bandages.

As she worked on him, she heard the thunder of horses and riders galloping up behind the Talamdorians. Looking up, she saw the enemy disengaging from the company and turning to face this fresh danger. She turned her attention back to Tremond, checked him again. His pulse was steadier, but his face was so white it was almost translucent.

He groaned, opened his eyes. "It's all right," she said. "I called a party of traders. They've come to save us."

Looking up, she saw that the fight was as good as over. Five of the six Talamdorians were dead, the other was a prisoner of the Yrusians. Thank God. Thank Ranu. It was over.

"It's over," she said. "We're safe."

She sat back on her heels, exhausted by the flow of healing. Then felt a warm hand on her left shoulder, augmenting her strength. She glanced round, expecting to see Shaunan. But it was the young Waymage, Rynam.

"Thank you, my friend."

It had been a close call. Ylonya was aching all over. She had never been so relieved to see her countrymen. The leader slid off his horse and strode towards her.

"Mistress Ylonya," he said. "Is all well with you?"

"Yes, thanks to your timely assistance. We are in your debt."

He bowed with some formality. "I'm glad we happened to be in the right place at the right time."

"How did you know we were in trouble?"

He nodded over to where a young Waymage in the traditional garb of ochre tunic and trousers was talking with Abigail, who was tending Tremond. He looked Yrusian.

"That one received a message from your Waymage," he said, "calling for help. Naturally, we came as quickly as we could."

"Why are you travelling with a Waymage?" Ylonya asked.

"We had dropped some trade goods off at the Fort of Ranu, and were asked to escort Waymage Rynam to the Vale of Berlysian, where he is to complete his training." He shrugged. "The pay offered was good, so we agreed."

"Whatever the reason, I am glad you were here."

"We would be happy to accompany you back to the Fort of Ranu," he said.

"Thank you," Ylonya said. "That would be most welcome. Now, you must excuse me. I have to check on Tremond. He has a bad wound."

The Yrusian bowed once more. No doubt he would be dining out on the tale for many seisdags. She headed towards Tremond and the two young Waymages.

"How is he?"

"He will be fine," Abigail said, "but I need to ask Shaunan to check on him, then we must get to Ranusheim without delay, so that the healers there can complete the process."

Ylonya turned to the young Waymage. "Waymage Rynam," she said formally, "thank you for bringing help. The Trade Master tells me you are on your way to the Vale of Berlysian."

The young man blushed a brilliant red and bowed low. "The pleasure is mine, Mistress Ylonya. I'm happy we were nearby."

"As are we," she said. "It was fortunate that you are one of those Waymages who is able to speak mind to mind."

"I didn't know I could," he said, "at least not over that distance."

"You need to practice," Abigail said, "and test how far it works. Or at least, that is what I had to do."

Ylonya hid her smile. What would the young Waymage think if he knew Abigail was not even an adept yet. Or maybe she was – she had certainly learned much on their journey.

Tremond was conscious again and struggling to sit up. She stooped to help him. “I am glad you are all right.”

“And so I am, thanks to Abigail,” he said. He flexed his arm carefully and winced.

“Keep it still,” Abigail said. “It will be sore for a while yet.”

“I am, once more, in your debt.”

Abigail blushed. “Now that you are healing, I must go and check on Shaunan, then introduce Rynam to her.”

Once the two youngsters had left, Tremond asked, “How did it end?”

“We were in trouble,” Ylonya admitted candidly, “but fortunately Abigail sent out a mental call for help and young Rynam heard it. So the Trade Master and his party came to our rescue. Five of the Talamdorians are dead and the other is our prisoner.”

“Is everyone else uninjured?”

“The normal scratches and bruises, no more,” she said. “The Trade Master has offered to accompany us back as far as the Fort of Ranu, to guard our prisoner. I think he will gain much status from it.”

Tremond grinned, a tired grin, but a grin, nevertheless. “Your reputation precedes you.”

She smiled back at him. “It would seem so.”

Ednor watched with satisfaction as the Yrusian traders searched the five dead Talamdorians for any valuables, before hauling them off into the nearby woods. He turned to the Yrusian Trade Master.

“My thanks, Trade Master. May I know your name?”

"I am Gorvis," the man said, his right hand open in the traditional gesture of friendship. "I am glad we happened to be nearby."

"As am I," Ednor said. "I am Ednor of Néartania."

Gorvis bowed low. "Lord Ednor, I am honoured to meet you." He paused, then continued, "But I wonder at the chance that brings such a mixed company into Lènium."

"State secret," Ednor said, and watched the man's face fall. "I am sorry, friend Gorvis. But know that your timely intervention was vital for the future of Veylindré. I will make sure the Wayzenmoot hear of your aid, when we reach Ranusheim."

He watched Gorvis process that information, then nod. "Fair enough," he said. "I should have known that any company which includes Mistress Ylonya would be on secret business."

Ednor could not help chuckling. "You know Ylonya well?"

"I have not had that privilege," Gorvis said. "But she is famous throughout Yrusian."

"Not only in Yrusian, Ednor said. "I would guess she is known throughout the Commonweal."

Gorvis nodded, then changed the subject. "We will accompany you back as far as the Fort of Ranu," he said, "so that we can hand over the prisoner and report the location of the bodies to the garrison."

"Thank you," Ednor said. "We ought to leave first thing in the morning. I'd like to reach the Fort of Ranu by nightfall tomorrow."

"I will let my traders know the change of plan," Gorvis said and left.

Ednor looked around and saw Aidren off by himself, looking glum. He walked over to join him.

"What's wrong with you?" he said. "You look as though you've lost a florin and found a copper bit."

Aidren hunched one shoulder, saying nothing. Ednor followed his gaze and saw Abigail and the young Waymage talking to Shaunan, and understood.

"They will only be with us for a couple more days," he said. "Then the traders will be taking Waymage Rynam to the Vale of Berlysian."

"Who did he think he was?" Aidren burst out. "It's my job to protect Abigail. And look at them now."

"Let it go, my friend," Ednor said. "Abigail knows your value. You have proved your worth many times over."

Aidren scowled, then shrugged. "I suppose so."

"I know so." Ednor said. "Come on. We're camping here tonight, then setting off for the Land Bridge in the morning. I for one would like something hot in my belly before then."

When they reached the Fort of Ranu on the afternoon of the second day after the fight, Shaunan was surprised to find three Waymages waiting for them, including her old friend, Joslin. It could not have been more of a contrast to their last arrival. It reminded her more of the time all those years ago, when she and Findoran had arrived as part of an expected intake of adepts for the Colaste a'r Teisen.

"I wonder how they knew we were coming," she murmured to Abigail.

A small smile curved the girl's lips. "That's simple," she said, a mischievous twinkle in her eyes that Shaunan was glad to see, "I reached out to High Waymage Valwyn and let her know we were on our way."

For what felt like the first time in seisdags, Shaunan burst out laughing. Which made Abigail giggle in her turn. Such a blessed balm for the soul.

She noticed Joslin cocking a quizzical eyebrow in their direction and pulled herself together. This would never do. "Your pardon, my friends," she said, making the age old gesture of friendship. "We are honoured to meet you."

Joslin stepped forward and kissed her on both cheeks. "Welcome back to Ranusheim, Shaunan." *But where is Ellyn? And the young man you set out to rescue?*

All desire to laugh left Shaunan. *Gone. Both of them.*

I am so sorry, my friend, Joslin said, then added aloud, "You are all welcome here. These," and she indicated her companions, "are Waymages Clauden and Ralea. We have come to accompany you back to Ranusheim. We should reach the city by early evening tomorrow."

"That is good. We have much to report."

You have the Master Bloodstone?

Yes, but at a great price.

That is understood. I will send word ahead to the Wayzenmoot.

Shaunan closed her eyes, feeling a weight lifted off her shoulders. They had reached the Isle. They were safe. But there was more to do. This story was not over yet. Not by a long way.

"We were attacked by a band of Talamdorians," she said, "just before the entrance to the Land Bridge. Abigail called for help and a group of Yrusian traders came to our aid. Five of the Talamdorians were killed, but the sixth is our prisoner. Our Yrusian friends," and she nodded across to where Gorvis and the others were waiting, "have him in their custody. But they want to hand him over to the garrison here, so they may continue on their journey to accompany Waymage Rynam to the Vale of Berlysian."

The male Waymage, Clauden, stepped forward. "I will tell the captain of the garrison to hold him securely, until the Wayzenmoot decide his fate."

"My thanks, Waymage Clauden."

A few minutes later, they were through the Fort and on their way to Ranusheim. Joslin brought her horse alongside her.

"Are you well, my friend?" she said in an undertone.

Shaunan met her eyes, saw the concern in them. "Not altogether," she said. "My heart has given me some trouble and I am weary and sad. But there will be time to speak of this later."

Joslin laid her hand on Shaunan's shoulder. *Of course. You can relax now. We will take care of you, and of the others.*

When they rode into the high, white courtyard of the Wayzenmoot complex, the sun was setting, bathing the buildings in warm orange light.

With an effort, Shaunan summoned up the energy to dismount. She was nearly done. Thank Ranu they were here at last. Numbly, she followed the others through the arch to the stables.

Aidren took the reins of her horse. “I will care for her,” he said. “You rest.”

She was not going to argue. Such a dear boy. He had grown so much on this journey.

Once they had tended their mounts, the six of them returned to the courtyard. Two of the High Waymages were waiting for them. Gwynmaer and Valwyn. Shaunan pulled back her shoulders and walked towards them.

“Welcome, Waymage Shaunan,” Gwynmaer said, and smiled at her. “Welcome, all of you. We are glad to see you here once more.”

Shaunan saw Valwyn whisper something to him. The smile dropped off his face. “I understand that one of you is injured,” he said.

“Yes, Tremond,” Abigail said. “We were attacked by a band of Talamdorians by the Land Bridge. He needs to see a healer.” She glanced over at Shaunan, then continued, “As does Shaunan. She is exhausted.”

Abigail! You did not need to tell them.

Abigail turned and glared at her. *Yes, I did. I'm not going to lose you too.*

Shaunan could see incipient tears sparkling in the girl's eyes. She bowed her head. *Do not fret, my dear. We are safe now.*

And I will see that you remain so.

“Waymage Shaunan, Watchman Tremond,” Valwyn was saying, “please come with me. Waymage Joslin will show the rest of you to your rooms. Food will be brought to you. We will see you on the morrow.”

Tomorrow. Shaunan could not think beyond the next moment. She followed Valwyn slowly towards the place of the healers.

The next morning, at fourth hour, the six of them were invited to Audience Chamber of the Wayzenmoot. Aidren walked close to Abigail, ready to protect her at a moment's notice. His past experience of these High Waymages had not been good.

Nonetheless, he could not help being awed by the beauty of the Audience Chamber with its circular table of Ranuswood and gorgeously painted curved ceiling. The twelve High Waymages were seated around the table in their golden robes, waiting to hear their story.

The six of them took their seats, Aidren between Abigail and Ylonya, with Ednor next to her, and Shaunan next to Abigail. Tremond took his place beside Ednor.

High Waymage Gwynmaer stood. "Welcome back to the Audience Chamber of the Wayzenmoot," he said. "Please tell us all that has happened since you left us." He resumed his seat, his expression one of polite attention.

Ylonya stood up, and began, "We crossed from Taellingsford in southern Lènium to Néartanis, where we met an old colleague of mine, Kendris. He advised us to travel through Yrusian rather than Néartania, it being a less obvious approach to Talamdor..."

Aidren listened in fascination as she recounted their adventures. She had a skill with words that he envied. When she told of Ellyn's brave sacrifice, her eyes met his for an instant, and he knew she was seeing that dreadful moment as clearly as he did. And when she related the tale of Jacob's death at the hands of Portak, he reached out for Abigail's hand, wanting to offer some physical comfort. Her hand gripped his, but her eyes were fixed on the High Waymages.

"...Then we were assailed by a band of Talamdorians near the Land Bridge," Ylonya finished, "and were saved by a party of Yrusian traders. And now we are here." She sat back down.

Aidren leaned towards her and murmured, "Are you sure you're not Lèniumen? You should be a storyteller."

She gave him a fleeting grin. "Thank you."

Gwynmaer rose from his seat once more. "Thank you, Ylonya. I speak on behalf of us all when I say how very sorry I am that two of your company paid the ultimate price to retrieve the Master Bloodstone. You have it here?"

"It is in my pack, in my room," Ylonya said. "Why?"

"We must examine it," the Ranusian Waymage, Vordan, replied, "so that we may discern clearly how it may be destroyed."

"I will bring it to you," Ylonya said.

Gwynmaer's eyes swept over them all. "It is a great achievement to have brought the Master Bloodstone here, in spite of many perils. The Wayzenmoot is in your debt. Rest now. We will speak again in a few days."

Four days later, Abigail and the rest of them were summoned to the Audience Chamber once more.

"Come with us," Gwynmaer said. "It is time for the Master Bloodstone to be destroyed, so that its evil power cannot threaten Veylindré again."

He led the way out of the Audience Chamber into the courtyard, followed by the rest of the High Waymages. Abigail and the others followed them through the tall, pointed arch which she knew led to the Golden Stone of Ranu. So this ritual, whatever it was, was going to be done in the presence of the holiest object in Veylindré. That made sense.

To Abigail's surprise, a large group of other Waymages were waiting for them – at least twenty. What was going on?

High Waymage Daefiel stepped forward, her pale blonde hair gleaming. "I have had a Truedream," she said in her soft voice. "All of you are necessary parts of this ritual, but Abigail will be the focus. In recognition of this, and of all you have accomplished on this quest, we have decided to raise you to the rank of adept."

Abigail could feel her cheeks growing warm. Adept? She had not expected this. Pulling herself together, she bobbed an instinctive curtsey. "Thank you, High Waymage."

"It is well deserved," Shaunan said. "You have done more in a few short seasons than many Waymages achieve in a lifetime."

The others clustered around her, adding their own congratulations. Abigail sensed their love for her, warm and supportive.

"Now," Daefiel said, "It is time for the ritual. The Master Bloodstone has great powers for evil, so each of us will need to support Abigail as the focus. Abigail, here is the Master Bloodstone, and the words you will need to say."

Abigail was glad to see that the Master Bloodstone was well wrapped – she would not need to touch it directly. Not yet.

"Shaunan and Ylonya," Daefiel continued, "you stand behind Abigail, with one hand each on her shoulder and the other linking the pair of you. Ednor and Aidren, you two stand behind Ylonya and Shaunan, and make the same connection between them and each other. Tremond, you must place one hand on Ednor's shoulder and the other on Aidren's. In this way, all six of you are connected to each other and can focus your strength on Abigail."

Would Shaunan be strong enough for this? Abigail would never forgive the High Waymages if something happened to her. But she had little time to think about it, because Daefiel was continuing with her instructions, this time to the other eleven High Waymages.

"We must form another circle, our left hands connected to each other's shoulders, while our right hands touch the shoulder of one of the company. Vordan and Valwyn, you must connect to Abigail, Ianlos and Shonala to Shaunan, Luciron and Tarmina to Ylonya, Perran and Onadia to Aidren, Gwynmaer and Bryna to Ednor, while Fenlar and I connect to Tremond."

Abigail was fascinated. She realised that each pair of High Waymages would be connected with someone with the Waymark of the land they represented. Except for Ianlos and Shonala – Shaunan did not have a Lèniumen Waymark. She guessed Ednor had been chosen for the Néartanian High Waymages, because he was part of the ruling family.

Daefiel turned to the other Waymages. "You must form the outermost circle, connected in the same way, to protect us all, enclosing both the two inner circles and the Golden Stone of Ranu."

After a bit of shuffling, everyone was in place.

"It is time," Daefiel said from behind her. "Each pair of High Waymages will say the words I received in my

Truedream, which will be repeated by the person they are touching, then Abigail will say the final words that will invoke the power of the Golden Stone of Ranu and cause the destruction of the Master Bloodstone. After each phrase everyone must focus on Abigail, both through the power of Augmentation, and by chanting, 'For only the Six can defeat the One.' Let the ritual begin."

Abigail unwrapped the Master Bloodstone. She hated the feel of it on her skin. It seemed to be trying to ooze out of her grasp, cold and inimical to her touch. She took firmer hold of it, in her left hand. She would not fail, not now. The price of reaching this moment had been too high. She could feel the power thrumming through her, as not only the other members of the company, but also the twelve High Waymages through them, and the twenty-four other Waymages, shared their strength with her, counteracting the evil of the Master Bloodstone.

She listened as each pair of High Waymages spoke in turn, invoking the presence of one of the Six. Their words were repeated in turn by each member of the company. Only Ednor added something, which made her heart swell with gratitude: "Beloved Néarta, I invoke your presence in the name of Ellyn, as we seek an end to this evil." After each invocation, everyone chanted, "For only the Six can defeat the One." She could feel the atmosphere changing, could sense the ineffable presence of each Goddess as they arrived.

The final pair, Vordan and Valwyn, met her gaze as they said, "Beloved Mother Ranu, we invoke your presence as we seek an end to this evil."

Her heart trembled as she repeated their words. She took a deep breath, then looked down at the paper Daefiel had given her, and began to read aloud, leaving a space after each phrase for the gathering to repeat the chant.

"Here, in the presence of the Six... and of the Golden Stone of Ranu... we command you, Talamu... to come out of this Stone and forsake your lust for power... Abjure your evil ways... Bc reconciled with your sisters, Lènia, Néarta, Dagâra, Yrusia and Garûna... and with Mother Ranu, who created you... May the power of this Stone be destroyed... that it may never be used again... to do evil and dominate others... In the names and presence of the Six, let it be so."

As she spoke the final words, the Master Bloodstone became fiery-hot in her hand – she could smell roasting meat and realised it was her own flesh burning. The Stone began to pulse with a sooty, incarnadine glow and a red, sticky substance began to ooze from it – blood. How revolting. She had to fight with every element of her being to hold on to it, to not let it fall. The pain in her left hand was acute and agonising..

We're nearly there, Abigail. Keep your attention on it. Do not falter now. Valwyn's voice, clear in her head.

She felt once more the power of her companions and the twelve High Waymages coursing through her, and somehow managed to find the strength to hold on. A golden beam of light burst forth from the top of the Golden Stone of Ranu, right over the heads of the company, enveloping the Master Bloodstone. An anguished scream full of an ancient frustration filled her ears, as Talamu gave up the fight. There was an unendurably bright explosion of light and the Master Bloodstone was gone.

It was done. Her eyes darkened and she slid into oblivion.

Chapter 22

When Abigail woke up, she was lying in a comfortable bed, cocooned in soft blankets. The light of late morning was shining in through the window. She moved her head and saw Shaunan sitting beside her. Where were they? She tried to sit up and pain shot through her left hand as she put weight on it. Memory came flooding back – the Master Bloodstone burning her flesh, the sickening stench of roasting meat. Her own hand, burnt and black.

"So you're awake," Shaunan said. "Good. You have slept for more than a day and a night."

Abigail looked at her hand, which was swathed in white bandages. "My hand – will it be damaged forever?"

Shaunan touched her good right hand gently. "No, it will heal. But it will take a while to mend completely – the Master Bloodstone had burned you down to the bone."

Abigail shuddered. "But it's gone now? I did it right?"

"Yes, it has gone, and so a great evil has been banished from the world. I am very proud of you, Abigail. No-one could have done better."

The joy, the pride in Shaunan's voice was balm to Abigail's soul. "I couldn't have done it without the support from all of you," she admitted. "I have never felt such power. It was almost too much for me to contain."

"It was an honour to be part of it."

Shaunan sounded so tired. "Are you all right?"

"Do not worry about me," Shaunan said, smiling. "Now that you are awake, I will go and seek my own bed. But I could not leave you before."

Abigail felt the tears sting her eyes. "I owe you so much."

"As Veylindré owes you."

"What will happen now?"

"We will leave Ranusheim in a few days, once your recovery is complete. And return home, I suppose."

"Home? Do I have a home?"

It felt like an important question. Ever since she had arrived in this world, she had been constantly on the move. She had no family, no – Jacob. Where could she go?

"Of course you do. Nordvein is your home. You are my adept, remember?"

A warm glow filled Abigail's chest. "I was so surprised when Daefiel said that. I hope that one day I'll be able to return here to do my final training."

"I am sure you will. Sleep again now, Abigail."

And as though Shaunan had laid a spell on her, her eyes closed of their own accord and she fell asleep once more.

A couple of short seisdags or so later – Ylonya wasn't counting the days – the remaining members of the company arrived in Taellingsford. After waiting until Abigail's hand was sufficiently healed for her to hold the reins without discomfort, they had left Ranusheim with the good wishes of the entire Wayzenmoot. They had said goodbye to Tremond at the Lènium end of the Land Bridge, as he turned north to return to Garûnalond.

"Will we be staying with Genira?" Abigail asked.

"Yes," Ylonya said. "I owe it to her to let her know how it all turned out."

"Good. I'm looking forward to seeing her again. But I'm glad we had the time to visit the Vale of Berlysian on the way," and she patted her healer's bag, which was plump and full. "My healing supplies were running low, and I've spent a good part of the money they gave me for becoming an adept on replenishing it."

An hour or so later, they were sitting around Genira's kitchen table, the copper pans gleaming in the warm light of an oil lamp, sharing a delicious meal of delicately poached fish, in a piquant sauce, with tiny new potatoes – the first crop in this Season of Growth – and fresh greens.

Ylonya pushed her plate away with a sigh of pleasure. "Thank you, Genira. That was so good."

"Let's clear away, then I want to hear the whole story."

Ylonya shot a glance at Abigail and Aidren. It would be hard for them to hear parts of it. Abigail nodded her acquiescence. Aidren shrugged.

Ylonya sat back and marshalled her story, while the two youngsters helped Genira restore the kitchen to its normal tidy condition. Then the three of them sat back down.

Genira cleared her throat, "I take it your quest was successful."

"Ye-es," Ylonya replied, "but not without scathe." Sitting here, she missed Ellyn with an acuteness that surprised her.

"A long tale goes better with wine," Genira said, fetching a bottle from the larder, and glasses from a cupboard. Ylonya took a sip, then plunged into an account of all that had happened since they had last been here. Genira was a good audience. She listened in silence as their story unfolded, with only a gasp of dismay when she heard of Ellyn's death. Eventually, the tale had been told. Ylonya sat back, exhausted. What would the Storytellers make of it, once it became generally known?

"I see what you mean by 'not without scathe'", Genira said gently. "I am so very sorry to hear about Ellyn and," turning to Abigail, "that your Jacob was both found and then lost again."

Abigail nodded her acknowledgement. Ylonya guessed the girl was struggling with tears, so she answered on her behalf. "Yes, our losses have been great, and we will grieve for them for a long time. Yet a great evil is gone from the world. Without the Master Bloodstone, we hope that the Talamdorians will stay behind their mountains and trouble us no more."

"What are you all planning to do next?" Genira asked.

"Abigail, Aidren and I will go home to Nordvein," Shaunan said, "stopping off at Luvodican on the way. Our news must be shared with the people we knew there. But I don't know what Ylonya and Ednor plan to do."

Ylonya felt her face grow warm. Ylonya and Ednor – how had Shaunan guessed? She cleared her throat. "I will have to report to Mistress Margera, and Ednor to Lord Éadulf and Lady Aethed. After that, we have not discussed what we're going to do next."

Shaunan stood up. "I am off to bed," she said. "Thank you for your hospitality, Genira, and for the delicious meal."

"You are most welcome."

Abigail and Aidren followed her, leaving Ylonya, Ednor and Genira alone.

Suddenly, Ylonya felt the need to be outside in the clear night air. “I’m going for a walk.”

“I’ll come with you,” Ednor said, as Genira said, “Here is the key. Please lock up when you come back.” The two of them grinned at each other.

Soon she and Ednor were wandering around the narrow streets of Tacllingsford for the sheer pleasure of walking in the moonlight. Ylonya felt a rare peace in her soul. It felt so good, just for now, to have no urgent task on hand.

“A copper bit for your thoughts?”

“I was just thinking how pleasant it was to not be rushing off to save the world for a change.”

Ednor laughed. “I know what you mean. All too soon, we will have to step back into harness once more. I must report to my parents and you to Mistress Margera.”

To her surprise, Ylonya felt a cold, empty sensation in her stomach. She did not want to walk away from Ednor, to never see him again. Abrupt tears were stinging her eyes.

“I – I suppose so,” she said, fighting to keep her voice even.

“Ylonya,” Ednor said, grabbing her hand, “it need not be the end for us. You are the most independent and brave woman I have ever known, and I know you could never give up your travelling life. But I love you. Mistress Margera and Guildmaster Brickon have proved that it is possible to make a marriage work even if much time is spent apart.”

Marriage? Ylonya's heart raced – she had not thought that far ahead. He was looking into her eyes with such love that she felt her reservations melting away. "Ylonya, will you marry me?"

"Yes," she whispered.

"Are we stopping here for long?" Abigail asked Shaunan the next morning.

"I would like to stay here to celebrate Yrusiastide – it will be beginning in four days."

"I'd no idea it was so close," Abigail said, "but I'm not sure I have the heart for much celebrating."

"I understand," Shaunan said, "nevertheless, we would struggle to find a ship willing to leave Taellingsford before the festival."

"I hadn't thought of that." Abigail paused, then continued, "And I suppose we'll be saying goodbye to Ylonya and Ednor too – didn't she say they were going to cross to Néartanis?"

"Yes, they will leave as soon as the festival is over. But before then, Ylonya will need to get her Goldstone recharged."

That conversation had been a seisdag ago. Abigail had found the festival difficult, as she had half-expected – it held too many reminders of previous festivals, with Ellyn and Jacob by her side, and she knew Aidren had felt the same. Shared grief had brought them closer.

And it had been hard to say goodbye to Ylonya. She had come to love the feisty, independent Yrusian, and was already missing her. But it was time to go, time to return to Nordvein, time to stop travelling.

As soon as Yrusiastide was over, she, Shaunan and Aidren had found a ship's captain willing to take them to Smithsport at the southern end of the Gulf of Dagâran. He told them that the Havimi had left the Sea of Ranu, so he did not anticipate any trouble. The weather was growing warmer and he assured them that with a following wind, they should reach their destination in between one seisdag and two.

In spite of her continuing grief, which was a constant companion, Abigail felt a frisson of excitement at being out at sea again. Something about the regular motion of the deck beneath her feet, the clean, fresh air making the blue and white striped sails belly out above her, and the gulls wheeling around them with raucous cries lifted her spirits. She was leaning against the forward rail, drinking it all in, when she heard footsteps behind her.

"This is better than riding," Aidren said. "I never thought I would say that, but I'm finding it quite –" and he paused, searching for a suitable word, "– exhilarating. This is only my second sea voyage."

"What about the ferry across the Gulf of Dagâran? Doesn't that make three?" she reminded him.

"I'd forgotten that. But that was a small boat, not like this. And we were only on it for a few hours."

A sad expression came over his face and Abigail knew he was remembering Ellyn's excitement about travelling outside Dagâran for the first time. She touched his arm, a gesture of shared empathy. They had both lost so much on this journey. Once more a wave of longing swept over her, and she had to bite her lip to stop the ready tears. If only they could have stayed in Nordvein. Or Luvodican. Jacob could have completed his training with Master Kalen, Aidren his with Master Sanderon, and Ellyn hers with Master Markhan. Then Jacob and Ellyn would still be alive.

"I wish we could have stayed in Luvodican," Aidren said, startling her.

"Are you reading my mind?"

He turned to her, surprised by the sharpness of her tone. "No. You know I can't do that. Why?"

Her lip trembled. "Because I was just thinking that if we had stayed in Luvodican, we could all have completed our training with our different masters, and – and Jacob and Ellyn would still be alive."

Aidren nodded in fierce agreement. Then he said, "Whenever I wished for things to be other than they were, my mother used to tell me, 'Never waste your energy on might have beens.' And I know she's right, but sometimes it's so hard..."

"I know," Abigail said softly, "but at least we have each other to talk to – someone else who understands what we're going through."

"I will always be there for you, Abigail."

"And I for you, my friend."

As one, they turned to lean against the rail once more. Thank goodness for Aidren. Between him and Shaunan, she was never alone. And now they were going home.

Was Nordvein her home? It was Shaunan's and Aidren's, so she supposed it must be. But would she fit in? She knew she would stand out – one white-skinned person amid all the dark-skinned Dagârans. But if Shaunan and Aidren didn't care, why should she?

It was good to be back in Dagâran, back in her homeland. Shaunan was looking forward to seeing Marinden again and sharing their story with her. But was also dreading breaking the news of Ellyn's passing to Master Markhan, and of Jacob's to Master Kalen.

The short journey from Smithsport to Luvodican took two days. Now, at the beginning of the Season of First Fruits, the countryside was humming with life – crops were ripening in the roadside fields and young calves, lambs and kids grazed beside their mothers, content to feed on the new grass and feel the warm sunshine on their backs. Shaunan felt herself relaxing as she reconnected with the natural beauty around her. Her grief for Ellyn could still catch her unawares, its sharp claws rending her heart, but she was beginning to come to terms with it.

They reached the South Gate of the city as the sun was setting, and a guard challenged them. "Who are you and what is your reason for visiting Luvodican?"

"I am Waymage Shaunan of Nordvein, and these are Aidren, a Warrior of Dagâra, and Abigail, my adept. We are on our way back home to Nordvein and wish to see First Waymage Marinden."

The young woman saluted. "I must test your Waymarks, Waymage Shaunan."

"Of course." Shaunan stood patiently as her Waymark and those of Abigail and Aidren were tested. Then she tested the guard's in return.

"Do you know your way to the Temple?"

"Yes, we do."

As they rode off through the narrow streets of Luvodican, Abigail said, “Such a difference from last time.”

“Yes, you were young in Veylindré then.”

“Do you remember the shock on their faces,” Aidren said with a grin, “when Abigail threw back her hood in the guardhouse at Myndorian and revealed she had no Waymark?”

Abigail smiled, a sad smile, but a smile, nonetheless. “Yes. I had no idea how frightening it must have been for them.”

“But now you belong here, with us,” Shaunan said.

“I hope so.”

“I know so,” Aidren said.

Marinden welcomed them herself, in spite of the lateness of the hour. “Come in, my friends. It is good to see you again.” *But where are Ellyn and Jacob?*

“Thank you, Marinden. It is good to be back.” *Gone. Both gone.* “I would be grateful if we could stay here for a couple of days before returning to Nordvein.”

“Of course. You are most welcome. I will ask one of the Temple servants to show you to your rooms. *I am so very sorry.*

“Thank you. I have much to tell you.”

Marinden touched her hand and Shaunan could sense the compassion radiating out from her. *Sleep well, my friend. I'll see you all in the morning.*

Aidren was pleased to be included in the meeting with First Waymage Marinden the following morning. The First Waymage listened in silence as Shaunan shared the story of the quest. He and Abigail chimed in occasionally, and Abigail took over the tale altogether for the Talamdorian part, when the Waymage had remained behind in Chorich Castle. Then Shaunan took it up again. Briefly though they spoke, the sun was high in the sky outside by the time they finished, and Aidren felt exhausted through having to relive it all once more. It had been fascinating to compare how Shaunan and Abigail told the story with Ylonya's retelling to Genira. The two Waymages enlarged on the roles of Ylonya, Ednor, Tremond, Ellyn – his dear Ellyn – and Aidren himself, while glossing over their own parts. He suspected a parallel conversation was going on in the silences between the words.

"I am so sorry for your losses," Marinden said, bowing her head for a moment. "Tell me more about the ritual that destroyed the Master Bloodstone."

"That is Abigail's tale to tell," Shaunan said. "She was the focus. It was the fact of her origin from outside Veylindré which made it all possible."

Abigail flushed, her creamy skin tinted a warm pink. Her exotic beauty could still take him by surprise.

"It was the hardest thing I have ever done," she began, "being the focus for so much power. And knowing that if I failed, all the long grief of the quest would have been for nothing."

But she had not failed. She had triumphed. Aidren's heart swelled – he was so proud of her. He had one remaining fear – that she would not be content to stay in Nordvein, after all she had experienced. He was not sure he could bear losing her too.

Marinden's voice broke into his thoughts, and he realised Abigail had stopped speaking. "Veylindré owes you a great debt."

"It was my privilege. I could not have done it alone. I only wish…"

Her voice trailed off. Aidren took her hand and squeezed it. She met his gaze, gratitude in her eyes.

"It has been a testing time of all of us," Shaunan said, "and our grief is real and lasting. I am dreading having to share the news with Master Markhan and Master Kalen. The loss of Ellyn and Jacob is hard to bear."

Hard to bear. She had never spoken a truer word. Aidren's chest ached with the grief of it. He felt Abigail's hand in his, warm and comforting.

"And we must see Master Sanderon," she said, "I'm sure he will want to hear all you have done since we left."

Master Sanderon. That was a thought. Maybe he'd be able to return to Luvodican, once he had seen the Waymages safely back to Nordvein.

Abigail could sense the rising excitement in her two companions, as they drew closer to Nordvein. She hoped she would be able to make a place for herself there. Because there was no going back – her old life had died with Jacob.

"Nearly there now," Aidren said, as they emerged from the Myner's Gap. "They are going to be so surprised to see us. I reckon they will have given us up for lost."

She had rarely heard him sound so excited. How wonderful it must be to have a home to return to. But they had said it would be her home now. She would have to get used to it.

"Then we will have to hand ourselves back," Shaunan said firmly. "And I will have to send young Hedwin back to Waymage Findoran to complete his training. His time here will stand him in good stead with the Wayzenmoot, when he goes to the Colaste a'r Teisen."

The Colaste a'r Teisen. Abigail longed to go there, to complete her own training. She shook herself – she wasn't nearly ready for that yet. She knew she had so much still to learn from Shaunan before that. It would be good to be in one place, so that she would have the chance to do some solid training, and opportunities to practise what she had learned, in a calm setting. Most of her learning so far had been on the move and in a hurry – Shaunan had taught her what needed to be done, in that moment. It was going to be very – different, trying to settle into the simple, static rhythm of village life after all their travelling.

The sun began to set behind them, behind the tall mountains of the Dagâran Range, which threw long shadows over their path. By the time they reached the outskirts of Nordvein, it was fully dark and they had to find their path by moonlight. Without thinking, she fished out her Goldstone out of its pouch and made light.

"Thank you, Abigail," Shaunan said. "We are nearly there now. I will be glad to rest."

Rest? Abigail had nearly forgotten there was such a thing. But she was glad for Shaunan's sake that the long seisdags of travelling were over.

Shaunan led the way to Nordvein's temple and ushered them both inside.

"Who's there?" A young man, clad in an adept's tunic and trousers, was striding towards the door. Then he stopped dead, a look of surprise on his face. "Waymage Shaunan? Is that you?"

"Yes, Hedwin. We are back."

They were back. Abigail squared her shoulders. Her new life started here.

The next morning, Shaunan showed Abigail round her still room, with all its rustling herb and bottles of potion ingredients. She was looking forward to being able to train the girl at leisure.

"Do I really have a home here?"

She sounded so sad, so uncertain. "Of course you do. You are my adept."

"What about Hedwin?"

"As I said yesterday, I will send him back to Waymage Findoran in Myndorian. He knew that his tenure here was only temporary, that he was here to look after the people of Nordvein in my absence. You are my chosen adept, and your place is here."

Shaunan felt the surge of relief from the girl.

"It's going to be so – so strange," Abigail said, "not being on the move all the time."

Shaunan chuckled. "That is the part I am looking forward to," she said. "It will give me the chance to train you properly, not on the run."

Just then, there was a knock at the door.

"Come in," Shaunan said.

It was Aidren and he looked excited. "What is it?" Abigail asked. She had obviously caught his mood too.

"It's – read this," Aidren said. "When I got home last night, my father gave it to me." He thrust a letter into Shaunan's hands. "I can't believe it," he continued. "Ednor put in a good word for me with Master Sanderon and they want me to return to the Hall of Warriors to complete my training."

Shaunan took the precious letter, which had the seal of the Hall of Warriors of Dagâra. She scanned it quickly. "And well deserved," she said, handing it to Abigail, who read it in her turn.

"Oh, Aidren!" she said, hugging him. "I'm so very pleased for you. When will you be leaving?"

Shaunan could sense an aching sadness in her and hoped that Aidren had not caught it. Luckily, empathy was not one of the powers of a Warrior.

"When the next ore train crosses the Myner's Gap, I will go with it. My parents are so proud of me." Then his voice changed. "How I wish…"

To Shaunan's surprise, Abigail finished his sentence. "How you wish Ellyn could have been here to see this. I know." She gave him another hug. "We are so proud of you too. And I know Ellyn would have been too."

"I hate to leave you," Aidren said. "Will you be all right?"

"Don't worry about me," Abigail said. "I'll be learning too. There are still so many things about Veylindré I don't know. Shaunan and I will be here when you get back… You are going to come back?"

"Of course I am."

Shaunan fought to suppress her surprise. When had the two of them become so close?

Shared grief has brought us together.

I am so glad.

Chapter 23

The longer days of the Seasons of Growth and First Fruits were behind them and the festival of Néartastide at end of the Season of Thanksgiving was approaching. The days were growing shorter again and all the harvest had been gathered in. Shaunan had been glad to slip back into her normal daily routine. She was sleeping better and felt that, as long as she was allowed to live here quietly, she would be able to serve the people of Nordvein for years to come. She was in her still room, preparing some salve for a miner's arm – she had cut it badly while underground – when Abigail walked in.

Shaunan took one look at her and asked, "What is wrong, my dear?"

"Oh, nothing. Just the usual." Abigail put her healer's bag on its peg and threw herself into a chair, despondency in every line of her face.

"The usual what?" Time to get this out into the open.

"It's so dispiriting when they all look past me when I arrive, hoping to see you. I had expected that they would have realised I am a good healer by now."

It was true. Abigail had learned her healing skills easily and well, and was by now nearly as good as Shaunan herself. Yet the people of Nordvein had been slow to accept her.

After breathing a swift prayer to Ranu, that the right words would be given to her, Shaunan said, "You must try to forgive them. They are simple villagers, who have little experience of the wider world of Veylindré. It takes them a while to get used to anyone new."

"It didn't take you and the others long," Abigail said, her resentment plain to hear. "I'm fed up with being treated as though I'm some kind of outlander."

"But don't you see? You look so different to them, with your blonde hair, blue eyes and pale skin. And they have heard part of the tale of our adventures. I expect they are a little afraid of you."

"Afraid? That's ridiculous." Abigail's eyes were flashing. "What is there about me to be afraid of?"

"Try not to take it so personally, Abigail. It is not meant so. Your service to them will prove your worth, in the end."

The girl looked down at her hands, breathing deeply. Good, she was trying to contain her anger. Shaunan walked over to her, cupped her chin in her hand and said gently, "They will accept you, sooner or later. Try to be patient."

Abigail's shoulders slumped. "I suppose you're right. But it's hard…"

What she would have said next, Shaunan did not know. They were distracted by the sound of running feet outside, then someone banging on the door.

"Waymage! Come quickly. There's been an accident underground. Some people are trapped."

All rancour forgotten, Abigail jumped to her feet, grabbed her healer's bag off its peg and ran outside. Shaunan followed more slowly. Each time this happened, it took her back to that dreadful day when she had lost Donan. She squared her shoulders and followed her adept to the mine.

After that, things had changed, to Abigail's relief. She was beginning to make tentative friendships with some of Nordvein's younger inhabitants, but there was none of the easy camaraderie she had enjoyed with Ellyn – her dear Ellyn. She knew they thought of her as the Waymage's adept and could not relax around her. So she preferred to spend most of her time with Shaunan. She knew she still had so much to learn. And with Aidren off in Luvodican, there was no-one else who had known Jacob, who had shared all the experiences of the quest.

Towards the end of the Season of Completion, they had travelled to Myndorian to celebrate Dagârastide, and Aidren had managed to get a few days' leave from the Hall of Warriors to meet them there. He had grown taller in his absence and broader too. But it was all muscle. It looked as though the training suited him. She found it hard to believe she had been a Ranusian for only one cycle of seasons. It seemed so much longer than that.

A few seisdags later, with the shortest day of the year behind them and the first shy green plants beginning to poke their leaves and shoots up above the ground, she and Shaunan were in the Waymage's still room – Abigail's favourite place in the entire village with its neat rows of glass bottles and dried bunches of herbs hanging from the central beam, filling the air with their subtle fragrance – when a rider from the Messenger Service arrived with a letter for Shaunan.

"I wonder," Shaunan said as she broke open the seal. She scanned the contents quickly, then looked up with a big smile on her face. "It is time, Abigail. I have been in touch with the Colaste a'r Teisen, and they have accepted you for training. You will need to be there just before Garûnastide, which is when the new Colaste year begins. There is enough time for you to get there, so long as you leave soon."

Abigail's knees gave way beneath her and she sat down abruptly. "I had no idea you had even written to them," she said. "Do you really think I'm ready?"

Shaunan nodded. "Yes, I do. I have taught you much, but there is more for you to learn, which can best be done at the Colaste, in the company of your peers."

"But how will you manage without me?" Abigail asked, then blushed. Shaunan had managed perfectly well for years without her.

"Do not worry about that. If I need to, I can always send to either Findoran or Marinden for some assistance. Both have adepts at the moment."

"But why Garûnastide? That is so soon – only a few seisdags. And Aidren's not back from Luvodican yet. I hate to go without seeing him."

"Garûnastide, whose other name is the Festival of Dedication, is the traditional time when all young apprentices and adepts are taken on by masters," Shaunan said in a tone that admitted no contradiction. "And you will be going through Luvodican on your way to Ranusheim. I am sure you will be able to see him there." She paused, then continued, "You do want to go?"

"Oh, Shaunan! Of course I do. But – I'm going to miss you, miss this quiet life. And I won't know anyone there."

"You will soon make friends. Come, Abigail, this is not like you. I thought it was your dream to train at the Colaste."

"It was. I mean, it is. It's just so sudden."

"I will speak with Brann to find out when the next ore train for Myndorian is leaving. You ought not cross the Dagâran Range alone."

Abigail jumped up, too excited to sit still. She was going to the Colaste a'r Teisen. At last.

"Abigail! What in the name of the Six are you doing here?" Aidren said.

He had walked out of the Hall of Warriors, hot and sweaty after a long training session with Master Sanderon and the other adepts, to find her waiting outside.

"Aren't you pleased to see me?"

He gave her a hug. "Of course I am. But why are you here?" He leapt to a conclusion. "Is Shaunan well?"

"Yes, she's fine," she said. "My being here has nothing to do with Nordvein. But Aidren, are you free now?"

"Yes. At least, I need to go back to my lodgings and have a wash, but if you can put up with the smell…"

She sniffed ostentatiously. "Hmm. You have smelt better." Then grinned at his outrage.

"I'm only teasing you," she said. "I have some exciting news."

They started to walk back to his lodgings. It was so good to see her. He hadn't realised how much he had missed her.

"What is it? If it's nothing to do with Nordvein, then it must be to do with you."

"You're right. I've been accepted for training at the Colaste a'r Teisen. That's why I'm here. I'm on my way to Ranusheim."

Her voice was positively clanging with triumph. Aidren gave her another hug. He knew how long she had hoped for this moment. "I'm so pleased for you. When do you start?"

"I've got to be there by Garûnastide. That's when they accept new adepts."

He whistled. "That's not long. How are you going to get there?"

"Shaunan suggested I ask First Waymage Marinden. She said she will know about parties of traders heading for the Isle."

Aidren came to an abrupt decision. "I'm going to come with you, to protect you. You shouldn't be travelling only with people you don't know."

And was rewarded by a radiant smile, which took his breath away. She was so beautiful when she smiled.

"Will Master Sanderon allow it? Aren't you in the middle of your training?"

"It's nearly over now. I think he might say yes if I explain that I'm accompanying you."

"Oh, Aidren, that would be wonderful. You're so kind."

He flushed and was glad it didn't show against his dark skin. "It's the least I can do. And he can only say no." He had another thought. "In fact, I might ask whether he would be willing to contact the garrison at the Fort of Ranu on my behalf, to see if I could be taken on there. That way, I could both complete my training and be close at hand if you needed me."

They had reached his lodgings by now. "Wait here," he said, "while I clean up. Then we'll go back to the Hall of Warriors together and I'll ask him today."

Once again, Abigail's face lit up. Did his presence mean that much to her? He could only hope.

When Abigail and Aidren reached the Fort of Ranu, they found a few other adepts, obviously waiting for a party of Waymages to take them to Ranusheim. Abigail took Aidren's arm, suddenly scared. What was she doing here?

He gave her a hug, then said, "I must report to the captain of the garrison. Good luck, my –" he paused and finished, "friend. May the Six be with you."

"Thank you, Aidren. And with you."

She watched as he strode briskly across the courtyard, then looked around, feeling a little lost. She saw a short young woman standing alone, washing her hands together nervously. She had very dark eyes and a wealth of black hair, which she wore braided around her head in a beautiful coronet. She reminded Abigail of Genira, so she guessed the girl might be Lèniumen. Maybe they could be friends. She walked over to her.

"Hello, I'm Abigail from Nordvein in Dagâran. Who are you?"

The girl turned to her gratefully. "Goodness, you have come a long way. I'm Raewe, from Plavin in Lènium," she said. Her voice was soft and musical.

"I wonder how long we'll have to wait here," Abigail said.

"The captain of the garrison said there should be some Waymages coming along by sixth hour."

Abigail looked at the sun, which was already high in the sky. "Not long now."

"Thank you for coming over to speak to me," Raewe said. "I was feeling a bit homesick."

"I expect we all are. But," Abigail said, the memory of how Shaunan and Findoran had met flashing into her mind, "now that we've found each other, let's stick together. Raewe's expression brightened as she smiled. "Thank you, Abigail. I'd like that."

Just then, the inner gates of the courtyard opened and a group of three Waymages came in. Abigail was grateful that she didn't know any of them. She'd have to be careful not to betray any prior knowledge of Ranusheim to her companion, or the other adepts. She wanted to be able to start fair, and find a place among them on her own merits.

Then heard a voice in her head and recognised it as Valwyn's. *Do not worry, Abigail. Your secret is safe with us.*

The Ceremony of Dedication took place a couple of days later, on the second afternoon of Garûnastide, in the presence of the Golden Stone of Ranu and the twelve High Waymages, resplendent in their fine robes. It was conducted by Reshin, whom Abigail knew was Chief Mentor of the Colaste a'r Teisen.

Some of the other adepts were called first, so Abigail had the chance to see what happened before it was her turn.

"Abigail of Nordvein, come forward." The old man's voice was as strong and resonant as ever. "Abigail, you have been called to the role of Waymage. Is it your wish to be trained as such?"

"Yes, Chief Mentor Reshin."

His grey eyes twinkled as he looked at her. He obviously knew who she was, what she had done. She was glad he would not betray it to her peers.

"Then say the Vow of Acceptance after me. I, Abigail of Nordvein..."

"I, Abigail of Nordvein,
vow that I will do my utmost to be true
to the Power of the Way,
to be obedient to my tutors,
to support my peers,
and to be diligent in learning
the skills required of a Waymage.
In the name of the Six, in the Power of the Way,
this is my vow."

"Abigail of Nordvein, you have sworn the Vow of Acceptance. Welcome to the Colaste a'r Teisen. May you learn well."

She bobbed a small curtsey to him, then walked back to where Raewe was standing. She had to stop herself from skipping, she felt so happy. This was it. Her training had begun.

But not quite yet. On the final evening of the festival, a band of Storytellers came to Ranusheim. To her acute embarrassment, they told the tale of the company's quest to find and destroy the Master Bloodstone. She was glad of the surrounding darkness, so that no-one could see her blushes, and wonder at them.

Somewhat to her surprise, Abigail settled in quickly to the new rhythm of life at the Colaste a'r Teisen. She was pleased to be sharing a room with Raewe and a strong friendship grew between them. The young Lèniumen was so different to Ellyn that Abigail soon stopped making comparisons when they sat to do their morning Immersion together.

And for the first time since coming to Veylindré, she fitted in. She was simply another Ranusian adept in a brown robe like everyone else, better at some classes than others. Most of the other dozen or so adepts were around her and Raewe's age, from all corners of the Commonweal. No-one knew of her past, for which she was profoundly grateful.

The training itself was fascinating. Long though she had spent in Shaunan's company, it was different when you were learning to take responsibility for an entire community by yourself. She began to understand that this was not only training, but a long, slow process of formation, raising them all to the status of Waymage.

The seisdags flew by and season followed season. As her knowledge of the power of the Way and the role of Waymages in harnessing it for the good of their community grew both broader and deeper, Abigail knew she had found her true calling. Where would she be assigned?

One morning, a few seisdags before Garûnastide, nearly a year after her arrival in Ranusheim, Chief Mentor Reshin walked into their classroom. As one, they rose to their feet and bowed to him respectfully.

"Good morning, adepts."

"Good morning, Chief Mentor Reshin."

"Please be seated. It is the view of your tutors that some of you are ready to be raised to the role of

Waymage. The following eight students will take part in the Vow of Assignment this coming Garûnastide."

Abigail held her breath as he began to read the names aloud. She gave a little gasp of joy when Raewe's name was called. Would hers be too? Name followed name and the adepts reacted variously, one bowing his head, another hugging herself, all clearly delighted.

"...and Abigail of Nordvein."

Thank Ranu, thank Ranu. She glanced around, saw the disappointment on the faces of those who had not been called, and tried to contain her joy. Reshin was still speaking and her attention snapped back to him.

"If you wish it, you will be permitted to invite family members and close friends to attend the ceremony. Please let Waymage Joslin know who they are as soon as possible, so that invitations may be issued and travel plans made. Adepts, good day."

As soon as he had left the room, a buzz of conversation began. Abigail and Raewe hugged each other.

"I'm so glad we will be finishing together," Raewe said. "Where do you hope to be assigned?"

Abigail gaped at her. She hadn't given it a thought. "I don't know. I expect I'll be sent back to Nordvein, to shadow Shaunan and then to take over from her in due course. What about you?"

"I have few ties in Plavin, so I'm open to being assigned anywhere." Raewe's dark eyes were sparkling. "I hope it will be somewhere near you, so that we can keep in touch easily."

"That would be wonderful."

As Garûnastide approached, Abigail's heart was full of a mixture of joy and apprehension. Where would she be assigned? She had hoped that Shaunan would be there to see her raised to the rank of Waymage, but received a message to say that her dear friend was not up to making the long journey. A spasm of guilt seized her – she should have stayed in Nordvein to look after her. But she knew Shaunan would never have permitted it.

At least Aidren would be there. She was looking forward so much to seeing him again – they had kept in touch by letter, but her training and his duties had not permitted them time to meet. He was the only "family" she had to witness her maging.

At last, the time came for the Ceremony of Assignment. She sat with Raewe and the other six adepts in the amphitheatre outside Ranusheim, watching the youngsters receiving their Ranusian Waymarks. Looking up into the audience, she scanned the watching faces. Yes, Aidren was there. Then, as on that Lèniastide long ago, the tutors of the Colaste and Chief Mentor Reshin made a second horseshoe in front of the High Waymages.

Reshin stepped forward. "I, Reshin, Chief Mentor of the Colaste a'r Teisen, am pleased to announce that eight Ranusian adepts have completed their training and are ready to be elevated to the rank of Waymage."

A thousand butterflies fluttered in Abigail's stomach. She clutched Raewe's hand tightly, felt an answering squeeze. Where would they be assigned? She hoped with all her heart that they would be close – she didn't want to lose touch with her friend, whose speaking mind to mind skills did not operate over any distance. Over the past year, she had grown almost as fond of her as she had been of Ellyn.

"Abigail of Nordvein, come forward."

Not sure her legs would hold her up, Abigail took her place in the centre of the double horseshoe.

"Abigail, you have completed your theoretical training in all aspects of becoming a Waymage. Do you wish to be raised to that status?"

"I do."

"Then repeat the Vow of the Waymage after me. I, Abigail of Nordvein…"

"I, Abigail of Nordvein," then she started to repeat the words after the Chief Mentor,

"vow that I will do my utmost,
to be true to the Power of the Way,
and to the rank of Waymage.
I will serve my community faithfully,
and guide them with kindness and wisdom,
remembering that all are children of the Six.
In the name of the Six, in the Power of the Way,
this is my vow."

"Abigail of Nordvein, you have taken the Vow of Assignment. Are you content to be posted where your gifts will best serve Veylindré and the Way?"

"I am."

Reshin smiled at her and presented her with a small wooden box, which she knew contained a silver brooch set with a golden yellow topaz to mark her status. "Very good. Waymage Abigail, you are assigned to Myndorian, in the east of Dagâran, to shadow Waymage Findoran, in the final years before her retirement."

Myndorian, not Nordvein? Abigail pulled herself together and said, "Thank you, Chief Mentor Reshin."

"May you follow the Way faithfully and serve the people of Veylindré for the rest of your days."

"I will do my best." Then she bowed to the tutors and the High Waymages and walked back to her seat where Raewe was waiting for her, her mind in a whirl. Findoran retiring? The idea gave Abigail a pang of anxiety. She'd not really thought of Findoran as old, and the Myndorian Waymage and Shaunan had graduated from the Colaste at the same time. What would Shaunan do without her?

"Raewe of Plavin, come forward."

Abigail held her breath as Raewe repeated the Vow of the Waymage. Where would Raewe be assigned? Let it be Dagâran, let it be Dagâran.

"Waymage Raewe, you are assigned to Taellingsford, in the south of Lènium, to shadow Waymage Anaya, in the final years before her retirement."

Taellingsford. Nowhere near Dagâran. Abigail tried to contain her tears, tried to be happy for Raewe. They would still be able to see each other sometimes, surely…

A couple of days later, the new Waymages left Ranusheim to begin the long journeys to their new posts. Aidren had completed his training at the Fort of Ranu, and had obtained the captain of the garrison's permission to return to Luvodican. So he was able to accompany Abigail back to Myndorian. He had only asked to be posted there so that he could be near Abigail. And he might as well have stayed in Luvodican –

the only time he had seen her had been at the maging ceremony.

Would there be any vacancies among the town guards in Myndorian? He'd have to see. For now, he'd just enjoy her company on the long journey home to Dagâran. He had missed his homeland more than he expected.

"Raewe will be coming with us part of the way," Abigail said. "She has been posted to Taellingsford."

The short, dark-haired Lèniumen girl came forward, her right hand open in the gesture of friendship. "It is good to meet you at last, Aidren. Abigail has told me so much about you."

Had she? That was a good sign. "It is good to meet you too, Raewe."

It took them two seisdags to reach Taellingsford, as the girls had insisted on visiting the Healer Hall in Berlysian on the way, to stock up on some of the more unusual remedies. Aidren liked what he saw of Raewe, but was could not wait to be alone with Abigail.

After a tearful farewell, Abigail turned to Aidren and said, "Ah, I'm going to miss her so much. Shall we visit Genira, do you think, before we leave here?"

He shook his head. "Better not. They'll be expecting you in Myndorian, won't they?"

"I suppose you're right. Let's go to the harbour and see if we can find a ship to take us home."

They were in luck – a ship with a cargo of healing herbs destined for Luvodican was leaving for Smithsport the next day. Abigail paid for both of them, in spite of his protests. "I have money for this journey from the Wayzenmoot. Save yours."

Over the next few days, they were together as much as possible. There seemed to be so much to talk about – Abigail's training at the Colaste a'r Teisen, Aidren's experiences at the Fort of Ranu. She was so easy to talk to.

"I wonder what Jacob and Ellyn would think if they could see us now," Abigail said one morning, as they leaned against the ship's rail, enjoying the Season of Growth sunshine on their faces, the fresh, invigorating air.

Aidren put his arm around her. She sounded so sad. "I think they would be happy for us, that we've managed to carry on."

She moved closer to him, snuggling in. "I hope so. Because I still miss them so much."

"So do I. But Abigail, we still have each other."

She turned to face him. "Yes, and I am so very glad of that."

"I will never forget Ellyn, but..." Aidren stopped, not sure how to say what he wanted to say.

"But?" her voice was light and teasing.

There were no words. He pulled her in and kissed her. For a moment she did not respond, but then, she was kissing him back, her lips so soft and warm on his.

After what seemed like a lifetime, they drew apart. "I love you, Abigail," he said. "I know you'll never forget Jacob but I want you to be my wife."

"Oh yes, Aidren, yes."

The Season of Growth was nearly over by the time they reached Myndorian. Abigail had enjoyed the last couple of seisdags so much, riding through the warm sunshine, past fields of standing crops or bleating sheep and lambs. And she was with Aidren. How would Shaunan take the news of their love?

They rode up to the South Gate of Myndorian and suffered their Waymarks to be tested. Then they made their way to the Temple, where Findoran would be waiting for her.

"Who wishes to enter the Temple of Myndorian?"

"Waymage Abigail and Aidren of Nordvein. I have been assigned by the Wayzenmoot to work with Waymage Findoran."

The gatekeeper bowed. "The Waymage is expecting you. Please wait here, while I tell her you have arrived."

Ten minutes later, Waymage Findoran came into view. "Waymage Abigail, welcome to the Temple of Myndorian. Come this way."

Abigail inclined her head. "Thank you, Waymage Findoran. And this is my friend, Aidren, a Warrior of Dagâra."

"Welcome, Aidren. I remember you from your last visit."

Aidren bowed in his turn. "Thank you, Waymage Findoran."

"Now," the stately woman said, "I have other guests. There are two people waiting to greet you in my chambers."

"Two?" Abigail said. "One of them must be Shaunan, but who is the other?"

"Wait and see. I would not want to spoil the surprise."

As they entered the Waymage's chambers, Shaunan walked forward to greet them. Abigail gave her a huge hug, but was shocked by how frail her friend felt in her arms.

"Oh, it is so good to see you!" *Shaunan! You've not been well. You should have told me.*

Don't worry about me. I am fine. Then added aloud, "and look who else is here to greet you."

Abigail looked across the room, where a familiar figure in a turquoise blue coat was beaming at her. "Ylonya! What brings you here?"

The Yrusian woman strode across the room and embraced her. "I thought it was about time I came to see you all. I had business in Luvodican, so I made a side trip to Nordvein. When Shaunan told me you were due back in Myndorian in a couple of seisdags, I decided to stay on and see you both."

"I'm so glad. How are you? Have you seen Ednor, or Tremond?" The questions came boiling out of Abigail. She was so eager for news of her friends.

Then she felt Findoran's eyes on her and blushed. "My apologies, Waymage Findoran. I –"

"I understand, Abigail," Findoran said. "Tomorrow will be soon enough for us to talk. Shaunan and Ylonya are staying in the Visitors' Hall and there is a room available for Aidren too. Chambers have been prepared for you near mine."

"Thank you." Abigail felt a little flustered by this attention. "That is most kind."

It is not every day I take on a new Waymage. Go and spend some time with your friends.

Findoran inclined her head to them all, and Shaunan led them to the Visitors' Hall. Soon they were sitting together over a simple meal of bread and cheese and fruit, sharing news.

"What have you been up to since I last saw you?" Abigail asked Ylonya.

"This and that," Ylonya's eyes twinkled. "Work for the Hall of Traders and the Guild. Although the war with Talamdor is over, there is still much to do. I'm in no immediate danger of unemployment."

Abigail laughed. "I'm glad to hear it. Have you heard from Ednor or Tremond?"

"I have indeed," and Abigail was astonished to see Ylonya's cheeks flush slightly. "Ednor is back at the border forts with his brother Réothed, but we meet up when we can. We – have an understanding. In fact, we got married last Garûnastide."

Ylonya, married? Of all the news, this was the least expected. Abigail rushed forward and planted a kiss on her friend's cheek. "Oh, I'm so happy for you. And for Ednor."

Aidren pressed forward to offer his congratulations too. Abigail touched his hand. This was the time. "We have news of our own," she said, blushing in her turn. "Aidren and I have decided we would like to get married at Ranustide, after the Season of Proving."

"My dear child," Shaunan said, "I am so glad."

"Would you marry us?"

"Of course," Shaunan said, "I would be delighted to."

After which, they talked for many times half an hour. Abigail was fascinated to discover that Tremond was heading a delegation to Talamunem City, in an attempt to better relations with Talamdor. "I can think of no-one better," she said. "I'm glad for him."

Chapter 24

Nine years had passed since Abigail and Aidren had returned to Myndorian. For the first five of those, Abigail had supported Findoran in her role as Waymage, and had nursed her through her final illness. To her surprise and pleasure, the Council of Myndorian had been unanimous in their desire for her to step into Findoran's shoes. So for the past four years she had been Waymage of Myndorian, had begun to train adepts of her own and, for the last couple of years, to mentor one brand new Waymage, Bronwin, who hailed from Fionnan in southern Dagâran.

The responsibilities of being the town's Waymage were many and varied, yet she had never been happier. All the same, she had come to value her morning Immersion greatly, as the time alone gave her the chance to re-ground herself in her vocation, to find some inner peace.

She was kneeling with her eyes closed, in silent communion with the Six and the Way, when there was a knock at the door. She blew out the candle and rose to her feet at once – a call this early rarely boded well.

"Come."

It was Brunan, the same Temple servant who had admitted them to the Temple all those years before, and he was holding a letter in his hands..

"I'm sorry to disturb you, Waymage Abigail, but this has just arrived from Ranusheim. I thought you'd wish to see it straight away."

From Ranusheim? "Thank you, Brunan," Abigail said, taking the letter from him. "I will open it at once."

The little man bowed and left, closing the door behind him. Abigail crossed the room and sank down onto a cushioned seat near the low oval table which stood in front of the stone hearth. Holding the letter in her hand, she gazed around the room. It had changed little since she had first entered it as a stranger to Dagâran, a stranger to Veylindré. The same gorgeous tapestries hung on the walls, but the scenes they depicted were now known and familiar, events from Dagâran's history. Now these chambers were her inner sanctum, a place to which she could retreat at need.

Picking up a slim, silver letter-opener – a gift from Aidren the previous Ranustide – she slit open the envelope and took out the message within.

"To Waymage Abigail of Myndorian, greetings!

This is to inform you that Marinden, First Waymage of Dagâran, has chosen to retire from her post at the end of the present year. After some consideration, we, the High Waymages of the Wayzenmoot, have decided that your unique experiences and talents have made you the most suitable candidate to be invited to succeed her as First Waymage of Dagâran at the Festival of Dagârastide.

Should you choose to accept this invitation, it will be necessary for you to report to the Colaste a'r Teisen this coming Garûnastide to undertake the required further training, which will take three seasons.

We understand from your reports that Bronwin, the young Waymage you are mentoring, is sufficiently experienced to deputise for you in your absence.

Please respond to this letter as soon as possible. May the Way guard and guide you."

Signed by all twelve members of the Wayzenmoot.

Abigail read it through a second time, sure that her eyes had deceived her. First Waymage of Dagâran! She had never aspired to rise so high. Being Waymage of Myndorian was honour enough for a lifetime.

Abigail's family lived in a small house in the Temple grounds. That evening, she walked across the grass deep in thought, anxious about the coming conversation with Aidren.

But that would have to wait until the children were in bed. She opened the front door and seven year old Ellyn barrelled down the hall towards her, blue eyes sparkling, her tangled golden brown curls a regular bird's nest. Closely followed by her twin, Jacob, a step to the rear, as always. How had she and Aidren managed to produce two such different children?

"Mamma!" Ellyn cried, a huge beam on her exquisite little face, raising her arms for a hug, "I've been so good today – I did my lessons and didn't get into trouble once."

Abigail dropped to her knees and embraced her daughter. "That's my good girl."

She looked across to where Jacob was standing, patiently waiting his turn. "And how's my best boy?"

"Good, thank you, Mamma," he said in his high treble voice, his deep brown eyes meeting hers. "I've studied hard and learned about val-er-ian and cam-omile."

Abigail smiled as she listened to him saying the names so carefully. She released her daughter with a kiss on the cheek, then held out her arms to her son. “Good lad. Come and give me a hug.”

She hugged her son gently, knowing that, unlike his boisterous sister, he preferred that. Then she stood up, offering a hand to each of them. “Come along, you two. Is Pappa home yet?”

“Yes, he’s upstairs getting changed,” Ellyn said, “and Mareen said we have to wash our hands cos supper’s nearly ready.”

“Off you go then.”

Then smiled as Ellyn dashed off, followed more sedately by Jacob. She loved them both so much. How would she be able to bear being parted from them for so long?

Mareen came out of the kitchen to greet her, wiping her hands on a cloth. “Good evening, Abigail,” she said with a smile. “Your supper’s nearly ready and Aidren is home early for once.”

“Thank you, Mareen. We’ll be with you in a few minutes.”

It had taken a while to establish this easy relationship with Mareen, who was worth her weight in gold, being one of those unflappable Garûnan servants who took everything in her stride. She managed the household efficiently and with a warm kindness, and the children adored her. Which meant that Abigail and Aidren were free to concentrate on their jobs, she as Waymage, he as the most experienced sergeant of the Town Guard.

“Has Harmin gone home?” Abigail asked.

Harmin was the twins’ tutor and came each day except Ranusdag to teach them.

"Yes," Mareen replied, a twinkle in her eye. "He said to tell you that Jacob is learning his herbs as fast as he can teach him and that Ellyn's concentration was better than usual."

"Ah, that is good to hear. Thank you."

"What's wrong, love?" Aidren asked once he and Abigail had put the children to bed. It had been his turn to read the bedtime story, and he had come downstairs to find Abigail sitting in front of the fire, a glass of wine in her hand, staring into the flames.

She met his gaze, her face troubled. "This came today," she said, handing him a letter, "and I don't know what to do about it."

Sitting down in his favourite armchair, Aidren opened the letter and read it. Then whistled loud and long.

"By the Six!" he said. "This is a great honour, Abi. Are you going to accept?"

She was plaiting her fingers, staring into the fire, looking younger and more nervous than she had for years. Aidren reached out and took her hand.

"Speak to me, Abi. What are you thinking?"

"Oh, Aidren," she said, meeting his eyes, "I don't know what to think. I realise what a huge honour it is, but I cannot think why they've chosen me." She paused, then added in a small voice, "And it will mean being away from you and the children for three whole seasons."

"I cannot think of anyone more suitable," he declared. "Look what they wrote: 'that your unique experiences and talents have made you the most suitable candidate.' I'm so proud of you, my dearling."

She flushed. "Thank you, that means the world to me. But can I really step into Marinden's shoes? I'm not sure I'm ready to be responsible for all the Waymages in the whole of Dagâran. Some of them are much older and more experienced than I am. What if I do it wrong?"

"That's why you need to do the further training," Aidren said. "Come on, Abi, this isn't like you. Don't worry about me and the twins – Mareen will look after us all. And those three seasons will pass really quickly."

Abigail sighed, a deep sigh that seemed to come from her heart. "You think I should accept then?"

"Haven't I just said so?" Aidren said. "Of course, it will mean relocating to Luvodican. We'll have to hope that Mareen will want to stay with us. And Harmin."

"What about you?" she asked. "You're in line for becoming captain of the Town Guard here, but if we move, you'll have to start again."

Aidren fought down a twinge of regret. "That's true," he said, "but there are plenty of opportunities for a good Warrior in Luvodican. I might even end up teaching in the Hall of Warriors."

He watched her face change as she made up her mind. "All right then," she said, "I'll do it. But I'll have to leave soon – it will be Garûnastide in eight seisdags."

"That's my girl," Aidren said, taking her in his arms. "You'll be brilliant, Abi. Just you wait and see."

The training at the Colaste a'r Teisen was very different to Abigail's experience of learning how to be a Waymage. Instead of being in a class with other adepts, she had one-to-one sessions with some of the senior tutors as well as with each of the twelve High

Waymages, who gently inducted her into her new responsibilities. She knew none of the High Waymages, who had all been elected since she had last visited Ranusheim. But was delighted to receive an invitation to dinner from the former High Waymage, Valwyn, and spent a very pleasant evening with her, catching up on all her news and sharing her own. And it had been wonderful to be back in Ranusheim, to sink into its deep peace.

As Aidren had predicted, the three seasons of her training had flown by. It had been interesting to learn that only Waymages with the gift of being able to speak mind to mind over distance were eligible for the role of First Waymage. She received regular letters from Aidren, enclosing brief notes from the twins. It had been particularly hard to miss their eighth birthdays, but she had sent gifts by way of a party of Yrusian traders who were heading for Luvodican. At times she missed them with a fierceness which tore at her heart and knew it would take some time for them to readjust to her presence when she returned.

Which would be very soon now. It would be Néartastide, the Festival of Thanksgiving, in a couple of seisdags, and her various tutors seemed to be pleased with her progress. With any luck she would be able to start the journey home straight after the festival, which would give her a few seisdags to prepare for the ceremony. Was she truly ready? She hoped so.

Following a smooth journey by horse and sea, Abigail arrived home one chilly evening, four seisdags before Dagârastide.

"Welcome home, Waymage Abigail," Brunan said as he took her horse. "Not that this will be your home for much longer."

"Thank you, Brunan," she said. "I'm going to miss you all very much."

The Temple staff and her adepts knew all about it, of course. She had called them together before she had left Myndorian, so that they would have as much time as possible to get used to the idea of her leaving, and to Bronwin stepping up to succeed her as Waymage.

"We'll be fine with Waymage Bronwin," he said with a smile. "She's shaping up to be a good Waymage. And," he added, "we're proud that one of our own has been chosen to become First Waymage of Dagâran."

She returned his smile, relieved by his positive attitude. She had become friends with him over the past decade and respected his opinions. As one of the longest serving Temple servants, he was a reliable indicator of the attitudes of the Temple's staff. If Brunan was happy with Bronwin and proud of her, she could stop worrying about the Myndorian she was leaving behind.

"Thank you, Brunan – I appreciate that."

"Get away with you, lass," he said gently, "and go home to that family of yours."

After a reassuring and relaxing evening with her family, Abigail walked across to the Temple to receive Bronwin's report and to start sorting out who she was going to invite to the First Waymaging ceremony in Luvodican. The invitations would need to go out in the next couple of days in order to give people the time to travel there.

First, she summoned Bronwin to her chambers. A gentle peck on the door heralded the girl's arrival and she slipped in quietly, an anxious expression on her face.

"Welcome back, Abigail," she said.

"Come and sit down," Abigail said. "I want to hear about everything that's happened these past three seasons. I know you've sent me regular reports, for which I've been most grateful, but I'd like to hear the highlights from your own lips."

Bronwin took a deep breath, then began. "The three festivals went well and the other adepts are coming along. I think that Jardin is nearly ready for his Waymage training."

"I thought he might be. I will write to the Wayzenmoot to let them know."

"On my word alone?"

The girl sounded incredulous. Time to bolster her confidence. "Of course, on your word alone. In a few seisdags' time, you will be Waymage here. And I know you will do well."

Bronwin flushed. "Thank you, Abigail."

As Bronwin continued her report, going into greater detail about the events of the three festivals, and about all the small matters which make up the life of a Waymage, Abigail recognised she would be leaving the Temple at Myndorian in good hands. Which was quite a relief.

She dismissed her with a word of thanks, then turned her attention to the invitation list for the ceremony which would elevate her to First Waymage of Dagâran, now less than four seisdags away. The High Waymages had informed her that every Waymage in Dagâran should be present, along with the First Waymages from the other five lands of the Commonweal, plus Lord Lesym and Lady Bélia, who still ruled in Luvodican, the leaders of the local guilds, and friends and family. And that the two present Dagâran High Waymages would be leading the ceremony. So although she didn't have to create the ritual itself, she would have many invitations to send out and replies to receive.

Aidren had been delighted to discover that the people of Luvodican's temple had decided to build a brand new house in the temple grounds for their new First Waymage and her family. He, Abigail and the twins, together with their faithful Mareen, had moved in a seisdag before the beginning of Dagârastide. As they walked through the rooms, Abigail exclaimed in delight, "This is so wonderful – how very kind of them."

"Quite a compliment to you, Abi," Aidren said, "that they've taken all this trouble."

And now it was Néartasdag, the second day of Dagârastide, and he and Abigail had invited a special old friend to stay. They had both kept in touch with Ylonya, who breezed in for a visit any time she was passing through northern Dagaran. The last time Abigail had seen her had been at Shaunan's funeral. The old Waymage had never quite recovered from the strains of the quest, and had suffered a final, fatal heart attack two years before. Aidren knew that Abigail still missed her – how proud the old Waymage would have been to see her now.

But, unknown to Abigail, Ylonya had visited Myndorian more recently, while she had been away in

Ranusheim and Aidren had given her certain instructions. So when she knocked on the door, she was not alone – Raewe, the Waymage of Taellingsford, who had been Abigail's best friend from the Colaste a'r Teisen, was with her.

"Raewe! How wonderful to see you!" Abigail said, hugging her fiercely. "And Ylonya, it's so good to see you too."

Ylonya, still wearing her favourite turquoise leather coat, beamed at her. "Aidren asked me to pick Raewe up on my way here," she said.

"Come in, both of you," Abigail said. "We've got all afternoon to catch up, and Mareen is cooking something special for dinner."

Aidren smiled at her excitement. How would she react to the rest of his surprise? Ten minutes later, there was another knock on the door.

Abigail jumped up immediately. "We're not expecting anyone else, are we?" she asked Aidren. "It must be someone from the Temple."

Aidren hid his grin behind his hand and let her open the door. Then heard her cry of astonishment. "Ednor! And Tremond! What in the world are you two doing here?"

"That's a fine welcome, Abigail," Ednor said, laughing. "Don't you want to see us?"

Aidren watched in satisfaction as Abigail hugged first Ednor, then Tremond. "Of course I do," she said, "but I had no idea you were coming. How did you know?"

Ylonya answered her. "That would be Aidren's doing," she said with a smile. "While you were away at Ranusheim, I dropped in and heard your news. Aidren asked me to bring Ednor and Tremond along to join the celebration."

"Oh, it's so gorgeous to see you all. I never imagined we'd all be in the same room together again."

"Well, it is a special occasion," Tremond said in his deep voice. "It's not every day a new First Waymage is installed."

"Come on in," Abigail said. "I have two very special people to introduce you to."

But one of them was already there. "Who are these, Mamma?" Ellyn asked, tugging at her mother's skirt.

"Some dear friends that Pappa and I haven't seen for years," Abigail said. "Ednor, Tremond, this is our daughter, Ellyn."

"She is as beautiful as her namesake," Tremond said.

Aidren welcomed their visitors into the main reception room, with its clean white walls and comfortable chairs, softly lit by oil lamps, where Jacob was sitting next to Raewe, questioning her about the uses of herbs. Aidren was sure his son would become a Lèniumen healer, or perhaps follow his mother and become a Waymage.

"And this is our son, Jacob," Abigail said. "Jacob, come and say hello to our guests. This is Lord Ednor, the ruler of Néartania and Tremond, the Wayzenmoot's ambassador in Talamdor."

Jacob rose to his feet and gave them a sketchy bow but found no words to say. Aidren hoped he would become more confident as he grew up.

The hours flew by as their old friends shared the more innocuous items of news and the twins entertained them all by their very presence.

Mareen had prepared a wonderful spread for the occasion (she had been in the secret too) and the wine flowed freely. It was the first time Aidren and Abigail had entertained in the new house and he looked around with satisfaction. The oak dining table seated them all comfortably and there were a couple of small tapestries hanging on the walls. But the Luvodican Temple staff had left it up to them to choose the final touches, which would be added in due course. Jacob was sitting between Abigail and Raewe and continued to pepper the Lèniumen Waymage with questions. Ellyn had chosen to sit next to Ylonya and was hanging on to her every word, as the Yrusian regaled the company with some tales of her adventures in the past few years, suitably edited for young ears.

"Come on now, it's bedtime," Abigail said, once they had all eaten their fill. "Ellyn, Jacob, say goodnight to our guests, then Mareen will take you upstairs."

Ellyn's lower lip drooped. "Can't we stay up, Mamma?" she pleaded.

"No, my love," Abigail answered. "It's the final day of Dagârastide tomorrow and you don't want to be too tired to enjoy it, do you? We'll go and see the storytellers if you're a good girl and go up to bed nicely with Mareen."

"I'll come upstairs soon," Aidren promised. He excused himself a few minutes later, saying, "One of us always tells them a story and tucks them in."

Abigail sat back with a sigh. "She does hate missing out," she said.

"You've got two lovely children there, Abi," Ylonya said. "Both as bright as buttons."

"I know. I can't believe how lucky I am to have not only Aidren, but the two of them. They keep us on our toes though."

"Ellyn reminds me so much of her namesake," Tremond said. "She's so lively and curious about everything."

Abigail sighed again. "Yes, I miss her still. But she lives on in our Ellyn."

"It wouldn't surprise me if she ended up with an Yrusian Waymark," Ylonya said, serious for once. "I sense a deep yearning to explore the wider world in her."

"Have a heart, Ylonya," Abigail said, "she's only just turned eight. But yes, I think you may be right – she was fascinated by your stories at dinner. And she's always asking questions about what's going on in the world. The two of them are so different, even if they are twins."

"Jacob is more like you," Raewe said. "He asked me some really intelligent questions about herblore."

"Yes, he takes life far more seriously than Ellyn does. Which comes from being the eldest, perhaps, if only by half an hour. I think he will turn out to be a Healer, or even a Waymage." She changed the subject. "Aidren should be back down soon. Then we'll be able to settle down for a quiet talk."

"So," Aidren said as he came back in and sat down, after refilling all their glasses, "we've told you our news. How about yours?"

"I'll go first," Ylonya said. "Mother has finally decided to stand down as Mistress of the Guild of Intelligencers and I've taken her place."

"I cannot think of anyone better," Abigail said, giving her a hug. "But that must mean you're doing even more travelling than before." She glanced at Ednor, who was sitting quietly next to his wife.

"Yes," Ylonya said. "It means that I don't see nearly as much of Ednor as I would like, but since Lord Éadulf passed away, he's had his hands full ruling Néartania."

"I was wondering about that," Abigail said. "I thought that your brother Réothed was the elder."

"He is," Ednor said. "But his long years in the border forts mean he has a key role in protecting Veylindré from the Talamdorians, so he decided to cede his claim to Néartania to me."

"Are you enjoying it?" Abigail asked.

Ednor pulled a face. "I wouldn't exactly describe it like that," he said. "But the people of Néartania have chosen me, so it is my duty to rule them as well as I can. I owe it to both my father and my brother. And," he added with a grin, "our journey with the quest gave me a unique insight into the other lands of the Commonweal, which has helped enormously. And Ylonya keeps me up to date on developments."

Aidren laughed. "I'm sure she does. I'm so glad you're both happy."

"How about you, Tremond?" Abigail asked. "How is life for you? The last we heard, you were in Talamdor almost permanently."

"Yes, the Lords and Ladies of Justice appointed me as Veylindréan ambassador to Talamdor some years ago. There's now a small, but permanent embassy in the main square of Talamunem City, which was quite a concession. The Talamdorians had centuries of distrust to overcome, but our willingness to aid them against the

Havimi helped. We're even starting to formulate trade agreements with Domlok and the Council."

"So Domlok still rules in Talamdor?" Aidren said.

"Yes. It has taken me some time to earn his trust, but I think I've done it."

"So the long grief of the quest was worth it," Abigail said softly. "We paid a high price to achieve it, but I feel more hopeful about the future of our world now."

Aidren hugged her. "Yes."

When Abigail awoke the next morning, she felt relaxed and serene. Seeing her old friends had distracted her mind from anxiety about the ceremony, which would be taking place that very afternoon, after the Ceremony of Assignment, which Marinden would be conducting as her final act as First Waymage.

Abigail had shadowed Marinden closely during the festival, making mental notes of all she had done. Finally, she felt prepared to take on the responsibility. It was a huge honour and privilege, but she felt equal to it.

"How are you feeling?" Aidren asked, watching her fix her Waymage's brooch to the left shoulder of her robes.

"Ready, I think," Abigail said, "but I can't quite believe it will be the last time I wear this."

Aidren hugged her. "I'm so very proud of you. The children and I will be cheering you on."

She kissed him. "Thank you. I'm not sure I could have done it without you."

"And now," Aidren said, "I must go and line up to get my Goldstone recharged. I'm so glad we only have to do it every five years now."

The morning flew by, then it was time for the Ceremony of Assignment. Abigail was sponsoring only one child at this festival, Kevan, the youngest son of one of the councillors of Myndorian. She had been working with him for a while and was sure he would become a good Waymage in the fulness of time. So she made sure she arrived punctually at the amphitheatre.

Abigail looked around the audience. Every Waymage in Dagâran was present, as well as the First Waymages of the other five lands in the Commonweal, and Lord Lesym and Lady Bélia. She also recognised a number of Guild Masters and Mistresses, some of whom she had met while mentoring the young people in her care. All would have their role in the First Waymaging ceremony.

She watched Marinden closely as the Ceremony of Assignment proceeded – she would be leading this ceremony at the next festival and wanted to do it well.

As the last child joined her parents in the audience, Abigail listened as Marinden closed the ceremony with her customary words, "People of Veylindré, once more we have welcomed new initiates into the Way of Veylindré. They are now adults with a responsibility to serve Veylindré and its people through following the truth of their Waymarks. It will soon be the time for feasting and celebration.

"It is also nearly the end of this Festival of Dagârastide. Until we meet again at the next festival, may you all follow the Way in truth and dedication. May you live in peace."

The sun began to slip below the horizon and gradually, the stars which made up the constellation of the Six became visible in the navy blue sky. Torches were lit all around the amphitheatre, so that the audience would be able to see what was going on.

Marinden raised her arms for silence. "As many of you know, I am retiring from the role of First Waymage at the end of today. It has been an honour and privilege to be your First Waymage for so many years and I will have fond memories of my time here in Luvodican."

An enthusiastic round of applause rippled around the amphitheatre, and Marinden was visibly moved by it.

"Thank you, my friends. I now have the pleasure of handing on the responsibilities of First Waymage to someone well known to many of you, Waymage Abigail of Myndorian. And I am honoured to introduce the two Dagâran High Waymages, Landon and Budella, who have come all the way from Ranusheim to perform this ceremony."

Another round of applause, cut short as the two High Waymages stepped forward, tall and imposing, gorgeous in their golden High Waymage robes, shot through with red and orange. A profound silence fell on the gathered people.

Landon spoke first. "Our greetings from the Wayzenmoot at Ranusheim. As the High Waymages serve the Way, so also do the Waymages of each community. The six First Waymages, one for each land of the Commonweal, are responsible for the people of their land, so that all may serve the Way in peace and amity. They are called to gather the people of the Way at each festival and to conduct the ceremonies which mark the passing of our year and the growth and unions of the people."

"They also liaise with each other," Budella said, "and with the High Waymages at Ranusheim, to ensure that the peoples of each land work together in the service of the Way. Waymage Abigail of Myndorian has been chosen by the Wayzenmoot to be First Waymage of Dagâran, and has undergone the requisite training at Ranusheim. Today she will be appointed to this role, in the presence of you all."

Abigail moved to stand before them, her heart beating fast under her Waymage robes. The other five First Waymages, representing the Isle of Ranu, Lènium, Néartania, Garûnalond and Yrusian, took their places in a horseshoe formation surrounding her. Then all her fellow Waymages rose from their seats in the front row, and joined them in the centre of the amphitheatre, forming a loose circle around her, the other First Waymages and the two High Waymages. Finally, Lord Lesym and Lady Bélia, together with representatives from the city's guilds, took their places to one side.

Landon addressed her fellow Waymages, "Do you believe Waymage Abigail to be suited to this role?"

And all the Waymages responded with one voice, their right hands on their hearts, "We do."

Budella asked the same question of Lord Lesym and Lady Bélia and the other five First Waymages, then Landon addressed the assembled Guild Masters and Mistresses. All answered, "We do."

Then Budella met Abigail's gaze. "Waymage Abigail, do you believe that the Way is calling you to this role?"

"I do so believe," Abigail answered.

"In the vow you are about to take," Budella said, "will you affirm your devotion to the Way, and your willingness to serve the people of Dagâran as their First Waymage, so that they and the land may flourish in the Way?"

"I do so affirm," Abigail said. Her stomach was churning and she could feel herself shaking. She hoped it didn't show.

"Waymage Abigail," Budella said, "repeat these words after me, 'I, Waymage Abigail of Myndorian…' and Abigail began to repeat the words after her,

"I, Waymage Abigail of Myndorian,
vow that I will do my utmost,
to live in devotion to the Power of the Way,
and to the rank of First Waymage.
I will serve the people and the land of Dagâran faithfully,
and will teach and guide my fellow Waymages
and the people of Dagâran with kindness and wisdom.
I will work with the other First Waymages,
in the wider service of the Commonweal of Veylindré.
I will always remember that all are children of the Six,
equally worthy of justice, equity and respect.
In the name of the Six, in the Power of the Way,
this is my vow."

At a nod from High Waymage Landon, the five First Waymages took out their Goldstones and held them in their right hands, touching her with their left. She felt a flow of power enter her, which exalted her. She remembered the last time she had felt this powerful, during the ceremony which culminated in the destruction of the Bloodstone of Talamu. Thank Ranu this was a happier occasion.

She sank into a blissful communion with the other Waymages and felt almost bereft when it ended. Then both High Waymages addressed her directly, "May you serve the people of Dagâran and the wider Commonweal well and faithfully."

Budella fastened the intricate and beautiful brooch of the First Waymage on her left shoulder.

"Thank you," she said, "I will do my best."

"Peoplc of Dagâran," Landon said, turning to the audience. "Please welcome Abigail as your new First Waymage."

Tears prickled at her eyes as the assembled people rose to their feet, their right hands on their hearts, and said, "We welcome you as our First Waymage. May you serve us well and faithfully."

How proud Shaunan would have been.

Then everyone burst into applause. Abigail blushed and bowed her head. It was done. She vowed in her heart to be the best First Waymage ever.

Then Ellyn broke free from Aidren's hand and rushed over to her. "Mamma," she cried, "I'm so happy for you."

Aidren and Jacob joined them. "We're all so happy for you," Aidren said.

Abigail returned to her chambers – so recently Marinden's – to change into her brand new First Waymage robes, which were laid out on her bed. Aidren had taken the children off to find something to eat. She was pleased to find some food laid out ready for her – she had been too nervous to eat much lunch. So before she changed, she ate some bread and cheese, washed down with a glass of Fionnan red. Then she dressed herself carefully and transferred the First Waymage brooch – a large, faceted yellow topaz in an elaborate silver setting – to the left shoulder of her new robe.

A few minutes later, she was on her way to the central square, where the ceremonial fire would be extinguished in the presence of the First Waystone of Dagâran. It would be her first ceremony as First Waymage.

Moving into the firelight, Abigail raised her arms for silence. "Holy Dagâra, Goddess of War and Metalworking, we have gathered in our customary way at the end of the Season of Completion to honour you. All year long, you have given us your aid and enabled us to follow the Way of Veylindré with faith and courage. Your Festival has been a time of remembrance, rejoicing and renewal, as we have honoured our dead, celebrated the marriages of our young people and welcomed our children into the fulness of the Way. Now it is time to put out the ceremonial fire, before we join together in a final feast in your honour."

She nodded to the four men who were standing to one side with metal tubs of sand. They walked forward, one to each corner of the bonfire, which was dying down to embers now, and dumped the sand on top of it. The flames were extinguished. A sigh went up from the gathered people.

Abigail waited for silence once more. "Now that the ceremonial fire has been put out, it is time for us to gather one last time in feasting and merriment, before we go our separate ways. May the Way be with you all. May it guard and guide you until we meet again."

The Stones of Veylindré – Glossary

Bangles of Control – Bangles made of talamunium, used to control all lower status Talamdorians.

Ceremony of Assignment – Takes place at each of the six Festivals, during which Waymarks are assigned to young people who have completed the Time of Testing.

Dagârastide, Festival of All Souls – Marks the end of the Season of Completion.

Dagârsdag – Fourth day of the Veylindréan seisdag.

Feolin – A loaf baked with meat and bread combined. Used as travelling food.

Garûnastide, Festival of Dedication – Marks the end of the Season of Awakening.

Goldstones – Tools used by Veylindréans to work the magic of the Way.

Golden Stone of Ranu – The master ranusfelsen stone, located in Ranusheim.

Lènia's Bruagan – A herb that can help restore lost memory.

Lènia's Nimbane – A herb which can counteract poison.

Lèniastide, Festival of Music and Storytelling – Marks the end of the Season of Dormancy.

Lethara – A drug used by healers to induce unconsciousness.

Néartastide, Festival of Thanksgiving – Marks the end of the Season of Thanksgiving.

Ranusfelsen – The mineral out of which Goldstones are made, and all Veylindréan temples built. It looks like a pale sandstone, but in the sunlight, hints of gold, green, red, orange, purple, blue and brown show through.

Ranustide, Festival of Wisdom and Lore – Marks the end of the Season of First Fruits.

Season of Awakening – Equivalent to early spring.

Season of Completion – Equivalent to late autumn.

Season of Dormancy – Equivalent to deep winter.

Season of Growth – Equivalent to late spring.

Season of First Fruits – Equivalent to summer.

Season of Thanksgiving – Equivalent to early autumn.

Season / Cycle of Proving – Time spent by a couple waiting to marry, to prove their commitment.

Seisdag – A period of six days, equivalent to our week.

Talamunium – A metal found only in Talamdor. Used as an alloy of silver, to overpower the will of any who wear the bracelet.

Temple of the Six – Seven-sided building which is a place of worship.

Test of Faith – Undertaken by all Talamdorians at the age of 12, to see whether they are worthy of becoming truebloods.

Time of Testing – A time of learning and testing undertaken at puberty by each person in Veylindré, to discern their goddess affiliation.

Truebloods – Talamdorians who have passed the Test of Faith, and are the ruling class of Talamdorian society.

Way of Veylindré – The magical / religious system of Veylindré.

Waymage – Local wise person / priest/ess of the Way. One in each community.

Waymarks – A special mark on the forehead of all Veylindréans, which shows their goddess affiliation.

Waystones – Pillars of ranusfelsen – one in each community. They help the inhabitants to access the power of the Way.

Wayzenmoot, The – Council of the Way. Located in Ranusheim.

Yrusiastide, Festival of Journeying – Marks the end of the Season of Growth.

The Stones of Veylindré: Characters

Characters from 17th century England:

George Crutwell – Witchfinder. Prophet of the One in Talamdor for 30+ years.

Richard Forster – A friend of Abigail's.

Mercy Paignton – Abigail's best friend.

Squire Petty – The gentry from Abigail's and Jacob's village.

Elder Sanderson – Presbyterian Elder. Pastor Winters' second in command

Matthew Sanderson – Son of Elder Sanderson. Pastor Winters sees him as a prospective husband for Abigail.

Thomas Winters – Presbyterian Pastor. Abigail's father and instigator of pilgrimage to the New World.

Mary Winters – Wife to Thomas, and mother to Abigail, **Isaac, Daniel** and **Faith**.

Captain Wood – Captain of the *Sweet Sarah.*

Characters in Veylindré:

Abigail Winters (Abi) – The heroine, from 17th century England. 17 years old.

Aidren – A young Warrior of Dagâra. Skilled with the sword. From Nordvein. Member of the Company.

Alaine – a weaver, wife of Rodis of Néartania.

Baldis – Agent of the Guild of Intelligencers in Céardochis.

Balmak – Portak's lifelong friend and lover.

Balon – A warrior who led the forces of Veylindré against the Talamdorians in ages past.

Barlan – An innkeeper in a village south of Myndorian.

Bélia, Lady – The ruler of Dagâran. Lives in Luvodican.

Bodan – A member of the Council of Nordvein.

Brann – A member of the Council of Nordvein.

Brickon – Guildmaster of the Hall of Traders. Ylonya's father.

Brunan – A servant at the Temple of Myndorian.

Donan – The former husband of Shaunan, now dead.

Ellyn – A young apprentice cordwainer, from Nordvein. Niece of Shaunan. Member of the Company.

Findoran – Waymage of Myndorian.

Gadaria – Dagâran silversmith, living & trading in Céardochis.

Gildon – Master Warrior of the Hall of the Warriors of Dagâra. Lives in Luvodican.

Gomlak – An agent of the Prophet, killed at the cove.

Grunen – A man of Nordvein.

Haldor – A young man of Luvodican, handfasted at Dagârastide in Luvodican.

Havimi – A race of pirates, living in Havim to the south of Veylindré.

Hedwin – Adept of Ranu, trained by Findoran, sent to Nordvein to cover for Shaunan's absence.

Jacob Wallingford – Abigail's boyfriend, from 17th century England. A talented smith.

Janissan – A young woman of Myndorian, handfasted at Dagârastide in Luvodican.

Jaradol – Messenger from Smithsport, to Lord Lesym and Lady Bélia.

Jordis – Son of Rodis, Néartanian farmer.

Kalen – A smith, living in Luvodican. Old friend of Shaunan's who takes Jacob on as his apprentice.

Kormak – Garûnalonden Watch officer (Portak in disguise).

Lesym, Lord – The ruler of Dagâran. Lives in Luvodican.

Lyma – A member of the Council of Nordvein.

Lymon – A boy at Ceremony of Assignment in Luvodican. From Myndorian.

Mardal – Yrusian trader and agent of the Guild of Intelligencers. Lives in Porusport.

Margera – Guildmistress of the Hall of Traders, and Head of the Guild of Intelligencers. Ylonya's mother.

Marinden – First Waymage of Dagâran. Lives in Luvodican.

Markhan – Master Cordwainer in Luvodican.

Mekin – Son of Mardal, has a withered arm. Encountered in Céardochis.

Meldar – Waymage of Nordvein before Shaunan.

Norin – A stable hand in village south of Myndorian.

Oltan – A guard of the East Gate of Myndorian.

Petan – The husband of Waymage Findoran.

Portak – Agent of the Prophet of the One. Uses the alias Kormak while in Veylindré.

Prophet of the One – The principal antagonist, ruler of Talamdor.

Raimun – Master Cordwainer of Nordvein.

Rewald – Waymage of Talmis.

Rodis – A Néartanian farmer on the road to Talmis, with whom the Company take shelter.

Sanderon – Sword Master at the Hall of Warriors in Luvodican.

Shaunan – Waymage of Nordvein. Abigail's mentor and member of the Company.

Shula – A girl at the Ceremony of Assignment at Luvodican. From Myndorian.

Tamin – Chief Messenger of the Prophet, responsible for sending and receiving messages from agents in the field.

Torlin – Trade Master at Smithsport.

Ylonya – An Yrusian guide and intelligence gatherer. Member of the Company.

The Stones of Veylindré – Places

Avarin – A mining village in northern Talamdor.

Berlysian – A settlement in the Vale of Berlysian, Lènium. Home of the Healer Hall and the Hall of Apothecaries.

Caethniss Castle – A border fort of Talamdor.

Caethwasim – A slave port of Talamdor.

Céardochis – The commercial centre for the many craft items made by the Néartanians. Home of the Hall of Clothiers and the Builders' Hall.

Chorich Castle – A border fort in Yrusian.

Claymont – A village in western Dagâran, on the River Redwater.

Coèdnis – Located in Néartania, on the edge of the Great Forest. Home of the Woodworkers' Hall.

Colaste a'r Teisen – The training school for Ranusian adepts, to turn them into Waymages. In Ranusheim.

Commonweal of Veylindré – A federation of six Lands: Dagâran, Garûnalond, Isle of Ranu, Lènium, Néartania, and Yrusian.

Cristail Keep – A border fort in Néartania.

Crullfeld – The location of a farming collective in Talamdor.

Dagâran – One of the six Lands of the Commonweal of Veylindré.

Deepwoods Keep – A border fort in Néartania.

Fenland – A substantial area of marsh and fen, which skirts the Inland Sea of Yrusian, to the north and west.

Fionnan – Centre of the wine-growing region in Dagâran. End of the Great South Caravan Route.

Fort of Ranu – The only entrance to the Isle of Ranu.

Garûnalond – One of the six Lands of the Commonweal of Veylindré.

Garûnashavn – The principal port of Garûnalond. Home of the Hall of Messengers.

Havim – Country of pirates and slave traders. Loose alliance with Talamdor.

Homing, The – The central settlement of the Fenland.

Iascan – The main centre of the fishing industry in Yrusian. Home of the Fisherfolks' Hall.

Inland Sea – A large inland sea in Yrusian, the southern part of which forms the border with Néartania.

Irnvein – A mining village to the north of Nordvein in Dagâran.

Isle of Ranu – One of the six Lands of the Commonweal of Veylindré.

Lèniashaven – The principal port of Lènium, where the shipbuilding industry of Lènium is based.

Lènium – One of the six Lands of the Commonweal of Veylindré.

Luvodican – The capital city of Dagâran. Home of the Hall of Weaponcraft and the Warriors of Dagâra.

Mathven – Located in Yrusian, a port at the mouth of the River Yrus. Home of the Hall of Mariners and Shipbuilders.

Mirunan – The capital city of Garûnalond. Home of the Hall of Justice and the Academy of the Watch.

Mistbourne Keep – A border fort in Néartania.

Mount Talamu – In Talamdor, mountain sacred to Talamu.

Muilléan – Located at the mouth of the Ranu River. Home of the Hall of Papermakers.

Myndorian – A town to the West of the Dagâran Range. Commercial centre for the mining industries of Dagâra. Home of the Hall of Metalworking.

Myner's Gap – A pass through the Dagâran Range between Nordvein and Myndorian.

Nailach – The northern port in Havim.

Néartania – One of the six Lands of the Commonweal of Veylindré.

Néartanis – The capital city of Néartania and its main port. Home of the Hall of Plenty.

Nellènium – The capital city of Lènium. End of the Great North Caravan Route.

Nordkeep – A border fort in Néartania.

Nordvein – A village to the east of the Dagâran Range.

Northern Range – A range of high mountains which divide the habitable parts of Garûnalond from the Northern Wastes beyond.

Plavin – A village in Lènium, home of Raewe.

Porusport – An inland port at the confluence of the Rivers Porus and Yrus. Start of the Great South Caravan Route. Home of the Hall of Traders.

Ranusheim – The capital city of the Isle of Ranu. Home of the Wayzenmoot and the Hall of Scriveners and Printers.

River Caethwas – Located in Talamdor.

River Choris – Located in Yrusian.

River Clearwater – Located in Néartania.

River Cristail – Located in Néartania.

River Elvan – Located in Garûnalond.

River Iascus – Located in Yrusian.

River Mistbourne – Located in Néartania.

River Porus – Located in Yrusian.

River Ranu – Located in Isle of Ranu.

River Redwater – Located in Dagâran.

River Roillon – Located in Talamdor.

River Yrus – Located in Yrusian.

Roillby – A village on the eastern bank of the River Roilldon in Talamdor, due east from Talamunem City.

Roilldon Fort – A border fort of Talamdor.

Rorschak – The location of a copper mine in Havim.

Rouliris – A town on the Great South Caravan Route in Néartania, north-west of Céardochis.

Ruslen – The capital city of Yrusian.

Silvin – A village in northern Talamdor.

South Plains Keep – A border fort in Néartania.

Taellingsford – Located at the southern tip of Lènium. Home of the Hall of Tradition.

Talamdor – The country of the enemy, ruled by the Prophet of the One.

Talamunem City – The capital city of Talamdor.

Tarrin – A village in western Yrusian.

Talmis – Centre of the agricultural region of Néartania. It hosts an annual Cattle Fair.

Ullmass – Site of the annual Wool Fair in Garûnalond. Beginning of the Great North Caravan Route.

Vale of Berlysian, The – Fertile area in the centre of Lènium.

Virunon – A village in south-west Yrusian.

Yrusian – One of the six Lands of the Commonweal of Veylindré.

Acknowledgements

I would like to thank my son, David, for suggesting, one day in October 2019, that I might enjoy writing a fantasy novel, for his many helpful suggestions and for his warm support throughout the process; Mike Richards for his encouragement and excellent advice; early readers Yvonne Aburrow, Stephanie Bisby, and Sue Jacznik; the members of Northampton Writers Group for their encouragement along the way; and Jon Davies for his efficient editing. And last, but not least, Maz, David and Becky Woolley, for being the best family in the world.

Printed in Great Britain
by Amazon

49135701R00208